THE RING OF A BELL

The Ring of a Bell

Ellen Kingman Fisher

CLIO MUSE PRESS
Denver, Colorado

The Ring of a Bell, by Ellen Kingman Fisher.
Copyright © 2024 by Ellen Kingman Fisher.
All rights reserved.

Published by Clio Muse Press
Denver, Colorado
United States of America

This book is printed in the United States of America

ISBN: 978-0-9994950-4-9
Library of Congress Control Number 2024909990

All images included in this book are subject to use according to trademark and copyright laws of the United States of America.

Cover and page design by Pratt Brothers Composition
Editing by Eva Fox Mate and Cotheal Linnell

Cover illustrations: early telephone image © Historical Images Archive / Alamy Stock Photo; puzzle image © extracoin / Vectorstock

Quantity Purchases: Schools, companies, professional groups, clubs, and other organizations may qualify for special terms when ordering quantities of this title.

For information, email: ClioMusePress@gmail.com

For my friends

"Life is nothing without friendship."
CICERO

Do you create your future from your past?

THE RING OF A BELL

ONE

Loud voices startled him awake, first a few and then more escalating in alarm. Herb tumbled from bed to look out the window and saw people gathering below, candles they held flickering light on their distraught faces.

"Mum, wake up," he shouted to the next bedroom. "Something's happened." He ran downstairs, took their coats off the hooks, and met her halfway as she came down in her nightclothes. "Here," he said. "No time to change." After helping her with her coat, they hurried to join the growing crowd, many wrapped in blankets and coats to protect them from the cold. From their block-long row house on the north side, they could see the billows of black smoke obscuring the stars and moon over downtown Boston. Neighbors huddled together for mutual comfort while they speculated.

"I can't tell if it's just the warehouses going up. It's too smoky," one person said.

"It looks like the center to me," one man offered.

"Mum, is it close to the high school?"

Sally pulled him close to her. "I can't tell."

Herb shuddered. Some of his friends lived closer to school than he did. They might not escape.

* * *

Rumors of death and destruction spread by word of mouth until newspapers published the known facts days after the Great Fire of November 9, 1872. The Saturday night conflagration killed thirty people, injured countless others, and burned 750 buildings in Boston's financial district.

Herb sat across from his mother at their circular wooden kitchen table, nicked and scratched from years of use. Sally grimly shook her head between words, reading aloud so he wouldn't have to wait to learn the news until after she finished. The fire had started in a warehouse but quickly spread to nearby structures. In a desperate attempt at a fire break, the fire department used gunpowder kegs to blow up buildings at the perimeter, only to expand the damage without halting the fire. Exploding structures hurled flaming projectiles, injuring spectators who went too close.

"The fire's brought everything to a halt," she said, giving him the paper.

"What about school?"

She shook her head. "The paper lists it as a closed building."

"For how long?"

"The paper doesn't have any details."

The sympathy Herb saw in her eyes revealed more without a word than the news articles. Herb left the table and went upstairs to lie on his bed. School gave everything meaning. He could not imagine life without it.

* * *

The fire had primarily damaged Boston's commercial buildings, and many lucky enough not to be destroyed were closed for repair. His high school was one of those not expected to reopen until the new year. People clamored for space to begin life over. A week after the fire, Mr. Wilkins, their high-and-mighty landlord, knocked at their door.

"Mr. Wilkins?" his mother said, surprised.

Herb watched from the shadows of the hallway as his mother opened the door wider to let the landlord enter.

"Is something wrong? We've already paid for the month."

Wilkins stepped over the threshold, wearing the same shapeless brown suit he always wore when collecting rent. His pock-marked face had an elongated nose that reminded Herb of a rat's.

She closed the door against the cold air. "The coffee's still hot. Would you like a cup?"

"No, no time for that." He shifted from one foot to the other in the entryway.

Herb stood quietly, watching and listening unnoticed.

"Rent doubles December first," Wilkins said, skipping any niceties.

Herb's mother gasped, covering her mouth with her trembling hand.

"I wanted to warn you before I come back to collect."

"Mr. Wilkins, that's impossible. Doubled? Surely, after all these years of paying on time—"

"I'm offering you a break."

Herb watched Wilkins' eyes narrow.

"I could rent this place for three times what you pay. Take the offer or find someplace else."

"At least give us time. With so much fire damage, finding a place won't be easy."

Herb felt a warm prickle inch up his back when the dirtbag shook his head with an unsympathetic sneer and moved closer to her. "Sally, maybe there's some bargain we could come up with." The man's jacket brushed against her shoulder as he leaned in, his lips close to her ear, whispering something Herb could not hear, but he saw her recoil and shake. Even Herb's adolescent eyes read a lewd proposition for a deal— he had witnessed the vulnerability of his widowed mother before.

Herb stepped out of the shadows of the kitchen doorway to be seen.

Startled, Wilkins broke away from Sally and strode toward the front door. Turning the knob, he said, "December first for the doubled amount."

Herb and his mother had no choice. They had to move.

Dislocation wracked Boston. The fire had left people unemployed, some without homes. Little, if anything, functioned normally. It did not take them long to realize the turmoil made it impossible to find another affordable place to live in Boston. Early the morning after Wilkins's visit, his mother left by train to search nearby towns. *Where will we end up?* The question churned over and over in his mind while he did his chores or tried to read.

When he heard his mum unlock the door at the end of the day, he held his breath, waiting for news. After she wearily hung up her coat, he saw worry written on her face. She shook her head. "Nothing we can afford, or at least that's safe," she told him. "I'll try again tomorrow."

The following day, he saw increasing desperation in her eyes.

"They jack up the prices when they see a woman alone and want to know where I'll get my money—as if I have no way to pay."

Herb was silently fearful. He had never seen his composed mother so undone. Without classes, he had little to do but run occasional errands for neighbors, as he often did after school. When a request took him close to where a friend lived, he went out of his way to knock on the door. He wanted to at least say one last goodbye instead of regretting never seeing his friends for the rest of his life. And yet, he could not think of what he might say. Should he tell Dick that he would never forget the kickball games? Would he thank Eddie for the fun of watching him when he skillfully talked unsuspecting newcomers into a marble game for keeps? Or say to Billy, who threw everyone into fits of laughter with his antics, a quick "See ya later, have a good life?" He loved those guys like brothers. Life would never be the same without them. As it turned out, he never had to figure out how to say goodbye because no one had been home. Had his friends, too, been forced to move, or were they temporarily away? Herb would never know.

In the second week of frantic searching, his mother came home mid-afternoon with haggard relief. "We've had a stroke of luck." She sank next to him on the couch, where he worked on a jigsaw puzzle—

his usual escape from tension. "I saw an advertisement for a two-story apartment in a long brick row of housing in Brookline. It wasn't the advertised place," she explained. "When I arrived, that landlord was listening to his next-door neighbor loudly complain about the occupants' skipping out the night before without paying rent. Both owners needed a tenant, but their first question was, 'Where is your husband?' I thought that would be the end, but one hesitated and then offered to show me through the apartment. I noted a few repairs that should be made. At the end of the tour, he walked around in a tight circle, giving me sidelong glances as he delayed. I took out cash for the first month. He took my money without commenting on fixing the deficiencies I had brought up." She nervously retrieved a receipt from her reticule. "It's close to the high school—one I learned has a good reputation."

They began packing, and on November 30, Herb watched a cartage company leave with everything they owned and head for Brookline, five miles away.

Their new two-story apartment was in a block-long, red-brick building with other similar units. They were arranged in pairs, with a stairway to two front doors as if connected duplexes—dated and ordinary but in decent condition, with little noise filtering through from the adjacent unit. The Brookline neighborhood was residential, unlike their place in Boston, which was fringed with commercial buildings.

Leaving his old neighborhood was not a big deal, but he might as well be throwing away his life by changing schools in his last year of high school. Herb knew he was shy by nature. He made friends slowly and, only over time, fit in. He was never part of the popular crowd at Boston High that laughed and congregated in an exclusive group, but he had a few close friends and a certain cachet for his high grades and athleticism. He felt comfortable in that role.

The forced move seemed easier for his mother because it changed little in her life. Despite her gregarious personality, she rarely socialized with other parents. Rather than attending teas and "at-homes," his mother went to Lyceum lectures and suffragist meetings, where she told Herb she fit in better with women of varied backgrounds. He suspected her decision was partly a choice but also from not being included. Their budget was modest, and his mum was a widow. "I don't need to be rich," she told him, "but it's essential to dress respectably. I'd rather cut corners here and there to afford nice clothing. Did you notice how tiers of ruffles are popular now?" she said one time, more to herself than him. He could tell she wanted her wardrobe to resemble the style of women from more prosperous neighborhoods, even if she could not mimic their lifestyle.

Monday, December second, was the worst day of Herb's life. He left for school early, leaving his mother unpacking their belongings. It was snowing heavy flakes, so wet they were slush before hitting the ground. With his first step through the double doors, he felt the other students' eyes watching him, undoubtedly sizing up his clothing, how he walked, and probably sensing the insecurity he tried to disguise with his defiantly clenched jaw. The school was a notch up from Boston High. The building was smaller but had newer and fancier architecture. None of that mattered. Herb would have given anything to be surrounded by the students, teachers, and architecture he knew so well.

The office was at the end of the first-floor hallway. The woman at the desk took what seemed like forever to examine copies of his previous grades.

"I'm sorry I don't have more. My school in Boston is closed . . . the fire."

Finally, after consulting a lot of papers on her desk, the woman handed him a piece of paper. "Here's your class schedule. You'll be late for the first period, but give the teacher this identification."

Just what I need. Late the first day.

The day was prolonged and confusing. He struggled to find the right classrooms, sometimes having to backtrack to a different hallway. No one bothered to ask if he needed help.

"How was school?" his mum asked.

Herb shrugged. "I'm behind in some subjects and repeating stuff in others." He did not tell her about enduring spitballs smacking the back of his neck during English class. The snickering stung worse.

At recess in the first week, he observed what games students played rather than trying to join them. One day, after the bell for recess rang, he went outside onto the playground. As he turned the corner, three bigger boys rushed at him and shoved him full force against a brick wall, smacking his face hard against the edge, sending shooting pain through his face. The boys dashed away before he could recognize them. The monitor, they probably knew, was conveniently across the field, out of sight.

Herb gingerly touched his throbbing nose to try to stop the blood streaming down onto his best shirt. Retreating to the boys' bathroom, he winced and dabbed his face with his handkerchief. For the rest of the afternoon, he wore his outer jacket to cover the stain that would never wash out.

Over the following weeks, Herb stayed up studying long after his mother had gone to bed. More than once, he awoke with his head on his desk after falling asleep at his books. He was determined to get the same high grades he had in Boston, but new material and unfamiliar teachers frustrated his efforts. He kept to himself, ignoring his classmates' stealthy hazing. The others had all gone to school together for a long time, maybe forever. He was an outsider, not part of any group.

As the months passed, Herb foiled the playground bullies with his athletic abilities. He gradually became a top pick for teams, and in the classroom, teachers praised his schoolwork. He relaxed a little.

The warped front door needed an extra tug to open and close, but Herb did it soundlessly. He wanted a few minutes to unwind before his mother questioned him about his day. Walking into the library—it was really the front room but lined with bookshelves, so that's what they called it—he set his school books on his desk and then slumped onto the sofa without taking off his coat. The air had been frigid during his after-school job delivering messages, and the room was cool without a fire in the fireplace. Clinking sounds of pots and dishes came from the kitchen where his mother was cooking dinner. On the large oval coffee table lay his jigsaw puzzle. He picked up a piece, searching for a fit. Before letting his mother know he was home, he wanted to match a few pieces. The thousand-piece puzzle of the London Bridge had been her Christmas present to him. So far, he had managed to connect all the border pieces; the others, categorized by color, lay spread around the periphery. Soon, he would hear his mother's cheerful voice: "How did you do at school?"

"Fine," he would say, and his answer would be true. He was already a top student, just like Boston, but in Brookline, he was a puzzle piece in the wrong place. He missed his familiar high school, where he had gone for over three years and, before that, eight years in a primary school. For all those years, his mum planned extracurricular activities for them to do in the city, especially trips to the museum.

Boston's museum was actually seven different museums. It touted half a million artifacts in its collections: birds, beasts, fish, statuary, and life-sized wax figures. Herb greeted them like friends, he had seen them so many times. He especially looked forward to watching specially designed productions, with stories and whimsical characters that made him laugh and clap with other children. On Sundays, when museums were closed, the two visited gardens or viewed historic buildings, trying to learn the architectural styles and history that his mother had studied beforehand. Many boys would have turned up their noses, but his mother had a way of asking questions: "Why do you think some buildings are constructed with brick and others with wood? How can mammals live in water? Which snakes are venomous?" She anchored history with dates but mainly described people's lives. In her free time, his mother read about what they planned to see. Then, she created stories, sometimes so vivid Herb felt as if he and his mum were part of events instead of learning about long-ago history or culture. Nighttime dreams often followed museum visits. He imagined marching to war as a gladiator or hiding behind a rock from a dinosaur. Going to the museum was heaven for his mother. "It's a free education," she liked to say. It was an attitude that rubbed off on him. The fire and having to move had wrecked everything.

"Herb, I didn't hear you. When did you get home?"

He jumped, startled out of his thoughts, sitting up straighter as his mother entered the room. "Just a few minutes ago. I saw a place where a puzzle piece might fit."

Sally, his mother, had light hair and a creamy complexion. His hair was a little darker, as was his skin, but their high, well-defined cheekbones gave them a family resemblance. He considered their personalities opposite. She seemed to move with an air of confidence, talking to any-one and everyone. She spoke little about her past, and he wondered if, somehow, she was embarrassed by what she might have been growing up. He wished his mum's air of confidence had been passed on to him. He often felt awkward and was reluctant to speak, except when some-one asked him to explain something. Then, he had a canny ability to remember facts and string together information so that it made sense. "Articulate," one teacher had labeled his trait. It was a characterization he relished and wanted to replicate—when he could find his voice.

Reading was something he and his mother had in common. Her proudest possessions were her books. The "library" was the best part of their home. She had finished high school but wanted to learn more. Herb knew she must have been a good student, even though she never bragged. He could not imagine how she had acquired a set of "The Hundred Classics of the English Language" and had read every one at least once, but she had. Herb liked looking at the titles on the spines that his mother had carefully arranged in an order of her own. Next to puzzles, reading was his favorite way to spend spare time, but he had not come close to reading the hundred books.

His mother walked over to stand next to him, her face flushed from the kitchen's heat. "Did you ask Mr. Brannan about going on?"

"Mum." Herb kept his gaze on the puzzle and knew he frowned. "We've already talked about that. There's no way I can go on to college. Even if I could get in, I'd have to have more than a scholarship. The small coins from delivering messages are a pittance when it comes to college costs."

"Your teacher encouraged you. What's the harm in trying?"

"He encourages everyone, even girls." Herb knew it was more than being nice to everyone. His teacher favored students who were eager to learn. Mr. Brannan quickly recognized Herb's curiosity about math and science, suggested books for him to read, and even lent him articles from magazines.

"What I would have given for a teacher like that," his mother said when Herb told her about how Mr. Brannan made conversations with students.

"Mine ignored most boys except the few whose fathers had money, and thought girls should stick to cooking and having children." His mother shifted positions as she considered. "I wanted so badly to go on with my education. It's such a feather in your cap and a ticket to security, but girls rarely have that opportunity. I certainly didn't." She straightened a picture on the side table, always needing to be busy. "What harm would it do to ask him about applying?"

Herb rolled his eyes. "I'll think about it. I promise." He stood up, half a head taller, his broad shoulders contrasting with her slender figure. "May I have a glass of milk? I'm thirsty even if it's cold outside."

"And bread and butter. Supper won't be for a while," she added.

"Thanks, Mum. I'll have a snack and then work at my desk. I have an overload of assignments for tomorrow."

Herb wanted to finish his assignments and have time to read the newest edition of *Scientific American*. The magazine was published weekly, and Mr. Brannan lent him his latest copy after reading it. Occasionally, it took a few weeks for his teacher to read a new issue, but the wait was worth it. Herb leafed through each one, absorbing as many details as possible but finishing them to return quickly and prove he was responsible enough to borrow another. Many articles described inventions recently approved by the U.S. Patent Office. Herb never tired of reading about inventions and how inventors came up with their ideas. He studied them to understand each step of the process, although he often had to ask Mr. Brannan for explanations.

The bell echoed through the school, signaling the end of classes. Students strapped up their books, chatting as they leisurely retrieved their coats and exited the classroom. Herb stayed behind. He was never really part of the laughing, teasing back-and-forth conversation anyway. The day had dragged on. Instead of his usual concentration, he could only think about what to say to Mr. Brannan after class about applying to a university. He remained in his seat while his teacher conversed with another student—a good student. Clara had milky white skin, unblemished except for a small mole to the left of her mouth. She braided her thick, dark hair and twisted it into a circle behind her head. A fringe of long eyelashes highlighted her prominent, watchful eyes. Not only was she pretty, but she was also one of his competitors for top grades. She was quiet, almost embarrassed about her high scores, as if girls should not have them. More than once, Herb had noticed Clara clasp her hands in her lap as if she were restraining them instead of raising one to answer. Only when Mr. Brannan called on her did anyone notice her intelligence. It was too bad, Herb thought. All those brains were wasted on a girl, although his intelligence might be wasted, too. He would be lucky even to have a future with some routine, repetitious, tedious job instead of physical labor, a job someone with his physique often ended up in.

After Clara left, Mr. Brannan picked up his gloves and briefcase, ready to go.

"Mr. Brannan," Herb called out, his voice sounding raspy in his ears. "Here's the *Scientific American* you lent me." Herb stepped up on the raised platform where the teacher's desk sat in front of the blackboard. "The best article was about Alexander Bell wanting to put the sound of a voice over electric wires." He thrust the magazine forward. "My mother went to a lecture Bell gave in Boston and told me about it; both father and son were there." Herb was thankful to have some slight connection that might impress his teacher.

"Oh, thanks, Herb." He took the magazine from him." I'll have the next issue for you soon. I always seem to be behind." Mr. Brannan paused to snap open his briefcase, slipping the returned magazine inside. "See you in class tomorrow." He walked to the door, plucked his hat and coat from a row of pegs that extended the length of the short wall, and rushed out.

Alone in the empty classroom, Herb ruminated before leaving. Expectations about going to college were probably unrealistic, even though he and his mother talked about the possibility. He knew she dreamed of college for him and reveled in his high grades. Herb sat down at his desk and stretched his legs to their full length. For him, busting his butt was worth it, more for the challenge of achievement than the remote chance that he could go to college.

Herb fumbled with the key to unlock the front door, his fingers shaking from the February cold. His mother was away at a meeting in Boston. When they lived there, she had gone to the city center every other week for a day or two, but her visits had lessened since the fire and having to travel from Brookline. Whenever she returned, she spent dinner time describing the lectures. Speakers came from all over, even a few from other countries. No matter what the topic, his mum offered up a question to make him think and express an opinion. Lyceum lectures were not the only reason she went. Sally was not just his mum but a volunteer for different organizations, especially those working to allow women to vote. He was not sure about everything she did while she was gone. He listened to her stories about attending lectures and meetings, which left big chunks of time without many specifics. Maybe she thought a boy would be bored by talk of women's rights. Had she asked him, Herb was unsure which way he stood on women gaining equal rights, including voting. Women like his mother and girls like Clara had as many brains as men, but their roles were limited to being first a man's daughter and then a man's wife, although his mother had been neither since he was born. He could not imagine Sally or Clara being able to cope with the competitive nature of business, and a job requiring physical strength would be impossible. And yet, should that exclude them from being part of local or even national decisions? He knew most of society believed women were unequal, but he had not made up his mind.

Because he had thought he would meet with Mr. Brannan, Herb had decided not to deliver messages. Usually, he walked to Washington Street amid Brookline's clustered commercial section with its mixture of grand buildings on main thoroughfares and others constructed of less expensive panel brick on side streets. Boys wanting to earn small amounts for delivering messages and packages crowded the general meeting place at the front entrance of a hotel. It was a job Herb had done in Boston before they moved, although then mostly for neighbors and local shopkeepers.

Unaccustomed to the system when he first came to Brookline, he'd approached the boys waiting for assignments; some wore decent clothes, like he did, while others looked ragged. As he got closer and tried to go forward to register for assignments, the others subtly shifted, throwing elbows and shoves to block him. When he pushed through, a foot slammed down hard on his instep. "Hey," he yelled, crooking his elbow to spring a fist at the culprit, but his assailant had melted into the crowd in an instant.

Earning money, even small amounts, was important, so he refused to give in to the ritual bullying. Disregarding comments, he muscled through, ignoring the burning pain in his foot, until he reached the desk and listed his name, age, and address in the errand boy registry. After a long wait, the desk clerk gave him two leftover messages, both to be delivered a long way away. Herb's left foot swelled painfully against his shoe. Wincing with every step, he limped through the unfamiliar Brookline streets to the addresses on the envelopes.

He had returned to the message center again and again, and after weeks of getting the dregs, he earned a reputation for dependability. Even then, though, he sometimes got stuck with the undesirables.

It was scrapping for dimes. Unlike the Western Union messenger boys, who worked all day and had regular pay, errand boys were paid little and hoped for a tip at delivery. Some recipients were grateful and generous, wanting to help young boys. A few snatched the missive and slammed the door without anything extra, even if the messenger had had to travel a long distance. Word of mouth spread names of cheapskates, and their messages stayed at the desk, undelivered or given to new boys who had not yet learned the pitfalls.

Herb knew not showing up that day would count against him. The desk clerk kept track. Herb considered him an okay employer, but the man still had favorites who got the most accessible addresses or high tippers. Nothing was ever wholly fair.

When he got home that afternoon, it was dark, and the kitchen was cold. He lit a lantern and held his hands against the chimney as it warmed while thinking about not meeting with Mr. Brannan. On the table lay a note in his mother's loopy handwriting, reminding him about what she had made for the next day's meals and a list of chores, with a final "good luck with your studies. Love, Mum." Herb missed the aroma of dinner cooking and his mother's questions about his day, even though he outwardly protested being quizzed.

He scratched a match against the cast iron stove and thrust it inside to light the small pieces of kindling. Once the kindling caught fire, he added larger pieces of wood. Until the oven heated, he could not warm up what his mother had left him, so he poured a glass of milk, took a handful of ginger snaps from the flowered ceramic jar, and ate them between gulps. She always made his favorites before she went away—probably out of guilt from leaving him alone.

When his mother was home, they chatted while he ate a quick snack at the worn kitchen table. She would be busy making dinner at the counter or the stove, wanting to know everything he had learned in all his subjects. She had a way of gleaning information without being pushy. Later, as they ate dinner, she'd quiz him about current events, never holding back her opinions about the news and, less often, describing social activities. Her thoughts on private matters were a mystery. He once asked, "Mum, do men attend your voting meetings? You'll need them to get the vote." He wondered about that and if she saw men at all. They never visited her at home.

Surprise had flickered across her face, and she'd nodded her head. "You're right; we will need them, but rarely do they attend. We'll have to approach them outside of meetings." Throughout their life together, his mother had kept her emotions buttoned up.

Clinking the lid back on the cookie jar, he picked up his books and went to the library. His desk sat in the far corner, at the end of the bookcase but close enough to the fireplace to keep warm. He lit a fire and went to his desk. It was a simple writing desk with two drawers on each side and a blotter and inkstand on top. His history book lay open, but the postponed conversation with Mr. Brannan distracted him from reading. He had taken extra courses, making late, weary nights, mostly because he was interested but also because his mother encouraged them as a way to bolster the possibility of college. He thought it was a waste of time to think about it. Acceptance was iffy, and paying tuition was even more questionable.

The savory fragrance floating into the library from the kitchen told him his dinner was heated. Without the usual conversation, he read the newspaper while eating. The Great Fire's effects on the economy still dominated the news with stories of unemployed workers and delayed construction projects. Finished, he cleaned the dishes and returned to his desk, revived. He thrived on knowing the answers when called on by a teacher, the opposite of the self-assured lot that lurked on the playground during recess, tripping and shoving the other students. They were bullies, too confident about getting ahead in life to worry about whether they studied or not, or they were so demoralized by the inevitability of their fate that learning did not matter. Herb turned to his math problems.

The hour was late by the time he damped the fire and lit a candle, the flame wavering as he walked up the stairs to bed. Instead of sleeping soundly, he debated his future. It was not the first time. When feeling upbeat, he came up with reasons to pursue college. Studying science would be a fulfilled dream, with the possibility of getting a good job. Just when he enthusiastically thought about those prospects, his mind would dart to the other side: college and science were impossible. He was tired of fantasizing about something that would result in disappointment. Issue after issue of newspapers described economies everywhere cascading down a steep, slippery slope into the mire and muck of depression. Boston going up in flames made local finances especially dire. *Better to be realistic. With graduation only a few months away and the economy the way it is, I should start looking for a job right away.* Herb startled awake, hearing the clock strike midnight, his bedding knotted around him. He spent the rest of the night agonizing over what he should do.

THREE

After his sleepless night, Herb's eyes were scratchy, his mind muddled. He absentmindedly held the long metal frame with two pieces of bread in the hot oven too long, burning his toast. Smothering the blackened bread with strawberry jam did little to improve its taste. Choking down mouthfuls, he tried to come up with reasons to reinforce his nighttime decision. He was going to drop out of school and find a job. He and his mother made do with income from a bank fund set up before his father's death, but getting a job would help their finances and give him a start toward the future. The jobs he was destined for did not need a high school diploma. *If I start looking right away, I might get a job before Mum returns.* He bypassed thoughts of her reaction. All logic had slipped away.

Frost collected on his slippers when he walked down the front path to retrieve the *Boston Globe* and begin his search of the help wanted ads. It was a part of the paper he rarely paid attention to. When his mother was home, they skimmed the headlines for important news before Herb left for school. By dinnertime, she would have read the newspaper front to back and be bursting for discussion. She insisted Herb state his opinions backed up with details. Growing up, he had stages of resenting the taskmaster part of her. He went petulantly silent but realized that those evening exchanges were part of why he could be "articulate" when prodded.

Herb flipped to the ads and then back to other pages to see if he had missed something. The few advertised jobs were in Boston for maids, cooks, and laborers. There was nothing in Brookline. *Brookline always gets short shrift.* That year, Brookline had turned down the bigger city's greedy desire to annex the small one for its many parks and trees. As a result, Boston's newspaper punished Brookline's rejection by excluding its local news.

Setting aside the paper to read the news later, Herb ignored the few dirty dishes and went to his bedroom. He knew that interviewing for a job called for something better than his everyday school clothes. That left his Sunday suit of dark wool, waistcoat, and trousers. He meticulously combed his light brown hair, applying a dab of macassar oil to keep it in place. Downstairs, he retrieved his warm coat, ready to make a good impression.

The direct walk along the curved paths to the central village was short, but he detoured on side streets to avoid students on their way to school who might wonder why he was going in a different direction. He had decided the local penny newspaper office was a good place to start. It was crammed into a small space on the first floor of a row of plain offices in sight of and contrasting with the town hall's grand Gothic architecture. Herb had spoken occasionally to the newspaper's owner when he delivered messages. While walking toward his destination, he concocted his rationale for being hired: the highest grades on his English papers, compliments on his writing ability, and the asset for a reporter of knowing the town from delivering messages. Newspaper work would not be bad lifelong work, he enthusiastically believed.

He knocked, and in only a few minutes, Mr. Myers opened the door. The pencil-thin man, wearing an ill-fitting gabardine suit and striped waistcoat, looked quizzically at Herb. "Do you have a message so early in the morning?"

"No, I've come to apply for a job because I'd make a—"

"Job?" Mr. Myers jammed his hands on his hips and let go with a torrent of words. "This has turned into a one-man office, and even at that, I'm barely hanging on. So many people are scraping by; a newspaper subscription is one of the first things cut to save expenses." His face was sunken below his cheekbones, with barely enough skin for a beard. "I have to get back to it." His hand clutched the doorknob. "I'm doing the work of three people." Myers began closing the door but paused. "Aren't you supposed to be in school?" Then, without waiting for an answer, he clicked the door shut, an inch away from Herb's face.

Herb stepped back, collecting himself. Instead of a job from knowing the newspaperman, he'd gotten a reprimand for skipping school. Herb stuffed his hands in his pockets and walked back and forth in front of the closed door, debating what to do next. He quickly rejected his previous notion of inquiring about a job at the general store. Whenever his mother shopped there, she bragged about his good grades. The question of why he was not in school was inevitable, and after a second thought, he realized there was no need for additional employees. Mr. and Mrs. Hazeltine owned the store, and their son, John, a few years younger than Herb, helped stock shelves and deliver goods after school.

With slow, heavy footsteps, Herb continued down the street. The lumber store extended half the block with only one wagon in front being loaded with purchases. Herb walked briskly to catch the employee before he returned inside. "No, we don't need workers," came the curt response, and the same came from the foundry and railroad station—there weren't even vacancies for mucking out the stables. "Don't you know about the economy, sonny?"

Herb gave an embarrassed nod. For months, newspapers filled columns with reports about the continuing demise of one business after another, not only in Boston but nationally and across the Atlantic. So focused on his own problems, he felt removed from the outside world.

His confidence sank a notch with each rejection like someone had socked him in the gut and stopped his breath. He had made a list of businesses, but by mid-afternoon, he was afraid to knock on the next door. He crumpled his list and gave up on Brookline. Boston was his only hope.

The following day, Herb boarded the train for the half-hour ride to Boston Commons Station. He had lost the confidence he had started with the day before and dreaded what he would see in the fire-damaged city. Since leaving three months ago, his life had been a scramble of changes and adjustments. There had been few goodbyes. Brookline was a short distance from the big city but a world away. Even before the fire, his Boston neighborhood had been one of change, and his school, too, gained and lost students every year and in between. Herb was one of the few who had attended school in the system since first grade; he was the constant to whom others turned for advice because he had been there so long and also because he was good at school and sports. He missed that stature. The fire forced people to move, and Herb could not stay in touch with his friends.

Signs of the fire's destruction were evident as the train got close to the city. Herb could not look away. Remnants of destroyed warehouses and other burned buildings were inescapable. He pressed his face against the cool glass, watching the grim backdrop as the train approached the station. *You numbskull, what did you think? Boston would be back to normal after three months?*

He walked down the train's aisle to the exit, feeling awkwardly out of place among older, better-dressed businessmen. His outgrown sleeves fell short of his wrists, and he tugged at them in a hopeless effort to make them longer to cover more of his gangly arms. He had never been to Boston Commons Station, so he had hand-drawn a map of the surrounding streets. After ten blocks of walking, he began to notice familiar landmarks, but the surroundings felt different. He stopped to think why the streets clogged with carriages and wagons in his memory were half-full. He remembered. A horse flu had swept down from Canada through the Northeast weeks before the fire. The death of so many horses the city relied on for passenger and commercial transportation was another blow to the economy. His heart lurched. At the bottom of his list of jobs was mucking out stable stalls. The realization hit him like a bucket of cold water—or more like horse urine. With fewer horses, even his job of last resort was unlikely, but he had to keep walking.

The center of the city briefly brought a wave of nostalgia for outings with his mother, visiting museums, or window-shopping around the holidays. That morning, the surviving buildings looked like forbidding fortresses, guarding the interior against desperate job seekers. On the back of his hand-drawn map was Herb's hopeful list of companies to visit about employment. Adjusting the map in the direction of where he stood, he determined his first stop, Western Union Telegraph, was only two blocks away. The office was in the basement of a prominent gray brick building with rows of arched windows across each of its four stories. Bold block letters stretched across the entrance: WESTERN UNION TELEGRAPH. Three steps down from the sidewalk was an office with plain bricks and no windows. Herb took a deep breath and opened the door, making a bell chime. The room was alive with a clack of machinery. The man behind the front desk—his name plaque identified him as George Smedley—rose to greet him.

"You here to send a telegram?" The man scrutinized Herb. "I hope nothing's amiss."

"Oh, no, I'm not here to send a telegram," Herb stammered. "I want to apply for a job."

"What's your rate of speed?"

"Rate of speed?"

"How fast do you type?" Herb flinched at the annoyance in Smedley's eyes.

"I don't type yet," Herb said, "but I can learn. I was thinking of being a messenger boy."

"Sonny, I have so many boys, and even men, begging for work," Smedley scowled, "I could fill this office twice. And those have some skill. Too many people are down and out these days." He sat back down to what he had been doing.

Herb froze for a moment while he digested the bad news and then wordlessly went through the door and up the stairs. He leaned against the brick wall, reexamining his map and list, when a dour man in a top hat passed, angrily pointing a finger at a small sign. Herb turned to read: NO LOITERING. *I'm not loitering; I'm trying to figure out my next stop.* He stood still, buttressing his courage to go on. *Jordan's Department Store. I'll try that.* As he walked the few blocks, he debated his approach. Anything in sales would go to older men, so instead of the front door, he went around to the back loading dock. The lack of activity perplexed him. A lone man sat on a lower step of an external staircase, bare knees showing through his tattered trousers. Hesitantly, Herb approached. "I'm looking for a job . . . maybe loading and unloading wagons."

"Get in line then, but that won't do you no good. The fire burnt so many warehouses, there's nothin' to load or unload." The unshaven man spit out a large glob of phlegm near Herb's foot.

"Where should I go next?"

"How the devil should I know?"

Herb recoiled, not realizing he had asked the question out loud. The bedraggled man struggled to stand up. "Why don't you go down to the dark side."

"The dark side?"

"The harbor! That's where the desperate go." He hung on to the stair railing for balance.

Herb quickly moved away from him to the far end of the lot. He did not have to refer to the map he had drawn. The route to the wharf was clear. His mother's words rang in his ears.

"Never, ever go near the crime-ridden area. It's dangerous, full of thievery, drink, and solicitation." She had continued with other vices before he could ask her what solicitation was.

Her warnings evaporated with his need for a job. Nervously, he hid his return train ticket between his skin and singlet, shoving the few extra coins for lunch deep into his pants pocket.

The stench of refuse assaulted his nostrils blocks before any water was visible. His eyes smarted from the acrid chimney smoke filling the air and blotting the light. Herb plunged down the narrowing streets, looking for signs on buildings—anything to indicate a place to work. Anxiously, he avoided eye contact with men slouched against walls. In their loose-fitting jackets, they could have been laborers or sailors without uniforms, their appearance desperate and menacing. He continued, cautiously peering down side streets as he walked. Before he could cross an approaching intersection, four stubble-chinned hulks swaggered forward.

Herb stepped sideways to veer around them, but they formed a menacing blockade.

The first man belched, close enough for Herb to smell his sour breath.

"Can you tell me where I can find someone in charge?" Before he could say in charge of what, a rough shove hit his back, made him stumble over an extended foot, and catapult forward. When his head smashed against the earth, his teeth pierced his inner lip. He tried to look up, but instead of focusing, his eyes sparked with stars.

"We're in charge, liver lily."

"I'm looking for a job." Herb remained sprawled on the ground, tasting blood. His wrist seared with pain from reflexively trying to break his fall with his hand.

"Job? Like sailing to China?" The leader laughed.

Herb thrashed to get up, but a foot on his arm kept him pinned to the street. Terrified by the prospect of being shanghaied, he remained silent. Pleading would only make him more vulnerable. The ruffians hovered over him, grabbing his jacket so hard they ripped his breast pocket from the fabric. They snatched his few coins from his pants pockets. Angry, there was no more, one clutched his tie and dragged him by his neck. Behind them, a whistle shrieked, and his head bounced off the ground when the man abruptly released his tie. Choking, he opened his eyes to see two blue-coated policemen above him.

"Don't you no-goods have anything better to do than fight?" shouted one of the patrolmen.

"I'm not one of them." Herb groaned hoarsely.

"Get out of here, or it will be jail for you."

"Find something useful to do," the second cop spat in disgust. Then, the two blue coats loped half-heartedly down the alley after his assailants.

"That's what I was trying to do," Herb mumbled to their backs. His head ached; his neck was raw and throat sore from being dragged by his necktie. Struggling up, he examined his clothes. His breast pocket hung down in a flap. He searched on the ground for his jacket's missing buttons. Trembling, he retrieved them from the ground and stuffed them where his money had been in his empty pants pocket. Dirt covered him, and he still tasted blood from his bitten lip. No one would consider hiring him now. With a jerk, he patted his chest in alarm. *Thank goodness*, he muttered. The return ticket was still under his shirt. He righted himself and stumbled down the alley. He needed to get home before his mother returned.

At mid-afternoon, the train was not filled with passengers. As he boarded, a woman stepped back with a frightened look and walked rapidly to another car. He must look like a vagrant. Ashamed, he turned away. *Stupid, stupid, stupid.* How could he have made such a foolhardy decision?

At the Brookline station, he stumbled off the train, hunched over, head down, to avoid explaining his disheveled appearance to anyone who might know him. Relief at arriving home without being recognized was replaced by thoughts whirling in his mind like dirt devils. *What am I going to tell Mum?* His hoped-for announcement of a paying job to support a new life had disappeared like water drops on a hot stove.

He searched his memory for where his mother kept her needle and thread. Sewing the pocket and buttons back on could not be that hard. In his bedroom, he removed his damaged jacket and, after a moment's contemplation, wadded it in the back corner of his small double-door wardrobe. He'd sew it later. *My trousers.* He stepped in front of the looking glass. *Only dirty.* He dampened a towel and wiped them off, wishing like fury his mother's eagle eyes would not notice remnants of dirt.

Scrambling down to the basement, he filled the coal bin from the delivery that had come through the chute earlier that day and trundled a basketful to the kitchen. The square-faced clock in the library rang five lingering chimes. Barely enough time. He lit the fire in the stove and retrieved the pot of stew his mother had put in the icebox before she left. Everything was in place. All he had to do was start his homework. A chill shot down his back. The routine of solving problems and memorizing was no longer necessary. He had left school. He paced and picked up the newspaper, but even the headlines escaped his concentration, and his jigsaw puzzle held no interest. Walking past the bookshelf, he had a momentary inspiration to complete all the unread books now that he was without school or a job. The titles blurred before his eyes. His life abruptly had no coherence, leaving him feeling lost and without direction.

The keys rattling in the lock made Herb jump. He considered racing up the stairs to pretend to be asleep, but what was the point? He had to face his mother eventually.

The cold walk from the station had tinted her cheeks. "Hello, dearheart," she said, entering the library. She leaned down, hugged him, and kissed his cheek. "Everything go all right?"

Bile percolated in his belly. "It went okay." He avoided her violet eyes. When he was little, his mum's usual question came laced with worry and remorse about leaving, but now that he was old enough to fend for himself, she inquired with less concern. Asking about her trips was unnecessary because she usually filled dinner times with stories about what she had seen and done. She was usually chatty and gay, explaining a speaker's topic or discussions with others who attended the Lyceum. Occasionally, she was quiet. During her quiet moods, she focused on him, asking what he had done during her absence. She was always keen to know about his studies, especially his grades. He let her mood dictate their dinner conversation—or lack of it. Without other family members to dilute their time together, Herb was good at sensing her disposition. Her facial expressions and movements revealed a more nuanced account of her trips than her words. He could read her moods, but he never deciphered what triggered them.

After her greeting of a glad-to-be-home hug, his mother returned to the entryway to hang up her coat and balance her hat next to her gloves on the shelf above. She left her carpet bag at the bottom of the stairs to take up on her way to bed later. Her burgundy silk dress rustled as she swept down the hall. He imagined her wrapping her well-worn white apron around her clothing and checking the stew. "It's getting warm," she called from the kitchen. "I was afraid you'd forget or let it burn," she said with a teasing tone.

Herb's arms hung slack, his wrist throbbing from being knocked to the ground. The desk, usually his favorite place, was repellent without tasks to accomplish so he half-heartedly continued working on his puzzle.

She called out again when he did not respond to her humor. "It's my good fortune to have someone to count on. Thank you for taking care of things while I was gone."

Someone to count on—someone who has dropped out of school and doesn't have a job. Herb desperately wanted to rush into the kitchen to explain what had happened and face the inevitable confrontation and overwhelming disappointment. His opportunities were those she had not had. He was ending his future and hers through him. She was the one who wanted him to continue to college; he was more practical. A steady office job would be fine; anything was better than mindless manual labor. She had told him she wished she had been able to go to college, and he suspected that was why she pushed *him* to get more education.

When they sat across from each other at the dinner table, his mum was in her usual return-from-a-trip-story-telling mood. "You should see Boston, Herb. Workers have hauled away some wreckage, and construction of new buildings has started in a few places. There's progress but still so much residue—piles of brick, burned timber, uncovered holes." She put down her fork, the slight lines of age tracing across her brow. "The extent of the fire could have been prevented. Do you think officials will ever fix the flaws that caused so much damage?" It was her usual way of making him evaluate issues with the expectation of answers supported by facts. An answer was forming, and he longed to engage in their usual repartee. However, he sat paralyzed. Any response might reveal that he had seen the city first-hand instead of being in school. He was also ravenous. He had not eaten since breakfast. He took a third biscuit and mopped the deep brown broth surrounding chunks of beef, potatoes, carrots, and tomatoes in his soup bowl.

"I guess I haven't read the newspapers as much as I should."

"Skipping the newspaper. That's unusual."

He could decipher question marks in her eyes.

"I stopped by the bakery on my way home and bought an apple cake. Would you like some?" she asked when his plate was empty, and his hands were still.

"Thanks, Mum. I'd like a piece, and then I'm going up to read in bed." He gulped down the cake and pushed back his chair. "I'm glad you're home." He hesitated. "We can talk more tomorrow." The dishes rattled in his hand on his way to the sink.

In the morning, Herb's mother pounded on his bedroom door. "Why haven't you come down for breakfast?"

"Mum, I'm not going; I don't feel well." It wasn't a lie because agonizing about what to tell her had kept him awake all night. Phantoms of what he would do next chased him through his dreams, and thoughts of facing her disappointment haunted him. He had buried his head under the pillow for so long he could smell the goose down, made moist from his breath. He wished he could end it all and suffocate in a soft grave of his bed.

His mother cracked open the door, her slippered feet scuffing softly on the wood as she moved toward the bed. "Herb," she looked down at him. Then he saw fear rise in her eyes. "What happened to your neck? It's red," she frowned. "Do you have a rash? Are you hot?" She laid the back of her hand against his forehead. He reached up to touch his neck. It *was* sore.

"No, no," he stammered. "I don't think I have a rash." Pushing himself up against his pillow caused a sharp pain in his swollen wrist. "I caught my tie on something, and it gave my neck a real jerk." He hated himself for lying, but he could not admit a thug had dragged him down a Boston back street. "That . . . that's not the reason I'm staying home. I ache all over."

"Herb, you haven't missed a day of school since you were little. I'm sending for the doctor."

"No, Mum, no!" He could tell his strangled response startled her. "Maybe I just slept funny. I'll try to get up."

"I'll make you some hot ginger tea. You still have time, but you better get going."

When he heard her footsteps recede down the stairs, he got out of bed to go to the bathroom to relieve himself, wondering if he might vomit as well. What *was* he going to tell her?

Only a few minutes passed before she was back again. "Herb," she said on the other side of the door. "When I picked up the newspaper, I found two letters in the box. They must have been delivered after I came home." She paused, "From the school. Come downstairs immediately."

"Okay," he murmured as he considered leaping out the second-floor window instead.

"Herb, did you hear me?"

"Yes," his trembling voice grew louder. "I'll be right down; I have to get dressed." *What were the messages from school?* He ached with fear.

His mother sat at the round wood table. A plate stacked with toast sat in the center next to the butter dish. Herb's stomach pinched at the sight of food. His mother wore her brown checked cotton dress tied with a dark ribbon at the waist. A cap of the same fabric gathered at the base of her neck kept the dust out of her hair when she cleaned. The thin line of her compressed lips stretched across her pale face.

"Open it." She nudged the envelope across the table toward him as he sat down.

With a glance at the envelope, his hunger vanished. John Brannan's name was on the return address. *Why would Mr. Brannan send me a letter?* Herb broke the wax seal, extracted the letter, and began to read.

13 February 1873

Dear Master Andersen,

I had intended to talk to you the day after I left my office in such a hurry. It was my daughter Diane's tenth birthday, and I had to hurry to pick up her favorite frosted chocolate cake before the bakery closed. I made it by minutes.

I wanted to explain why I left in such haste and to learn what you wanted, but you have been absent. Let's have that conversation after class when you return.

Regards,

John Brannan

Herb's mind stood still as he tried to absorb the letter. *Mr. Brannan really had wanted to talk to me. It wasn't a brushoff. And now I've messed everything up.* Emerging from his concentration, he caught his mother's steely look. She moved the second, already unsealed envelope close to him.

13 February 1873

Dear Mrs. Andersen:

I am writing to inquire about your son Herbert's unexcused absence for the past two days. We presume it was not because of illness, or we would have heard from you. You may not know that Brookline High School, like all public schools, is reimbursed for student days attended. Herbert's grades have been commendable since his arrival last December. Nevertheless, truancy will not be tolerated.

I want to discuss the ramifications with you and your son after school. Please affirm by messenger that such a meeting is possible.

Yours in closing,
Headmaster David Quincy

"What does yours say?" she asked.

"It doesn't say much."

His mother picked up Brannan's letter, her hand unsteady as she read. Finishing, she slowly shook her head, her eyes brimming. "In a short time, a teacher has shown interest in you, and not only that, but your grades have gained the respect of the headmaster—until this week. Why weren't you at school?"

Herb could not lift his eyes. He rested his elbows on the table, protecting his throbbing wrist; his head cradled morosely on the other hand. "Mum, I'm sorry. It's not what I meant to happen."

"You've worked so hard all your life, and now, just when it really matters, you choose to throw everything away. You were always so predictable. What has happened?"

"There's nothing to throw away. Someone like me does not get to go on. College is just for rich kids, so high school no longer matters. I might as well get a job now. Or I thought so. The fire and depression have mucked up everything." Herb scraped back his chair and stood up. "I'm sorry."

His mother eyed the wall clock. "We're through for now, but you will go to school this morning, and we will meet with the headmaster afterward. Get going. You can't afford to make another mistake."

Students glanced curiously at Herb as he slid into his desk, chest pounding from the run to make it on time for his first class. He hunched his shoulders, head bowed, attempting to blend invisibly with the desk. A whispered voice said, "Mr. Smarty Pants is back." It was followed by a spitball to the back of his neck. Then, a friendly hand shoved his shoulder. "Were you sick?" It was David Hall, a recess kickball friend. Herb nodded back just as Clara brushed by, going out of her way to pass his desk. "Glad you're back," she murmured, surrounded by a flutter of giggles over her detour.

The chatter hushed as Miss Elliot, the history teacher, entered. After hanging her coat on a hook and placing a thick book on her desk, she scanned the room and smiled when her eyes connected with Herb's.

Herb was flabbergasted. *They were sorry I was gone.* Why, he was not sure. Did his teachers and fellow students respect his hard work, regardless of his newness and lack of a family name? Maybe others recognized an unrealistic dream of making something of himself more than he did. It was a heady thought worth dreaming of when he went to bed that night . . . if he survived that long.

"Good morning, class. Today, we will begin studying the third volume of Gibbon's *Decline and Fall of the Roman Empire*."

Miss Elliott's voice temporarily jolted him back from his anxious thoughts, though not for long. Most of the day, the specter of what the headmaster would say to his mother invaded his mind. When the last bell rang after science class, Herb gathered his materials and headed toward the door.

"Herb, I'd like to speak to you," Mr. Brannan said.

"I can't right now, Mr. Brannan. I'm sorry." A tremor jangled his spine as he hurried out of the classroom through the crowd of students congregating in the hallway. When he reached the main hallway, he spotted his mother farther down the long corridor. The narrow black hat pushed forward on her light hair bobbed up and down with her stride. Students parted respectfully when she passed, looking around to figure out whose mother she was. Her erect figure in a stylish wool coat left an unmistakably favorable impression.

By the time he pushed through the other students to catch up, she had already spoken to the clerk in the anteroom. "We have to wait here until the headmaster is ready," she explained. They wordlessly sat in two straight-backed, wooden chairs.

In ten minutes, Mr. Quincy appeared. He was a short, heavyset man with a beak-like nose poking from his fleshy cheeks. Wiry gray whiskers cascaded from his sideburns to his beard.

Herb felt the scrutiny of his gold-brown eyes, enlarged by his spectacles.

"I don't believe I've met either of you."

Herb heard a glint of surprise. Perhaps the headmaster had not expected an attractive woman and a robust boy who was both muscular and a top student to be called in about truancy.

"Come into my office." His walk was more of a waddle than a stride.

They followed him into a plain room with few decorations except bookshelves stacked with books and papers. Tidy piles of papers lay on his desk next to his inkstand. Mr. Quincy waited until they were seated before walking around it to sit down and glower at them. Herb perceived his mother's posture straightening a notch. Despite the stakes of losing the dream of her son continuing his education, she would not cower.

Herb saw annoyance flick across the headmaster's face, perhaps at his failure to cow her.

"Mrs. Andersen, did you allow your son to miss two days of class this week?"

"Herb had a task he thought he needed to do in Boston. He suspected I would disapprove, so he went without permission," she answered truthfully.

"Did he ask his father?" Quincy's jaw muscles worked behind the flab as he waited for her answer.

"I'm a widow."

He took another careful look at her and then turned to Herb. "What task was more important than school?" Headmaster Quincy's eyes were piercing him like needles.

"We moved from Boston right after the fire," Herb shifted nervously. "I wanted to see what happened to Boston," his face warmed, "and I wanted to see if there were any jobs."

"Jobs? You're only three months away from graduating. How could you think of leaving?"

"I wanted to see what was possible," Herb faltered. "It was a mistake. I need to finish school."

"Well, your actions have put that possibility in jeopardy."

Herb silently quivered like a vole under Mr. Quincy's predatory owl eyes.

"Our high school is paid for each day a student attends. You have cost us money; if you don't want to attend, we can allow someone outside Brookline to take your place."

His mother sat ramrod straight in her chair.

"It's regrettable when someone of your ability doesn't take opportunity more seriously."

Herb wondered if the headmaster looked directly at him to avoid his mother's penetrating violet eyes.

"I promise not to miss any more school." He hated the pleading sound of his voice.

"Your case would have been closed," the headmaster idly moved the stack of papers from one side of his desk to the other, "but Mr. Brannan and Miss Elliot have put your name on a list of those seniors who will graduate among the top of the class. You have now negated those commendations and maybe even a chance to graduate."

"He's had excellent grades here and at his previous high school," his mother said. The sound of her voice, struggling to conceal her desperation, washed Herb with guilt. She cared so much about his opportunities.

"Mrs. Andersen, I'm sorry for the loss of your husband, but clearly, a boy needs the strong discipline of a man to raise him properly. We shall see what happens, but I can't guarantee anything." Mr. Quincy rose from his desk chair. "You know the way out."

The sanctimonious principal's dismissal was so fast that Herb and his mother did not move for a moment, but there was nothing to do but leave. Instinctively, Herb knew it would do no good to try to stand up to him. He could tell his mother felt powerless, too, and it was his fault.

They trudged home, silently linked by the headmaster's disparaging words. When they got to their apartment, Herb escaped to his studies, relieved to have the weekend to catch up from two missed days. But as he sat at his desk, staring down at his notebook, his mother, not his assignments, occupied his thoughts. His earliest memories were of her attention, which was caring but not indulgent. Rules were definite. Most of the time, he was her preoccupation, but not always. Regular gaps in time occurred when she went to overnight meetings in the city or even to Providence. When he was little, she hired someone to stay with him. "She's a substitute grandmother since you don't have one of your own," his mum had explained. Sometimes, his caretakers were what he might wish for in a grandmother, with warm hugs, storytelling, and game-playing. A few, however, ignored him. Thinking Herb had not noticed, one slipped food from the cupboard into a satchel to take home and gave him a cracking back of the hand about any request for more than a glass of milk. At a young age, he'd resolved never to complain or confess, and his mother's return had always made everything right . . . or almost.

With the comforting aromas and sounds of his mother cooking in the kitchen, Herb put memories aside and began his homework. An hour later, she had to call him twice for dinner to break his absorption in his homework. He had finally solved the last math equation. He stood up with satisfaction, knowing only a few in his class would succeed at all the calculations. Just in case, he would double-check his work after he ate.

Since the kitchen butted up against the other half of the duplex, it had no windows. The plumbing was inside the shared common wall. Windows were located on the front and back of the apartment building instead of at the sides. A small downstairs closet contained a pull-chain toilet and sink. Upstairs, the bathroom abutted the other half of the house. Sometimes, the sound of running water came from next door, but he and his mother were less concerned with the noise than grateful to have indoor plumbing upstairs and down.

He pushed aside the temptation to apologize for skipping school. The conversation with Headmaster Quincy and his snotty judgment about not having a man in the house had piqued Herb's curiosity. His mother had told him that his father had died around the time he was born and had left an insurance policy to take care of them, held and invested by State Street Bank and Trust in Boston. The threat of being expelled from school and searching for a job made him curious about his father's work. Why hadn't he asked more questions about him? His mother had told him how fortunate they were that his father had ensured they would not be left destitute. That seemed all that was important about someone he had never known. Thinking more carefully, he realized how little he knew about his parents' marriage and short life together. Now that he was close to graduating and making decisions about the future, he wanted to know where he came from to better understand where he might go. The few times he'd asked, his mother had redirected the conversation. He'd assumed speaking of her dead husband was painful. Or perhaps she considered the past behind her and therefore unimportant. She had always made a point about looking forward instead of back. Had she ever thought of having men as friends? Men and women attended the lectures she went to, but he had never known her to go out with men. Her volunteer work in the suffragist movement was in the company of other women whom she talked about most. He scanned her face—the oval shape, high cheekbones, attractive eyes, and frame of light hair. She was focused on cutting small bites of her porkchop instead of her usual conversation. Her thoughts were elsewhere. Was it worry about his staying in school or something else or even someone else?

"Mum, you said pictures of my father were lost when we moved a long time ago. What did he look like?"

He felt a twinge of guilt when his mother furrowed her brow and half closed her eyes. Her expression was sorrowful, as if the subject was too painful to discuss. "He was handsome and strong . . . smart in lots of different ways, but that was a long time ago."

Despite causing her discomfort, Herb wasn't quite ready to let the topic go. "I'd really like to know more."

She took a deep breath. "Now that you're becoming a man, you have the same physical features—tall and broad-shouldered. Your hair is a blend—not as light as mine or as dark as his. He has . . . had," she stumbled, "intense chestnut eyes. You're just as smart, but he was forceful with his knowledge. He always had to be in command." She caught Herb's eyes. "Quiet intelligence like yours has advantages." Her eyes took on a dreamy look as her mind revisited the past.

"How did he die?"

His mother jumped as if pricked by a needle. "I've told you before, he was sick and couldn't recover. There's nothing more to add." She got up and took the empty plates from the table. "You must have lessons to make up for your absences. From the looks of it, getting back in the good graces of the headmaster is not going to be easy. If he expels you from high school, your future is over."

Herb flinched as if she had slapped him, remembering the thugs in the back streets of Boston and picturing life there. "He likes my grades," Herb reminded her. "But he wouldn't care if I left. He favors high hats. I've seen him bow and scrape when the fancies come to the building."

"Herb," she stopped abruptly, midway to the sink. "That's just an excuse. You caused this problem," she fumed. "So much is at stake. I've tried to give you the opportunities I never had. You're right; we don't have much, but you do have intelligence, so education and hard work are your ways to get ahead. Don't waste them." She snatched up the empty serving bowl. "Mistakes can damage the rest of your life. Trust me, I know."

Her comments shook him. She had never mentioned mistakes. He looked up at her stricken face. "What mistakes, Mum?"

She shook her head, saying no more. His last glance before she turned to carry the rest of the dishes to the sink caught an expression of despair. Was it because she had unintentionally disclosed something?

Herb completed the rest of his missed work in only a couple of hours. It felt good to be doing homework at his desk, but it was only half satisfying. He still had to face Mr. Brannan and a few other teachers. He had let them down, too.

In bed that night, his mother's words about mistakes plagued him. Instead of his usual temptation to retreat into a shell and make problems disappear as if they did not exist, he kept cogitating. To him, his mother was invincible. She strove to be organized, control situations, think things through, and question everything before making decisions. Mistakes were in opposition to her persona. Curiosity about her life and the longtime mystery of his father now nudged and poked at his consciousness, insisting that he find answers to questions he had never asked.

SIX

At school on Monday, Herb brushed off more questions about his absence by saying he had been absent because of a family matter. He just shook his head when friends asked something like, "Your grandparents?" His excuse was not a lie. Getting a decent job was a family matter, even if it had been a stupid idea.

Instead of waiting for his teachers to call on him, he raised his hand to prove he deserved to remain in school. The day breezed by until it was finally time for mathematics and science, taught by Mr. Brannan. They were his favorite subjects. At the end of class, he wanted to explain why he had declined his teacher's invitation to meet with him the previous Friday. Mr. Brannan was the opposite of the headmaster, who always projected an aura of being a notch above, reinforced by any opportunity to diminish others. He wielded power through authority and self-designated superiority. Mr. Brannan gave students a sense of accomplishment when they succeeded and inspired them to strive for more. Herb looked forward to meeting with him.

At the beginning of class, Mr. Brannan wrote a series of problems on the blackboard for the class to solve. Herb wanted to be the one to work out all the answers. Clara caught his eye as she sat down. Herb saw a hint of uncertainty in her cornflower blue eyes, eyes that usually blazed with quiet confidence. She was going for the same goal he was—perfection. He had spent hours over the weekend reviewing equations, making sure of his answers.

"All right, class, let's see if we can understand the six problems before the bell rings." Mr. Brannan was slight in build, sometimes outsized by the older students, but because of the force of his intellect, no one would ever call him small. He reached up to start the equations at the left topmost area of the blackboard. "This is the beginning of trigonometry, our work for the last months of school." The scraping of feet in the back row sounded resistance. "Who wants to write the answer to the first equation on the blackboard?"

Herb did not hesitate before raising his hand. Standing at the blackboard, he wrote and explained, step by step, how he had reached the answer.

"Well done, Herb," Mr. Brannan said. He looked at the others. "If you didn't get the correct answer, copy Herb's explanations. Learning trigonometry is a building process, so the rest will become impossible if you don't understand the beginning."

In the end, Herb had done all six problems correctly, and Clara five. Most others only made minor errors, keeping up with Brannan's well-explained directions. Only the boys in the back slunk down in their seats and said nothing, but their cockiness allowed them to swagger out of class when the bell rang, their arrogance something others were reluctant to confront.

"We'll continue working on these until everyone understands them. I don't want to leave anyone behind." Mr. Brannan wrote equations on the blackboard. "Here is the new set of problems for tomorrow." The final bell drowned out his final words, forcing him to repeat them: "Copy them before you leave."

Herb had rehearsed what he should say to Mr. Brannan several times but still held back. His feet would not move. *Talk to him tomorrow. That will work just fine.*

"Herb," Mr. Brannan's voice jarred his thoughts. "Do you have time? I'd like to discuss the—"

"I'm sorry, Mr. Brannan—"

"If you have obligations, we could talk before school in the morning."

"No, no, I didn't mean that." Herb's palms were moist. "I'm sorry I walked away so fast last Friday without saying why."

Mr. Brannan stepped down from the teaching platform. "Here, have a seat," he said, gesturing to Herb's desk while he took the one next to him in the front row. "You're right. A little explanation would have helped." His eyes softened as they focused on Herb. "I guess I was guilty of that, too, when I rushed out to buy a birthday cake. Maybe it's a lesson for both of us." A half smile turned up his lips.

Herb nodded with a full exhale of relief. "Thanks."

"Now, let's talk about more serious matters."

Herb grimaced.

Mr. Brannan reached over to pat his shoulder. "Headmaster Quincy has told me the trouble you're in about missing school. I've worked for him for over a decade." He shifted in his seat as if considering whether to say more. "I know him well. He likes his position as head, maybe a little too much." He coughed. "Let's just leave it at that."

"Do you think he'll throw me out?"

"Hmm, I'm not sure. Hopefully not." Brannan frowned. "Even for him, that would be harsh when you have excelled in every class. What he might do is influence your decision to go to college. Applications require a recommendation from the headmaster, not just teachers."

"That's not fair." Herb's insides twisted.

"No, it is not, and unfortunately, it will not be the only obstacle in your life that's . . . not fair. Let's see if we can counteract any negative influence. Your job will be to keep up your grades. I'm not sure what I can do, but I'll look for opportunities." With that, Mr. Brannan stood up and stepped onto the platform to his desk. He opened his briefcase and pulled out a magazine. "Another issue of *Scientific American*. I haven't had time to read it, so here." He held out the magazine. "This time, I'll read it after *you* finish. Maybe you can tell me which articles are worth spending time on."

Herb took the proffered magazine. "Thank you, Mr. Brannan." He wished he were the type who was effusive, but that was not him, and Mr. Brannan probably knew it. "I'll start right away."

"No rush," He waved a hand at his cluttered desk, "but electromagnetism is the cover article. I'd be interested in your take on it. Thanks for staying, Herb. I need to organize my papers before I leave, and then I have an errand." He shook his head. "I always seem to be given something to pick up on the way home."

His complaining tone was unconvincing—Herb suspected he did not mind doing errands.

Herb carefully rolled the magazine and tucked it inside his jacket. "Thanks again. Bye, Mr. Brannan." Leaving the classroom, Herb felt like he was walking on air. The tension of the past week began to release. *Mr. Brannan wants my opinion on . . . what did he say?* Taking out the magazine to skim the cover, he read "electromagnetism." It was tempting to read the article as he walked, but after a moment, he rolled up the magazine and put it away. He'd go home and do his homework before allowing *Scientific American* to absorb him.

"Herb, is that you?" His mother called out just as he closed the front door.

I don't know who else it might be. "Yes, Mum," he said, loud enough for her to hear as he hung his outer jacket on a hook.

"What happened at school?" The staccato of her shoes on the kitchen floor quieted as she stepped onto the hall carpet. "Did you see the headmaster again?" Her brow knotted with concern.

"No, Mum, but I did talk to Mr. Brannan." He unrolled the *Scientific American* and showed her the cover. His success with trigonometry and his conversation with Mr. Brannan gave him calm confidence. "He wants my opinion about this."

She arched her eyebrows. "Well, that's an accolade from a teacher. What about your chances of staying in school?"

"Mr. Brannan wasn't sure what Headmaster Quincy might do, but he'll try to put in a good word when he has a chance."

"Not entirely reassuring." His mum's voice caught, her worry for his future palpable. "But at least you have someone on your side."

He did not miss the apprehension in her eyes before she quickly turned back toward the kitchen with, "I'm still worried."

After putting his books and the *Scientific American* on the desk, Herb sat at the kitchen table while his mother poured him a glass of milk and set it next to a plate of warm gingersnaps. A subdued mood linked them, both pondering their thoughts instead of talking. Herb preoccupied himself by eating, convinced that his mother's lack of conversation came from the blow he dealt her with his wrongheaded miscalculation that risked graduating from high school. He knew her well enough to realize that a fresh batch of gingersnaps was a nuanced message that she was not as judgmental as he feared. Even though furious about his miscalculation, she understood it was a mistake—a terrible mistake rather than misbehavior. He dipped a gingersnap in his milk and closed his eyes as the pungent taste sank into his tongue. No other gingersnaps measured up to his mother's. He reached for another, not able to extinguish the folly of his actions, which threatened his future and must have seemed like a slap in the face for all she had done for him. Sometimes, his logic got ahead of him.

She sat across from him, drinking hot tea from a flowered china cup. "What exactly did Mr. Brannan say?" The black rim around her violet irises seemed more pronounced when she was tense.

Herb bit back a sigh, preparing himself for a conversation he knew would not be a usual after-school chitchat about classes and assignments.

He stuffed the entire gingersnap into his mouth, "He said—"

"Don't talk with your mouth full."

Swallowing in a gulp, he had to wait until the big lump cleared his esophagus. "Mr. Brannan hoped my good grades would keep me in school."

"But?"

"But, even if they help, missing school might hurt my chances of going on."

His mother's eyes pressed shut.

Herb suspected she was holding back tears. Pressure spread in the center of his chest, shortening his breath. He rued being the cause of her unhappiness. His job search had been a boneheaded attempt to make life easier. Instead, he had made everything harder.

"Mum, in all my school days, I've barely ever missed a class, even on account of being sick. Upsetting my future on account of two days out isn't fair."

After a noticeable intake of breath, his mother spoke. "You've just learned the truth, and it's a painful lesson. Life is not fair, especially for people like us. We weren't born into wealth. One mistake can erase everything we've strived for. Children end up in factories, men work as laborers until they become too crippled to stand, and women are stuck in menial positions, or worse . . . all for a few coins to survive by. Education is a way to escape the hardships of the laboring class. That's why it's so important to do well in school."

Any response escaped Herb. His argument that a college education was the only way to do well in life would fall as flat as griddle cakes. Seldom had he heard his mother speak with such passion. Their kitchen interior replicated the darkness and quiet outside as the day's traffic diminished and streetlamps came on. Soon, the chandelier above the table provided the only interior light.

His mother broke the silence first, a grim look on her oval face. "Maybe all is not lost, Herb. We will keep working and avoid mistakes." She pushed back her chair. "Why don't you light a fire in the library to keep you warm at your desk? You probably have homework."

"And a *Scientific American* to read." But the burden of her despair was his, too.

"Electromagnetism? Tell me why you found this most interesting, Herb."

Herb and his teacher sat in the front row of student desks precisely a week after the fearful meeting with the headmaster. Mr. Brannan knew how to get him to talk. He didn't waste time on the idle jabbering that bored him. If it was a discussion with meaning, Herb was willing to say something. Mr. Brannan always offered that to him.

"It has to do with a scientist named Maxwell and his experiments with electricity and magnetism. Here's the interesting thing." Herb turned to his teacher, full face. "It might be helpful to what the Bells are doing." He watched Mr. Brannan's puzzled expression. "Do you remember my mother went to a lecture by Alexander Graham Bell and his father, describing their interest in sending sound with electricity?"

Mr. Brannan nodded. "Now that you remind me, I do."

"Well, electromagnetism might be useful in sending sound over wire." Herb shook his head. "Scotland is a small country, but something about it must stir up inventions. Both Maxwell *and* the Bells are Scots."

A smile slid across Mr. Brannan's clean-shaven face. Herb thought his forehead was broad because it had to be wide enough to contain his big brain. From there, his cheeks narrowed into a small chin.

"I must say, you've gotten ahead of me. If only all students were like you, Herb. It would make teaching an even greater reward." He left the front-row desk chair to step onto the teaching platform, preparing to leave. "I'd like to have another conversation about this when I've finished reading the article and given it more thought." He picked up his briefcase and stepped down. "I'm glad to have someone to discuss it with."

Herb savored his warm, reassuring handshake.

On his way home, the past week's events gripped Herb. The grim realities of the job market, thugs about his age thrashing him, the headmaster threatening expulsion, and, worst of all, disappointing his mother. Then, a ray of sun shone through the black clouds of his thoughts. His teacher had praised his comment on electromagnetism and the Bells. The balance of the week weighed heavily toward failure, but he had managed one peaceful breath. Even the raw ring around his neck and injured wrist pained less noticeably.

The walk from school took Herb through parks and along serpentine paths, which often confused visitors with their turns and loops but had become enjoyably familiar since their move. Brookline's parks contained a profusion of trees—oak, birch, Eastern white pine, hemlock—giving the town a rural setting despite its substantial population. The landscape blurred into obscurity as Herb's thoughts returned to his family. Not even a wedding photograph existed of his parents, which was one of life's milestones often captured by a camera. "Lost," his mother had said about pictures and "dead" about relatives before switching to another topic that absorbed the conversation.

Extended family members had not mattered. He and his mother did fine together. He was a cotton shirt boy, not one who wore flannel to school so he could go directly to work, either at home or for someone else. Clothing symbolized one's station in life, but his mother had made clear, actions and education were even more critical.

"You're home early," his mother's voice came from the kitchen after he had shut the front door.

"Any more troubles?" she asked warily as he entered the kitchen's cozy warmth.

"I decided not to deliver messages because I met with Mr. Brannan."

Her eyes brightened. "Come, tell me about it after you change your school clothes."

Herb settled at the kitchen table, describing his conversation while eagerly breaking a piece of bread from a freshly baked loaf. The butter liquified as he spread it. The first mouthful was one more bright spot to an already good day. "I told Mr. Brannan that my favorite article was about electricity and magnetism. It listed all sorts of uses. If I understand it right, I think those ideas might help Mr. Bell's experiment to send sound over electrical wires." He tore another piece of bread, eating the soft texture first, then the crust—the tastiest part.

"I went to a lecture by the Bells."

"That's why I thought of them," Herb said, looking up at her. "Mr. Brannan said we could talk more about the article after he read it."

His mother's attentive eyes told him she was calculating what it all meant. "I told you Mr. Brannan is on your side."

Herb nodded. "Miss Elliott and maybe my other teachers, but they're only teachers. Mr. Quincy has the authority. He's the one who matters." He took two gulps of milk. "Mum, if a college accepted me, like you want, how would we pay for it?"

She lowered her gaze to her floral-patterned teacup. Herb waited for an answer while he ate more bread. He imagined the twists and turns of her mind like a ceramic model of the brain he had seen in the Boston Society of Natural History. Her eyes moved from side to side as if scouring information inside her head. Pride swelled as Herb, not for the first time, admired how smart she was.

"There may be a way." Her eyes connected with his. "I don't even know the cost. I guess the amount depends on which college. They probably have different tuition." She mulled it over. "Going on with your education would give you respect for the rest of your life. No one could knock you down." She stared across the kitchen as if looking into the future.

"Yes, but Mum, where would the money come from?"

Her head jolted as if his words had snapped her back to reality. The set of her mouth told him it was, at the moment, a place she did not want to be. "Our money comes from the fund your father left us." Her words wobbled.

Questions swirled in Herb's head. *His father must have established the fund at a young age. Since he didn't die suddenly, he must have had time to plan—odd if he was sick.* However, he would have to wait for an answer; his mother's compressed lips warned him not to ask more.

Words of praise scrawled on his assignments rewarded Herb's efforts to submit flawless schoolwork. He eschewed making a single mistake. As winter proceeded, his confidence grew. When he included a bit of humor in an answer during class—"the French Revolution was a real pain in the neck"—laughter followed. It meant the other students were paying attention and laughing with him, not at him.

"Very good," Miss Elliot responded. "It's nice to see you smile," she added, smiling back at him.

Spring was cool, not ready to release winter's grip and allow crocuses and daffodils to push up through the dark earth, but Herb did not care about the weather; he had made friends. At recess, his muscular build made him adept at kickball, tug of war, and foot races. Winning was important there, too, and the other boys had noticed his ability. Another born athlete, Jim, had rusty hair and freckles on his face and hands. His humor was subtle. After Herb had made a miraculous goal, instead of congratulations, Jim remarked with a sly grin, "I think you went a lit-tle left; go for the center next time." Ben was unbeatable at marbles and talked all through the game—about what Herb could never precisely remember—but his conversation entertained them while his deadeye aim captured marbles. The mischief-makers, with their sneaky tripping and jutting elbows, kept their distance after Herb subtly stepped into the fray to oust those picking on weaker kids. Herb tended to go through life with little conversation, yet a constellation of boys and sometimes girls surrounded him admiringly and depended on his implicit protection.

EIGHT

"May I have a word with you before you leave?" Mr. Brannan said from his desk on the platform as Herb came into the last class of the day.

"Yes, sir," Herb said, concealing his curiosity. He slipped his metal-nibbed pen in the indentation next to the ink-well as he considered what Mr. Brannan wanted. Had the headmaster spoken to him? Then he relaxed. *Scientific American. I'll bet that's why.*

The usual hubbub ended the day—students talking back and forth, putting on their outer coats, and saying parting words to Mr. Brannan before he slid into the student desk next to Herb. Herb liked the side-by-side camaraderie, so close he got a whiff of hair cream. Mr. Brannan did not have to be pompous and act above everyone. He kept order, even with the boys in the back, without whacking knuckles with a ruler. Science and math, the classes he taught, were not easy, not even for the best students like him. However, Mr. Brannan had a way of explaining complicated information step-by-step so no one was left behind. There was no way for anyone to avoid his questioning. Students had to stay alert, even the dull and recalcitrant. Herb liked to be called on. Science and math were his favorite classes, and Mr. Brannan was his favorite teacher.

"Herb, I'm impressed that you connected electromagnetics to the transfer of sound." He thumbed to the page with a turned-down corner.

"My mother goes to lectures and then tells me all about them when she comes home. It's almost like I go to lectures with her. It's one way I learn."

"Well, she must have a good memory to recall so many details—you, as well, young man." Brannan had put his briefcase on the floor next to him. "You took one piece of information from the article on electromagnetics and speculated that it might be useful for something else." He clapped his hands and rubbed them together like over a fire, apparently eager for what was next. "Anyone in Boston with half a wit knows of the Bells' work with the deaf here. I did a little research about their latest projects." He rapped his knuckles on the desktop in enthusiasm. "The younger Bell, Alexander—has taken a position at Boston University. His title is impressive. Let me read it. It's a mouthful." He looked down at the page he had marked. "'Professor of vocal physiology and elocution at the Boston University School of Oratory.' He also privately teaches deaf students."

"Do the Bells research sound and electricity at the university?"

"That's one of the places. They also have a laboratory at their home in Brantford, Ontario, and another in a downtown Boston office. Last year's fire did much to damage the university's buildings." He held up his hand. "Don't worry, the science building survived."

"Lucky! So much didn't."

"Indeed. It got me thinking." He chuckled. "My wife says that a new thought from me is dangerous."

Herb detected humor and affection for his wife twinkling in Mr. Brannan's eyes before they turned serious. "Your grades at Boston High School and Brookline should allow you to go on. I suggest you consider Boston University. It's close and well-known for science and mathematics."

"And Mr. Bell's there, too," Herb said, finding it a challenge to assimilate that revelation.

Brannan nodded. "Because of his reputation, Professor Bell attracts proven scientists and machinists. As an undergraduate, you would be unlikely to study with him, but an application to the university might still be worthwhile."

Herb hid his trembling hands on his lap, speechless.

"I hesitated to mention it to you because of the inevitable hurdles. Only a few of our students go on to a university, and many of those have what might be called an inside track." Brannan stood up restlessly, walked to the door, and turned back. "I want you to remember that there are ways to get ahead other than college if it doesn't work out." He slid into the student desk beside Herb again.

"I should try." Herb's answer came instantly, as if directly from his mind to his voice without thinking. "A college degree is the ticket to money and respect."

After a long inhale, Brannan responded slowly. "Money and respect are two different things, Herb. Be careful. You may fail if you believe that going to college is the only way to gain respect and money." He leaned closer. "You're curious and have the desire to learn. Those are reasons to consider going on."

Herb nodded guardedly, afraid his words about money and respect had sounded wrong, even if he believed them.

Brannan glanced toward the window. "Has the day gotten away from us?" he asked, plucking his pocket watch out of his waistcoat pocket. "Not really, just overcast." He stood up again. "We've done all we can today. I'll request an application from the university. You can discuss it with your mother."

"I know she'll approve," Herb said. Success linked to college education were words borrowed from his mother. Neither could deny the lack of tuition money in their budget. His mother had weakly hinted that there might be a way, but he feared he would eventually have to confess they had no money for tuition.

"It's agreed then," Mr. Brannan said, rubbing out the reality. He stood up but paused before stepping up on the platform to his desk. Instead, he turned back with what Herb read as a sympathetic concern. "Remember, we're just approaching the hurdles; we aren't over them yet. The application requires the headmaster's endorsement and signature. I would be less than honest if I didn't warn you to be prepared for disappointment."

"Mr. Quincy?" Herb struggled to hold back the full force of the emotion he felt.

"He's one hurdle. We'll do our best, but sometimes success is out of our hands."

When he entered, the apartment was cool and did not smell of cooking. "I'm home, Mum," he called out. "There weren't too many messages to deliver today."

"I'm back here," she answered from the small pantry behind the kitchen where they stored dishes. She came through the kitchen still dressed in a tan silk dress with indigo diagonal stripes that met at her waist like an arrow point, just above the fullness of her skirt. "I got home late, so I'm running behind. Would you chop some wood and make a fire in the stove while I change my clothes?"

He put on his work clothes and headed to the backyard. The sounds of the end-of-the-day street traffic diminished with the growing dark, just as one window after another in the surrounding buildings brightened with light. The pile of kindling wood was almost gone. Sometimes, the family on the other side of the duplex borrowed what he had split and took a long time, if ever, to replace it, making unanticipated work for him. He admitted that sometimes the shortage came from his bad habit of procrastinating about splitting wood. He put it off until only pieces of kindling lay in the dirt, but once he started, he found pleasure in the rhythm of his muscles expanding and contracting with each swing and blow of the ax. Physical motion activated his mind as well as his body.

He pondered his conversation with Mr. Brannan, reining in his galloping emotions, afraid of the disappointment of rejection, not only for himself but for his mother and Mr. Brannan. The wood pile grew as he considered and chopped, first slender kindling and then larger pieces. He filled the bushel basket with the firewood and lugged it upstairs to the kitchen, dumping most of it into the open bin by the stove and layering some in the stove. Sometimes, they used coal as fuel, and sometimes wood. The library fireplace would not be lit until after dinner when he studied at his desk while his mother read in her easy chair. He touched the kindling with a match, and the stove came to life in a slow progression toward cooking temperature. After the kindling caught to a full orange glow, Herb added two larger chunks of wood, lingering until they caught.

"I'm glad you're here," his mother swished in, a long, black shawl wrapped around her casual dress. "I don't like coming home to a cold, empty house." Then her eyes connected with his, silently acknowledging how often Herb did that when she traveled.

"It will warm up soon," Herb said, reversing roles. He washed his hands before removing the airtight top of the ceramic jar and reaching in for a handful of gingersnaps. Sitting at the table, he watched his mum's graceful movements in front of the stove. She made a one-handed effort to clutch her shawl and, with the other, grasped the frying pan.

"I went to a local 'votes for women' meeting today," she said over her shoulder.

"Mm?" he mumbled, chewing.

"We talked about the Civil Rights Act. It's caused some consternation since it passed. Do you think it should stand?"

That was his mother, constantly pushing with a question. She wanted to discuss what she had seen or read about. He would have been happy simply to listen, but she always added a question to force him to think of an answer and make his opinion flawless to her examination. Her trait annoyed him sometimes, but he realized the practice had helped him excel in high school.

After a moment of thought, he answered, "The war was fought to ensure everyone has the same rights—in transportation, public accommodations, and, ideally, probably education—there shouldn't be discrimination."

"And what about the vote?"

"Yes," he said less certainly. "That's discrimination, too. Politics seem to be going backward right now," he added.

She nodded in agreement. "They often do. It's too bad that only a dozen women attended the meeting. Women here in Brookline are making a reasonable effort, but well-known speakers go to Boston, where they draw a bigger crowd," she said, adding a scoop of coal to the blazing firebox. "The Brookline ladies are friendly on the surface, but they all know each other, and it takes time to break in, especially when . . ." her voice faded off as the firebox clanged shut.

You have no husband. Herb could have finished but left the sentence hanging and changed the subject. "I talked to Mr. Brannan after class."

"About the article?"

"No, about college." Herb's voice rattled. "He suggested looking into Boston University for next year."

"That's good," his mother said, putting a spoonful of lard in the frying pan and moving it to the hottest circle of the stove. Then she whirled around, looking at him with a start. "Wait. What did you say?"

"He's going to request an application, but he won't go ahead without your consent." She set her spoon on the counter with a clatter.

"Does that mean you really might have a chance?" Her violet eyes reflected the glitter of the chandelier's light.

Herb was uneasy. His mother had as much invested in his success as he did. His going on would validate her careful work in raising him or cause her enormous disappointment if he somehow failed.

"I shouldn't have mentioned it until we see if it's possible, but Mr. Brannan won't go ahead unless you agree." He squirmed, causing his chair to scrape against the wood floor. "Mum, where would we get the money?" Herb glanced at her, then vaulted up, the chair crashing behind him. "Oh, no!" The lard in the pan she had forgotten on the hot stove was burning. They knocked into each other, both searching for a hot pad. Grabbing one, Herb shoved the pan to the stove's far corner. Breathing in the acrid smoke sent him into uncontrolled choking. Flapping a towel while she ran down the hall, she opened the front door to let out fumes. Then she raised the small window in the bathroom for cross ventilation.

She collapsed back into the straight-backed kitchen chair. Her usually neat blond hair had escaped from its hairpins and hung at odd angles around her forehead while the chignon half unrolled down her neck. "Oh, Herb, what did you get as a mother?" She closed her eyes briefly, then opened them, moisture welling within—from smoke or emotion, he could not tell.

"Mum, it's okay; it's just lard," he said, his throat thick with phlegm. Righting his fallen chair, he sat across from her, feeling as if he were somehow responsible.

"You're right," she said, clamping three hairpins between her lips and retwisting the chignon. After fastening it, she said, "It's lucky I hadn't put in the pork chops—dinner would be ruined." She stood up and walked to the sink. "We can talk more about college at dinner; I'm too frazzled to discuss it right now." She pinched her nose. "My goodness. It will take forever to get enough air through to rid the draperies and upholstery of the smoke."

Seven sonorous chimes rang from the clock in the library just as his mother called him to dinner. On the tablecloth, an old one with a pattern of flowers faded almost colorless with laundering, she put down two plates filled with pork chops, potatoes fried in the drippings, and sweet apricots she had put up the previous fall. She heaped his dish with food and hers with a modest portion because of her unwavering attention to her figure. She ate in small bites, wanting to know every sentence of his conversation with Mr. Brannan.

Herb alternated between eating and talking as he watched her expression seesaw from enthusiasm to apprehension. Advanced education was a crucial prize for her son since it had been out of her reach and maybe that of her family. Did other deprivations grieve her? He wondered. His mother had described little about her childhood, but the consequence of his truancy had begun to unveil how carefully she kept details about the past shielded. How much had she orchestrated the particulars of her life . . . their lives? Did fears of the past ever leave someone? Why had he never insisted on knowing?

Concern writ clearly in her eyes, she once again sidestepped his question about money for tuition. "I've been thinking about attending a forum in Providence." She redirected her eyes to her plate instead of him. "I might fit in an inquiry about money for college." She put a forkful of pork in her mouth and slowly chewed.

"Mum, I thought our money came from a bank in Boston." He stopped eating. "Why Providence?"

Her eyes flashed with a touch of annoyance. "I might as well go to the women's meeting since Providence is not so far away. It will take all the effort we can muster to get the vote—in Brookline, Boston, Providence. . . ." After a brief hesitation, she added, "As long as I'm there, I could meet with someone who might be helpful about tuition money. I met him long ago through some business dealings." Her tone was emotionless, and she still avoided Herb's eyes.

What business dealings? Herb wanted to ask but held back. Any man she might know, be it through business or pleasure, wasn't his affair. And yet, long after slipping under the covers that night, he pondered his mother's upcoming trip. *Who could she possibly be visiting?*

His mother left for Providence on the Wednesday following their discussion. Her absences were a familiar routine, ongoing since he was too little to remember. His mum arranged for someone to watch after him. Before she left, she sat down with him to tell him where she was going. Sometimes, her destination was as close as the city's center; other times to Providence. Hovering over a special notebook she had given him, they had handwritten a calendar, writing the days when she would be gone. "Let's put a star by the day I'll return," she said with a cheerful voice. The notebook was the last thing he looked at before he went to bed while she was gone, crossing off one more day that his mother was away before he blew out the candle to go to sleep.

He missed her—her voice, her hugs, the books she read to him. In Boston, they had lived in a brick duplex with long steps up to the front door and a few paces across the landing to the other front door. The Robinsons moved in next door when he was around eight, and Mrs. Robinson became his caretaker during his mother's absences. Her husband, Jim—he called him "Mr. R"—was a bulky man with an oversized head, tall and slope-shouldered, who said work was so close he could walk. Herb imagined maybe it was at a post office, sorting mail because Mr. R had told him he saw all the mail but did not deliver it. His wife, Roberta, or "Robby," matched her mate with a broad forehead topped with a full head of gray hair interlaced with strands of pure white, always pulled back in a tight knot. Her wire-rimmed spectacles, attached to a looped chain around her neck, often rested on her pillowed bosom. "Mercy, me," she used to tell Herb, "when my eyesight got worse, and I needed these," she'd say, tapping the spectacles, "I spent my life searching for where I put them. Now they're chained to me, except for the bed and the tub," she'd finish with her raspy laugh that always grated on his nerves. Robby and Jim had raised four children, who had grown up and left home long ago.

"I'm grateful for the money, Mrs. Andersen, and being only a few steps away from Jim at mealtimes eases my mind. He'd starve to death on his own," Herb overheard Robby tell his mother one time. Soon after, Mr. R started coming to eat with them.

Most of the time, Robby was like a comforting grandmother. Still, Herb had vague recollections of her not being home when he returned from school. Other times, she would tell him, "Be a good boy, now, and play with your toys. Robby will be back in a sec." After the big hand of the clock had advanced an hour, he would fearfully search for her, but a knock on her door went unanswered, leaving him abandoned and scared, with only his worn, stuffed rabbit for solace.

When Herb was about twelve, Mr. R retired and was always home. Sometimes, when his wife was gone, Mr. R's door would open when Herb turned the key to his own. *He must listen for me to come home.* He tried to rush in and shut the door, but Mr. R came behind him to spend the afternoon.

"Thanks for coming over, but I can take care of myself," Herb said more than once, walking rapidly down the hall for gingersnaps and milk, but Robinson always followed him to the kitchen and sat at the table smoking while Herb ate his after-school snack. The smoke burned his nostrils, and he found the man creepy, with his wheezy breath and bloodshot eyes. One time, when his mother was not due to return for two more days, Robby had gone to take care of her ailing mother. Herb dreaded having the old man as his caretaker. The man lumbered after him when Herb did his chores and sat close to him, smoking like a smokestack when Herb studied or worked on puzzles. To escape, Herb decided to join the afternoon kickball game a few blocks away. He changed into old clothes and told Mr. R where he was going.

"I don't think you should go there, Herb; not all those boys are nice. I'm responsible for you."

"I'll be careful," Herb said as he walked out the door. *They might not be nice, but they're better than you.* But he knew the old man was right about some of the boys because he had played kickball there before. The shouts and laughter became more distinct close to the playground. As he approached, he saw silhouettes of full-grown bodies, cigarette smoke mixed with breath from the cold air rising above their figures. When mostly younger boys played, it was a contest of kickball and keep-away. When older boys, discontent from being idle, especially during the economic downturn, waded in, it was a game of power. Eyeing the big boys, Herb had known it would not be all fun that afternoon. At twelve, he had the disadvantage of a slight build, but he was fast and agile. Herb could break away from the pushing and shoving of competition with the ball at his feet toward the goal if the game was fair. As he joined, the older boys simultaneously moved like wolves in a pack, sauntering into the scrum with the bravado of size and age. Their game of the day was trip and push. Herb helplessly watched one of them stick his full-sized foot out in front of a runner while his partner followed up with a shove to the smaller boy's shoulder, making it impossible for the child to recover his balance. The boy fell hard, landing on his elbow. Curled in a ball on the ground, he clutched his arm, rolling and moaning. "It's broken."

"Sissy . . . mama's boy," the tormentors taunted. With the game stopped, the ruffians migrated back to the fringe, bored with their abuse yet still a menacing presence.

When the game resumed, Herb reluctantly joined, but the free-spirited action had disintegrated. Play had transformed into slow motion, with everyone fearfully looking over his shoulder against attack. He hated it, but had to stay with Mr. R lurking at home. He surveyed the players, imagining the reasons other boys remained until evaporating daylight forced them to go home to whatever fate awaited them.

After school the following day, he opened the door quietly and locked it behind him. He could not stand one more day with the Robinsons. It would not be long until they came looking for him. They had a key to the front door. Guilty thoughts plagued him as he did his chores. He knew his mother assumed everything was all right when she left because she had carefully hired surrogate grandparents to look after him. She had no way to understand. He filled the coal buckets, chopped wood, and stoked the stove before sitting at his desk. His concentration snapped with the knock on the door and Robby calling his name.

"My mum is coming home early today," he said through the wood. "I don't need you."

The clock chimed five before he heard the clinking of the key turning. His breath stopped until he heard her familiar voice. "Herb, I'm home." Breathing hard from coming up the outside stairs, his mother closed the door and met him in the foyer with an affectionate, homecoming hug. Usually, Herb allowed only a few seconds before separating; this time, he stayed in her comforting reassurance. Her furrowed brow told him she noticed.

"How did you do while I was gone?" she asked, still holding him.

"Okay," he said, finally pushing away.

"I'll change my clothes, and we can talk while I cook. What do you say?" She pulled him back for a brief kiss on his forehead before she retrieved her carpet bag and went upstairs.

Herb entered the kitchen to put a match to the kindling arranged in the stove's firebox. He poured another glass of milk and sat at the table, despondently tracing the tablecloth's patterned flowers with his finger. No matter what, he would not be cared for by the Robinsons again.

Two weeks later, his mother said, "I'm going to Boston for a Lyceum conference. They've asked me to be on the planning committee. It's quite an honor."

"I'm not having anything to do with the Robinsons," he spat back, standing up with his fists balled beside his skinny body.

He watched her sparkling eyes cloud with surprise. "They've always been there for you to fix your meals and see to your needs while I'm gone."

"No!" he said, moving to the hallway.

She stood across from him just inside the kitchen doorway. "I can't go away and leave you. You're too young to be by yourself overnight."

He watched her struggle to comprehend his unexpected reaction. "I'll run away if they come here again." Herb felt a tremble go through his body. "I'm going to bed; I'm not hungry." He turned toward the stairs and left her behind. His stomach turned, knowing he had likely made her feel guilty and possibly question whether she could continue the life she was living—one he doubted she could give up.

Breakfast was a standoff. His mother's eyes were red-rimmed, her lips downturned. Herb had not glanced in the mirror, but his sleepless night must have been apparent. Every hazed blink felt grainy. "Will you tell me what happened?"

"Nothing happened!" He would go back to bed rather than saying anything about the Robinsons. There were no words to express his raw emotions, and anything he said would sound like blame. She could not give up traveling. Except for him, life with meaning was elsewhere. "I can stay by myself."

"Won't you be lonely?"

"It won't be that hard. I have school and puzzles and can run more errands for people."

"I have an idea," she said firmly but gently. "Let's each write down the pros and cons of staying alone and propose rules." She held his eyes with hers. "Or, call them guidelines for when I'm gone. We can compare them and work out an agreement."

He could tell she had been thinking about a solution before their conversation, probably all night.

They had later agreed on what he could or could not do and people to go to in an emergency. They visited Dr. Howard at his office, five blocks from where they lived, to ask if Herb could turn to him with sudden medical needs. By the time they had moved to Brookline, Herb had been on his own for five years when his mother traveled.

After his mother told the Robinsons she no longer needed them, they moved. He was still too emotional to feel bad for them. Herb suspected the extra income from caring for him had made the difference in affording rent on their tight retirement budget. After they left, next-door renters came and went. Some paid Herb to run errands and do small jobs. Others remained strangers he and his mother seldom saw. The last renter before they were forced to move was a thin, pasty-faced man, often unshaven, who did not come out of his house often. His mum occasionally made double portions of food, suspecting the neighbor had little money. Mr. Jacobs was friendly when Herb delivered the extras. "Everything's in the dumps, and so many are down and out," he wanly said. "I 'preciate your generosity."

Books, puzzles, and his studies were companions away from school, especially when his mother was away. He occasionally went to other boys' homes but did not need constant company like some of his friends. Herb was independent, not a recluse. Nevertheless, his mother's return from a trip dissolved any loneliness and gloom he had unconsciously suppressed.

TEN

The dimming outside light made the puzzle pieces hard to see. His shoulders were stiff from hunching over, and his neck cramped from bending close to his puzzle, but he was too lazy to get up. When he heard the key unlock the front door, he stood up to light a lantern. "I'm home, Herb," she trilled.

"How was Providence, Mum?" He heard her remove her coat and put her hat and gloves on a shelf. His match touching the lantern wick made a golden pool of light on the table as she entered the library. "Ooh, you've made progress on the puzzle since I left." She put her arms around him. "Hmm," she looked over his shoulder, "I think I see a fit," she teased, knowing it maddened him when she tinkered with his careful way of proceeding.

Herb rolled his eyes. "This is my third time doing this; it should go faster than the first two times."

"Someday, you'll have enough money to buy all the puzzles you want," she told him. The light shone on the dark circles under her eyes. "I'll be back after I change."

He heard the familiar rustle of silk when she picked up her luggage to go up the stairs. "I'll light the stove, Mum. I didn't want to do it too soon and waste wood before you were home."

"Good decision, Herb," his mother said wearily from the stairs. "You never know what will cause a delay when you travel."

Herb leaned over the table. "Hah!" He snapped in a puzzle piece and had to restrain himself from searching for more fits.

In the kitchen, he lit the small kindling, and while waiting for enough flame to add bigger chunks of wood, he put forks, knives, and spoons on the table, pondering what to expect from dinner conversation. She always had something to tell him about a trip, almost as if to have homecoming fun to make up for being away. After so many years of the routine of her return from travel, he could read her moods. Sometimes, she was lighthearted, brimming with delight, and recounted what she had learned at a meeting, so the information also became part of his knowledge. At other times, she was thoughtfully somber, even though she still had things to relay. Events she left undefined made up as much of her life as what she revealed. Again, Herb was struck by the secrecy that surrounded his mother.

This time, his mood was different, too. His burning curiosity about the mysterious businessman and what he might have said about college tuition heightened his interest in her Providence trip.

The logs spit and crackled when the flame engulfed them. Herb had been lazy while his mother was gone, and he had yet to bring up a new batch from the damp basement to let them completely dry. He floated a hand above the stovetop—it was getting warm but not hot enough to cook or boil water.

The stiff soles of his mother's brown button-up shoes made little noise as she entered the kitchen. They matched her lightweight wool dress, the color of strong coffee. Until recently, it had been a cold-weather going-out dress, but she had worn it so often that the cuffs and hem had frayed. Now, she only wore it at home.

"The women's meeting in Providence was so-so," she said, removing the pieces of chicken she had placed in the coldest part of the icebox before her absence. She filled a bowl with flour, salt, and pepper to dredge the raw pieces. Herb's mouth watered at the thought of the tasty, fried dish.

"Everything has gotten so political." Flour dust puffed as she whacked a drumstick to make her point. "There's little difference between the National Women's Suffrage Association and the American Women's Suffrage Association, yet they disagree without a chance of merger. It seems to me they would be much stronger together."

"Which one do you favor, Mum?" He wanted to sound interested but was impatient to hear about her meeting with the mysterious businessman.

"The NWSA, probably because it has a more national focus." She shrugged. "Of course, politics are played nationally as much as within each state. The police arrested Susan Anthony when she voted," his mother said, irritation drenching her voice. "Anthony was born in the United States, and the Fourteenth Amendment gave all citizens the right to vote. Yet, they arrested her, fined her one hundred dollars, and negated her vote. That's politics." She banged the frying pan on the stove in frustration and added a dollop of lard. Pausing momentarily before saying, "I won't let this burn this time," she looked over her shoulder with a har-rumph. "Sorry, these meetings get me agitated, but we won't give up. Your daughters will vote," her expression changed to a happy smirk.

Her statement surprised him. The idea that he would have daughters who could vote seemed like science fiction rather than something that would actually happen.

The chicken sizzled as she carefully added one piece at a time so the fat would not splatter. She had covered herself with her well-worn apron.

"Mum, what else happened in Providence?" Curiosity had kept Herb at the table while she was cooking instead of going to the library to study or work on his puzzle.

"The meeting was well attended. Many of the women I had met before. We've become friends through the cause. . . ." She stopped, clearly notic-ing his expression. It was not what he wanted to know.

"I'm almost done here. Let's talk while we eat." After cooking the chicken, she added sweet potato slices to the hot grease. When the orangey flesh turned crispy brown, she served the chicken, potatoes, and steamed spinach. She mounded Herb's plate high.

"The day after the meeting ended, I met the man I told you about." Her eyes looked tired and cautious. Her slender shoulders were tensely hunched, far from her usual gracefully erect posture.

"Who is he?" Herb asked, his fork hovering over his untouched food. He could barely stand the suspense.

"I met him many years ago." Her eyes were unfocused as if going back in time. "I was so young then, not much older than you are now. I worked in the downtown Providence area . . . at an inn, with a restaurant on the first floor and sleeping rooms above. It was a gathering place for residents to eat and where visitors could stay the night." She kept her eyes on her plate, not on him; she had never told him this part of her life.

"My first job was cleaning rooms, but one day, the young man who delivered food to the tables didn't show up. The owner, Mr. Davis, came huffing up the stairs in a dither and found me where I was changing sheets. He almost shouted at me to go down and help with the food. They were backed up and customers were impatient.

"It was more than an everyday tavern. Downtown businessmen came there for lunch. There was even a ladies' dining room where women could come for a meal." She stopped to take a deep breath and drink water. "Even though I was little more than a maid, every morning, I came in the most respectable clothing I could put together and made sure my hair was neatly combed. Some unknown being somehow took care of me that first day in the dining area." She tilted her head at the ceiling as if angels were flying around the chandelier as she remembered the day. "As nervous as I was, I kept my composure. Later, I discovered that the customers spoke well of me afterward, even those in the back room—the one with the Ladies Reading and Library Society members.

"The manager, Mr. Davis, rewarded me with a new job and even more pay. It was still barely enough to get by on, but every once in a while, I was given an extra coin by a diner." She cut off a piece of chicken and ate it before looking up at him. "I discovered the women met fortnightly. One day, a friendly woman asked me if I liked to read. It surprised some that I could read and that it was my fondest occupation. From then on, they brought a book to lend me . . . and after a while, even more, that I took the best care of and returned the next time they met. When I served them, I studied the ladies carefully, observing every detail of what they wore, how they spoke, and even their manners. My job became an education."

"What about the man?" Herb asked. Only chicken bones remained on his plate, but he waited to ask for seconds until she had finished.

"I met him there, too," she said, her words slowing with hesitancy. She scooped up a forkful of spinach, chewed, and swallowed. "As I said, most customers in the main eating area were businessmen. Of course, there was always a share of travelers, but many diners came from the nearby offices. They were respectable, or most of them were. Mr. Davis was paternal for some reason, although he was not old enough to be my father. Maybe having three daughters of his own made him protective. If a man was fresh, and Mr. Davis was around, he handled things in an instant; often, though, I had to fend for myself. I was grateful for Mr. Davis. He was a funny-looking man who was unattractive and overweight. The waistcoat over his stomach was so tight it looked like the buttons might explode if he took a deep breath. His double chin, maybe there were two," she smiled, "folded over his collar, almost touching his tie. The waistcoat and jacket he wore reached to the tops of his knees; his trousers were a checked pattern of one color or another, and beneath them were wide square-toed shoes. He kept a top hat on a hook near the front desk for when he went out," she said, taking a last bite of food.

"Mum, could I have a little more, please?" Herb asked, removing his silverware from the plate. He might as well keep eating while she continued her story. "And, what about the man?" he asked again.

His mother stood up and spooned the remaining contents of the frying pan onto his plate. "You're growing so much you'll eat me out of house and home," she said, returning the pan to the counter.

"Sorry."

She smoothed her skirt beneath her and sat down again. "He was one of a group of successful businessmen who ate lunch there frequently. He was in the cartage business, sending supplies of every description to all parts of the country, especially up and down the Atlantic coast. His business became prosperous during the war and continued to grow afterward, but at that time, he was just starting. He was probably not quite thirty. He was muscular, broad-shouldered, had a squarish face, brown hair, chestnut eyes, and a big full mustache." She glanced at Herb and gave a nervous twitch. "You might call him reserved, but he could forcefully hold his own in debates with older, more prosperous men around the table. For some reason, he remembered me and greeted me by name whenever he came to the inn. I learned that an easy way to get a tip from men was to learn a little about their business, so I paid attention to snatches of their conversation when I passed by, remembering who did what. I also kept up with events. Instead of discarding the newspapers customers left behind, I collected and read them at the boarding house where I roomed. Every once in a while, I would mention snippets of information, although I had to be careful because being too friendly would imply something else," she said, reddening. "One day, I remarked about the cartage business and how difficult it must be to get enough draft horses to carry heavy loads. He was surprised and appreciative that I understood one of the challenges of his occupation. There was no time to say anymore because I was rushing back and forth to the kitchen. One person was hardly enough. Mr. Davis had me working breakfast and lunch . . . and sometimes as a backup, at dinner, although I never liked that. It was a different crowd, and drinking brought out the worst in some of them.

"The next time he came in, he waited until others at his table had left before he told me there was another problem at his business. To add to the shortage of horses, demand for carting had increased. He was busier than ever, soliciting business, ensuring the freight came and went where it should, and keeping his records straight. That part, he explained, was sometimes left undone. The stacks on the desk were growing higher and higher, so finding what he wanted was impossible. He asked if I wanted a small job after I finished lunch duties at the inn, putting his business records in some sort of order. The pay he offered was fair and meant I wouldn't have to work an extra shift for dinner. His office was a short distance from the inn and the same back to the boarding house. Mr. Davis did not object. His business was growing, too, and needed someone full-time for dinner instead of part-time."

During the story, his mother looked dreamy. Finally, she looked directly at him. "I said yes."

"Really?" Herb asked, nonplussed. Before now, his mother had told him nothing about a working life. He had not thought much about it but assumed she had lived with her parents. He did not know when they died. He tried to imagine her being a waitress or arranging someone's business papers.

"Going through everything at the beginning took time," his mother said, shaking her head as if she remained surprised that she had gotten the job. "He had an assistant who was more a salesman than an office assistant. I didn't know anything about haulage and the types of income and expenses of that business. I started by sorting documents into different stacks." Her laugh sounded hollow. "Fortunately, he was too busy to notice that I was often in tears trying to make sense of them. There was no order. At first, I put everything with the same name together, understanding nothing. Slowly, so impossibly slowly, after going through the papers over a dozen times, they began to make sense, and I developed a system. Weeks after I started, my employer rushed into the room where I worked at a long table and asked me to find a receipt. The supplier was waiting, saying my employer had not paid him. I thought about where I had put it and went to the box. I ruffled through the papers," she moved her fingers one at a time as if going across the files, "and pulled it out. You can't imagine how pleased he was . . . and how relieved I was." She groaned. "I was so anxious."

Herb had so many questions he wanted to ask. How long had she worked at this office? Had she met his father there? Did she ever leave the inn? When had she last seen the businessman before their recent meeting? And, most importantly, what did he say about the question about money for college? He glanced at his mother. Her tired eyes drooped over half-rings of dark circles. The trip had exhausted her, and, most likely, telling her story had, too. She had revealed quite a bit, but there were many ambiguous details he longed to know. From her worn-out appearance, he suspected it would be another day when he learned more about the relationship with her acquaintance, but he could not wait to know about the money.

"Mum, what did he say about a financial arrangement for college?"

She hesitated. "He's considering it." Her voice wavered as much as the answer.

"Does it depend on if I'm accepted?"

"He considers everything carefully." Her tone filled with annoyance. "He's probably determining whether it is a good investment," Herb heard almost a scoff in her voice, "and if money should be given for all, or in part . . . or if it should be lent." Her reaction was a determination to make things work, but she cloaked any optimism about the outcome if she felt it.

The Providence meeting changed nothing for Herb. He persisted in an almost obsessive effort to ensure the highest grade in every class. Nothing short of perfection would suffice. He spoke up more, disregarding the barely audible catcalls of "smarty pants" or "teacher's pet" whispered from the back of the classroom or the retaliation in the hallway of camouflaged elbow knocks to his ribcage. A teacher's grade of "A" on an English paper with the comment, "Good job, you might strengthen your writing style with more adjectives," signaled to Herb the work was flawed. He would have to do better until there was nothing but positive critique. His mind churned when he noticed a high grade on an assignment passed down the row to a well-heeled student. He couldn't help but wonder if it was given for true merit or because of a father's financial status.

April had been dismal, filled with cloudy, wet days. Even when it was not raining, the atmosphere was saturated. Their kitchen was a maze of never-dry laundry, with the collapsible drying racks perpetually filled beside the stove. They draped more sodden clothing over the backs of chairs or hung it from doorknobs. Herb's shoes were always sopping. Avoiding puddles did no good. The soggy ground squished around his feet on his way to school or to deliver messages. Whenever he returned home, he removed his shoes and put them close to the stove or fireplace, only to find them cold and clammy the following day. Bed was the only dry, warm place, and he sometimes felt chilled even there.

When Herb entered the classroom the Monday after Easter, Mr. Brannan asked, "Can you stay after school today?"

A nervous feeling rippled in Herb's chest. Was it bad news of some sort, such as a word from Headmaster Quincy? Since moving to Brookline, he had never relaxed. He worried about his studies, repeatedly reviewing assignments to make sure they did not fall short. Every day, he regretted his stupid attempt to get a job since it gave the headmaster the power to prevent him from being accepted into college. Then, if he did get into a university, there was the question of finding funds to pay for it. His mother could not support him forever. But how would he meet his expenses if he were independent? Fast on the heels of this question came a new one: Could he leave his mother on her own? She would soon turn forty-four.

Weary from worry, he forced aside his uncertainties and concentrated on science class. When it was over, Mr. Brannan stepped down from the platform and sat at a front-row desk beside him. Outside, rain pattered against the tall windows, making the classroom gray and gloomy.

"I'm not sure why it took so long," Mr. Brannan said. "I finally got the Boston University application." He smoothed two pieces of paper on the desk's writing surface. "Because the college has suffered damage from the fire like so many others, it won't accept as many students as in previous years. That means greater competition." After a pause, he said, "Another factor is at play. If not to Boston University, this might be the right time to apply somewhere else. Institutions of higher learning are multiplying, and the number of students accepted is, too. Did you know some now regularly admit women? Imagine! Eliza did not attend college, but Diane and Vicki will be able to apply. We've already begun talking about it at the dinner table."

Herb smiled, anticipating his mother's pleasure when he told her that news.

"First things first," Brannan rubbed his chin thoughtfully. "Let's at least go over the application to make sure we want to proceed."

"No question, I want to proceed!" Herb said so vehemently his teacher jumped. He hastily added, "I mean, I want to go over the information." Was there any question he would apply, no matter what?

Mr. Brannan faced him. "There are a few things we have to take care of," he cautioned. "Remember, people with opinions of their own make these decisions. It's a little like the difference between grading a math examination and an essay for history class." He chuckled. "That's why I teach mathematics and science. Mathematics consists of numbers—the answer is right or wrong. History depends on the reader. Oh, sure, you have to get your nouns and verbs right and back up your thesis with facts." He chuckled again. "But a lot depends on the reader's views. That's the position we'll be in. Everything we do may be right, but it may not be enough to pass the muster of others."

Herb moaned at the possibility of doing his best only to come up short, his mother's reaction, Mr. Brannan's disappointment, and his view of himself.

"You need two teachers' endorsements. I would be happy to be one of them, and I've thought of plenty of examples to support my recommendation. I'll also state how you will benefit the university." He laced his fingers and rested them on the desktop. "Do you have an idea for the second recommendation?"

Herb took his time. English was a possibility; he got high grades on tests and research papers. Then he considered the teachers. His history teacher mirrored his mother's ability to make the past come alive. Plus, she seemed to appreciate his humor and understand when he went quiet. His decision was clear: "Miss Elliott."

Brannan nodded. "A good choice. You're fortunate to have options." His hazel eyes gleamed. "There's not a class you don't do well in, but history will demonstrate another side of your intellect along with your obvious aptitude in the sciences. I've heard my colleague comment about the quality of your work, and I'll put in an extra word for you. Here, take this and copy the instructions." He handed Herb a typed document. "You can give them to her when you ask for her support. If she responds positively, and I have no doubt she will, both of our recommendations will go to Headmaster Quincy for his approval and signature." Brannan hurried on to the next topic, not dwelling on the headmaster. "Is your mother willing to sign the application?"

"She wants me to go," Herb said, knowing her heart would sail over the moon to have him attend college.

"I wish I didn't have to ask, but there's the question of money." Brannan's brow furrowed. "Do you have resources to pay tuition?"

Herb swallowed. It was the question he'd feared, and he could not lie to Mr. Brannan, not in the face of the man's kindness and support. "I'm not sure. Do you know how much it will cost?"

Mr. Brannan's eyes closed halfway, as if shuttering out the answer. "Seventy-five dollars. Each year," he said, with a wince.

Herb's eyes widened. "By the time a degree is granted, it costs as much as a house!" His heart sank. He could not fathom that education cost that much.

"I never thought about it that way." Brannan paused, as he often did, as if to be certain he'd say the right thing. "It's about the same as a small house and, like a house, it would be an investment for life."

"But I wouldn't have anything to show for it." The concept of nothing but a piece of paper to show for that amount of money was incomprehensible.

"Not in bricks and mortar or anything else of material structure; you're right. However, a college education would more than pay for itself over the course of a successful career. Once you have it, no one can take it away." Mr. Brannan fidgeted with the application. "Mind you, there are plenty of people who do quite well without going to a university . . . most, to be honest. Higher education is a big commitment, and there are other ways to learn." The skin between Brannan's eyes bunched. "I may have been wrong in even suggesting it."

"No, not at all. It's a good idea. My mother thinks it's a good idea," Herb said, afraid Mr. Brannan was reconsidering his recommendation. "The cost is a surprise, that's all. My mother is trying to get the money together." He shrugged. "But nothing's certain yet."

"The best thing to do is to go home and tell your mother everything you've learned. She may have a different perspective when she considers all the information. You can let me know what you decide. Take your time," he said, standing up, ready to leave. "There's no real rush, but you can't delay too long. Start as soon as you feel ready." He handed Herb the application. "Take this with you; you can copy what you need for Miss Elliott if you decide that's the road you want to take." He stepped up on the platform, arranging papers and putting some in his briefcase before he met Herb's eyes again. "Remember, Herb, whatever you and your mother decide will be right—there is no wrong choice. You'll just be taking one path instead of another."

A path to what kind of life? If only I could see the end of each path. Herb brooded silently. *Does anyone ever know the end of life's path? Maybe those who follow in their father's footsteps do.* He slowly stood up. "Thanks for getting the application, Mr. Brannan." Glumly, he walked to the long row of pegs to retrieve his Macintosh raincoat. Only Mr. Brannan's coat remained; everyone else had left. "I'll let you know what my mother says." Herb carefully protected the application under the Indian rubber canvas wrapped around his books.

He entered their apartment, chilled from the walk home in the rain. It was a baking day, but the yeasty scent of baking bread offered him a little comfort. He hung up his drenched coat and carefully unwrapped his books to make sure no drops had seeped underneath. He left the application on his desk in the library and went to the kitchen. "It smells good, Mum. All of a sudden, I'm ravenous."

"Pour yourself a glass of milk and get the butter while I take these out. I baked six loaves—we'll see how far they last into the week." His mother smiled as she tipped one of the metal pans and ran a knife around the edges. The still-steaming bread slid out onto a wire cooling rack. When the loaves were free of their pans, his mother transferred one to a plate, added a knife, and handed both to Herb.

"How did your day go?" she asked.

He sliced off a quarter of the loaf and spread butter, watching it languorously seep into the airy texture. He took a bite and chewed slowly, savoring the taste and delaying his mother's inevitable eruption of conflicting emotions about the application. He suspected her reaction would be a magnified version of his own—a sense of being overwhelmed by expenses, uncertain outcomes, and fear of failure.

"Mm," he intoned appreciatively after swallowing his last bite. "May I have another?"

She nodded and waited while he sliced another piece.

"Mr. Brannan gave me the Boston University application today."

His mother inhaled sharply and did not release her breath for a long moment.

"First of all, tuition is much worse than I imagined," Herb said, wondering why they were going through this pointless exercise. "It's not only the cost; I have to get two recommendations plus Headmaster Quincy's signature. Who knows how that might turn out? All my teachers are my supporters, but I swear Mr. Quincy does everything he can to put up roadblocks, not just for me. I'm not sure he has any fondness for students." He took a deep breath. "And then, what if I do get in?"

He compulsively sliced another piece of bread. His mother sat across from him. Her brown checked work dress was visible above the edge of her white apron—almost translucent from so many washings. Even when she cleaned vigorously, her light hair stayed neatly in place. He glanced across her shoulder to make sure all the pans were removed from the stove's hot spots. They did not need another grease fire and smoke during this conversation.

She remained composed, but Herb saw extra interest flash in her eyes, or maybe it was dread. He could not tell. "Boston University costs seventy-five dollars a year."

Her chest rose and fell with short breaths. "I expected going to college would cost quite a lot, but I never really thought about how much."

"I don't have to go, Mum. Even Mr. Brannan said that most boys don't and still do fine."

He gazed at the table, avoiding her eyes, although his mother's thoughts were easy for him to imagine from past conversations. She wanted him to have what had eluded her: assets that led to a secure existence. Her opinion had always puzzled him since her knowledge and assured demeanor were a success in his eyes. He was always proud of her. It wasn't just that she dressed well—although she did, even when it was only the two of them. On their frequent excursions to museums and art galleries, he was often aware of other visitors standing close, listening to her cheery, intelligent explanations about what she had learned through her reading.

"Mr. Brannan is right, but you should still try." Less confidently, she added, "I need to think about how we might manage the cost." A hard edge had crept into her tone. She pushed back her chair. "Now, I must cook. You might as well tend to your studies; dinner might be a little late . . . but I suspect you're not starving," she smiled, lightening the mood with a sideways glance at the half-eaten loaf of bread.

Three days later, at breakfast, his mother said, "I've decided to go back to Providence for a few days."

"Another suffragist meeting?"

"No, something else I have to take care of."

"The businessman?"

"Yes." She hesitated, her eyes flitting from side to side like a rabbit looking to escape from a fox. "I told him about your situation at our last meeting, and now that we have more details, he may have some ideas. He knows a lot about finance."

"Why would he be interested in helping me?" He said it to her back— she had turned to close the oven door.

"He's interested in all sorts of things," she told him, firmly putting the words together. "And he should have an interest in this."

His mother's departure for her second trip to Providence prodded Herb to work on the Boston University application. The day after they had discussed tuition costs, Herb had told Mr. Brannan that his mother had agreed to sign the application and had begun to explore ways to pay for tuition.

Before history class, Herb asked Miss Elliott if she was free to meet at the end of the day. She eagerly agreed. When classes had ended, Herb explained his desire to attend Boston University and his need for a recommendation, and she said, "If you go, it means success for the rest of us, too. It's a bright spot for the school." Miss Elliott was older than Herb's mother, but not old. She was taller than most other teachers—both men and women. Perfectly round spectacles perched on her pronounced, beak-like nose. Behind her back, she was fondly nicknamed "Miss Crane" because of her height and posture, which canted forward, and a frizz of blond hair resembling a topnotch. Students had learned the crane was a well-known symbol of wisdom, which fit her, too.

History had never been one of Herb's favorite classes. The logic of mathematics and science appealed to him more, but he had liked Miss Elliott from the start. Her teaching was different. It was not a session of memorizing names and dates. Instead, she told spellbinding stories about long-ago times and places: the Roman Empire, India, and other cultures, like Africa, with its tribal systems, valued family relationships, and strong respect for older members of society. Her realistic details transported him to different countries as if he were living there, experiencing the people and events. She wanted students to understand the lives of the past—both leaders and ordinary people, as well as geography and politics.

Sitting at her desk chair, Miss Elliott plucked the pencil resting on her ear underneath the wiry poof of blond hair. "Herb, tell me everything you need so I can write it down. When did you say you need it?"

"April fifteen." He went over the brief instructions. "I'm very grateful, Miss Cr . . . Elliott."

Her smile flashed. She knew her nickname. "Ten days, that's more than enough time. We can go over it when I finish." Miss Elliott stood up and extended one arm around his shoulders with a squeeze. "Best of luck. Teachers like to cheer on students who want to learn more."

Miss Elliott's wholehearted support surprised him. He searched his memory. Did teachers at Boston High go out of their way to help students? He liked some of them, but they were more distant, coming to teach and leaving afterward with little interaction with students outside the classroom. Maybe Miss Elliott and Mr. Brannan were interested in him because he wanted to attend college. He was not sure, but personal attention by two Brookline teachers made changing high schools almost worth giving up the familiarity of the past.

At his desk, alone in the evenings while his mother was in Providence, he fretted over the required two essays, each 500 words. The first asked what he had enjoyed most in high school, and the second, what he planned to study. He hated open-ended questions like that. Mathematical tests requiring straightforward answers better suited his personality. The surrounding book-lined shelves and heavy draperies absorbed his audible groan. He felt his stomach knot as he took paper from his desk drawer. He had no idea what made the difference between admittance and denial. "What do they want to know?" Herb asked the emptiness. Mr. Brannan's words came back to him: "Essays are not all that matter. You have many accomplishments in your favor. Look at your courses: arithmetic, algebra, geometry, and four years of English and history."

"Civics and rhetoric," Herb had added.

"And all with good grades from two high schools."

Herb had smiled. He *did* have something to show for his hard work.

"If you were applying to the most prestigious colleges, you would have more to prove. You know," Brannan had raised his hand high above his head to illustrate, "a top hat, expensive fabrics, and, of course, lineage to prove you're a gentleman."

Herb had laughed despite his nervousness.

"With its wide range of students, Boston University makes more sense and emphasizes teaching science, which happens to be your interest."

The pages on Herb's desk remained frustratingly without words, but remembering Mr. Brannan's comments bolstered him. He decided to explain why math and science were his favorite subjects. They were like doing a jigsaw puzzle, looking for logical pieces and determining how they fit together. He also liked the different characteristics of algebra, geometry, chemistry, and biology. The mental exercise of analyzing helped with other subjects, even English and history. Analytical skills would benefit his other studies and be helpful for a future occupation.

In the second essay, he explained that he wanted to pursue science to invent things that would make life easier. He used Alexander Graham Bell's work with deaf people as one example and the telegraph as another. The ideas came quickly, but the writing was slow, as he struggled to include detailed explanations to make a compelling case for admission.

On half-used scraps of paper, he penned his thoughts, crossed them out, and started again . . . and again. After two hours, he crumpled the scribbled sheets and tossed them in the trash bin. Disgruntled, he left his desk for the coffee table and couch to work on his latest puzzle—a Bierstadt painting of Yosemite Valley with geometric peaks lining each side of the river. One thousand pieces would keep him busy for a month, but his essays had to come first.

TWELVE

His mother returned from Providence, seeming to Herb to be edgy and distracted. Her conversation flitted from one topic to another with little concentration, and she asked none of her usual questions about school, what errands he had run, or even recounting the highlights of her time away. She lost herself cooking a dinner of roast pork with potatoes and onions, making gravy with pungent drippings redolent with sage, salt, and fat. When she baked a roast, whether pork, chicken, beef, or turkey, she stretched it into the rest of the week, mixing it with other ingredients for additional dinners, using the bones for soup, and cutting thin slices of the meat to make sandwiches for his school lunch.

Wary of her mood, he quietly watched while she served dinner. She added the outer portions, the skin crinkled into a brown, crispy crust, to his plate. After his first bite, he said, "Thanks, Mum; it's my favorite part."

Then, he asked. "What did you learn in Providence?" He could not stand not knowing any longer. She sighed, her lips narrow and firm. According to her tacit rules, *she* was supposed to relay information about what she did when she was ready; Herb was not supposed to ask.

Now that he was older, childhood rules were at cross purposes. He needed to know if the meeting with the man would allow him to submit his application. Even more than that, he wanted to learn more about the carefully guarded past. He was increasingly aware of how carefully she tailored words—telling him some things and leaving out others. His teeth clenched with festering resentment about not knowing the whole truth.

"He met with me again." Her words scuttled his ruminations. "He said he'd researched Boston University." She twisted her napkin. "I told you he was thorough. He learned what Mr. Brannan described to you—a benefactor had given the university a million dollars' worth of buildings and other real estate in his will. The university had insured everything," she continued in a low, serious tone, "but because of the extent of the fire, insurance companies quickly ran out of funds. In *his* opinion, the university might never recover, and it would be unwise to pay tuition, not knowing if it will survive."

Her evident anger surprised him, but he felt it, too. "The most important building—the one where Alexander Graham Bell teaches—survived. The science building is the only one *I'm* interested in." He was disheartened that someone would turn down a proposal without understanding what was important.

"He hasn't turned it down completely." She appeared emotionless, but her tightened fists revealed her inner agitation. "He suggested that you look into a scholarship."

"Scholarship?" Herb did not believe what he was hearing. "Where would I get a scholarship?"

"I don't know, and neither did he." His mother writhed as if the turmoil of pleasing two people with opposite agendas left her feeling trapped. "Could you ask Mr. Brannan's advice?"

"I guess so," Herb groaned. He had warned himself not to raise his hopes, but he had anyway. "He's done so much already; asking another favor is embarrassing."

She nodded, appearing as dispirited as he felt. "Maybe he knows of something. It wouldn't hurt to ask." Her eyes glistened with unspilled tears.

"I will." He could not procrastinate because the deadline to apply was not far away, and the application required a tuition guarantee.

When they met after class, Mr. Brannan made light of the lack of funding with a cheerful expression, put on like a particular piece of clothing to create the right impression. "You know land grant colleges out West are cropping up like weeds in a garden, enticing students with generous scholarships. Maybe you should consider going to someplace like Colorado Territory."

Stories about fortune seekers traveling west had filled the news throughout Herb's lifetime, but he could not imagine going. He assumed land grant colleges taught about farming, but nothing that interested him. His expression must have revealed his thoughts because Mr. Brannan's smile vanished.

"Herb, I'm sorry. It was just one of those random thoughts. Going to the West doesn't appeal to everyone—in fact, not most people." He reached over and patted Herb's shoulder. "There are scholarships for Boston University," he continued earnestly, "but they require full documentation of finances. A person has to open up records for every dollar and cent." He hesitated as if considering whether he should say more. "The other problem is that you'll need a man's signature for the finances. Does your mother have anyone to do that for her? Her father? A brother? Any close male relative?"

Herb shook his head. "My mum's had a lot of deaths in her family. We have no relatives."

"Unfortunate." Mr. Brannan laced his fingers, pressing one palm against the other in thought. He finally picked up his pencil, opened his notebook, and jotted down two words Herb could not read. "The way I see things now," he said, looking up, "is for you to go ahead and tell your mother about the scholarship situation. Maybe she can think of something we haven't. And we will continue with the application with a note that tuition payment is pending."

Herb was silent, scouring his brain for ideas. Vacantly, he perused the classroom—the blackboard, with its tipped chalk holder missing a screw; the narrow, ten-foot-high leaded glass windows that let in the sun, shining on the desks, their surfaces marked and nicked by students with varied abilities and expectations. His shoulders slumped.

"What's the use? There are too many obstacles to overcome."

"We both knew, and I suspect your mother did too, that college acceptance would be far on the horizon of possibilities. Lofty things always are. You still have to try them. Have I ever told you about the Marquis de Lafayette? He changed his coat of arms to *Cur Non*—Why Not. That motto seems to apply here. It doesn't mean you're a failure if things don't work out."

"Thank you, Mr. Brannan. I wouldn't have any chance without you," Herb said, but pessimism strangled his enthusiasm.

Herb's mother paced back and forth in the library, muttering about the effrontery of anyone examining her finances or demanding to know where her money came from. "As if I haven't taken care of myself . . . of us . . . alone for years."

For the first time, Herb wondered how she had worked around the necessity of a male signatory all these years, but he kept his questions to himself. Nor did he tell her of Brannan's far-fetched notion of moving to the West, where land-grant colleges solicited students. Since the suggestion, his newest jigsaw puzzle, the Bierstadt painting of a storm cloud over the Rocky Mountains, reminded him of Colorado whenever he worked on it.

THIRTEEN

Streaks of gray clouds blotted and unblotted the sun the day he graduated. Herb was happy with how many classmates congratulated him. The preceding week, Brookline High named him the top student. However, the honor of giving the valedictorian speech went to a wealthy merchant's son who was going to Harvard. Clara was at the top in a special category for girls.

At gatherings like this, he observed his mother at her best—attractive and confident as she talked to many parents. Cliques collected, but many families praised his mother for Herb's performance. It was impossible to ignore the top student.

It was all playacting for Herb. His mind halted and lurched with anguished thoughts to say the right things to students going on to college. He and his mother had held their breaths for over a month each time the mail was delivered, waiting for Boston University's decision. Two slim letters had arrived in the same day a week before graduation. The first announced that Boston University had not accepted him because of a lack of tuition payment.

The second, addressed to his mother by her business acquaintance, said he would not pay Herb's tuition for the fall semester. If Herb did well in the fall and got a job to earn part of the tuition for the winter, he would consider a proposal for contributing the rest.

The letter had trembled in her hand as his mother read it. He'd watched her clench her jaw, sensing anger as much as abject disappointment. He'd understood her long-held hope for a successful future for him through a college education had disintegrated into a million irreparable pieces. Rejection was hard to stomach, particularly when it came from lack of funds, not lack of ability. "He knows you don't have enough money to attend the first semester and that the trust fund is reduced when you turn eighteen, so it's not even a real offer," she'd said so quietly that he'd barely heard her. With difficulty, he refrained from questioning her. *Did she say he knows you don't have enough money for the semester, and the trust fund is reduced when I turn eighteen? Were those separate thoughts, or did she say he knows both? Why would he?*

Toward the end of the graduation reception, Herb watched Mr. Brannan excuse himself from a group of parents and stride across the room.

"Congratulations on raising a remarkable son," he told his mum after they were introduced. "This may be the end of classes, but I like to keep track of my favorite students—and, Herb, you are one of my best—even at seventeen. I'd like to keep in touch. I'll lend you my *Scientific American,* but only if you agree to meet and discuss the articles," Brannan said with his usual chipper disposition.

For Herb, congratulatory remarks like those were the day's highlights. The rest of graduation was buried in the dark mire of his future, shared, he was sure, by his mother.

Herb had to find a job to meet the slim prospects of partial tuition and, more importantly, pay his expenses. Their income would be less after August twentieth. Prospects for employment were scant. The economy had only declined since his bruising search for a job in Boston. In different iterations, headlines routinely declared: THE DEPRESSION OF 1873 CONTINUES —THE WORST IN HISTORY.

A sleep-tormented night followed graduation. Twisting in his sheets, he had nightmarish visions of hoodlums kicking and yelling at him as he sprawled helplessly in a trash-strewn back alley. The slam of the door in his face by cackling, skeletal business owners felt so real that, in the morning, he ran his hand across his forehead to check for a bruise. He could not rid himself of hopelessness. The prospect of being unemployed made him afraid; the specter of having to accept a dead-end position that slowly destroyed him made him shudder. What is a future without hope? He knew he was not alone in asking the bleak question.

At breakfast, Herb and his mother ate in silence. Monday morning after graduation signaled the beginning of his new life. Herb's routine of attending school had ended, and only a few chores at home remained undone. After breakfast, he dispiritedly worked on his newest jigsaw puzzle at the coffee table. He quickly connected three gold pieces of the sun shining through the dark clouds of the background of the Rocky Mountains. He sighed and wondered if life would ever again be as peaceful as putting together puzzles. Forcing himself away from the table, he perused *The Brookline Courier* and *The Boston Globe* for job advertisements but found nothing suitable. So, he walked to the two-story, mansard-roofed Brookline Library to look at city directories. He made a list of businesses, guessing what kinds of workers were employed and if there were any openings—none, he suspected, but he had to start somewhere. He would begin by going to places close to home and continue farther away until he found something.

A glance in the looking glass reflected a satisfactory image, even to Herb's self-effacing eyes. His mother had bought him clothes for graduation. A single-breasted jacket, closed with four buttons, was constructed of dark wool tweed, casual but smart, a waistcoat, and trousers that fit well, accentuating his muscular shoulders, trim waist, and long legs. He was the size of a full-grown man, but his whiskerless face gave away his youthfulness.

His first stops were shops in Brookline, where he knew owners from running errands and delivering messages. They congratulated him on being a top student, a fact listed in the local paper, and apologized for saying, "No help needed." Some took time for a conversation about the distressed economy and business hardship caused by residents cutting back on spending. "Desperation is everywhere, and I don't see an end to it," one told him gloomily. The farther away from home Herb got, the more abrupt the answers came from men he had never met. He tried different approaches:

"I'm willing to take any job. I'm always industrious."

"I just graduated from high school with the best grades."

"I need to earn a little for my mother and me; anything will help."

Too many others were out of work and destitute. The forced optimism Herb began with was chipped away with each rejection. After walking miles in a futile effort, he came home at the end of the day, footsore, hungry, and demoralized. His mother did not question him, but he felt worthless.

After exhausting Brookline prospects, he had to face the dreaded inevitability of Boston. A job there would require extra time, the cost of daily train fare, and moving away from the smaller, friendlier environment he considered home, but it was his only resort.

The following morning, he arrived in the city where he had lived most of his life. It resembled little of the vibrant city of his childhood with still-evident signs of fire damage. Herb knocked at the doors of banks, garment makers, grocers, pubs, repair shops, and factories. He responded to each rebuff with humble politeness, disheartened that his options were becoming nonexistent.

The day Herb went to the naval shipyard, an unblemished June sun warmed the air. He knew nothing about mechanics and repairing ships, but desperation drove his mission. Getting to Boston from Brookline and then across the Charles River to the harbor on the north side required two trains. It was mid-morning by the time he got there. He secured his paltry coins for lunch and the return trip inside the same clothing he had worn the first time he looked for a job—he wasn't about to risk his new suit in an unfamiliar neighborhood. Approaching the river, he watched the brisk activity of men pushing conveyances back and forth along the dock. One man—evidently in charge—barked orders to the others. As Herb walked toward him, his feet were pushed out from under him, and his head jerked back. He sprawled on the ground, trying to figure out what had happened. He looked up.

A thick-bodied man with a florid, unshaven face stood over him, glaring. "What the devil do you think you're doing, sonny," he snarled. "Butting in line will get your balls cut off. Get to the end, or you'll be too crippled to work."

Shaking his head to clear it, Herb turned to see a line of men slouching against a building in the sun, seemingly waiting for the slim chance at a job. He rolled over and got to his hands and knees, his wrenched back throbbing in pain.

"The line ends up there," the brute shouted.

There were too many to fight. Herb staggered past the glowering faces to take his place at the back. Infrequently, the boss summoned the first man in line, and the rest shuffled forward a few steps. Herb was hungry, but there was no chance to leave for food or water. The sun seared him as it inched up in the sky, clear skies without clouds or smoke. Men straggled in behind Herb. When he had to urinate, he turned close to the soot-streaked brick and let go, as others had. The stench mixed with chemical-laden fumes. A stringy-haired man with ragged clothing cradling a bottle of whiskey unsteadily bumped him. "A dime a slug," the foul man slurred. Herb turned his back.

He'd had nothing to eat or drink since breakfast but could not leave his place in line, even though he estimated only ten men had been taken at the front, leaving six ahead of him. He calculated it would be at least forty-five minutes to an hour before he got to the front and a chance. As the line inched forward, the man with a bottle collected nickels and dimes, secreting each in a small cloth pouch before handing over the bottle, then wiping the top with his shirttail and giving the bottle to another. Each taker gulped a full portion before handing it back. Herb could tolerate his thirst no longer and offered a dime. The man on the other side of him leaned in with a snort and tipped the bottle, sending whiskey pouring into Herb's mouth in a long, burning stream down his throat and up through his nostrils.

"That'll cost you extra next time, laddie," the owner snarled, sharply kicking Herb's shin.

The spreading warmth from the alcohol made him lightheaded and loose. A glance at his pocket watch showed he had an hour before he'd have to catch the train to return home in time for dinner. Once takers had emptied the first bottle, the provisioner passed a full one. Herb had given three dimes when he blearily consulted his watch again. Only a few people remained ahead of him, but too many to make it to the front and still catch his train. Leaving the line, he staggered toward the train station. "Sorry," he apologized each time he bumped into someone passing in the opposite direction.

Passengers leaving work for home filed into the first of the two trains he needed to take. Herb flopped into one of the few remaining seats. He could no longer stand up, even if he hung onto an overhead strap. With a jolt, the train started, giving him the odd sensation that the car was whirling in a circular motion instead of moving forward. The experience was eerily similar to a carnival ride he'd taken when he was ten, one which promptly caused him to upchuck when he got off. He clutched the train's leather seat, trying to hold everything down. The dizziness would not stop. His train connection was two stops away, but using the latrine could not wait. He stumbled off when the train stopped. Through blurred eyes, he spotted it. With no time to close the door, he heaved and retched until he was sure his stomach had gone into the stinking hole with the vomit. Shaking, he leaned back against the wall, wiping his mouth with his sleeve; still unsteady, his mind was a little clearer. Under the pitched roof of the outdoor station, he looked at the schedule. The numbers wavered in and out of focus. It was half an hour until the next train. He had missed his connection for the second train and would have to take the following one, arriving in Brookline an hour later than he had told his mother. She would worry.

Finally on the train to Brookline, Herb watched the passing scenery through a nauseous blur, sitting ramrod straight so he would not fall asleep and miss his stop. Close to the end, he patted his jacket, sending up a whiff of puke. With a prolonged release of steam, the train stopped, and he staggered home in the twilight of the setting sun.

After dropping his keys three times, he managed to unlock the front door with a sharp pang of dread at facing his mother. She burst from the kitchen when she heard him, moving so hurriedly her feet almost tangled in her brown-checked work dress. Relief washed over her until she got close. Her arms, extended to embrace him, pushed out in rejection. "What happened?" She stared in horror at his stained and poorly sewn jacket pocket. "Surely, you didn't go job hunting looking like this?"

Head spinning, he thought he might lose consciousness or throw up if there was anything left in his stomach.

His mother's anger kept him upright.

"What's that smell?" She took a step closer, nostrils flaring. "Whiskey!" She reached up and grabbed her hair as if she would pull it out by the roots, a gesture he had never seen her make before.

"Answer me. Have you been drinking?" She asked, clearly as baffled as she was angry.

"Yes," Herb said numbly, putting his palm against the wall to steady him. "I didn't mean to."

"Never, in all my years as a mother, did I think my son would be a drunk." She trembled with rage.

"Mum, I'm sorry," he reached out to her, but she stepped away.

"Go up to bed. You'll answer to me in the morning."

Rays of light sifting through the curtains woke him. Raising his head from the pillow hurt so much that he wondered if he could get out of bed. Focusing took effort. Somewhere through a haze, he had heard the clock below. Eight strikes, he thought he counted —breakfast was usually at seven. Tight, squeezing pain clamped his stomach, either from vomiting or going without food for a day. The most crushing awareness came from remembering his mother's stinging words and the shame of her disappointment. After struggling to dress, he gripped the banister and slowly walked downstairs to the kitchen. He sat at the table in everyday clothing. No interviews would happen that day.

His mother was bent over, cleaning cupboard shelves with a rag—a summer project to prepare them for new jars of put-up vegetables and fruits for winter. Herb suspected she had chosen a kitchen job to be there when he came down.

"There's toast on the table, and you can pour a glass of milk. Do you want anything else for breakfast?" she asked, not looking at him.

"Coffee, please, and I can make it, if there isn't any." He looked up into her unforgiving eyes as he walked to the stove. "I'll try to explain, Mum. I'm sorry."

She pulled herself up from her chore. "There is no reasonable explanation," she said, jamming her fists into her waist, arms akimbo, then dropping them by her side.

Trying to form thoughts through the fog in his brain, he awkwardly described the long line of rough and abject men waiting in the heat for a chance at an interview. After completing his saga, he put his empty cup aside. The coffee worsened his stomach, but it stayed down with the toast. His mother's posture was as rigid as her expression was grim.

"Getting a job at the shipyards seems hopeless, but I heard some men talk about the textile mills at Lowell. Seems they're hiring more men than mill girls these days."

"Shipyards? Textile factory?" His mother sagged into the chair across from him. "A common laborer after your high grades?" Her eyes closed as if she could not focus. "You can't," she said, begging and ordering all at once.

"There isn't anything else."

FOURTEEN

Lowell was a direct connection from Boston, twenty-five miles to the northwest. Herb peered through the window at the changing environment. As they got close, he was astonished by the uniformity of the buildings. The architecture replicated the order and precision of a factory system, yet trees and patches of grass gave verdant breathing space to row after row of brick structures. The train stopped with a long squeal of brakes; Herb watchfully stepped down three iron steps to the platform, wary of the good-for-nothings who liked to prey on strangers—the types he had already encountered in Boston's back alleys and shipyard and who, no doubt, infested a factory town as well. The bag that held his possessions was oversized and heavy but at least had a shoulder strap to make it more manageable. He kept one arm free, on guard to retaliate against thugs. In his duffel bag, he had put his waterproof Macintosh, a canvas quilted jacket, underwear, socks, four shirts and trousers, an extra pair of shoes, various sundries for hygiene, and a portable writing kit with powdered ink and pen. His beloved puzzles and books were left behind. He had brought everything he needed to exist because he was not going back. Lowell was the last chance for a livelihood.

Herb had used the Sanborn maps at the Brookline Library. He skimmed through the descriptions of each building, which were written in detail for insurance purposes, and took more time learning about the history. The Lowell Experiment began in the 1830s when families and girls were used for making textiles. It was the largest industrial complex in the United States. Before the South fought to separate, Lowell wove the cotton produced in the South. Since the end of the war, Lowell's textiles had transformed from fine fabrics to coarse cotton shipped to the southern states to make simple clothing.

At home, he had found more information on his mother's library shelves. Charles Dickens wrote *American Notes* after a visit to America in 1842, admiring the country's friendliness and way of life, "except for its egregious system of slavery." Dickens wrote in *Hard Times* fourteen years later: "Lowell had been planned at the beginning with production efficiency, democratic morals, and social structure to contrast Britain's cramped, cruel conditions."

When Dickens returned to America in early 1868, Herb's mother had attended his Boston lecture. Herb had only been twelve, but he remembered her bubbling enthusiasm. "Even after he'd harshly criticized some parts of our country, the audience loved him." She described Dickens as frail at fifty-five yet able to give a two-hour lecture with only one break. "He knew his material so well, he spoke without notes," she had told Herb.

Remembering Dickens's words about Lowell's intent, Herb observed the surroundings as he walked south from the long, two-story railroad station and, in two blocks, turned west on Merrimack Street. The network of canals and bridges interwoven among the streets made the route confusing. Block after block had rows of narrow, four-story buildings. He guessed they might be boarding houses or dormitories for workers, including the mill girls he had read about. In contrast, other blocks had two-story buildings with taller structures behind them, made of the same red brick and architectural design. He wondered if they were places of work because the signs did not always identify what went on inside. In some sections, factory smokestacks sent up dark plumes of smoke, rising to mix with streaky white clouds across the pale blue sky. No matter the uses of the various buildings, lawns and green grass surrounded them, often dotted with trees in lines as orderly as marching soldiers.

The high, early July sun burned with heat, the humid air suffocating with odors of chemicals and horse droppings. Traffic was sparse—most people, he guessed, were at work or home. The confusing layout of streets made him occasionally backtrack when a bridge led to a lane he was not looking for, but his deviations were short. He reached his destination of the Massachusetts Textile Mill office only half an hour after exiting the train.

Before he entered, he wanted to get a sense of the size and walked the perimeter. The complex sprawled over four blocks. Retracing his steps, he stopped at the door with "agent" stenciled on a glass pane. He paused to wipe drops of sweat from his forehead. Taking a deep breath, he entered a small office lighted by two second-story windows above. Stairs led to a mezzanine containing several desks. The man sitting at the single desk in the entryway swiveled in his chair when Herb opened the door but did not rise.

"Need something?"

"I've come for a job in the mill," Herb said, walking a few steps closer. The man at the desk, whom Herb assumed was the agent, was average sized and seemed to have remnants of muscles that had become mostly flab. Herb ventured that he might have been a laborer who had moved up a notch, whether because he was deserving or simply a political player like Headmaster Quincy, Herb could only guess.

With his knobby, work-worn fingers, the man shifted his spectacles to the few remaining hairs on his pate. He moved his eyes deliberately, taking his time examining Herb, and then he shook his head. "No."

Herb felt his shoulders sag like a puppet losing its strings. He wanted to say he had a high school degree. He was at the top of his class, hard-working and strong, and his mother was a widow. Instead, he turned to leave. *Why bother?* Anything that came out of his mouth was wasted breath.

"Wait a minute, lad." The man rose unhurriedly. He had grizzled white sideburns and a nest of whiskers on his chin. "I'm the agent, Frank Battles," he said as an introduction. Herb heard a hint of Irish in his speech and speculated that Battles was not new to the country but not born in it.

"Turn so I can see your back."

As Herb turned, the agent grabbed his bicep and squeezed it.

"Well, you're soft. You've never done real labor, have you? There's promise, but your lily-white hands will be pulp before they're calloused."

"Labor?" Herb thought of his wood splitting and carrying coal buckets up and down the stairs.

"It'd be a waste to have you in the mill; the young boys and mill girls can do that job." The man shuffled over to his desk and searched through a pile of papers. "Ah ha." He bent over to write on the back of a card. He handed Herb a card printed with *F. F. Battles* on the front and scribbled with the note *George Richardson, Lowell Machine Shop,* on the back. "I know the super there."

"Thank you. Is it nearby?"

"You came on the train, I guess." The man looked up, red veins lightly visible in the whites of his blue eyes.

Herb nodded.

"Go three blocks past the train station on Dutton and turn left over the tracks. It's not the easiest to find because the complex has canals on three sides." With an amused smile, he said, "It's like a moat, but not for protection, for transportation. The Pawtucket Canal leads to the river and then on out. Look for the tracks going down into the bunch of buildings. I don't guarantee a job's available, but I heard George was looking for muscle. You'll develop them soon enough if he puts you to work."

"Thanks, Mr. . . ." Herb turned the card to reread it. "Battles. Thanks a lot. I better get going."

More than once, his mother had remarked about Herb's good sense of direction—his internal compass, she called it, but in Lowell, nothing was on a grid, and there were many bridges and different railroad tracks. As he walked, he ate a slice of bread and a hunk of cheese he'd retrieved from his duffel bag and washed them down with water from his flask. He had learned his lesson about going without food. Somewhere, from the endless maze of buildings, came three chimes. It was mid-afternoon. He found the left turn and then the well-marked building in another block. *It has to be labeled because everything looks alike.* He pushed open the office door. Standing at a high desk, a muscular man with a neck like a tree trunk bent over his work. Herb's fingers almost flew to his ears to plug them against the din of clanging and hammering in the background. The man was clean-shaven, except for a dark, shaggy mustache that matched his full head of hair. He had not heard Herb enter.

"Hello," Herb called out, and then again, louder.

The startled man frowned at him, with eyebrows so thick they nearly formed an unbroken line above his eyes. "Whaddaya' want?" He barked.

"I'm here to see Mr. Richardson." Herb cautiously held up the card with the name on it. "Mr. Battles sent me."

He took a minute to give Herb the once-over. "That old piece of horse shit. Why'd he send you? It's no word on you."

Doomed again. "He said you might need a worker."

"What kind of work?" The man stood up, moving the stool out of the way with an awkward movement of his right arm. Herb noticed his shoulder jutting out at an odd angle. The man's gray fabric duster reached below his waist over worn tan-colored work pants. His dark eyes scrutinized Herb more deliberately. After a long moment, he offered Herb his gnarled hand to shake. "You got it right," he said. "I'm George Richardson, the super here."

Herb nodded acknowledgment. "I'm willing to do any job you have. I work hard."

"What work have you done?"

"I just graduated from high school—"

"Har, Har, Har. That's all I need. A schoolboy wanting a job."

Herb did not reply. He needed a job enough to beg, but he would not. He read this man like other bullies he had encountered. They took advantage of weakness. Fair enough. He wouldn't show any. He straightened. "If you need a hard worker, I'll apply for a job. I'm Herb Andersen."

Richardson stepped back with a limp and reached for a stack of papers on his desk. "We might need a laborer in the ironworks. Well, Sonny, come over to the table so we can talk about the job and sign papers if we both agree. What did you say your name is?"

"Herb Andersen."

"Well, Herb, I don't know if I'm doing either of us a favor, but I have a job. Our shop keeps all the machines running, with repairs and new parts. Sometimes, we make alterations when someone has a better idea. It's work that will blister your hands—and other parts—in the heat of the fire. Machines do more and more work, but there's still a need for the kind of labor that breaks your back. That's what I can offer."

"I'll take it." Herb wouldn't let fear crowd out the relief of a possible paycheck.

Richardson nodded slowly, once more examining Herb. "Be here tomorrow at seven. You work seventy-two hours a week, with Sundays free. Lunch breaks last half an hour. Bring your own food and lots of it—that's your main meal. You get porridge in the morning and boiled potatoes or whatnot in the evening. You'll start at two dollars a day with more later, depending. Pay used to be collected at the company office, but now it's collected here," he said gruffly.

Emotion overcame Herb. He had a job but had fallen steeply from the lofty position of top student. "You won't be sorry, Mr. Richardson."

After signing the necessary document and tucking his folded copy in his jacket pocket, Herb turned but stopped. "Where's the best place to look for a room?" There was no turning back now.

"Hmm," Richardson rubbed his chin. You might see if there's a vacant spot at the Line House on Merrimack Street. You'll find mostly

Americans there. It used to be that families and mill girls did the jobs, but nowadays, workers come from all over Europe. Lately, hundreds of French Canadians have crossed the border to settle and work here. Workers group together, depending on where they're from," Richardson said. "Where do you come from? Your speech sounds American."

"Brookline," Herb said, wondering about any prejudice Richardson might have.

"How many generations here?"

Herb stumbled for an answer, even though he figured it should not matter about his ancestors since he would be doing the work. "Except for my mother, all my relatives are dead, but both my mother and I were born here."

Richardson nodded. "You'll have to put up with the sound of trains at the Line House, but you'll get used to noise in Lowell. Most of us are half-deaf from it. Step outside, and I'll point the way. Let Mrs. Wright know I sent you."

The Line House was easier to find than his previous two stops. Once he located Merrimac Street, Herb followed it until he saw the sign on one of the buildings on the right-hand side. He still had no sense of the city's overall layout. It twisted and turned, with buildings of varying dimensions set around small squares in one area while stretching for four standard blocks in others. Each structure had a black peaked roof and long, narrow windows, all roughly the same size throughout the city, except for churches with unique architecture and steeples. The address he sought was on a tightly packed block. Four three-story buildings crammed the short side of the block, and a jumble of others with a variety of dimensions filled the long side. The building had four windows across each of the three stories. When he entered, he found the first door on the left imprinted with "office." His knock brought out a stout woman, as wide as she was tall, with fleshy jowls and blue eyes that peered through thick spectacles pinched on her flared nose. A whisker or two sprouted under her chin. Remaining in the doorway, she described the available lodging.

"I'd like to see the cheapest."

"All right, then, let me show it to you."

Herb followed Mrs. Wright up the stairs. Between labored breaths, she explained that rent included a cot, bedside table, and blanket for a quarter a week; a lantern was extra. "All twenty of you share the bathroom at the back. It has a toilet and sink."

At the second-floor landing, she paused. "There's a bathtub on the first floor. Let me know if you want a warm one—that costs a nickel. You can get into the cold leftovers any time they're available."

Ten cots, with single-drawer tables beside each, were lined up on each side of the wide, open, low-ceilinged third floor. The available bed was in the middle on the right side. There were hooks above each bed but no shelves or cupboards to put things away. Personal items lay at the bottom of or under each cot. With everyone at work, the beds were unoccupied.

"If you're interested, you'll pay each week in advance."

"Do I smell something, like bleach . . . or maybe vinegar?" Herb's spirits sank at the thought of living in something as impersonal as a barrack.

"We disinfect everything once a week to cut down diseases. The health department inspects and fines us if we don't."

Mrs. Wright must have noticed his discomfort. "There are rooms that house four or eight in the next building," she suggested. "They cost more."

"I'll take the cot," he said, slowly pulling two dimes and a nickel from his pants pocket. He kept his coins in three different pockets and strapped the one-dollar notes his mother had given him to his chest. From the looks of the place, he'd have to sleep with the money on his person. The room was a perfect target for theft, without any way to lock up anything. He felt like a sitting duck, ready to be shot, plucked, and roasted.

That afternoon was his last free time until Sunday, three days away, so he needed to get a sense of the town. Saying goodbye to Mrs. Wright, he departed with his duffel, afraid to leave it unguarded.

Children were leaving school, dispersing through the streets, laughing and chattering on their way home. Seeing them, some with their mothers, made Herb melancholy about the life at school that was now over for him. Shops clustered the main thoroughfares. He walked those first, alongside groups of women shopping for daily provisions, but the prices were more than he wanted to pay. Instead, he explored side streets, often strewn with piles of dung and fetid garbage, but on these streets, he found markets and small stores with lower prices. He bought a loaf of bread at the bakery; at two other shops, he purchased a wedge of cheese, a tube of salami, and two apples. That would suffice for lunch, that night's supper, and lunch at work the next day. He paid for them and stuffed them in his duffel bag.

On a bench under a tree in one of the many small, green parks, he sat and tore off pieces of bread, matching them with slices of cheese or salami he cut with his pocket knife. Passersby kept their eyes on him with a look of suspicion as he ate in the park. *They must wonder why I'm not at work.*

The July sun had begun its arc down to the horizon when piercing whistles from one end of the city to the other signaled the end of the workday. Lowell transformed as men in dirt-encrusted, sweat-stained work clothes meandered out of factories, crowding the streets on their way to their next stop—some in conversation, some silent. The number of people made jostling and bumping unavoidable on his way back to his new "home." Walking nonchalantly, he tried to envision everyone's destination. Some strode with purpose—those who had a family and dinner waiting, he supposed. Others entered saloons, and most went into the markets and shops or stopped at street vendors who had appeared early in the evening. The scent of cooking meat and the shrill cries of hawkers competing for business filled the air. Unrecognizable languages overloaded his ears; some English was so thick with accent that he could not understand it. Everything was so foreign that he could have been anywhere in the world.

At the Line House, he found residents straggling back from work, retrieving stored possessions from beneath their cots and adding any purchased items to them. A few joined the line for the washroom. Herb sat on his cot and arranged the food he had purchased on his nightstand.

Weary, he stretched out full length and closed his eyes. It may have been a few minutes or an hour when nearby movement roused him. His first wide-open glimpse was of a man standing beside the cot next to his. From Herb's recumbent position, the man seemed so tall his head nearly touched the ceiling; his bulging muscles flexed as he set down a duffel bag.

"My name is Herb," he said, sitting up cautiously while thinking. *What the deuce am I doing here? I won't make it in Lowell if you need to be a giant.*

"I'm Jeff." The man eased down gently on the cot. He was graceful for his size. "Are you new to Lowell or just to Line House?" he asked with an unidentifiable accent.

"Both."

"Gotta job?"

"I start at The Lowell Machine Shop tomorrow."

Jeff nodded without comment and pulled an item of clothing out of a canvas bag.

"You?" Herb asked.

Before Jeff could answer, the door flung open, hitting the wall with a reverberating crash. Everyone stopped what they were doing to watch the culprit grab the doorjamb to steady himself as he stumbled in. Herb guessed him to be in his mid-twenties. He was medium height and shirtless, wearing only a dark gray bib overall and his short-billed hat at an angle. Surveying the room, he seemed unsure where to go. His scanning stopped when he saw Herb. "Looky, looky, what do we have here?" Keeping his feet wide apart to maintain his balance, the man walked unevenly to Herb's cot, expelling a breath rank with alcohol in Herb's face.

"Let's see what the new boy has," he said, tipping toward the night-stand; he lunged for Herb's hunk of cheese, knocking into the cot as he did so. Herb drew back his fist, ready to punch.

As if propelled by a spring, Jeff came up; his brawny hand gripped the other man's upper arm as if it were a twig and removed the cheese from his grip. The man's loopy return swing missed Jeff.

"That's enough, Ricky." With a shove, Jeff pushed the stumbling man away. "Go sleep it off. And apologize in the morning." He returned to his cot. "Too many curs have to raise their hackles and piss on every tree to prove whose territory it is," he said to Herb. "It's always the ones who think least of themselves who act that way."

Inside the Lowell Machine Shop, a stoked fire burned around the clock, ready to keep metal malleable. Herb's skin seared from heat. There was no comfortable place to be. His hammer blows vibrated through his bones, each one jarring all the way up through his skull. Dirt invaded his pores, and noise throbbed in his ears.

He learned to identify other workers by the rhythm of their ringing blows. The cacophony of hammers had become commonplace, each blow confirming what his life had become—monotonous hard labor with little hope of anything more. The routine should have given him time to think, but the persistent noise shattered any chances for meaningful thought. He knew it was probably better that way. Recognizing life like this could go on forever would have driven him mad.

When the whistle signaled the end of each workday, Herb only desired to sit or lie down after the hours of interminable standing. Workers were only permitted off their feet during meals. He made friends—or, at least, companions in misery—through conversations at mealtimes and walking to and from the Line House. Eight men on the third floor worked at the Machine Shop, and others had similar jobs at foundries or construction sites.

After a month, he had little to show for his labor. George Richardson had charged him a quarter for acting as his agent. Herb had spent more of his precious salary to replace his gloves with a more durable variety and for bandages to cover oozing blisters. Another expense was a towel for handwashing and wipe-off bathing with water from the sink. The square of soap his mother had stuck in his duffel bag had worn down to a sliver, so money would soon go toward a new bar. Mrs. Wright rented lanterns for the bedside; otherwise, there was a light at the entry and one by the lavatory. Too tired to read at night, Herb had foregone the luxury of light on his nightstand. His landlady did laundry for a price. Before he paid to have her wash them, his clothes were stiff with dirt and sweat, and he could no longer bear to put them on.

Food was his most significant expense. Breakfast provided at work was a thin gruel of grain boiled in water or occasionally milk. Sometimes, hard and tasteless oatcakes were included. Potatoes and bread were the staples at dinner. The lunch he brought sustained him, although he begrudged the time it took to shop on his way home or, sometimes, over his lunch break when he risked the penalty of a dime for returning late. With experience, he had learned the markets and vendors with the lowest prices. His body demanded as much food as he could afford—a robust body was all he had to offer.

Sunday was a day of rest for most of the world, and for manual laborers, it was a day of recouping from exhaustion. Herb never got enough rest to recover—his body always felt spent.

The third floor of the Line House was half empty on Sundays. Those who lingered were tempted by gambling, horseplay, or any other diversion to relieve tension and depression. Others went to a saloon for camaraderie. Herb felt the tug of companionship such pastimes brought. Any activity that blotted out the cruel monotony and physical exhaustion of life in Lowell was a welcome activity for many workers. Most of the time, Herb preferred quiet relaxation during his little time outside of work. He craved fresh air and sat in a park for hours when the weather was mild. Lowell's parks and trees added a drop of life to the otherwise mechanical surroundings. Using his imagination, he could almost forget about the long future.

Herb used Sundays to write to his mother, although avoiding descriptions of the grim monotony of factory work left him with little to say. His mother's regular letters were reminiscent of her chatty conversations. They described her meetings, travel, and events in the news. On one stifling August morning, two letters arrived, the first from his mother and one from Mr. Brannan. It was the second his former teacher had sent, but Herb had not responded. What was there to say? Any words would focus on the humiliation of his current life. In his letter, Mr. Brannan wrote a few paragraphs about school, students, and Brookline. He enclosed a ripped-out *Scientific American* article entitled "Improvement in Transmitters and Receivers for Electric Telegraphs," a report about Alexander Bell's recent patent. "He is still experimenting with electro-magnetics for telecommunication," Brannan wrote. "I regret you're not here to discuss it."

Herb had not been home for two years. In 1875, the depression that struck in 1873 still had the country by the throat. A quarter of workers in some cities were unemployed. Desperate for pay, they were willing to step into the maw of the factory beast to survive. A worker dared not miss a day or stand up against injustice. Herb wondered if he would ever see his mother or the people he knew again. He had rejected her offer to take a train to visit him, refusing to expose the shame of his existence.

Life in Lowell went on as pervasively regimented as the factory machines. Winter days were piercingly cold, with furnaces giving off close-by blistering heat rather than warmth. On the third floor of the Line House, rising heat from below gave too little warmth in the winter and suffocating heat in the summer. He passed the hours of the day enduring reality.

So far, Herb had met no one with whom he had much in common. Lowell workers had different aspirations—often unintentionally. Most came from generations of hard labor. The tradition of using a back instead of a mind to get along too frequently was a script without an end. It was difficult to imagine any visiting a museum or reading *Scientific American.* Some had been forced to drop out of school, lying about their age or making other excuses because of the pressures to earn money as a son or a husband for their family. Young immigrants who came to the country unable to speak English often bypassed required schooling or sat through class in a blur of unrecognized words. They were put into labor as children with no horizon of other possibilities.

Different as his fellow laborers might be, their conversation was enjoyable during moments of relaxation. Jeff, the gentle giant on the cot beside him, had become a comrade. He was without formal education but principled, refusing to put up with bullies picking on the underdog. "Life is too tough to add that crap," he said. Another friend, Joey, originally from Ireland, was clean-shaven and had curly brown hair and melancholy blue eyes. Small and slight, only with resolute spirit did he conquer the rigors of keeping up with brawny men like Jeff. Joey often asked Herb to join him at a saloon or pub, as he called them. They were places where merriment, fired by drink and folk music, temporarily freed the spirit. Occasionally, Herb acquiesced, finding the atmosphere infectious. He joined in with a Guinness, but eschewed a repeat of the nauseous, spinning drunkenness he had succumbed to at the Boston wharf.

On a frigid day, Herb considered buying an extra blanket for his cot, but theft was too likely. While looking at blankets at the general store, he was surprised to find a small jigsaw puzzle. Jingling the coins in his pocket while he considered, he impetuously splurged and bought it. At the Line House, he laid it out on the table he had traded for his smaller nightstand. Herb matched pieces, using the dim light from the entryway to see. He finally had a small pleasure to pass time in the evening. After four nights, the picture of a sailboat began to emerge. He was a quarter done. The pieces of the multiple sail looked so similar that he had trouble deciphering the pattern in the scanty light.

Loud yells jolted him from his concentration. Two roustabouts were in a rage with each other. Herb glanced up in time to duck as a nightstand hurtled past his head and careened into his table, scattering puzzle pieces through the room. Men erupted from their cots, throwing punches one way or the other, not sure which side to be on. Herb yanked the man who threw the nightstand, shoving him to the ground. He was fed up with mindless abuse of others. The next sound was a high-pitched whistle so piercing Herb thought his eardrums had burst. Charging through the door, Mrs. Wright kept blowing until her breath ran out. Motion stopped.

"I'll call the cops," she shouted breathlessly. The men shrank away to tend their bleeding noses and bruises as they put the room back together. Herb's puzzle pieces were scattered, with no way to know how many were missing. He heaved fistfuls of the puzzle into the trash, not even bothering to look for any remaining pieces. He felt like pounding something. The loss wasn't just a cheap puzzle but so much more. It was a link to the past and the one small entertainment he'd cared about at Lowell.

Herb never let his guard down. He was always ready to defend himself at the Line House or Machine Shop. His sturdy build was an advantage, but sabotage lurked, as it had on the high school playground, kickball field, or wharves. He moved through the workweeks with flexed muscles, ready to retaliate when the hostility from overwork and underpay exploded into aggravation at some injury, real or imagined.

Letters from his mother, and occasionally John Brannan, were Herb's only real fragments of reality. They pulled off the cover protecting the landscape painting of his existence and prevented him from escaping the truth. Great waves of homesickness washed over him as he read his mother's most recent letter, remembering home and unfulfilled dreams. He dreaded falling into an abyss of sorrow from which he could never surface. His future seemed unfathomable.

Carefully putting the latest letter in a box with the others, Herb propped himself against the wall behind his cot. The curved position always hurt his back, but there were no chairs, and the pillows all had bedbugs. His mind ran in two directions: one to home and the other to his supervisor, George Richardson, with his crooked shoulder and shuffling gait. Physical infirmity was the dead-end fate of so many laborers, but Richardson was one of the lucky ones who had somehow gotten out of laboring and still had a paycheck. Herb had heard plenty of scuttlebutt at meals when the super was out of earshot about men with broken bodies or delirious minds who were too damaged to rise from a bed. He tore two pieces of the three-day-old newspaper he had pulled from the trash bin and twisted them into plugs to stuff in his ears in a useless attempt to drown out the mindless horseplay across the room while he considered his future.

If he could not imagine anything worse than his current life, then there was little cost of doing something different, even if it was like jumping off a cliff with no known ground underneath. Herb leaned back and put his head against the wall, his eyes closed, turning possibilities over in his mind. The paucity sent him another notch lower into despair. He almost dozed off to escape his miserable thoughts when he jumped at the sensation of something against his arm.

"Are you all right, mate?" Jeff asked, patting his arm a second time.

Herb drew in a long breath and sat up straighter. "Is anything all right here?" He shook his head to clear it.

"We all go through spells and then get over them," Jeff said, lowering his hulking body to his cot and bending to remove his boots.

Herb nodded. *That's what I'm scared of.*

Always one of the first to arrive in the morning, Super George Richardson liked to keep track of anyone late so he could dock him coins he probably kept for himself. Herb found Richardson at his desk, drinking a cup of coffee, likely after a full breakfast at home. Herb had never seen him eating a bowl of the watery gruel served to workers. "Super," he said, taking another step toward the desk, waiting for Richardson to raise his head.

"Yeah, you want something? You'll miss breakfast if you don't get in line."

"I'm giving notice. I'm leaving at the end of the week. I'm going home." Herb saw a genuinely startled look in Richardson's eyes.

"Anything wrong?" the older man replied suspiciously. "We don't give breaks."

"No, nothing's wrong." *Not anything—everything.*

Richardson's mouth twisted with an ugly snarl. "I always knew it was a mistake to hire you."

Herb barely forced down his anger. He had learned his job quickly and soon matched most of the men in output at the end of each day. Never had he been part of the repeated altercations ignited by frustration. He knew George Richardson wanted to goad Herb into reacting in retaliation for leaving—he undoubtedly resented losing a good man.

"As you said, I better get in line, or I'll miss breakfast." Herb turned and walked to the group of men, immediately striking up a conversation with his friend, Joey, who was ahead of him. He would make sure to say goodbye to him and others before Saturday.

At the end of that day, Herb bantered with the other men as he arranged his tools in an orderly row, ready to quickly pick up when the morning whistle blew. His arms were stretched wide to loosen his stiffness when George Richardson shuffled across the floor. Herb was surprised at how fast he was moving toward him with his stiff-legged limp.

"Andersen," he said. "Here's today's pay. You're through here."

The men wheeled around to observe the confrontation.

"I gave notice for the *end* of the week," Herb said defiantly.

The others returned to their end-of-the-day routine, dumbfounded, not daring to risk their fate by saying anything.

"What you did don't matter, you worthless piece of shit." Spittle spewed from Richardson's lips. "Good riddance. There's three better waiting to replace you, schoolboy." He swiveled on his good foot and hobbled away.

"What happened?" one man whispered. "You never caused no problems."

"He'll regret losing you," another added. There was fearful, muted agreement, knowing a job was valued, no matter what the circumstances, during a depression.

"Let's get out of here," Joey said. "I say we go to the pub and give Herb a send-off."

A few men muttered about having obligations, but a dozen shook off their other plans and went. Other workers had arrived before them, and when the news spread, the pub became a brew of grumbling and grousing about fate and wishing Herb well with spirited teasing and compliments.

"Do you remember Herb's first gloves?"

Another laughed. "Sunday school gloves. They dripped blood until he bought new ones and toughened up."

Laughter and comments went around the table.

"And what about getting so close to the fire that blisters covered his back?"

"Hard worker."

"Smart."

"Slow to rile."

"Loyal."

Herb sat in a daze, listening to the comments. He had thought himself anonymous, but now he knew better.

By the time the crowd thinned and he got up to leave, Herb was tipsy, not only from the second mug of stout but from the closeness he had never realized existed. His farewells to Jeff and the other third-floor men brought a whiff of sentimentality but no regret.

On the morning train, Herb took stock of his finances. He had kept an accounting of every cent he had gotten. He had listened to the talk on the third floor about pay and knew he had made the lowest wage. On his year anniversary, he had asked for an increase, and surprisingly, Richardson had agreed, knowing full well that it would not have come unless he had asked. He would have asked again if he had stayed past his second anniversary, just a few days away. With scrimping and saving, he had twenty-two dollars to show, plus the three dollars he would return to his mother. The money would last a while, but it was not enough to pay for a semester's tuition. After two years, his application would be invalid anyway. He was not sure whether two years of experience in Lowell would be worth anything. The shortage of jobs was still pervasive.

What was he going to say to his mother? That he failed was obvious. He had mailed a hastily written letter the night before, telling her of his return on Sunday without any details. Herb would beat the letter home since he had put the letter in the mailbox before he knew he would not work until the end of the week.

He was clad in his one good jacket and trousers, unworn since he arrived in Lowell. Most of his clothing could be thrown away unless he worked as a laborer again. His jacket felt snug around the shoulders, and his pant legs clung tightly to his muscular thighs, but the belt was notched in a hole. He had scraped away his stubble with a razor but regretted not having time for a haircut and shave. He dozed most of the way on the train, a somnolent escape from inescapable problems.

Sun shone fuzzily through the heavy air. He breathed in Brookline's familiarity. The serpentine walkways, grass-carpeted parks, thick-trunked trees, shops, and houses felt welcoming. His duffel bag weighed the same as when he left; his money was bound to his chest, and his front door key was tucked in an interior pocket. With a shiver of apprehension, he pictured his mother's greeting, but she might be away on one of her trips. His absence gave her more freedom. He was unsure what he would do if she were not at home, but there was nowhere else to go, so the answer was obvious.

He banged the brass door knocker at the top of the steps, waited, and then banged again. The door opened a crack and then farther.

"Yes?" his mother asked inquisitively. Her sudden scream knocked him back.

"Herb, is it you?" Her hands fluttered from her cheeks to her apron pockets and back again. "What are you doing here?" She hesitated. "Why didn't you?" Then she reached up and hugged him.

Her slender body and familiar scent brought Herb a forgotten peace. She held him for a long time until she unwrapped her arms to pull him inside the foyer.

"Do you want a glass of milk?" she said, incongruously, as if deciding what she should do with this son who'd become a stranger. "I've stopped baking cookies." She laughed, obviously still trying to take stock of his homecoming. "Look at you, Herb." She stepped back. "You're a man now."

"Is it all right that I'm here?" he asked honestly, not presuming he still had a right to be there.

"Yes, I'm so happy." The question of what had happened was in her eyes but not her words. A sense of belonging returned instantly.

"Let me take my duffel upstairs. Don't worry about making dinner for me. I don't expect to barge in and have you feed me."

"It's no trouble. I'm so glad to see you." She almost danced with glee, her small feet stepping to and fro, as if she did not know any other way to express her elation. "It's lucky I just returned from shopping, so I have food in the house." She smoothed her work dress. "Oh, it will be so good to have company at dinner."

In his bedroom, the blue quilt lay across the mattress, neatly ending over a mound of feather pillow. Puzzles lay stacked on the shelf, waiting to be put together. *Was it a dream? Was he really home?* Moving towards the wardrobe to put down his duffel bag, he was startled by his reflection in the square-looking glass above his chest of drawers. He brought his face closer and then stepped back for a longer view. In Lowell, an under-sized piece of polished metal hung above the washroom sink, producing a distorted image to guide a razor while shaving. The only sight of his physique had been brief reflections in store windows—undefined and incomplete. Muscles had added breadth to his already broad shoulders. His face, angular and hard, with the stubble he had not gotten quite clean, gave him a rugged appearance. He looked as different outside as he felt inside.

SIXTEEN

The hot, humid, midsummer day left the house airless and stale, even with windows opened for cross ventilation. Herb sat on the familiar low couch, a Chesterfield his mother called it, with its deep buttoned, quilted leather upholstery that still looked presentable even though it must have been older than he was. Two matching chairs crowded on either side, with dark wood end tables in between, offering ample space for lamps, beverages, and miscellany. His desk and chair completed the library, comfortably confining after the expanse of the Line House's third floor. He spread out the Bierstadt puzzle to begin again after not finishing it before leaving for Lowell. Physical idleness propelled his mind to work overtime. He longed to walk through the Brookline parks, free of encroaching industrial structures. Still, his courage flagged at the thought of meeting someone for whom he had once run errands or delivered messages. He wasn't ready to answer questions about life as a laborer in Lowell. Worse would be admitting he was once again without a job. Had he left, or had he been fired? Frankly, he wasn't sure, but either would be an embarrassment.

Sites he remembered beckoned him to go out: the library, kickball ground, and even Brookline High School—not necessarily the building, but a few teachers, especially Mr. Brannan. Herb's psyche was at a low ebb due to the absence of the intellectual challenge that he had thrived on growing up. Teachers' recognition and respect of other students, though often unspoken, had created his self-image. Nothing remained of what he once was. He wasn't even a common laborer any longer.

In the bathtub that night, Herb's fingers turned white and wrinkly from staying in the temperate water for so long. He stepped out and wrapped himself in a towel. When the last gurgle of water sucked down the drain, he went to bed. Sinking into the mattress, cushioned by the bed's suspended straps, his mind went calmly dark until morning. Startled by the first light glinting through his bedroom window, he jumped from bed to dress for work until he remembered where he was and fell back into an exhausted, peaceful sleep for another hour.

After breakfast, he split wood, carried coal, and even washed the high windows to contribute something to being home, although it was evident to him that just his being there was enough for his mother. She expressed pure appreciation through her exuberant conversation. He listened to her rather than talking about his life. When she left to go shopping, he luxuriated in the quiet library, reading the current edition of the newspaper, untouched by splotches of garbage from a thrown-away copy in a trash bin. Working on his puzzle activated the joy of mental stimulation. Relaxation came bit by bit, like a reptile shedding its too-tight skin, leaving the old behind in preparation for new growth. Yet, Herb's tranquility was only on the surface; heart-squeezing anxiety about what to do was not far below.

After three days, he had to escape the solitude and overthinking. He wore his graduation suit, ignoring the constricting fabric on his muscular shoulders and thighs.

"Mum, I'm going to see if Mr. Brannan is at home," he said casually, papering over the dread of explaining that he was jobless to anyone he might encounter, especially deplorable Headmaster Quincy. "He tutors students in the morning during the summer and should be available now that it's afternoon. I ran an errand for him once, so I know where he lives." Herb had debated sending his former teacher a message but decided the visit should seem as impulsive as it was. A message to say he was coming would imply that Mr. Brannan should do something for him. Dropping in as if he were passing by suggested no obligation.

His mother looked up from the morning *Boston Globe* she was reading. "What a good idea." Her expression seemed one of relief that he would do something other than hide away in the apartment. "I'm going to make a meatloaf, and it will hold—stay as long as you want."

The walk took him through the town center and then, on the other side, to a neighborhood that was a mixture of single houses and apartments. Herb scanned the walkway for anyone he recognized coming toward him. What he would do to avoid someone, he was not sure—hide behind a tree? He muttered at his ridiculousness. The change in his physical stature over the past two years had surprised his mother; maybe others would not recognize him when he passed, but he knew they would and would want to know what he was up to.

The Brannans lived in a small, two-story, white-clapboard house with a steep-pitched roof and two especially tall, red brick chimneys at the back. Herb stepped up on the gray-painted front porch, the same color as the low fence around the lot's perimeter. The brick house had greenish-blue trimming. At his knock, a woman, who looked to be in her thirties, opened the door. "May I help you?" Her welcoming face was framed with light brown curls, her butterscotch eyes alert and questioning. She wore a vibrant blue dress with lace at the neck and three tiers of ruffles.

Herb almost asked if the Brannans still lived there, but she was such a likely match in age and healthy slim figure, he said, "I'm Herb Andersen. May I talk to Mr. Brannan, if he's free?" He faltered to explain why he was calling. "He used to be my teacher, and I'd like a word with him, but only if I'm not interrupting."

"I'm Eliza Brannan," she said quickly with a smile. "Step inside while I go back and get him." Two curly-haired young girls—Eliza's replicas—peeked around the corner from the next room, hands cupped in whispers to each other.

Mr. Brannan came down the hall, inserting his arms through the sleeves of a loose-fitting frock coat as he walked. "I couldn't believe it when Eliza said your name." He grasped Herb's hand. "Imagine seeing you." He stepped back. "And look at you now."

"Thanks for your letters, Mr. Brannan. I'm sorry I didn't write."

"No bother," he said, his hazel eyes gleaming. "Are you here for something in particular?" He paused briefly. "If not, I'd enjoy a talk. It's been too long since anyone quizzed me about *Scientific American* articles."

Herb felt the weight of tension slide off his shoulders. "Do you have time?"

"If you don't mind a bit of clutter, let's go back to my study." Mr. Brannan started but turned back so suddenly that Herb almost bumped into him. "By the way, we're no longer student and teacher. Call me John." He resumed walking toward his study. "I don't know what this room was designed for, perhaps an oversized storage place, but it has a window, and it's out of the way from the rest of the household." He removed a stack of newspapers from a burgundy leather chair, its cushion sagging from use. "Have a seat."

The room was not untidy, just overloaded. Every space was filled with reading material. Herb scanned the shelves of books, newspapers, a stack of *Scientific Americans*, an encyclopedia, a dictionary, and an atlas. A pitcher filled with water and several empty glasses sat on a small round table, ready to serve visitors.

John had turned back corners of magazine articles as markers. Their conversation began with those, then migrated to the stagnant economy. "There are still increasing job shortages, which depresses everyone's pocketbook and mood," John said.

Herb felt as if in a trance. It was the first wide-ranging conversation of anything more than schoolwork or university applications that he had had with another man. He had to be reminded three times to call John by his first name. Herb and his mother were close and discussed current events, but conversing with John was different. Their conversation lasted for two hours with occasional, thoughtful lapses of silence before John gently asked him, "Are you still at your job in Lowell?"

"No." Herb shook his head. "I've come home to look for a job."

"Well, it's not a pleasant proposition in this economy, but there can be gain from starting something new." John rubbed his unwhiskered chin. "Would it be helpful for me to make inquiries since you've been away?"

Herb nodded slowly.

"Job prospects are dismal; I don't know if anything will turn up."

"I'd appreciate knowing about anything." The thought of searching for another job must have made his expression as grim as he felt.

"I suspect the most available jobs will be menial," John glanced up with a frown. "This is Tuesday." He pressed the heel of his hands on the chair arm to stand up. "Can you come back on Sunday afternoon, at about the same time, after my church obligations? I might not know anything by then, but if not, there's plenty to discuss." He offered Herb two magazines. "I think these will be of particular interest. Let's discuss them when you return."

At the front door, John said. "Thanks for stopping by, Herb. I live in a world of females." He chuckled. "I love them dearly, but it's not the same as man-to-man."

They clasped hands, Herb noticing the softness of his teacher's palm against his rough, calloused skin.

"I look forward to our next conversation," John said.

The way home evoked a friendly memory of delivering messages. Herb knew every street and alley. Twittering and chirping sounded as he walked. Wrens and finches perched in the trees, and swallows flew from branch to branch. Had there been any birds in Lowell? He could not remember. Clopping hooves sounded on the cobblestones; people bunched together or separately, going on one errand or another, but Herb no longer worried about meeting someone he knew. His conversation with John Brannan had made a change. It wasn't anything material, and maybe nothing would come of it, but somehow, a scintilla of self-respect had crept back. Herb's shoulders pulled back as he straightened his spine.

The day after meeting with John Brannan, Herb began his job search. The results were dauntingly similar to two years previous. Some stores had closed or changed names. When he returned home each day, his mother greeted him with the same cheerful face, pasted on, he suspected, to console him and, perhaps, herself, about the endless financial depression.

"Some people remembered me, like Mr. Brown at the feed store. He said it was beneficial to have two years of work experience. They'll keep me in mind when business improves."

"Something will turn up eventually," she always said. In his mind, and he suspected hers, too, the specter of a return to Lowell loomed. Even there, jobs were no sure thing, particularly because he had quit one job there. Or, worse, was fired; there was no telling what kind of twist George Richardson had put on his exodus.

"On Monday, I'm going to Boston. I doubt business has picked up there, but I have to try. Before then, Mr. Brannan—he's asked me to call him John," Herb raised his eyebrows, not yet used to the idea. "He wants to meet with me again on Sunday afternoon. We both like to talk about science, although he knows much more than I do, of course."

"Herb, how wonderful to have continued contact with a teacher. It's impressive." His mother was in her favorite chair, reading. Summer sunlight shone through the library's double-pane window. Finished with the newspaper, she put it on the coffee table. He knew she would bring it to the table for her inevitable interest in his opinions about articles when they talked at dinner.

"He says my constant questions test him, and he likes that." He glanced at her with a slight smile. "I wonder where I learned that? Maybe we should ask him for dinner, where he would really face the examiner."

His mother laughed at his teasing. His humor was a small crack in the carapace of tension he had worn since high school.

"I was going to say that Mr. Brannan makes a good father figure, but when I met him at graduation, I realized he is not quite old enough to be your father, although it would be possible. He must be what? less than twenty years older than you? More like a . . . mentor," she concluded.

Pausing, Herb shrugged. "Perhaps even a friend."

Throughout his life, his mother had diligently worked to be both father and mother: She set rules and enforced them. When he was sick or hurt, she nurtured him, taught him how to manage finances, and exposed him to the world through museums and newspapers. Yet she had not given up her life. Over time, he came to understand that it was a standard she set for herself as a parent, along with her high expectations for him. It was not her responsibility to be his friend. John was a friend.

The sun came out Sunday afternoon after an early morning rain, leaving a steamy aroma of woody mulch and damp on Herb's walk to the Brannans.

"Welcome," Eliza greeted him. "John has been looking forward to seeing you again after your last visit. Our daughters—Vicki is ten and Diane, twelve—and I are not all lace and frills. We're a family of readers, and we like to discuss different subjects," she explained. "But John relishes talking science with another man."

John came down the hall, buttoning the dark gray jacket that reached his knees, the clothing he had most likely worn to church.

"I'm glad you could come again so soon." John's handshake lingered. "Making contacts has been a bit discouraging, but I might have come across something," he hesitated. "I'm not sure what you'll think about it." He stopped. "No use my blathering. Let's go back to my study so I can describe it, and you can see what you think."

Curious, Herb thought. *He's in a dither.*

In matching burgundy leather chairs, they sat down across from each other, reminiscent of their occasional after-class conversations, sitting side-by-side at front-row desks.

"Herb, I sent messages to old friends, former students, anyone I could think of—here in Brookline, Boston, and Providence." He shook his head. "We're all helpless prey in the lion's jaw of the economy. There's little but discouragement."

"Thanks for doing so much, Mr. Bran—John. I've met the same deadlock here, so I'm going try Boston."

"Boston." John's eyes brightened. "That's exactly the place I wanted to talk to you about." He rubbed his palms together and then rested his hands on his lap. "I don't want you to get the wrong idea about this. You need to be doing something with your fine mind." He rubbed his palms again. "The one job I found is that of janitor and sweeper for the Boston University science building." Apology suffused his face. "I know it's not what you might have hoped for, but there may be some advantages we can't quite recognize yet. It's two dollars a day, and a need to take the daily train to and from Boston will eat into that."

"A janitor?" Herb's voice faded as images of janitors ran through his mind. They were the kind of men who were not smart enough to do anything else—disparaged and called derisive names.

"There's one little twist that may make it more appealing. Alexander Graham Bell teaches there and also has a small lab there. He has two other labs: one in the city center and one at his family home in Brantford, Ontario."

Herb exhaled. It was an appealing thought to be in the same Boston University building as Bell, but the idea wrenched him. He could have attended the university had things been different. This job would be so opposite of being a student. He cleared his throat, "I need to take anything, and it's not too far from home." He sighed again. "The physical labor is surely less than in Lowell."

"One more thing. Mr. Bell is known for being compulsive about security. Your fine reputation in high school is one reason you were offered an interview . . . tomorrow morning at eight, but only if you want. It's up to you, Herb."

SEVENTEEN

When Herb applied to Boston University over two years before, John described it, and Herb visited the library to find out more. He learned that Isaac Rich, a wealthy merchant, had bequeathed many of his real estate holdings to the university in his will. He died in 1871. The Great Fire damaged or destroyed all but one of the buildings—the four-story red-brick, Federal-style science building.

Herb arrived half an hour early for his eight o'clock appointment and waited on the entryway under the eaves to escape a gentle mist of rain. He carried his mother's tall, black umbrella but had not unfurled it. After a while, he heard a latch click and the right side of the double door opened. A man stuck his head out.

"Ah, you're here. Herb Andersen, I take it?"

The man at the door was much less muscular and not as tall as Herb. His full head of white hair graduated to gray in his sideburns and beard, covering much of his lower jaw, but the skin above his thick, moist lips was bare.

"I'm Mr. Shields, Robert Shields." He shook Herb's hand indifferently. "I manage the building. I will take you on a tour, and then we'll go to my office."

Herb followed the building manager, who walked, toes out, in a stride that resembled a penguin's waddle. Half of the first floor contained the university's administrative offices. Classrooms for teaching oratory and elocution were on the other side, including a small private classroom where Bell taught his deaf students. Combined rooms for lectures and laboratories filled the upper three floors. Some were standard lecture halls, with blackboards, an instructor's desk, and student desks filling most of the room. Some, however, had long tables with beakers and other equipment on top and chairs around them.

"Students must like these rooms, where they learn by doing," Herb commented, trying to make conversation as they walked through the rooms.

"All our students are happy learning here," Shields said without elaborating.

In the basement, Shields pointed toward the lab with an office at the far end. "This is where Alexander Graham Bell does his scientific experimentation." Long tables held mechanical devices, spools of wire, and beakers of chemicals. "He works here with his assistant, Thomas Watson. That is when Bell isn't teaching, and Watson's not at his mechanic's job."

Shields led him in the opposite direction down the hallway of the basement. Eight-foot windows lined both sides, lighting the otherwise dark, underground space. Gray linoleum covered the floor, giving a sense of cleanliness. The furnace was at the far end of the hallway with a nearby closet. Shields opened it. "Here are the cleaning supplies," he gestured to a jumble of brooms, mops, buckets, and other cleaning supplies. With one glance at the helter-skelter assortment, Herb knew he'd have to organize the closet to make any sense of what was there.

"This," the building manager canted his head toward an undersized square table and chair between the broom closet and a washroom, "is where the janitor may sit during breaks." The space fell into the shadows between two windows but was better than Lowell's long, crowded tables on hard-packed dirt floors where rats competed for scraps.

After twenty minutes of touring, Shields took Herb to his office, where he asked him to sit in a straight-backed chair. Mr. Shields waddled to the other side of a flat-top desk and sat across from him. The desk showed the nicks and scratches of wear but was distinctly neat. Papers on both sides of the blotter were piled in perfect alignment, with an inkstand and pens in front. Other papers and books filled shelves along the walls.

"You've heard about the fire?" Shields's gray eyes watched Herb through wire-rimmed spectacles.

"Yes, sir. I used to live in Boston at Twelfth and Elkington, on the north side, but we had to move to Brookline after the fire. I haven't been back much since."

Shields nodded. "Mr. Brannan communicated with me last week. He indicated high regard for you, both in grades and character."

Herb hesitated, wondering if he should embellish the description or mimic the undemonstrative style of his interviewer. He decided to risk enthusiasm. "I was lucky to have Mr. Brannan as a teacher. He teaches mathematics and science, but has a special interest in science and inventions, like me."

"Well, science and invention are some of what we do here," Mr. Shields's voice was monotone.

Herb could not imagine Shields inventing anything.

"Mr. Bell's small laboratory is here; he has a bigger one downtown. What he does is confidential and held with the highest secrecy. A commitment not to reveal anything is demanded." Shields's pale eyes were squinty, and his mouth turned down as he spoke. "That means anything you touch, hear or see. Will you pledge to that?" Shields's cheeks reddened in his first show of emotion.

"Yes, I promise to keep everything private."

Shields acknowledged what Herb said with a wary expression. "Are you going to come in from Brookline every day or get something near the university?"

"I'll come in from Brookline." Herb could not afford to move and was not sure he wanted to go back to Boston.

"All right then," Mr. Shields pushed a sheet of paper toward Herb. "Sign this agreement."

Shields had not verbally offered the job, but Herb's name was typed at the top. After reading the scant document listing hours, pay, and a covenant of confidentiality, Herb signed and dated it August 2, 1875— eighteen days before his twentieth birthday.

Because work started the following morning, Herb busied himself with projects when he returned home: splitting extra wood, filling the coal bin, and dragging around the ladder to dust and polish the tops of bookcases, light fixtures, and windows. He wanted to do extra chores for his mum before work consumed his hours. Except for splitting wood, the jobs were something his mother customarily did since she had no help, and once explained: "Even though my chores are the work of a scullery maid, doing them myself is an easy way to pinch pennies. I'd rather have a little extra to spend on my wardrobe and travel. Nobody knows I do my own housework."

Over a dinner of pork chops stuffed with buttered breadcrumbs and bacon, cabbage, and vinegar salad, boiled potatoes, and bread, he said, "I wish I'd found something better, but it's not the worst job, and I need the pay."

"Just so you don't get stuck. There's a certain impression that janitors can't do anything else because of . . . " his mother hesitated as if wondering how much she should malign a job he had just taken, "a perceived lack of intelligence. It's easy to get locked in that image with no way out." She began clearing the dishes. "Right now, I'm happy you have a job in a safe place and don't have to return to Lowell."

Shields lurked in the corners during the first week of work, furtively following Herb around every floor. He appeared out of nooks and recesses, reprimanding him for using water on wood and insisting he swipe the long duster twice over every surface to remove the motes and cobwebs. "Only swiping in one direction won't catch all of them."

On the fourth floor, Herb clutched a stack of papers while dusting with the other hand. Rushing footsteps and a hissing voice startled him.

"Don't touch anyone's papers!"

The papers cascaded to the floor.

"Oh no!" Herb gasped.

"I thought Brannan said you were bright," Shields said, looking down at the papers. "I'm not so sure."

"I'm sorry. You scared the wits out of me." Herb carefully scooped up the papers and watched Shields walk out the door, fearing he had lost the job he'd barely started. After straightening the papers and replacing them on the desk, he looked at his watch. One o'clock, time to stop for lunch.

At his small table, he took out his lunch, regretting that he was in the basement instead of a student in an equipment-filled classroom upstairs. But it was better than Lowell. The temperature was mild instead of a searing fire, and he liked the closed-in privacy. Best of all was the quiet. From his chair, the only noise was indistinguishable conversations in the lab at the other end of the corridor. He had just finished the first half of his sandwich when he heard approaching footsteps.

"Ah, who do we have here?"

Herb jumped up. "Mister Shields said I was allowed to sit here." He half expected his employer to leap from a corner, threatening him with termination for talking to someone.

The man who addressed him was tall and composed, with a boyish look. His smooth ash brown hair, parted neatly on the left, contrasted the frizzled mutton chops and beard covering all but his chin. His friendly chestnut eyes peered through oval-shaped spectacles.

"I'm Tom Watson. And," he paused, "I don't want to be presumptuous, but are you another new janitor?"

"I'm Herb Andersen, the janitor, and I'm new. Another?" he asked, surprised by the implication.

"Well, I've only been here a year, but there have been others. Sorry to disturb your lunch; I work mornings at Charles Williams Machine Shop and am just arriving for the afternoon . . . and often the evening." He laughed. "I'm on my way to the toilet before I begin." He shifted to walk past Herb. "It's a real convenience to have one down here." In a few steps, he entered and closed the door of the small washroom. Herb sat down again and returned to the crusty round loaf of his bread, three hunks of cheese, from which he had made a sandwich. He brought a large water flask from home, but having the washroom so close meant water was available. Watson breezed by on his return, giving Herb a nod in passing. Unsure if he should converse with anyone, Herb kept silent.

Over the succeeding days, the time Shields spent following Herb lessened. Whether work obligations or a gained confidence in Herb's abilities kept him in his office, he could only speculate. The upstairs laboratories would remain empty until classes began in a week, but there was plenty to do. Whatever other janitors had preceded him had let dirt and grime collect in the out-of-the-way corners and back shelves. Herb attacked them with rags soaked in soapy vinegar water. He even washed the windows of the first floor. He was amused when a scientist came in and paused, saying, "Let there be light!" with an arch of his eyebrows. "Keep it up," he added before walking over to a table laden with mechanical devices.

Herb stood by his bucket, yearning to ask what the man was working on.

Saturday, at seven o'clock, Mr. Shields came to the basement with Herb's twelve dollars. "Here's your pay for six days. I expect to see you Monday morning *on time*."

Herb bristled silently. He had arrived early every day and had done extra projects after finishing the regular tasks. He wiped away the insult, knowing he should feel grateful for having survived the first week, even as a drudge. He tucked the money in his trouser pocket but would transfer it underneath his shirt before leaving for the train. In Lowell, he had devised a wide fabric strap that he wrapped around his chest and over one shoulder. Within the strap were extra pieces of fabric he'd sewed on as pockets. A similar strap wrapped around his waist. The straps hid the bulk of his money, but he kept a few loose coins in his jacket as a throw-off for thieves, who would be suspicious if his pockets were empty.

Because of his work hours in Boston, his mother delayed dinner-time until eight so they could eat together. The aroma of food cooking welcomed him that Saturday. He hung up his jacket, reaching beneath his shirt to pull out his pay. The modest amount to contribute to their upkeep barely erased the humiliation of working as a janitor. It was lowly but less physical than Lowell.

After washing his hands, he slumped into the chair across the table from his mother. She had served two plates of sliced venison, potatoes, and baked apples.

He handed her his money. "Here, Mum, this will help with food."

Her face brightened as she counted it, then frowned. "Did you keep enough for yourself? You'll have expenses."

"Right now, my only expense is train fare. I'll keep more next time; I want to pay my share."

"Thanks," her eyes softened. "We're a team, and you *are* doing your share."

"Mum, you won't believe who I met today."

Meeting Mr. Bell's affable assistant, Tom Watson, brightened the dinner conversation, even though telling her about meeting him made Herb ache with regret and envy of a man of similar age with a much loftier position.

Summer lingered green; autumn was not yet showing its colors. Scarlet roses in full bloom climbed over and through the fence that enclosed the Brannans' front porch. Herb breathed in their scent in the heavy air as he approached the house. John sat in a slat-backed rocking chair with an identical rocker sitting empty beside him. "Welcome." He got up to greet Herb when he saw him coming down the path. "I hoped you wouldn't be too tired from work to make it to our Sunday conversation. I'm outside because none of my usual techniques with cross-ventilation have worked in my study today. It's hot out here, but there's air, and the overhang will keep the sun off. Have a seat." He gestured toward the second rocker. "Forget protocol and hang your jacket on the back of it. The heat's too much for anything but shirtsleeves." John removed his dark gabardine jacket and draped it over the back of his rocker, leaving on his waistcoat.

As he returned to his seat, Eliza pushed open the screen door, carrying a large glass pitcher filled with fresh-cut lemon slices floating in lemonade. Diane and Vicki followed, giggling shyly.

"Mr. Andersen has been here before. Please say hello," Eliza requested of her daughters. Vicki and Diane caught his eye with a flutter of eyelashes and bashful hellos.

"Would you permit them to call me Herb? I'm not ready to feel so old."

Eliza and John looked at each other in silent communication. "I think so," John said, "since we're friends, but looking at you would confirm a grown man."

"We'll leave you to your talking now," Eliza said. "The lemonade is lukewarm, but I couldn't spare ice with this heat. Come along, girls." They looked in Herb's direction and then followed their mother. The screen door banged as John's family went inside, all three talking simultaneously.

"Everyone is always happy here,"

"Oh, there's plenty of drama. And you can't imagine how girls can tease each other . . . and inflict verbal wounds," John said, but his voice brimmed with affection. "Maybe sibling rivalry is preparation for life— testing the limits of what you can get away with or what compromises are necessary to move forward." He wrapped his hand around his glass and then shifted to take a sip, his lips puckering with the apparent tart sourness of the citrus before he continued with a chuckle. "When there's caterwauling, I escape to my back room." He looked across at Herb. "Another lesson: hiding from problems. That's my tendency, but little gets solved through avoidance." He reached for the pitcher. "More?"

"Please."

John refilled both glasses and set the half-empty pitcher on the table. "Now, *I* am going to remain silent and listen to the details of your new job. Don't hold back. Give me the roses *and* the thorns."

The pleasant atmosphere enveloped Herb. Male companionship, lemonade, rocking chairs, fragrant roses, and having a job loosened him like a champagne bottle popping its cork. His usual reticence was supplanted with volubility as myriad thoughts and emotions swirled through his mind. "In Lowell, I worked with laborers, most without formal education, using muscles for pay—too worn out to think about much else than a tired body at the end of the day and return the next morning for another. At the university, I'm surrounded by people who use their minds instead of their bodies. It shames me to be in a lowly position around people with high dreams. And I'm letting down my mum's high expectations for me." He wasn't sure he was brave enough to consider dreams of his own.

"You know what worries me most?" he asked John. "It's that I get stuck as a janitor, or worse, a laborer, for the rest of my life." He rocked slowly as he talked. "The men in Lowell often came from families of laborers. When times were slow, and exhaustion didn't crush our ability to talk, they described their family lives. Some, of course, were from other countries, but no matter where they came from, they'd followed in their father's footsteps." Even though Herb had exerted no energy, sweat beaded on his forehead from the humid day. He swiped his face with his handkerchief. "Once a laborer, always a laborer; once a miner, always a miner, once a sweeper, forever a sweeper." He felt John's temptation to interrupt, but it did not come.

"On the other hand, some of my classmates and those you taught have gone on to lofty positions in banks and commerce, just as some girls married well. That's another continuation within a family that's hard to break into instead of out of." That was his mother's worry, he realized, failure to advance. He stopped the rocking chair's motion. Was this something she had experienced? She had been widowed at a young age, left with a child to raise alone. She had not been able to share ambitions with his father. Herb understood that his mother's life had been filled with sacrifice. Yes, they'd always had a roof over their heads and food on the table, but all the responsibility was her's.

There was a deep silence, like one after a foghorn's blare—long and noticeable.

"Your assessment is not altogether off base," John said at last. "I come from a lineage of schoolteachers, including my father, mother, grandparents, many cousins, and uncles. The Brannans confirm your point. I'm proud to be a schoolteacher. We never make a fortune, but we are well respected, or at least most of us. I guess that comes from our store of knowledge and the expectation of carrying on society's values—aspiring to good ethics, industriousness, integrity, and being members of sound families. You know," he glanced at Herb with a smile, "being someone who follows the rules. Societies want their children to learn those values, even if they as individuals sometimes choose to profit by abusing them."

Flies buzzed over the lemonade pitcher in another stretch of silence.

"Herb, would it be too presumptuous to ask what your father did? Or what you remember of him?"

Herb tipped back in the rocker. John had read his mind. "I don't remember him at all. By the time I was old enough to understand anything, he had already died. My mother has said his work involved some business, but other than that, she's stayed pretty silent about him. It's probably too painful for her to talk about. Always being alone must be a burden. I'm just coming to understand that. Aside from that topic, my mum talks a lot," he said, chuckling, "about what she thinks is important. You would have liked to have her as a student. She is curious about everything and wants to learn more."

"I'm sure I would have liked to have had her as a pupil. And an interest in learning more reminds me," John rose, steadying himself from the rocking chair. "There's a *Scientific American* I know you'd like, and now that I know about her interest in learning, you can share it with your mother. I left it in my study. I'll be right back."

With the bang of the screen door, he was gone. For the second time, a discussion with John aroused so many thoughts that Herb had trouble returning to reality. What imprints did his father's footsteps leave that he might or might not be bound to step in? The thought jumbled his mind. Family relationships, the environment in which they lived, and the surrounding economics influenced the aspirations of life, maybe as much as something biological, like brown hair.

"Here it is, Herb. Sorry, it was buried under something, and I couldn't find it at first. It's about Professor Bell, the very man working in your building. The idea of a tradition of occupations you alluded to has merit, but plenty of people break out of where they came from. I don't deny the obstacles, but I assert the possibilities. Let's talk more about that in the future. Our talks are becoming a tradition I relish."

On Herb's walk from the Brannons, the humidity-saturated air slowed movement and thought. Herb felt like he was walking through a deep pool with every step exertion. When he got home, he found the apartment no cooler inside than the temperature outside. After his conversation with John, he wanted to think clearly, but even shaking his head to get rid of his drowsiness failed in the heat.

"Hi, Mum," he said, entering the kitchen. She was working at the kitchen table, setting up her reading material, inkpots, pens, and paper. He had told her they could share the desk in the library, but she'd instinctively known that he needed a workspace of his own. Her kitchen encompassed the facets of her life—cooking, studying, and organizing. They shared the library for reading and doing puzzles. The mostly unused parlor had tufted sofas, thick velvet draperies, and lampshades dripping in red fringe. The formal dining room seated eight, but he could not remember a dinner for eight, only occasional meetings with women who circled around the polished mahogany table, debating and discussing.

"How was your meeting?" she asked, looking up from the newspaper, her eyelids low and sleepy-looking. "I'm sorry. I know it was more of a conversation than a meeting. What did you talk about? More science?"

"He gave me another magazine." Herb put the *Scientific American* on the table and removed his jacket, lazily hanging it on the back of his chair. He reached for a glass and began to open the icebox.

"Be quick! It's barely cool in there, and there's no ice delivery until tomorrow."

He poured a glass of milk in record time and sat down at his place at the table. "We talked about jobs and how many men follow, one generation after another, in the same occupation. In Lowell, entire families worked as laborers, and here in Brookline, a grocer has his son and his grandson helping while he trains and teaches them the business." He sipped the rich white milk, remembering the tart lemonade at the Brannans and John's question. "Mum, what was my father's occupation? I'd like to know if I might follow in the same type of work."

His mother's posture was rigid, her violet eyes wide and alert.

"He was—" Her voice trembled. "He was in the business of transporting things." Her lips pressed down resolutely before she continued with a frown. "One generation following another may be customary, but that's not always true. Traditions pass on, especially when there is a strong influence. Herb recognized her habit of picking and sorting her thoughts, like going through fruit at a market, choosing the best, what to say, and how much. Disciplined to consider her words before she spoke, she rarely blurted out anything. Her filtering and weighing everything annoyed him. He itched to have her reveal everything and let the listener decide what was important.

"Anyway, if you work hard, you can break out of the tradition of an undesirable job. Some do manage to go onto a higher level after a lowly upbringing." His mum tossed the idea down like a skein of tangled yarn without adding enough information to unravel the specifics that would answer his question. "Oh." She fanned her face with her unfolded napkin. "This heat is fraying my nerves."

"Am I like him?" Herb was undeterred.

She whirled around, glaring, but then her eyes softened, erasing her look of annoyance. "As I told you, you're beginning to look like him, the older you get. Not altogether. Your hair is a little lighter, but in structure, you do. As far as personality, he was domineering and you're more thoughtful. I wouldn't say you're much like him." She turned away from him toward the sink. "I'm going to finish my business and then read my book. It's a biography of Jane Austen. She depended on her family's library the way I do ours, but the Brookline Library didn't have this book, so I bought it at the bookstore. Indulgent, I confess, but owning a good book is always worth the expense."

EIGHTEEN

A forty-five-minute lunch break was listed in his contract, but up to that day, Herb had never taken that long. At the most, he spent fifteen or twenty minutes eating his bread, cheese, and fruit. Sometimes, he brought a book to read, but he never used the allotted time before returning to his cleaning, even though he wasn't paid for the extra minutes or allowed to leave early. Curiosity dared him to risk leaving the building, but not without notifying Mr. Shields, who thrived on power and permission.

Herb found Shields in his office at noon and his door open. "Mister Shields, I'm sorry to bother you, but I have an errand. I'll be back before my lunch break ends." He smiled noncommittally. "I've cleaned the three floors of classrooms, and I'll work on organizing the closets this afternoon."

Herb's reference to extra work was ignored.

"What errand?"

"A short trip to the library." *Not that I need permission or to tell you where I'm going.*

"Do you own a library card?" Shields's tone was patronizing.

"Yes, but I'm researching, not checking out a book. I better get going. It's a fifteen-minute walk each way, which only gives me fifteen minutes to work." He gave a half bow of deference but turned and left before Shields officially granted permission.

Dashing down the street, Herb arrived at the library in twelve minutes, dripping with sweat. Wiping drops from his brow, he hurriedly asked the librarian for directions to the city directories. Tables were crowded with patrons languorously reading, enervated by the heat. Even newspaper pages made scant rustling in the damp air. Without a space to sit down, Herb balanced the 1855, 1856, and 1857 directories—the volumes of the year he was born and the two after. His mother never referred to his father by name, but he remembered her speaking once of William . . . William Henry. However, no William or W. H. Andersen was in the three directories. He glanced at the wall clock. Time was up. He slid the directories onto the shelf and lined them up evenly with the others. He would have to come up with something else; he had no idea what, but thinking was impossible while running back to the university in Boston's heat.

Mr. Shields stood on the landing four steps up from the expansive entryway, casually shuffling back and forth as if he just happened to be there. Yet the pocket watch in his hand was a giveaway.

"I'm back," Herb called out, not stopping as he made a sharp right turn down the steps to the basement in time; his underarms were wet with sweat. *You're going to get yourself fired with your brazenness.* He quickly changed to his work duster, filled his bucket, grabbed rags, and went up to clean the closets. There was no time to have lunch. Eating would have to wait until a brief afternoon break.

He passed through the empty entryway. Shields had apparently returned to his office and missed Herb sloshing the bucket up to the third floor for yet another extra project. From the looks of them, the storage closets had not been cleaned for a long time, maybe since the building was constructed. Some of the instructors nodded as they passed. Mostly, he was as unnoticed and inanimate as the rest of the room's equipment.

Life had developed a humdrum rhythm. Herb's days were filled with train rides, mopping, sponging, polishing, and a litany of Mr. Shields's add-on work and criticisms. But mostly, he was ignored. Herb felt no sense of accomplishment nor real fear of being fired. The tension and camaraderie of shared suffering in Lowell had been replaced by solitary plodding, Sunday, and visiting John was his respite. Some of their discussions were spontaneous topics they happened on, while others Herb suspected John had conjured up and was testing his ideas by listening to Herb's response. Added to his pleasure from time spent at the Brannans was pride in becoming skilled at fixing almost anything at work and home.

On August 20, 1875, Herb turned twenty. That Sunday afternoon, a thunderstorm threatened to turn his umbrella inside out on his walk to the Brannans. John's project of the day was to create games to interest reluctant students in science. Herb forgot about his rain-dampened clothing. It was typical of John to encourage all students to be as enthusiastic about learning as he was. He took every opportunity to teach—a trait Herb guessed had seeped into John's bones through his lineage of educators.

Surrounded by inkpots and papers, the two of them thought of brain twisters, especially about inventions, suggesting them out loud as they came to mind. John valued Herb's ideas as much as his own. They laughed as they discarded far-fetched ideas, like filling a pen with ink to be carried by the owner from place to place. They exclaimed when others made sense, like a carpet washer. Some of their ideas made Herb laugh harder than he ever remembered. He and John were so raucous that Eliza peered around the corner to see what was happening.

"Gentlemen?" She gave them a broad smile at their shared pleasure. In the end, Brannan had a list of science problems he hoped would engage students and many crumpled papers of useless ones. Herb did not mention his birthday, but unknowingly, John Brannan had given him gifts of respect and intellectual engagement.

On the way home, the undiminished storm hurled heavy drops on top and under his umbrella. Distant thunder boomed like a voice warning against the routine of insignificance.

The whipping wind had sent drops under his Macintosh. He hung it up in the foyer, its drips gliding to the mat underneath the row of hooks. His mother was in the dining room. Usually dark, the six-globe chandelier was lit and had colorful, thin ribbons hanging from the curved brass arms.

"Happy birthday, Herb." She looked up, gleaming. "Let's celebrate your birthday away from the kitchen for once." She reached for his umbrella, still in his hand. "I'll open this near the fire to dry."

"Thanks, Mum." Spreading his arms to warm himself, he said briefly, "I'm wet to the core. I'll change and be right down."

It was his first birthday at home in two years. His mother had cooked roast beef—top round instead of the usual pot roast. When it was cooked, she removed it to a platter. And then, into the pan of beef drippings and fat, she poured a batter of eggs, milk, and flour. He had watched her make Yorkshire pudding since he was little. She poured the batter into a pan greased with fat drippings. After fifteen minutes of cooking, the mixture had risen high. The crust, where the dough had come into contact with the drippings and fat, was crisp, pushing up a light pudding with a puffy texture on top. She cut it into squares and arranged them around the roast, rimmed with carrots and potatoes. The dinner brought back memories of similar celebrations—his mum could make meals fun even with only the two of them. For dessert, she baked his favorite carrot cake, with thick cream cheese frosting as white as clouds.

After a bite, he looked up and asked, his voice trembling. "Mum, did my father ever see me?"

Startled out of the relaxed, celebratory ambiance, she looked sad. "No, I wish he had. It's a regret, but it no longer matters."

It might matter to me. "My birthday made me wonder. What was his name?"

His mother restlessly twisted her napkin before placing it by her plate, which usually indicated that she had finished, even though she had eaten only a few bites. Her eyes narrowed as they did whenever she was flustered.

Herb pressed a bit as she reached for the wrapped birthday present on the console. "Was it William? William Henry?"

She nodded in wary acknowledgment and pushed the present toward him. "Here. Open this. You have little spare time, but I know you like challenges."

Momentarily debating between the carrot cake and the birthday present, curiosity won over. He moved his unfinished dessert to the side to untie the dark blue ribbon and rip open the paper wrapping. He lifted a box. "A new puzzle. Thanks, Mum." He turned the box right-side-up to examine the picture. "Pikes Peak," he said, recalling an article he had read. "It's in Colorado Territory, where the gold rush was. Of course, they never found gold very close, but Pikes Peak was the most visible symbol." He inspected it more carefully, "This is going to be a challenge. The mountain's covered with snow. A thousand pieces, and a lot of them white. I may have another birthday before I finish it."

He talked in torrents to avoid asking about the past he knew troubled her. "Funny, Mr. Brannan once suggested I go to Colorado for college. They need students in the West, and it might be easier to afford."

His mother drew in a sharp breath.

"It wasn't a serious comment," Herb added hastily. "Mr. Brannan likes to keep things light when I get too serious and keep me thinking about different options. He has a card on his desk with his motto: CURIOUS, NOT COMPLACENT."

His mother was quiet, not reacting to what he said for a moment. "Interest in learning is one thing; idle curiosity is another." Picking up her plate to go to the kitchen, she changed subjects. "If you ever want to use the dining room table to do puzzles, it's especially pleasant when the sun shines." She raised her eyes toward the sound of rain pelting the panes.

"Thanks, that might be a good idea. I can already tell this puzzle will need space to spread out." He cut himself another piece of cake, opened the puzzle box, and carefully tipped it to gently spill the pieces, keeping them away from his plate.

At various stages of his life, he and his mother had argued when his need for his individuality tested her desire for control. Still, their common dependency on each other maintained an unbreakable bond. His insistence on answers about his father had created a turbulent mood, as if his new puzzle pieces had been shot out of a cannon, landing in disarray, some pieces still drifting in the air.

An all-week lyceum with visiting lecturers took his mother to Boston in mid-September, causing the usual flurry of preparation before she left. It felt odd that they would be in the same city where they had resided for most of his life, but this time occupying separate worlds.

On Monday, Herb decided to risk leaving the university again during his lunch break. This time, he planned to go to city hall to search for his parents' marriage certificate or birth record with his father's name.

"Mr. Shields, I need to go out again during lunch hour. I'll be back on time."

"Not a minute late." Shields's mouth scrunched with displeasure.

Herb bolted out the door and down the street, where fellow pedestrians paused to look curiously at his rapid pace. *They must think I'm either being pursued or pursuing someone.* Half running, he scanned the faces ahead with an irrational dread of meeting his mother coming or going from her Boston meeting. He would be struck dumb if called upon to explain what he was doing.

At city hall, a young, red-haired clerk eagerly offered to help. With an Irish lilt, she said, "Give me the names and the dates as close as you can come."

"Herbert Andersen, with an 'e' at the end, was born August 1855. I'm looking for a birth certificate and a marriage certificate for Sally Andersen, also with an 'e.' Look at the years between 1849 and 1854, please." His face warmed. *She must wonder why I want that information.*

She looked unconcerned when she turned to a bank of filing cabinets and opened the top drawer. Her fingers danced over the tops of the files, stopping every once in a while to read more carefully. Herb's eyes moved down from the files to her trim waist, not drawn into such an extreme that a man could encircle it with his hands as was in vogue, but a healthier, more appealing shape, with naturally rounded hips filling a dark-blue skirt without a bustle. Her copper hair hung down, captured by a fine net that fanned out between the puffed shoulders of her white blouse. When she turned toward him again, he took a second look at her clear, light complexion. Auburn eyebrows arched above Wedgwood blue eyes. He had barely noticed her face when he arrived he was so focused on his task.

He noticed now.

"I'm sorry to disappoint you, but there isn't a marriage license or a birth certificate. It isn't unusual," she rushed on, her blue eyes captivating him. "Babies are often born at home, and some people don't bother registering their marriage. Churches don't even send us information regularly." Her melodic voice reminded him of the Irish ballads he'd heard sung in pubs in Lowell.

"No need to apologize. It's not your fault," he said, but his shoulders slumped with disappointment. "I wasn't expecting to find anything, but I needed to make an effort."

"Are you trying to find Herbert Andersen or another Andersen?" she asked politely.

"I'm Herb." He glanced at her ringless hands. "Do you mind telling me your name, Miss?"

"Anna McGilvery. Spelled the Irish way, it's Á-I-N-E, although I've changed the spelling and pronunciation to sound more English." She paused. "You know, I wonder if the spelling of your name might have been changed in the records by accident or intentionally. Do you want me to look again, but this time for Anderson with an 'o'?"

The mere sound of her voice sent vibrations through his heart. "No . . . I mean, yes, but not now." He took out his pocket watch. "That's kind of you, but I need to get back to work." He'd have to run again to make it back in time.

"If you write down your address, I could send you any information by post or messenger."

Herb did not dare have information sent home, where his mother might see it, or in care of the university, where Shields might ask questions. "I can't thank you enough for the offer, Miss McGilvery. I'll have to come back." He turned toward the door, then looked over his shoulder. "I look forward to coming back." His audacity surprised him. At that moment, what he wanted most in life was to see her again.

His stride on the way back was more a run than a fast walk. *It would be my luck to be stopped by the law as a suspected thief, running away with stolen goods. That would doom my job.* At the university, he entered the front door with nothing more than a glance at Mr. Shields, pacing in the lobby. At the bottom of the basement stairs, a glimpse at his watch showed two minutes to spare. He traded his jacket for his work duster and grabbed a bucket to get to work.

"Boy . . . boy!"

Herb paused, one foot on the upper step, ready to ascend. A slender man with curly, onyx-black hair, a beard, and a trim mustache approached him, gesturing with his hands.

"Yes, sir? Did you want me?" Herb asked.

"Yes, I called you." The man paused. "For a moment, I thought you were one of my deaf students when you didn't answer."

"I beg your pardon. I didn't know you were talking to me." *No one ever talks to me.* "I was on my way up to clean the floors."

"Never mind." The man looked at Herb with eyes so dark they looked like jet marbles. Between them, above his nose, a pronounced crease made him look as if in a state of deep concentration.

"My assistant is out; would you help me move some batteries?"

"Of course," Herb said, setting his bucket on the floor and resting the mop handle against the wall.

"I'm A. G. Bell, by the way. Follow me."

Too stunned to introduce himself, Herb followed Bell. *He's not that old, probably not yet thirty.* Wires and equipment filled the laboratory they entered. He had seen the room, but Mr. Shields had told him to clean there only if specifically asked and to do nothing to disturb the laboratory or the office beyond.

Bell pointed at the bulky mechanisms they needed to move. "It's not just one; a bunch of them need to be put in a box, but I don't want to separate them. Here." He canted his head. "Lift that end of the box, and I'll take the other. We need to carry it to my desk in the office."

They moved together through the door, Bell backing out of the lab and through the doorway of the small office.

"An electromagnet?" Herb asked before his mind had fully formed the thought. It looked exactly like the drawing in *Scientific American.*

The heavy box tipped dangerously toward Bell. Herb tried to maintain the balance on his side.

"Let's set it down here, but mind the other equipment," Bell said, lowering his end. "You know what it is? Have you been looking around when we're not here?" he asked accusingly.

"No, not at all. I read about it in a *Scientific American* my teacher lent me."

"Yes, yes, you're right." Flustered, Bell moved around the office. Most of the equipment was in the laboratory, but he grabbed a towel and covered something in one corner of the office, more like an alcove. "It all has to be top secret when you're solving problems. You never know who wants to take your ideas." Bell looked straight at him. "What is your name anyway? Why is a sweeper interested in electromagnetism?"

"Herb Andersen. I meet with my old—" Herb stumbled. John was not really old, although he was older than the man he was now talking to. "My former high school teacher, every Sunday, to discuss things. We're both interested in math and science."

Bell's dark, suspicious eyes did not release his.

"He knows a lot more than I do," Herb finished.

"Is he working for someone? Someone doing experiments?" Bell squinted his eyes.

"No, he isn't. He likes to teach students, that's all." Herb was about to explain that John lived in a household of females and enjoyed the company of a man, and so did Herb, but he already sounded foolish, so he stopped.

"Remember, everything back here must remain confidential." Bell took a few steps and said, "Maybe I should move it off-site. No, No." He shook his head before looking back at Herb. "Don't enter unless requested." He began to turn, then stopped. "What did you say your name is?"

"Herb . . . Herb Andersen. I've never even cleaned this area."

"Good." Bell's tone was softer now. "Thanks for your help, Herb. And keep up your learning. It's always a benefit, no matter the circumstances."

The rest of the afternoon, Herb could not get his mind straight, leaving rags behind and then having to search for them, letting the broom handle fall to the floor with a crash loud enough that it might have reverberated down the staircase to Mr. Shields's office, three floors below. He thought only of his conversation with Alexander Graham Bell. Had he imagined it? His mother would be astonished when he told her he had met the man whose lecture she had attended, but that conversation would have to wait. She would not be home when he got there. She was in Boston, although exactly how close to him, he did not know.

That evening, he pulled out the already-prepared food his mother had left in the icebox. As much as he could build and fix mechanical things, he found cooking a mystery. After he depleted the refrigerated food, he would rely upon jars of put-up vegetables and fruit, plus bread and cheese. He lifted the lid and found gingersnaps in the cookie jar. His mother always made sure he would not starve or even have to shop at the market, even though he had managed it in Lowell.

Bell and Watson—the men he had met at different times in the university basement, had been pictured in the *Scientific American* article. Herb's mind spun.

His Pikes Peak puzzle lay on the dining room table, with ample space for spreading out. He had sorted the pieces but had connected only a few. Used to entertaining himself over a lifetime of his mother's absences, that night, searching for the right puzzle pieces unexpectedly created a mood of isolation. His thoughts turned to Lowell, where the constant melee of unfiltered conversations and fisticuffs had often made him crave solitude. Despite little commonality, he had enjoyed the company of some who lived in the Line House. He missed being around men his age—and women when he'd had the opportunity at pubs. Visions of floating red hair and soft blue eyes distracted his usually focused mind. *Anna.* He plotted to make one more mad dash to city hall. *For what? Fifteen harried minutes, with the risk of losing my job if I'm late returning?*

He connected two light gray puzzle pieces—both shadowed snow at the mountain's peak—and hunted for another fit. Shields made him nervous. Apparently, other janitors had been hired and fired. He connected two more pieces and pictured Anna's pretty face again.

Risk or not, he was going to see her again over lunch hour.

"Oh, you're back," Anna said with a quizzical smile.

Is she happy to see me?

"You left so fast last week; I wasn't sure if you wanted me to look for more information."

"I'm sorry," Herb said. He had worn his best jacket and shirt and slicked down his hair. "I was in a rush to get back to work. I only have a short lunch break at the university."

Her blue eyes widened.

He shook his head. "It's not anything important. I sweep up," he confessed, wishing he could say he was a student or teacher. "But I have met Alexander Graham Bell." He winced, wondering if the security-conscious Bell would want his name bandied about.

"Is he the younger or the older Bell? They're both quite famous for teaching the deaf."

Herb almost swooned. Anna was not only beautiful but also intelligent. "Alec is the son."

"That's right. I'll see if I can remember." She turned toward the files, making her red curls swing. "Do you want me to look for Andersons with an o? It will take me some time because there are more of those than the ones with an e."

"If it's not too much bother."

"Not at all; it's my job." Her eyes were as blue as deep pools he could fall into.

"Unfortunately, I can't wait; I have to go back." He brazenly said, "Could you meet for a meal so we could talk about it? Maybe tomorrow evening?" It was the last night his mother would be gone. When she hesitated, he worried that he had been too forward.

"Yes, I might. My brother, Sam, works in a public house. As long as he's there, it's probably okay for us to have a meal together."

"Seven thirty? I leave work at seven, so I might make it earlier, depending on how far away it is. What's the name and address?" Herb was so giddy that he suspected he'd float back to work.

"McLaughlin's Pub—at the corner of Maple and State Streets."

He nodded. "Tomorrow, then. Thank you, Anna."

"I'll see what I can find about Andersens—both o and e."

Herb's heart swelled at the thought of seeing Anna again. Then, it plummeted to the ground when he spotted Mr. Shields standing at the top step of the entryway.

"This is becoming a habit, Herb. We did not envision you coming and going during work."

Herb's first thought was that it had been worth seeing Anna, even if he was fired. He withdrew his watch. "It's twelve forty, sir." His tongue fumbled over the polite address. "I'm back in time. I'll change my jacket now and start my cleaning again."

"That's a handsome jacket for doing research. What exactly are you up to?"

"I-I—" Herb fell silent. He did not know what to say to the man. Any response would likely land him in trouble.

Behind him came a voice. "Oh, there you are, lad. You can be of use again." Alexander Bell, now next to him, looked up the stairs at Shields. "We need to change the location of one of the long tables without taking everything off it. It was good of you to hire someone with muscles. It won't take long. I'm sure you won't object." Bell kept his gaze trained up.

Herb barely disguised his vindication at Shields's obsequious response: "Not at all. Glad he can be of help," he said with a slight bow. "Take all the time you need."

"Come along then, boy." Bell turned to look at Herb. "What did you say your name is? I'm sorry," he said, frowning. "It's one of my many flaws. I can't remember names." The Scots accent rolled the "r" on both ends of "remember."

"Herb . . . Herb Andersen, with an e."

One more day without being fired. All well and good, but it was not even the best part of his day.

NINETEEN

From the chilly November evening, Herb entered the overflowing warmth of McLaughlin's Pub. He joined the crowd in the vestibule, waiting for a break in the music to be allowed to enter. Like him, the others appeared to be scanning the interior for someone they planned to meet, or perhaps someone they wanted to avoid, in this proxy for home or escape. Rich, amber wood covered the ceiling and walls of the high, two-story room. On the second floor, filigreed railings matched the dark wood of the small round tables throughout. The linoleum floor had a pattern of black and cream squares, except for the red-diamond design under the chairs at the long bar stretching the room's length. Bottles, necks pointed down, ready to serve, filled the wall behind the bar. The pub was lighted with bright globed, kerosene lamps suspended from the ceiling on silvery metal chains.

When the music stopped and the crowd surged forward, Anna came around the corner. She must have been waiting just inside at the end of the entryway. Her red hair was swept away from her face in a chignon. "Did you have any trouble finding it?"

Herb had no idea how to greet her. Should he shake her hand? Hug her? Afraid to touch her, he resorted to letting his arms hang by his side. "It was easy to find, and I like it. It reminds me of pubs I occasionally frequented in Lowell, but this is much nicer."

"You were in Lowell?" Her blue eyes were curious and nonjudgmental.

"I worked there for two years; I've only been back in Brookline a few months." He wondered if she considered a laborer in Lowell worse than a university sweeper. He wasn't sure where he ranked the jobs himself.

"Brookline?"

Before he could answer, a man stepped between them. "Anna, is this the bloke you told me about?" Herb could tell this was her brother. His auburn hair was a shade darker than hers, and he wore a full, russet beard. He had the same blue eyes.

"I'm Herb. Your sister's been assisting me at city hall."

"Sam," he introduced himself, returning Herb's handshake with a sturdy grip, making him wonder if Sam, too, had once been a laborer. "I'm glad to hear Anna's been helpful. I'm not surprised." Sam cracked his knuckles. "I also want you to know I'm one of three brothers and two sisters. My brothers and I take care of our sisters. You'll answer to us if there is any doubt." His demeanor was matter-of-fact, not hostile, but definite. "You'll be keeping everything to business. I reserved the table across the room, where I can keep an eye on you."

If Sam's bossiness bothered Anna, she did not show it. "Follow me, Herb. We'll look for the reserved card. It's always crowded here."

Herb eyed Sam, moving toward the bar, wanting but not daring to take Anna's arm to guide her through the throng. Soon after they sat down, a waitress came to recite their food choices. The matronly woman wore a simple gray gathered skirt and white blouse with a paisley shawl around her shoulders. She shifted impatiently as they took time to decide. Anna ordered corned beef, cabbage, and a ginger ale. Herb requested lamb stew and a pint of ale.

Anna leaned forward toward him. Her gauzy white shirtwaist, partially hidden under a blue wool stole, was like white clouds against the sky. "I researched the Andersons, as I told you I would."

The overhead lamp highlighted her red hair and blue eyes. He was intoxicated before his first sip of ale.

"There were lots of Williams, but none combined with Henry or even an 'H.' I'm sorry. Do you have any suggestions about what else I might look for?"

"Don't worry." He reached out to pat her hand like his mother did when she consoled him. Then, with a swift look toward Sam at the bar, he jerked away as if her hand were a snake. "It was a long shot. I thought I should try."

"Why do you want to find him? Is he a relative? You have the same last name."

"I'm not sure—"

The sudden music drowned out his voice. At the side of the room, a man wearing a green plaid kilt had begun strumming a lap harp, accompanied by a robust woman plucking a much larger, four-foot gilt harp cradled in her arms. The tempo harmonized with the thump of a third player's small, circular, hand-held drum. The brilliant sound reverberated through Herb as if they were playing the strings and beat of his heart. The music was more hypnotic than that in the pubs he had frequented with Joey in Lowell because Anna sat across from him.

By tacit understanding, they listened to the song. During an intermission, the waitress brought their food and disappeared as two musicians, one with a flute and the other with a fiddle, replaced the original trio. Listening to the music and eating gave Herb more time to consider how to answer Anna's question. What exactly *was* he looking for? Knowledge of his father? What had *his* life been like? Would Herb follow in his footsteps, even though he had never met him? Herb's mind was confused about what he wanted and, more importantly, how much to share with Anna.

"How's your lamb stew, Herb?" Anna asked during the next break.

"Delicious. And your corned beef?"

"Tasty." She locked her blue eyes on his. "Sam works here, but I'm not allowed to come often, so this is a treat. Thank you."

They continued eating, again lapsing into contented silence as the musicians played. At the next intermission, Herb moved his empty bowl to the table's edge, along with the coins to pay for their dinners. "You asked who I'm searching for, and the answer is simple. My father died right around the time of my birth, but my mother doesn't like to talk about it. I thought, perhaps, the legal documents would tell me some specifics."

Anna observed him with intent interest.

"Do you know the date of your father's birth or death?"

"No," he shook his head. "Not exactly. I wish I did."

"What about his occupation?"

Again, Herb shook his head, exhaling a deep sigh of frustration. "I don't know much about that either, I'm afraid. All Mum has told me is that it was related to transporting things."

Anna paused while the waitress collected dishes and money from the table. "I'm good at finding people; that's my job, and I've learned a lot about how to do it since I started working with vital statistics. However, we'll need a little more information before we can find any answers."

We? Herb raised his eyebrows. Did Anna consider this her project as well as his?

A bevy of musicians fringed a cleared space with their collection of instruments: harp, fiddle, accordion, banjo, bodhran, whistles, and flute. The music began again, this time a jig. Couples hurried from their tables to the open dance floor—step, step, lift one knee, then the other, faster and faster.

Anna tilted her head toward the dancers, a question in her eyes.

Herb shook his head, opening his eyes wide. "No," he mouthed.

Anna laughed, showing straight, white teeth outlined by unadorned lips the color of raspberries. She raised her voice over the din. "You're not Irish, then?"

"No." Blood rushed from his head at the thought of joining the dance floor. He had never danced to any music.

They sipped their drinks. Talking was impossible until the musicians stopped playing. When they did, Anna's eyes lost their liveliness. "Herb, it's time for me to leave now. Sam works the early shift and will get off work soon; he'll walk me home."

"I'd be glad to."

She shook her head. "I had such a good time. Thank you. If you can think of any more clues about your father, I'll gladly help you."

"I'll try." Standing beside her, he said softly, "Anna, could we meet here again? Getting to city hall on my lunch break is hard, and I want more time with you."

"We could work during the music breaks," she teased.

"What about next week?"

Anna nodded and bent her elbow a little.

The touch of taking her arm left Herb breathless. He steered her through the noisy revelers to the bar, where Sam was pouring drinks . . . and keeping an eye on his sister.

Coming home to the aroma of dinner the following night made his stomach growl. Not that he had gone hungry during his mother's absence, and last night's dinner, more the memory of Anna's presence than the lamb stew, still occupied his thoughts. "Hi, Mum. How was your week?" He gave her a quick hug.

"So, so," she smiled, returning to stirring gravy in a pan, an apron covering her brown checked dress. The familiarity warmed him, and yet burgeoning discontent nudged him, too. The scene was comforting, but living it forever would not satisfy him. His mother's "so, so" gave an inkling that she was also feeling discontent, though about what he was unsure. Having a grown son still at home? The snail's pace of the suffrage movement? Or was it something else he was unaware of that she did not want him to know?

After washing his hands, Herb poured a glass of water before sitting at the kitchen table. What he wanted was an Irish pint and a redhead's companionship. Silverware already gleamed on a fresh tablecloth. His mother usually liked company for a few minutes as she began preparing dinner, but not when concentrating on measurements and getting the heat right at different locations on the stove and oven. Being together for those few minutes while he ate a snack was a pre-dinner start of a conversation about the day they would recommence while eating. In between, she continued cooking, and he did homework, read, or worked on a puzzle. That night, he wanted to talk to her before she served dinner. His sitting down early did not seem to bother her.

"After the lectures, some of us had time to go to the Boston Museum. Do you remember going there, Herb?" She looked over her shoulder at him, still stirring.

"Mum," he laughed. "How could I forget it? We went almost every Saturday. It was my second home."

"All those different museums under one roof. We would start with a new one every Saturday, and just when we'd finished, the museum had added something else, so we would have to start over again. And, remember the afternoon children's performances in the theater on Saturdays? It took you until you were six to be able to sit still," she laughed.

Recalling, he said, "They were long, and then they continued afterward in my dreams . . . and sometimes nightmares, but mostly, I didn't want performances to end."

"You memorized the names of the animals in the museum exhibits."

"Not always well-received." He took the plate she handed him filled with slices of roast lamb, mashed potatoes covered with mushroom gravy, and cubed acorn squash. "I was sent to the principal's office because I insisted that I had seen a duck-billed platypus."

She pulled out the chair and sat across from him. Soon, mother and son were lost in eating and individual thoughts. Hunger satisfied, he paused. "Mum, what was my father's occupation?"

"Herb, I've told you; it was so long ago, it no longer matters." Her tone let him know the pleasure of museum memories had disintegrated. "I know you have come to the supposition that sons follow fathers, but that isn't always the case and certainly would be less so without daily influence."

He had a nascent awareness of how she adroitly avoided information about the past, deftly sidestepping the subject with excuses or skipping to another topic.

"I know I won't be like him. You're the one who shaped my life with museums, books, and discipline, but I still want to know."

The strain in her expression remained. "His business was haulage, drayage, cartage—taking heavy things from one place to another."

"Was his name the same as ours?"

She ignored his question. "Herb, you need to let the past be the past. He has never been a part of your life. That's not how I wanted it, but it is how it turned out."

His mother thumped down a bowl of butterscotch pudding. She refrained from dessert to save her figure, but instead of continuing the conversation while he ate, she started washing dishes. After his first help-ing, he spooned seconds of the smooth, amber-colored dessert into his small glass dish. Questions that had never demanded answers filled his head. Was his father's death so awful that she could not bear to remem-ber? Or was there something she didn't want him to know? Something about her phrasing struck him as odd. *He has never been a part of your life. That's not how I wanted it.* She'd spoken almost as if there'd been a choice.

He shook his head. Was he being ridiculous? Or was his mother hid-ing something?

"Let's stay out on the porch," John said, greeting Herb at the door. "We just can't miss this spectacle." He tilted his head toward the riotous patchwork of late autumn colors. The sun, floating in the cloudless sky, amplified the colors of flaming sugar maples, orange beech, and the gold of hickory and chestnut trees. It warmed the air enough for sitting out-side in a coat.

With each visit, the difference in their status became less pronounced. All four Brannans welcomed Herb's arrival. Vicki and Diane had lost their shyness and were eager to show him drawings or other projects. Eliza had to coax them away. The entire family had become Herb's mentors, friends, and a paragon of family interaction.

"I've spent so much time at your house, usually your office; I should describe where I work since you can't visit." Herb relaxed into his chair, gently rocking back and forth. "My office, if you can call it that, is in the basement, where I store the tools of my trade—bucket, mop, broom, and rags." He read John's curiosity about where the conversation was leading. "It's also where the washroom is. You never know who you'll see on their way to the necessary. I have talked to the famous scientist, Alexander Bell, and his assistant, Tom Watson, as they walked to and from." Herb could not remember being in such a jolly mood. He continued, painting such a thorough picture of Bell thwarting Shields's attempts to discipline Herb that John slapped his thigh with amusement. More laughter came when Herb switched subjects, describing the Irish pub and his terror that he might be forced to dance a jig. He didn't mention he'd been at the pub with a young woman. His interest in sharing more about his life still stopped short of talking about Anna or his search to know more about his father.

At their meeting the following Sunday, John described the academic year as too routine. "Headmaster Quincy is still with us, demanding control of everything." Here, John bit back a grin. "A little like your Mr. Shields, I suspect. There are always men who need power to compensate for their inadequacies.

"My students are about the same as always. There are a few bright stars and the same portion of dim lights, though most fall in the middle. Few test me with curiosity the way you did and still do." He unfolded himself from his chair and paced as he talked. "I'm feeling a need to add a little 'oomph' to studying math and science." He reached the end of the porch and pivoted to return. "I have an idea, but I want your take on it. What if we challenge ourselves and, at the same time, my pupils to keep up with what Bell and Watson are doing? It will be energizing to understand the connection between electricity and sound. My students might be inspired to learn more by following new scientific exploration."

Both the idea of working together and keeping up with invention surprised Herb. He moved his rocker forward to a straight-up position to respond. "I'm interested, but I'd need to be as cautious as a mouse with a cat lurking." He rocked back again. "As you told me, Mr. Bell is obsessed with secrecy."

"Perfectly understandable. It's not fair to do all the work and have someone else swoop in and take all the credit . . . and money." John returned to his rocker. "I've read about that very thing happening. Most inventions come from improving one idea from another, a stepstone process of many minds, not just one. What I'm suggesting is sketching a general background of the road to the invention rather than discussing their work specifically. We'll become amateur inventors and bring the students along with us," he finished, grinning at Herb.

"As long as I don't show too much interest in what's happening in Bell's laboratory or accidentally reveal a secret, I'm on board."

***

Walking home, the secrets of Herb's life, not those of Bell's, were on his mind. He had hidden his research at city hall from his mother, knowing it would upset her. Similarly, he had not explained to Anna his motivations for asking her to investigate. Last, John did not have an inkling of his interest in information about his father or about Anna, for that matter.

***

On the first day of the week, Herb was tempted to make another dash to city hall. He wanted to tell Anna the new information he had learned about the haulage business. However, something held him back. The concept of having a father had blossomed from an undefined need, but it was irrational to believe that learning his father's characteristics would change what he had become without him. Did he hope somehow the ghost of his father would improve his prospects? The exact opposite had at least an even chance. Some personal blemish or ill behavior on his father's part could forever twist Herb's life into a coil of complications. A new thought had occurred to him because of his mother's secrecy. Making information known about his father might somehow affect her. Like locusts invading trees, his need for a paternal connection was getting out of control. His head throbbed. Before meeting Anna on Thursday, he would have to decide whether to continue his pursuit. The easiest course of action was to admit that he had come to a dead end and lay the matter to rest as idle curiosity. Gaining more importance than his curiosity about his father was his interest in Anna. He wanted to assure her of his desire to see her, with or without a mission of investigation.

TWENTY

Haunting Irish melodies played by bagpipe, harp, and flute—life's sorrows put to music—met Herb when he pulled open the door at McLaughlin's Pub. People jammed the entryway, waiting for a break in the music before moving forward to get a table or to find friends. He was not sure Anna would be there. They had quickly agreed to meet again at the same time and place, but she might have changed her mind in a week. Or her brother might have nixed the idea of her seeing him again. Herb stood, waiting and worrying, until the last of the droning sounds ceased vibrating up his spine.

Propelled forward with the crowd, he searched the interior for her distinctive red hair. In a moment, she appeared from around the corner, just as she had before. With a questioning look rather than words, he asked permission to take her arm and was repaid by a glowing nod and the offer of the crook of her arm. He placed his fingers along her elbow, guiding her rather than linking arms more familiarly. She motioned toward the same table at the far end of the room and in sight of anyone at the bar.

When they got there, she plucked off the reserved card and put it in her reticule while Herb pulled out her chair.

"How are you?"

Awestruck by her presence, Herb tried to think of something more clever than "fine." He failed.

Anna filled the silence seamlessly. "Did you learn anything new?" Her blue eyes sparkled as she looked across at him.

"Yes, he was involved in hauling."

"Hauling? Hauling what?"

"Drayage."

"Drayage?" She frowned.

"He apparently had a drayage or cartage business that hauled heavy things locally but not over oceans or great distances."

"Oh, now I understand. Details help," Anna laughed. "Let me see what I can do with that information. It may lead to nothing," she warned, "but I'll try."

They ordered dinner, he with a pint, and she with ginger ale. Talking to Anna was as natural as speaking with his mum or John. The interludes of music made conversations easier for him. They allowed him to think about what to say next. He asked about her family and how long she had been in the country. As the evening went on, something close to shouting was necessary to be heard over the accelerating decibels of music and voices. Herb didn't mind the noise because Anna's interest in everything, her knowledge, her beauty, her very presence besotted him.

At nine-thirty, he walked her across the room to the bar. "Next week?" she asked before they were within earshot of Sam.

"Next week," he said simply instead of jumping out of his skin with enthusiasm. He longed for an embrace and a kiss on her raspberry lips, but he did not want to risk his life by being shot by her brother. He and Sam exchanged perfunctory nods as Herb turned to leave. Walking toward the door, he was tempted to join the Irish jig that had just begun. His feet and spirit sprung wings.

"How was your evening?" his mother asked at breakfast, inquiring, not prying. Herb had told her he would not be home for dinner the previous night because he had planned to go out but had not told her with whom.

"Remember I told you about going to an Irish pub in Lowell with Joey? He was born in Ireland, like so many of the laborers there." Herb took a tentative sip of his steaming hot coffee and decided to tell his mother about Anna. "I met a girl at city hall. She's Irish, and one of her brothers works at a pub, so it's a good place to get together." Herb rushed on with a description of the music, people, food, and ambiance so his mother would not have time to ask him what he had been doing at city hall. "Some call a pub a 'meeting house,' and you can see why from the amount of activity. Anna says it's like a second home for the Irish. They often have such small dwellings, both in Ireland and here, that pubs give them a chance to include more people. Like I said, her brother was there last night, too, so it was proper." It was impossible to hide his enthusiasm.

"It's wonderful that you're with people your age," his mother said, adding hot coffee to her cup. "I've never been to a bar or pub. The thought makes me nervous." She scanned his face. "But I can understand why people in a new country would want to gather with others from home." After giving him a smile he read as supportive, she sat at the table with her freshly toasted bread and began reading the morning paper.

Herb smiled, certain she was dying of curiosity about Anna and had willed herself not to prod for more.

On Sunday afternoon, Herb could no longer hide his interest in Anna. With more embellishment than his usual spare words, he told John Brannan about meeting her and their two dinners at the pub. "I've never seen such a beautiful woman. Her hair is the color of sunsets, and her calm blue eyes sparkle like fine china. You wouldn't think someone with such beauty would have intelligence, too, but she's as bright as they come."

"It sounds to me like you've hit pay dirt."

Herb blushed. "My mother's pleased, too," he said, then frowned. "I'm trying to save every penny so I can help out at home, but I could tell my mum was happy about my making friends and not put out about my spending." Herb's lips curved. "Maybe not so happy about my going to a pub, but she kept her judgments to herself. After two years of absence, she's glad for my company and realizes I'm an adult who wants the company of people my age."

"I concur wholeheartedly with her about companionship. It's part and parcel with school, but often harder to find after that—everyone needs friendship." He filled his water glass. "You'll see your redhead again Thursday?"

Herb nodded, feeling the flush come back. "Thanks for listening. My mind is on her a lot, but I've also been thinking about our conversation last week. Have you made any decisions on proceeding?"

John looked momentarily confused at the abrupt change of topics, and then Herb saw the light dawn in his eyes. "Ah. We covered the waterfront with our conversation last week, didn't we?" He swiveled toward his desk and reached for a couple of sheets of paper.

Glancing over, Herb saw a hand-drawn chart.

"We talked about Bell's insistence—maybe that's too mild a word—on secrecy," John said with a chuckle. "At any rate, I've thought about how we can learn about the new science without breaking confidentiality. And I mean *we* because this will help us both if you're game."

Curious, Herb wondered what project would tie an inventor, a teacher, and a janitor together.

With the cooling fall weather, John looked more like a teacher than when he wore less formal, warm-weather clothing. He had replaced the casual, lightweight gabardine jacket he wore during the hot summer months with his familiar wool tweed jacket. He appeared as if about to begin a class lecture. "We'll start at the beginning and learn all we can about electricity. That has a double benefit. As we learn, we can think of exercises to assign to my math and science classes. That way, we will all benefit." His eyes gleamed with what Herb knew was his endless ardor for learning and teaching. "You would gain a broad knowledge of electricity, so Bell doesn't think your interest is in what he's working on, and who knows?" John cocked his head. "You might be of some value to him in the future." He brushed his palms together in enthusiasm. "If you were going to start at the beginning of electricity, where would it be?"

Herb slumped in his chair and stalled, hoping his former teacher would provide the answer, but John calmly sipped water from his refilled glass.

The mechanisms of Herb's brain ground like rusted gears as he searched to remember. The silence felt like forever. In reality, it was only a few seconds before he snapped his fingers. "Benjamin Franklin and his kite."

"You've got it," John leaned forward to give Herb's shoulder a congratulatory pat before reaching for a stack of *Scientific Americans* from his desk. "Eliza tells me we're going to have to build an addition to the house for all my magazines, clippings, and books," he said, chuckling affectionately. "I searched every single issue, and you can see I've concocted a timeline," he tapped his hand-drawn chart.

John explained that since its beginning in 1845, *Scientific American* had written articles describing United States patents and explanations of worldwide inventions. "Just a few months ago, in April, the U.S. Patent Office gave Bell a patent for vibrating steel reeds that allowed four messages to be sent over a wire simultaneously, saving time and the cost of installing additional telegraph poles, wires, and receivers." As if his chair could no longer contain him, John stood up.

"Now, as we know, Bell is working on something beyond that. It will involve electricity, but beyond the taps and clicks over a wire. Let's start with knowing everything about electricity and then go on to possible uses." John had divided the *Scientific Americans* into similarly sized piles. "Would you be willing to take this stack and summarize the articles on electricity? I've turned down corners on the pages of relevant articles." He added his hand-drawn chart on top of the stack of magazines. "I was short of time to make a second timeline, but I'll lend you mine, and you can copy it, so you'll have one, too. Neither of us has many extra minutes, but we can discuss what we find during our Sunday meetings. It will add to our already enjoyable conversations."

"How was your afternoon with John Brannan?" His mother was reading in the library when he came home.

"Always interesting." Herb walked through the room and put the pile of magazines on his desk. He had not used it often since returning from Lowell.

"What do you have there?" She swiveled her neck to see what he had set down. "It almost looks like homework."

"That's exactly what it is."

"But you're no longer in school." She looked perplexed.

Herb shook his head, laughing. "I told you, Mum, teaching is the blood that runs through John's veins. He loves to learn and loves to get everyone else to learn. He can't help himself. We're going to find out everything we can about electricity." He extended his arms toward the ceiling in mock hopelessness. "I can't think when I'm going to have time to read all this." Then he laughed again, knowing he welcomed the assignment.

"Can you include me in this? Electricity? I want to learn more." She inserted a bookmark and closed her book. "I'd better finish dinner. I boiled lobsters while you were at John's. They're cooling, and we can have them for a light supper since we had Sunday dinner earlier. Let's eat in an hour." She uncurled herself from the corner of the couch. "Bring one of the magazines to the table. I'd better start learning right away."

TWENTY-ONE

Familiar music and spirited conversation welcomed Herb at the entry of McLaughlin's Pub Thursday. He and Anna gently leaned against each other as they pushed through the infectious gaiety of the crowded room. Anna occasionally stopped at tables to introduce him to her friends, switching back and forth between lilting Gaelic and English while studiously pondering him from under her long lashes. From the looks of others, he could tell his best trousers, waistcoat, and jacket counted in his favor even though the muscles he had gained since buying the clothes strained the fabric. At least they did not label him a janitor. Thankfully, Anna excluded that from her introductions.

At "their" table, the waitress, once more wrapped in her paisley shawl, chalk-white shirtwaist, and drab gray skirt, arrived to take their order. "Nice to see you again. You're here more often than usual."

"Doris, this is my friend, Herb."

"How do you do?" She winked at Anna and gave Herb a reassuring glance.

After Doris left with their order, Anna explained that waitresses served the same tables each night, adding to the pub's camaraderie.

Anna spread two sheets of paper on the table before their dinner arrived. "Unfortunately, I don't have anything useful to report." Her creamy brow creased with light lines. "I looked up cartage companies in Boston in all the ways you described them." She pointed to the list on the first page and Herb became distracted by the freckles on the back of her hand. "Then, I researched the owners and employees of the companies." She looked up at him. "Of course, the employees probably change more frequently than the owners. Do you have any idea what position William Andersen might have held?"

"No, but based on what little I know, I'd guess he worked in an office instead of loading and unloading carts."

Anna nodded. "My next step was to forget about the last name of Andersen and look for William H's. There were several, so I did a little more tracing in the registries. I can give you the dates men with that combination of first name and initial lived in Boston during the time you're interested in. I only have a date of birth for one. I wish I could have done better." She scooped up the papers as Doris interrupted with a tray full of steaming bowls, soda bread, a dish of butter, ginger ale, and a pint. At Doris's suggestion, he and Anna had chosen an Irish stew with onions, carrots, and potatoes immersed in a dark, savory broth. *Lamb stew in an Irish pub with a beautiful Irish girl.* After his years at Lowell, eating alone and piecemeal, Herb thought he might be dreaming. The richness of the stew enhanced that feeling. He scooped spoonfuls of the flavorful medley and then dipped pieces of bread into the remaining broth. He would have asked for a second bowl if he had been home. Instead, he sliced another piece of bread, careful to leave enough for Anna.

She had only finished half her meal when she asked, "Some cartage company offices are in New York, New Haven, and Providence. Should I look at those, too?"

Herb finished chewing and shook his head. "No, you've been burdened enough with my silly goose chase. It isn't important anyway." With his napkin, he swiped the hairs above his lip; they were the beginning of his growing a mustache.

Anna's eyes had a soft fire about them. "It's no trouble. I like this kind of mystery; it's like a puzzle. My boss says that's why I'm good at my job. It's the only reason he hired a girl, especially an Irish one, and maybe because he takes credit for my work."

She likes puzzles. Herb felt giddy. He reconsidered her question. New York was the bigger city and might have had more businesses, but Providence was closer, and his mother had rarely been to New York or New Haven but often traveled to Providence.

The music had begun again. Enthusiastic revelers rose, swaying shoulder to shoulder, swept up with emotion, as they sang a ballad of the Irish famine. Herb spoke over the song. "Would you mind looking at companies in Providence?"

"Not at all." She wrote "Providence" on her paper in a round, rolling script and then rose to join in the sad lament of the man who had to steal food in the 1840s to feed his family during the famine. She grasped Herb's hand and pulled him beside her, moving with the music. Most of the thick, Gaelic brogue was incomprehensible, but he wordlessly swayed with her, enjoying the closeness. When the music stopped, their bodies remained imperceptibly touching. Finally, she released his hand, and they sat down.

"We haven't had an easy time in this country. We only get low jobs, if any. Mine is an exception, but living here is better than Ireland during the famine." Anna finished the last swallow of her ginger ale. "My grandparents on both sides remember it well. They don't want us to forget what we didn't experience—the 'Great Hunger.' Not having enough food, even for children, and watching friends and relatives starve left long, deep scars. Irish dinnertimes are full of stories about the pain that made kin leave our homeland and the misery of those who stayed behind." She pointed at the revelers. "Look around. You can see that we like to be with our kind—others with the same heritage—laughing and talking is only one part. Too often, discontent is drowned in Guinness or Irish whiskey."

Her eyes met his but did not stay. "My father is one of those. Sam won't allow my sister and me to touch a drop and keeps a stern eye on our brothers. He serves as a barkeep for the money but grudgingly."

Before Herb could tell her how much her honesty meant, a harp's slow, melodic strains overwrote their conversation. The haunting music echoed sentiments of starvation and despair, and through notes so ghostly, they resonated in Herb's non-Irish soul.

December tensions crackled through Boston University as frazzled students completed their examinations and harried professors rushed to grade them before the Christmas recess. The mood was equally strained in the basement, with Bell and Watson conversing in hushed voices and frequently departing for their central laboratory downtown. Both scientists had begun to greet Herb by name as they brushed by him in the lower levels. Occasionally, they asked him to assist in moving laboratory equipment, always with a word of thanks. Some professors on the floors above made out-of-the-ordinary requests when Shields was out of sight. One agitated instructor for whom Herb had done odd jobs asked him to compare the answers of math exams against the key. Herb sat down with a stack of booklets and marked a check for correct answers and an X for wrong ones, adding the percentage grade at the top by the students' names. Reading the questions and answers, Herb found he was as knowledgeable as many college students, but he was in the basement while they were in the classroom. It was a bittersweet truth.

"Thank you. Don't tell a soul," the professor begged, his relief at crossing one task off his list palpable.

"Any time, Professor Brown." Herb treated everyone in the building with a politeness bordering on submissiveness. He was well aware of his station. Most instructors and students considered him an anonymous drudge, too menial to be acknowledged. Shields kept track of Herb's whereabouts, although Herb's familiarity with a few professionals, especially Bell and Watson, had eroded Shields's control and threats. Herb walked a fine line. His familiarity with instructors was an advantage unless and until Shields felt it a threat. If a dispute arose, Herb wondered if anyone would stand up for him against the officious building manager.

Herb was allowed two days off for the holidays. One was Christmas, and the second was New Year's. Both fell on a Saturday that year. In the weeks before, Herb joined the throngs of seasonal shoppers and dashed from one store to another during his lunch break. He wanted to find just the right gifts for his mother, John, and Anna. The forty-five-minute time constraint put him in a dither, just as it had during his trips to city hall. He entered unfamiliar shops with scant time to scrutinize their merchandise. It helped that the store owners, eager for customers, often suggested items to purchase. Boston's rebuilding since the fire three years before had progressed slowly. Its economy remained more depressed than the rest of the country and much of Europe.

Books were an easy fallback as gifts for his mother and John, but he continued looking for something more original. What to give to Anna put him in a quandary. Jewelry was too forward, and he decided against a lace handkerchief because most were Irish-made, and she likely had one already. At one pub dinner, Anna had told him about Irish lacemaking. It was a logical fit for the women of her homeland, she said. Needlework took little equipment—only a bobbin, scissors, and linen or cotton thread. The patience demanded of lacemaking was especially suited for rural women with few diversions. Irish women had sold their precious lace to help feed their families during the Great Hunger. The poor benefited by supplying lace for the rich.

After days of deliberation and indecision, Herb finally decided on a floral-patterned eyeglass holder for the spectacles his mother had started wearing to read. For John, he bought a set of nibs for his pen. And for Anna, after so much back-and-forth that one storekeeper eyed him suspiciously, he chose a small leather reticule with an attached strap to hang over her shoulder. It was personal but not intimate.

Two days before Christmas, evergreen wreaths and swags of boughs topped with crimson velvet bows filled McLaughlin's Pub. The fragrance of pine did only a little to dilute the smell of cigarette smoke and hearty food. Anna met him, wearing a form-fitting bodice of rosy cotton that cinched her waist and flared into a voluminous skirt of lace-trimmed ruffles. They strolled to their usual back table, talking to pub patrons. Her close friends now addressed Herb by name. Conversations were brief but friendly. Even Sam wished him a Merry Christmas with a firm handshake. After Doris had left with their dinner orders, Herb extracted the tissue-wrapped present from his jacket. After a glance around, Anna untied the bow. Her cheeks flushed pink as she separated the paper, gently lifting out the purse.

"How pretty," she said, feeling the fabric and examining both sides. "The strap will be useful." She lifted her head, again scanning the room. "Thank you," she said, stealthily squeezing his hand. "I have something for you, too." She pulled a small, wrapped package from her satchel.

"A notebook," he said after unwrapping it. He opened the soft, tan leather cover to reveal the blank pages.

"I know you're researching; maybe this will come in handy."

"Much better than slips of paper. I have dozens and can never find the right one." He gazed across at her, yearning to kiss her.

Transferring the contents of her reticule to the purse he had given her, she pulled a sheet of paper with writing on it from an oversized satchel. "Do you remember we discussed looking for cartage companies in Providence?"

He nodded. "I hope you didn't spend too much time."

"Not too much." She pointed at the names on the list with a pencil. "Unfortunately, I didn't find exactly what you were looking for. There was no William Andersen at all, either with an e or an o, and no combination of W and H worked either. But look at this." She circled a name and address: *Sinclair Cartage, Proprietor William H. Sinclair.* Their eyes met.

"Hmm, no Andersen, but a William H. and a cartage company. Hmm," he said again. His heart beat rapidly as he pulled a pencil from his pocket and opened his new notebook. "Useful already." He felt his hand tremble as he jotted the company's name and address on the book's pristine first page.

"Here's a little more. The company has been in business since 1835, making it forty years old, and William H. Sinclair was born in 1810, making him sixty-five." She looked across at him. "I'm sorry, that's all I have. Do you want me to research New York City or New Haven?"

"No." Herb calculated the years. The man at the cartage company was forty-five years older than he was, making him nineteen years older than Herb's mother, which was quite an age difference. But it was a haulage company, and the first initials were correct. It was a leap to make any connection, but not impossible.

"Let me think about this a little longer. I've probably reached the end of the road, but thanks for your help and for the gift." He held up the tan notebook. "I have a new project. I'm studying electricity, and I have plenty of notes to take. Let me tell you about it." He carefully tucked his new notebook in the inner pocket of his jacket and used his napkin to wipe his upper lip. His mustache had grown in nicely. It wasn't bushy yet, but it would be soon. "Would you like some dessert while we talk?"

He could tell she was thinking, perhaps about her cinched-in waist, just as his mother might before eating dessert.

"Would you be willing to split something?"

"Sure, what would you suggest?" He grinned at the thought of half instead of his double portions of everything at home.

"Irish Christmas cake?" Her blue eyes sparkled. "It's a spice cake filled with fruit and nuts and frosted with white buttercream frosting. Ma's is the best, but it's good here, too."

Herb rose partway from his seat to catch the waitress's eye. Doris was unaccustomed to their ordering dessert. When she left with their order, Herb turned back to Anna. "I'm becoming Irish," he said with another grin.

"It's a heavy responsibility." Her eyes twinkled back at him.

The cadence of their conversation was as distinct as the rhythm of the pub's music: listen for half an hour and talk during the fifteen-minute break. Anna talked fast and fluidly. Her accent and speed were often hard to keep up with, especially over the noise in the background. Herb spoke slower, lacing his words with his subtle humor, although more than once, the endings of the stories he tried to make humorous were drowned out by the beginning of the music.

There was little they did not share. He told her about his mother, his Sundays with John Brannan, and his work at the university, including talking to the famous Bell and Watson. She described her mother, sister, and brothers. Her job at city hall came from an accidental connection at the pub. She had worked at city hall for over two years. "But," she said, "you never know when you might be let go. Some people want nothing to do with the Irish."

They did not talk about their fathers.

TWENTY-TWO

January was frigid. Wind-whipped air, saturated with moisture, pricked like needles on any uncovered skin. Herb's mother had given him a heavy wool coat and thick gloves lined with rabbit fur for Christmas. The clothes were nothing fancy, but they were warmer and more presentable than the well-worn, quilt-lined canvas coat that had lasted through his two years at Lowell and less restrictive than his graduation suit from almost three years ago. After Christmas, he bought himself a long plaid scarf he discovered in the dry goods store's "reduced" bin. He could not resist the discounted price or the tag that proclaimed "Made in Ireland." He wound the long scarf around his neck and face so only his eyes showed when he walked to and from home, the train, or the pub. When Anna first saw it, she smiled. "Ah, Herb. I recognize the plaid. The green and blue represent the deep green Irish fields and the typical blue of the countryside sky. Clothes won't make you Irish, though," she teased. "But your mustache has a hint of red. It does look a little Gaelic."

They had just arrived at their table, and he stood with his back to the rest of the room. He impetuously leaned down and pressed his lips against hers. Kissing her electrified every fiber in his body. Anna let the kiss linger for a few seconds.

"It tickled," she told him after they had separated. His chest rose and lowered in quick breaths, and he noticed her short breathing, too.

He pulled out a chair for her, nervously casting his eyes around to see if anyone was watching them. He took his place across the table. "I don't think anyone saw."

She smiled cautiously. "Nothing goes unnoticed at a pub—some forgiven, some not."

"I want to kiss you again."

"Me too." She glanced at other tables. "Too dangerous!"

Herb nodded. *It is too dangerous because I don't want to stop at a kiss. I want to know every sensation of your body.* His eyes met hers. "I'm lucky not to have Sam's fist in my face, but it would be worth it."

In John Brannan's study, the round table usually used for beverages had been cleared and replaced with a two-foot-high stack of metallic disks held by metal rods embedded in a circular base. "Eliza is out of sorts about this," he whispered to Herb as they entered the room. "She says I keep adding things to the room and never subtracting." He shrugged. "She's probably right."

Herb glanced at the rows of shelves neatly lined with books or carefully stacked objects. Every surface was occupied. "Why do you have a battery in here?" He stepped closer to the tower of disks.

"We've come this far in our study of electricity." His voice rose a decibel in enthusiasm. "I plan to take this to my science and math classes tomorrow. You're familiar with batteries, but maybe not the history. Alessandro Volta devised the first one," he pointed to the mechanism on the table, "at the beginning of the century. His design is still used today. These disks alternate between zinc and silver. A cloth soaked in salt water or sodium hydroxide goes between each disk. Voila!" he said, dramatically, "electric current. All sorts of experiments came from Volta's battery, and scientists are still experimenting with uses for batteries." John picked up several of the zinc disks. "It's the storage part that makes it most useful, instead of having to generate electrical power each time, as in the past."

Herb thought of Bell and Watson and some of the equipment he had moved for them at the university.

"How do you think the students will like it?" John almost danced with enthusiasm as he began layering disks.

"Most will be interested." Herb lifted the battery to feel the weight. "You might have to go over the mechanics more than once. I don't recommend telling them everything in one day."

Remembering high school brought up images of Herb's former classmates. Batteries and the potential of electricity would have interested many of the boys. Girls might be bored. Science was not supposed to make sense to them. Herb smiled at the thought of his former competitive classmate, Clara. She had relished science and mathematics. Studying batteries would delight her. From John's occasional news of past students, Herb knew Clara's parents had been able to send her to Smith College, where she was studying science in hopes of going to medical school. Between Clara, Anna, and his mother, Herb had developed a certainty that women should be allowed to vote and pursue whatever they wanted.

"Careers come faster for some than others," John had said, careful not to focus only on the most successful of his former students when he reported news about them.

Herb was the only janitor, but through John's and Anna's respect, he now took a little more pride in his work. It was not the worst occupation. True, one or two boys who'd sat in the back row had used their father's prestige and money to attend renowned colleges, but, given the poor job market, many of those without that advantage had added to the labor pool.

"Would you mind making another stack?" John interrupted Herb's thoughts. "Follow what I do. I want to have three models for students to look at closely. The one I've already made is a vertical stack of discs; we'll make two more, this time horizontal in a trough, so the liquid doesn't run all over everything."

They stood side by side, placing small cloth squares soaked in a saline solution between each metal layer while proposing ideas to spark young imaginations. As always, some of the farfetched ones made them laugh.

"Let's make them want to learn math and science and then be inventors," John said.

Shields had quickly picked up on Herb's knack for fixing things. "Might as well add maintenance to your job description," he smirked. Herb was as aware of the savings from not having to call an outside repairman as he knew Shields was. Herb's to-do list grew every day as Shields added one task after another. What should have increased but did not was his pay. Even a small amount would have helped his budget, which must have been obvious. Herb added one more adjective to character traits he did not like in Shields—cheap. Other than the lack of compensation, Herb was okay with the added assignments. He liked interacting with the professors and the scientists when he repaired their equipment. It added variety and human contact to his day. His mind wandered with the routine of mopping and dusting. Lately, he daydreamed about going to Providence to learn more about the cartage company. Without days off work and everything closed on Sundays, he had not figured out a way. Idly, he schemed how to leave work. Saying he had a sick relative? He quickly nixed that idea, remembering the lesson of his truancy during high school. One lie led to others and would eventually snare him in a web of dishonesty. Asking for a day off, even without pay, was futile. Mr. Shields would invoke his power of refusal with relish. Insisting might have worse consequences. Herb had proved his worth to the faculty and was less worried about being fired than during the early weeks, but complete confidence was impossible with the mercurial Shields's need for control.

The following week, Shields approached him with a gleam in his eye. "I've ordered shelves for every classroom desk. They're to be attached under the seats for students' items. The hauling company will deliver them and stack them in the basement." Shields brushed off a piece of lint from his dark gray jacket. "You'll need to start as soon as they come." He lingered in the doorway, daring a reaction.

It galled Herb that Shields was taking advantage of him, but he would rather die than show it. Unlike the two scientists in the basement, Shields never addressed Herb by name, requested extra work with a "please," or thanked him. Shields turned to leave, looking smug after giving his order.

Before Shields got too far, an unpremeditated idea came to Herb. "Mr. Shields, Mr. Bell and Mr. Watson have asked me to attend to several jobs. That will take time. What if I stay a couple of hours later each night to work on the desks?"

Shields grinned, uncovering his yellowed teeth, obviously delighted by the offer of fourteen-hour days instead of twelve at the same subsistence wages. Herb had already saved the university money with his special projects and repair skills and also relieved Shields of the nuisance of hiring someone to do maintenance work. Shields would take everything he could get from him, Herb knew.

Herb stood across from him, his muscular strength opposite the administrator's flabbiness, and took a chance. "Don't worry about paying me extra. I'll keep track of my hours, and when it adds up to a day's work, I'll take one day off."

Shields's head snapped up from his shoulders, stunned by the bold offer. His face jutted forward, his pursed lips beginning to form words. Herb imagined he could almost read the beginning of "You're fired." Instead, he watched a frown ripple Shields's brow and guessed why. He had observed the university's most esteemed scientists rely on Herb to move and clean the lab, all while keeping its secrets. Herb knew that if the man fired him, it would not go unnoticed. The manager, his heavy-lidded gray eyes simmering, said nothing before he waddled farther down the hallway.

Herb smacked his fist into his other palm in an unexpected surge of confidence. He had stood his ground and won a victory by outthinking his officious boss. He was not altogether powerless. But a word of caution sounded in his head. Men like Shields would not tolerate being bested without retribution, especially by underlings. Herb had to be careful. He would do what he was asked by working late every night, except Thursday, his night with Anna at the pub. After each desk had a lower shelf, he would have to fight not to be trapped forever in fourteen-hour days—a routine Shields would relish. By living at home, Herb owed his mother more than making minor repairs and contributing to rent and food. His mum needed his company, even if not all the time.

Turning over each desk and mounting the shelves was cumbersome at first. Soon Herb developed a system of laying the pieces out for a dozen desks and drilling the beginnings of a hole for each screw. By the second day, his work was efficient. Soon, the mechanical work freed his mind for other thoughts. He was eager to tell Anna of his conversation with Shields and the possibility of time off to go to Providence. His mind seesawed back and forth with how much to reveal. Her curiosity about the person he sought was evident, but she had been too polite to ask. *She's either guessed or is close to the truth*. He turned a completed desk upright and pushed it in line with the others. Tipping over another desk, he tucked four screws in his pursed lips and began installing the lower shelf, and continued his thoughts. His situation must be mysterious. In Anna's realm of records and documents, missing people were commonplace, but was anyone else so unfamiliar with his father that even his name was unknown? Herb tightened the fourth screw. Another desk finished, but the question unanswered.

Searching for his father was problematic, but more so was revealing his actions. The three people he cared about most, his mother, John, and Anna, knew of his growing interest in his father, and only Anna had knowledge of his quest, but not entirely. If he told one, what about the others? Realization within him was growing that he had to weigh the compulsion of knowing his father's history with the consequences, especially for his mother. And yet, understanding more about his father was an irrational part of defining himself. He argued back and forth with himself to forget his interest and drop his hunt to avoid the risks, but he could not erase the desire from his soul.

Having wrangled a potential day off work to go to Providence, Herb burst with a desire to tell Anna everything, if only because he needed her advice on how to carefully investigate the cartage company. If there was any information of value, he needed to avoid mucking up the opportunity to discover it. He knew from his past job inquiries that the wrong approach could bring the quick and final closing of a door.

On Thursday, the workday passed quickly. Herb was preoccupied figuring out how to frame his inquiries while in Providence. Explaining that he might have a connection with the man at the cartage company would raise questions he was not sure he wanted to be asked.

With long strokes of his mop, he was finishing the floor of the last room on the third floor—his final assignment before he could put away his bucket and mop and head to the pub. Poking the stringy rag mop back into the suds, he did not hear Mr. Shields come up behind him.

"Herb."

Herb's lurched reflex knocked over the bucket with a metallic clunk. A pool of used gray water fanned into small streams that trickled slowly toward the room's corner. Herb wheeled around to face Shields, barely suppressing his fury. Shields loved to slink like a phantom, appearing from the shadows to surprise and control.

"Yes, Mr. Shields," Herb righted the bucket as its contents continued to seep across the floor.

"I just talked to Professor Bell. He is going to move the lab from the basement to the Williams building where Watson works." Shields touched the gold chain across his waistcoat. In his dark jacket and softly striped trousers, he resembled a banker rather than a building manager. "Instead of working on chairs tonight, I need you to help load a wagon with some of their equipment," Shields said, looking at his watch.

"I'm sorry, sir. This is a day I have to leave on time." Herb steadied his hand on the mop handle, trying to anticipate the manager's response.

"That's right." Shields made a surprised face. "You leave early on Thursdays."

"No, sir. I leave on time on Thursdays." Herb felt like shrieking or even punching the flabby asshole. It was too late to get Anna a message before she left work for the pub. If Herb refused Shields's demand to help the university's most celebrated academic, he gave Shields cause for firing him. Herb felt a cyclone lodged in his brain.

"I'm afraid this has some urgency," Shields said, sliding his watch back into its pocket. "You'll have to stay tonight, but don't worry, you can make up for it and leave at the usual time tomorrow." His tone held a taunting note.

Herb wanted to say, "Go ahead and fire me," but calling Shields's bluff was too dangerous. In the present economy, men begged for work, and the tradeoff between hard labor in Lowell and the university environment made the low pay bearable. This fact silenced him. The job had particular advantages for him. Not only was his job without heavy labor, but the university was within walking distance of Anna's office and the pub. He acquiesced with a nod, refusing to give Shields the satisfaction of hearing him complain.

"After you clean up the mess you made," Shields said, victory gleaming in his eye, "go to the basement and report to Bell and Watson." He wheeled and walked to the stairs; his footsteps rang in the silence.

Herb seethed at the manager's calculated meanness.

He finished the floor and sprinted down to the basement, banging his mop and bucket into the cleaning closet.

"Evening, Herb," Tom Watson came down the narrow hallway from the washroom. "Thanks for offering to help us load and unload." He stood next to Herb, shorter and less muscular. "I told Shields we could manage independently, but he said you would insist." He clamped his hand on Herb's shoulder. "Thanks."

Herb barely suffocated his anger. Shields had offered his time when it was not even necessary. "I'm happy to help," he muttered. "Let me get my jacket."

"It should only take an hour. The wagon's already here. Bell and I will meet you down the hall."

"Only an hour" was enough to ruin everything.

Watson was right. The job took a little over an hour. Herb loaded most of the equipment, all of it tightly wrapped for both protection and secrecy. The two scientists spoke in hushed tones, enveloping the move in a shroud of mystery, in great contrast to their usual, more audible back-and-forth banter. Herb wanted to ask if their work had outgrown the lower-level laboratory or if Bell was leaving the university altogether, but the clandestine mood kept him quiet. The driver covered the load with a large canvas tarp he'd laced to the wagon's sides, even though the evening was dry so far. Once he'd made certain his load was covered, he waited for the three men to board to go to the downtown laboratory to unload. After everything was carried up to the space on the third floor, Bell extended his hand with coins.

"Thanks, you don't have to." Heat rose in Herb's cheeks. "It's still work time for me." He paused for an opportunity to return the money, but after Bell's firm head shake, he slid the coins into his pocket.

Bell stepped forward, his dark hair tousled from his labor, and shook Herb's hand. "We've discussed it. Eventually, we want you to come to this lab. It's a big space where I can spread out and concentrate, even if we're with other scientists. I've decided to give up most of my teaching and focus on something else. I'll talk to Shields about you possibly moving here when the time comes. It will take a while." His dark eyes sparked. "I know he keeps you on a short rein. It's started raining so the cart driver will take you back to the university. Thanks for your help." He shook Herb's hand. "I hope we didn't keep you from anything."

Outside, an icy drizzle had begun, too wet for snow, though cold enough. Herb and the driver stepped up to the damp plank board seat, and the driver flicked his whip, clucking the pair of chestnut bays into action. The trip back to the university, where Herb had left his waterproof Macintosh, took only a few minutes.

Running to the basement, he plucked his heavy coat from the hook and fled. His stride was just short of a run as he raced down the slippery streets toward the pub. What would Anna think about his not showing up? It was the height of disrespect that he would never intentionally show her. Herb's sense of despair erased any pleasure he'd derived from Bell's praise. Dodging people in his haste, he burst into McLaughlin's crowded entryway at eight-thirty, an hour late and very wet. He removed his hat, using his fingers to comb his hair and mustache as he searched hopelessly for Anna. The sweet, shimmering sounds of the harp slowed and then quieted as the musician finished her finale. A crescendo of talking replaced the music. Herb walked through the room among occasional waves or calls of greeting. Herb returned only a brief nod—unable to cinch in his desperation.

Even his acquired friends could not calm him or slow his movement through the room toward "their" table. Then, he stopped. Four unfamiliar people sat jammed around the circular table where two usually sat. What had he expected?

Pivoting, he scanned the bar's ebony wood, stretching the long length of the room. Herb slowly let his eyes take in all the details. Mirrors reflected rows of glasses and crystal decanters, all sparkling in the refracted light. The expanse called for three barkeeps to meet the demand, but only two were tending bar. Making his way across the room, he approached the one he thought was named Jimmy. "I'm looking for Sam. Is he around?"

The stocky bartender had muscles that could quickly stop altercations if needed. He scowled. "Sam left early to take his sister home."

Herb inhaled a discouraged breath. The man's unstated meaning was clear. Herb had stood Anna up. "I had an emergency at work. Please explain why I—"

But Jimmy had already turned his back to refill an empty mug. Another voice, slurred and thick, called out. "Hey, what's the holdup? Gimme another round."

Herb stood, stymied. There was nothing more to be done at the pub. He rotated toward the door and went outside to walk in the sleet to his train.

TWENTY-THREE

Although Herb half expected Shields to invoke some made-up rule against a janitor sending a message, he schemed how to send it. An errand boy usually arrived an hour after the building opened. Herb busied himself cleaning around the entryway. The boy came in the door whistling an off-note-tune. He brought messages and would take away hand-deliverables from the university to their designated destinations.

Herb rushed toward him, nervously scanning the first floor for Shields. "Here," he handed the boy the envelope addressed to Anna at city hall. "I need to have this delivered this morning." The previous night, Herb had written the distraught note, explaining his absence at the pub and pleading for her forgiveness. "Here's something extra for your speed." He gave the boy twice the necessary number of coins to ensure the letter's timely arrival. "It's important that she gets this right away. You'll know her by her red hair, perfect skin, and deep blue eyes. She's smart too." Herb ached with the thought that he might never see her again.

"Smitten with the Irish, are ya?" The skinny boy seemed years younger than Herb; pimples dotted his pasty skin. "I'll deliver it unless I take a fancy to her myself, although the Irish don't suit me." His taunting laugh showed his crooked teeth. "Don't worry; downtown is where I'm headed next."

Herb watched him jog up the stairs to the offices, his footsteps echoing down the hallway.

Down below, he rolled his mop and bucket out of the janitor's closet with a leaden heart. Bell and Watson were gone, and with them, a good part of the appeal of the job. He imagined them continuing their work, engaged in a repartee of who was doing what in the science community and what they might try next. He was sure it was a conversation similar to those he had heard in bits and pieces as he ate lunch or came down to the basement for extra supplies. Few details of their discussions had come through, but the men's genuine affection for one another had been apparent. As a mark of his respect, Watson always referred to Bell as "Mr. Bell" or "Graham Bell." Their bond reminded him of his friendship with John Brannan.

"Have you heard the news?" John was waiting at the door when Herb arrived on Sunday. He held up a *Scientific American*. "Bell has received a patent. Let me read it so I get it right: for inventing transmitters and receivers for electric telegraphs."

Herb's lips moved, but no sound came out for a few seconds. "They've really done it?" He could not wait to sink into a chair in John's study and learn more details.

"Just in time, too," John continued. "He beat his chief competitor, Asha Gray, in filing for a patent by only half a day."

"Is the sound of a voice really carried over wires?" Herb felt lightheaded, trying to grasp the scientists' success.

"From what the article says, 'yes and no.' Ten days after the award, he and Watson were able to make it work. From one room, Bell said, 'Mr. Watson, come here, I want to see you.' Watson heard that request in another room by wire, but the contraption doesn't work consistently."

"Gray can still beat him?"

"Not for a while, at least. The patent's provision allows Bell a certain amount of time to perfect his invention. It won't be of any good for selling or attracting investments until they do."

Herb almost reached down to pinch his ribs to see if he was dreaming. How could he be so lucky to know the men who had invented such a thing? He looked across at John. "I finally realize that ingenuity and labor are only the first step to creating something. The next is having money to bring an idea to life. No wonder scientists keep their tinkering undercover." He squeezed his brow in a frown. "I overheard Bell bemoaning his shortage of money. He told Watson he gave up all but two of his deaf students. His tutoring apparently brought in most of his income, with a little coming from teaching at the university. Tutoring and teaching take time away from his inventions. My third revelation," he said, laughing at himself for being such a dunce: "Inventions not only have to work; they have to produce revenue."

"Here we are, still standing at the door. Where's my hospitality? Come back to my study."

Sitting in his familiar burgundy chair across from Herb, John continued, "Discovering solutions takes one attempt after another—often, one failure after another."

Herb recognized this refrain. It was a concept John frequently preached to his students, no doubt as an encouragement to keep striving for success despite failures.

"Both failure and success require money," John continued. "Convincing investors that your project is useful enough to bring profit is a cutthroat game. Another reason inventors want to keep their work under wraps. With so many challenges, it's a wonder any of them succeed."

"Fortunately, they do, and Bell wants to transmit sound over electric wires." John rubbed his palms together in glee. "We've talked about occupational traditions. Sound and hearing are in *his* blood. His grandfather, father, and brother work in elocution and speech. His mother and fiancée are deaf. It's natural for him to want to transmit the sound of a voice."

"It hasn't come quickly—something else I now appreciate. My mother heard him lecture about the possibility years ago."

"From the patent, we know he's close, and it's no secret that others, like Gray, are on the same quest—he has competition." He tented his fingers. "Hmm. The struggle to succeed gives me an idea. Bell and Watson have built on the technology of the telegraph. What do you say we think of inventions built on other inventions? Just think what it could demonstrate to students?" John's lips tipped up with anticipation. "We could show how one improvement leads to another and mankind's constant desire for advancement. Always striving is what sets humans apart." Still in his easy chair, John set the magazine containing the account of Bell's patent on the small round table as he considered what to include. He tapped, tapped, tapped his pencil as he thought.

Ordinarily, John Brannan's projects immediately fueled Herb's responses. He relished participating in an intellectual game, getting caught up in the match of who could come up with the best ideas and the reward of John's thigh-slapping guffaw: "That's a good one."

Over time, Herb realized John's habit of skipping from one question to the next, never satisfied with the status quo. His mother was the same way, asking: *What if? What next? What more?* Those lessons had wormed their way into Herb's soul. But this Sunday, his drive to know failed him. His mind was too tangled with thoughts of Anna.

Herb worked on his routine tasks at the university. With the scientists gone, his job felt less demanding and less rewarding. He tried not to think too much about when Bell might talk to Shields about having Herb work at the downtown lab, but what consumed most of his thoughts was overriding anxiety about not hearing from Anna.

His breath stopped each time an errand boy arrived to deliver messages and collect others. Sometimes, it was the same boy to whom he had given his missive for Anna, sometimes not. The pimple-faced boy with the crooked-toothed smile had promised that he had delivered Herb's message, but no answer had come. Herb could no longer stand not know-ing what had happened. He had to go to city hall to personally apologize and explain why he had not come to the pub on time. He also wanted her advice about going to the cartage company in Providence. He had almost earned enough extra hours to make the trip. He had documented dates, hours, and work in the soft, leather-bound notebook Anna had given him. He would give his boss no opportunity to renege, although Shields had more power to do whatever he wanted with Bell and Watson gone.

As usual, when he left the building, he noted the exact time of his departure. In a half-walk, half-run, he reached city hall in twelve minutes. Running up the stairs, he stopped so abruptly that his shoes made a loud screeching sound, skidding against the marble floor in front of the infor-mation desk. Anna was not there.

"Can I help you?" the startled clerk asked. Instead of the lissome red-head, a squat woman in her fifties stood behind the desk, her dark hair streaked with gray. She wore a black wool jacket over a shiny gray dress. Leaning forward, she peered at him through round wire spectacles. "You scared the bejeezus out of me. Is something the matter?"

"I'm . . . I thought . . . I'm here to see Anna," Herb said helplessly.

"Of course, many people expect to see her. She's well-liked. But never mind, I'm Miss Hansen." She straightened a stack of paper. "I haven't been here long," she smiled reassuringly. "But I'll try to help."

Herb stepped closer to the desk. "Could you tell me what happened to Anna?"

Miss Hansen frowned at him, perhaps expecting a question about a vital statistic, not her predecessor, or maybe she had heard too many questions about Anna. "She must have done a good job. I've heard she got promoted and is at a different office." Miss Hansen glanced down and bit her lip as she stared at the stack of documents that appeared to be unfilled requests for information.

Shifting his weight from one foot to the other, Herb asked. "Can you tell me which office? Where can I find her?" His fingers trembled as he fidgeted with his watch.

She shook her head. "It was just idle words that let me know. I'm not sure the rumors are even true." She frowned and picked up her stack of papers. "If you need me to pull anything from our files, you'll have to fill out a request." With an unmistakable air of dismissal, she walked away.

Wait. You can't leave. I need to find Anna. Herb's insides crumpled. He had pinned his hopes on being able to explain everything to her. Hope of that was lost, and there was no time to ponder his next step. He had to be back at the university, where Shields would be waiting at the top of the entryway steps, pocket watch in hand, timing every second of his absence.

By March, every student desk in the science building had a shelf below its seat for storage. Some used them, but plenty of others plopped their books on the floor beside the desk, as before. When Herb considered it, maybe Shields's make-work project had backfired. Instead of keeping him under his thumb doing a made-up project, as Shields had most likely intended, the extra work had allowed Herb to accumulate more than enough hours to take a day off. Herb did not feel it was a complete victory yet. He had to calculate the timing of a trip and then succeed in going to Providence. Unless he devised a foolproof plan, he could expect Shields to waddle down the hall, waving his hands in mock urgency, with a last-minute task to prevent him from leaving. Another "do it or be fired" order that Herb could not refuse. His mother, too, was an issue. Most of her meetings and lectures were in Boston, but some were in Providence. He did not want to board the train to Providence and accidentally find her seated, prim and proper, in one of the cars. What would he answer when she asked, "Why are you going to Providence?" He would shrink from admitting that he was tracing his father. The mere thought rattled him so much that he stumbled over the empty bucket, whacking his shin hard with the mop handle. That was the first of one minor mishap after another. His nervous distraction carried over into his evening.

From the moment Herb walked into their apartment, he was sure his subterfuge was obvious without words. His mum had a sixth sense about the motives behind words, and he proceeded as if tiptoeing across a tightrope.

"I've been cleaning all day . . . I guess we both have," she said, giving a tired laugh as he entered the kitchen. After the few minutes it took her to carve the pot roast, she brought him a plate stacked with sliced meat laced with brown gravy, roasted carrots, and potatoes. Herb's mouth watered at the sight. As usual, her plate held a third as much.

He waited for her to take her first bite before he cut a piece of bread and dipped it into the gravy, savoring the taste. "Mum, who's coming to speak to the next Lyceum?"

She gazed across the table at him. "Mark Twain. Do you remember him? His real name is Samuel Clemens. His short stories made you laugh when you were younger."

Herb nodded, his mouth too full to reply. He needed to know the date and location of the talk.

As if on cue, his mother continued. "He's coming to Boston to publicize his new book, *The Adventures of Tom Sawyer*. I already have a ticket. It's going to be a sold-out auditorium." She took a small bite of a carrot.

Herb worked at cutting a piece of meat. "Is it soon?" he asked, trying to act more interested in the food than his question.

"Next week, as a matter of fact. I might add on a side trip, but I haven't quite decided." She went quiet, thinking.

Side trip? His mind raced wildly. *Not to Providence!*

It was not until Sunday's noon dinner that his mother told him Mark Twain would lecture on Wednesday. She would leave for Boston Wednesday morning and be home Friday afternoon. "I may not be home in time for dinner. You don't mind being left to your own devices, do you?"

It was more of a statement than a question, but he answered it anyway. "No, I don't mind at all. I'll make extra and have something waiting in case you're hungry when you return." He looked up at her and smiled, trying to keep track of the two conversations he was having: one with his mum and one with himself. He imagined his trip to Boston and then changing trains for the one to Providence. She had not been specific about a sidetrip.

She laughed, her eyes sparkling with gratitude. "Thanks, Herb. Don't go to any trouble. I know you'd rather repair things than cook. I don't eat much."

"You save dinner for me when I work late. I can do the same for once." Then, his mind blanked because she was right about his lack of cooking skills. "Don't expect too much," he warned. "When I make a meal, I just put food on a plate. It's not exactly cooking."

"I appreciate the thought." Her violet eyes softened, expressing unspoken affection. Once they had finished eating, she stood and began to clear the table. "Are you going to see John Brannan this afternoon?"

"Yes—I'll tell him about Mark Twain." He considered whether his former teacher would be interested. "Most of his reading has to do with math and science, but almost everything interests him." Herb collected the remaining dishes and took them to the sink. "You can bet Eliza and the girls will want to know."

Monday morning, he arrived early at work, dusting and cleaning around the administrative offices so he would not miss Shields's arrival. After the administrator appeared, Herb gave him time to take off his topcoat and look through his schedule before knocking on his open office door frame. Shields's automatic greeting soured when he saw Herb instead of an instructor.

"What is it?"

Herb remained in the doorway since Shields had not invited him to enter. "I'm ready to take Wednesday off in return for my overtime work."

Shields's eyebrows almost collided, so intense was his frown. "There are no free days."

"I've earned more than two days off, but I'm only asking for one of the agreed days now." Herb remained unwavering, forcing a calm exterior while his insides churned.

"Where's your proof?"

"I've kept track of the time, and professors have noticed my overtime work to put shelves on student desks."

Shields looked down at his date book, muttering unintelligibly as he went through the obvious sham of examining his calendar. "Wednesday?" He shook his head. "I'm sorry that won't work," he said with a barely veiled smug look. "We have a group of businessmen meeting in the building to discuss campus expansion. It's a crucial discussion, and I may have to call on you for extra duties."

"I can get everything ready Tuesday afternoon," Herb protested.

"Impossible; something might happen that day. Thursday might work. I hope that doesn't spoil your plans." Shields stood in triumphant dismissal.

Herb dropped his gaze to his feet, hoping he looked downcast in somber disappointment. "Thursday, then." He stepped away from the door and, once he was out of sight, leaped in the air and clicked his heels together, as he had seen done in a circus act. The move almost sent him tumbling onto the floor. *I'd need more practice before I'd be hired as a clown.*

His plan had worked. He had figured Shields would reject any day he proposed, so he had asked for Wednesday while hoping for Thursday. Thursday was a bit of a risk because his mother might go to Providence from Boston that same day, but the odds were as great that she would stay in Boston. Even if she did take a side trip to Providence, their ending up on the same train together would be a fluke. He decided to chance it.

Thursday morning, Herb's clothing lay neatly draped over the back of the bedroom chair: a dark wool tweed jacket that ended mid-thigh, a waistcoat, dark, narrow trousers, a white shirt, and a wide ribbon tie. His mother had given him the clothing as a birthday gift the previous August. They were the best he owned. He inspected himself in the looking glass. The clothes did not look worn or out of style.

He had taken time to trim his mustache, which had grown full and slightly more russet than his light brown hair. It was not a janitor he saw in his reflection. He did not expect to meet with anyone, but his mission demanded a substantial persona, even if not yet achieved. Drizzle filled the cold air. Herb buttoned his warm overcoat and borrowed his mother's umbrella. She had already gone, so he would take it.

In Boston, he stood on the station platform waiting for his connection to Providence, fidgeting nervously as he scanned the growing number of passengers coalescing on the platform. His eyes locked on a feminine figure well in the distance, wrapped in a beige overcoat like his mother's; a broad-brimmed rain hat covered her light hair. His heart pounded as he ducked behind a pillar. Guardedly, he moved his head around the edge for a fearful peek and let out a loud gasp of relief. The woman was the same size but had nothing of his mother's graceful bearing and stride. Weak-kneed, he remained by the pillar until his train pulled up. He crowded past the exiting passengers to find his seat. Apprehension that his mother would somehow appear made relaxing impossible. To do something with his hands, he folded and unfolded the map he had drawn without glancing at it. He had memorized the central downtown Providence streets.

It was mid-morning when the train arrived in Providence. The architecture of the recently constructed Union Station awed him. Having only been in the old one, Herb took time to examine what he had read was the world's longest building before continuing his mission of finding the cartage company.

Puddles made walking tricky. The sky was gun-metal gray, threatening but not raining yet. Washington Street and the three-story red brick building, edged in blocks of creamy white stone, were not difficult to find. After pausing to rehearse his reason for coming to Sinclair Cartage, he entered. The reception counter stood to the right of a wide polished stairway leading to the upper floors. In the twenty steps it took to reach the counter, Herb felt the scrutiny of the heavyset clerk, sure he was evaluating his age, clothing, stature, and perceived economics. The man's expression was noncommittal, and Herb guessed the clerk struggled to label him. Herb was too old to be a messenger boy, not elegant enough to be of the upper class, but someone with enough presence not to be ignored—the image Herb intended. Herb did his own evaluation. A spiderweb of red veins spread across the clerk's bulbous nose, his cheeks were florid, and his eyes drooped. He had not had an easy life.

"I'd like a price for sending a heavy carton from here to Boston."

"For you or your employer?" The clerk was still taking stock.

"Myself."

"What are the dimensions and contents of the carton?" His focus did not leave Herb.

"It's six feet long by five feet, and it weighs nearly two hundred pounds," Herb said about his nonexistent package. "It's a scientific device. I can't say for what," his tone was confidential. "All the pieces are separately wrapped and will be reassembled upon arrival." His self-assurance grew with the fabricated story.

"Would you fill out this form?" The clerk slid a document across the counter. "I'll consult my chart for the cost. It will only be approximate, you understand, until we have the exact weight and specific addresses for pickup and delivery."

The clerk turned and walked to his desk. Two men chatting while slowly descending the stairway distracted Herb from the form. The slimmer, younger man, clad in a morning coat and tweed trousers, noticeably deferred to the other, who wore a rich wool jacket trimmed with a braid and worn with gray trousers. They carried top hats. At the bottom stair, they paused for a few last words. Herb studied them. The older man was broad-shouldered, close to six feet tall. His hair had remnants of light brown but was mostly gray, except for his mustache, which was more russet. His square face held a demeanor of respectable industriousness. His eyes caught Herb's for an instant before the two men shook hands, settled their hats on their heads, and exited the building.

"A preliminary estimate is ten dollars," the jowly-cheeked clerk startled him back to his reason for being there. "That's just an estimate."

"Excuse me," Herb said. "Can you tell me who the older man is?" He canted his head toward the door. "The one who just left. He looks familiar. I might know him from somewhere, but can't place him."

"Oh, then." The clerk's eyes widened. "You know the top. That's William Sinclair. The owner. Does that ring a bell?"

Herb's breath caught, realizing he had just seen the man he was searching for. He was tempted to run out the door after him, but it was impossible.

"Do you want to fill out forms now?" The clerk asked with a touch of impatience at Herb's distraction.

"Uh, no, thank you. You've given me the information I need."

"Would you like to leave your name, sir?" The clerk looked curious.

Herb hesitated. He was not sure he wanted to reveal his name, but not answering the expectant man would seem odd.

"Herb Andersen," he said before turning to leave.

"Good day, Mr. Andersen," the clerk called after him.

Herb's mind twisted in a knot after not only finding the cartage company but also catching sight of the man who headed it. He walked a few blocks before he could clear his thoughts. Finally, he pulled out the map he had drawn and a list of sites he wanted to explore in Providence. He had gone to the library to learn about the town. After the Revolutionary War, Providence developed a strong manufacturing economy in machinery, precision tools, silverware, jewelry, and textiles. A few minutes' walk to the west brought him to the Nicholson File Company Mill complex— the site he wanted to compare with Lowell. Nicholson manufactured armaments for the North during the Civil War. The seven-acre site contained a dozen or more dark red-brick buildings, some with dormers and all with regular rows of three windows side-by-side, framed at the top and bottom with wide bands of light gray stone. Although much smaller in scale, the site was reminiscent of Lowell, and the noise of the hammering and machinery, even at a distance, evoked the trapped feeling Herb always got when he thought of the plight of factory workers. As he knew only too well, most were desperate enough to submit to what amounted to bondage, sometimes for life.

The wet weather did not deter him. He occasionally unfurled his umbrella against the rain and otherwise used it as a walking stick. Crossing over the river on College Street, Herb walked to Brown University and strolled by the campus's elegant century-old buildings. On narrow pathways through the expansive lawns, he brushed shoulders with passing students. Boston University differed from Brown, just as Lowell differed from Nicholson File. The real difference, he regretfully understood, was between those who worked as laborers at factories and those who had the celebrated opportunities of academia, not always based on merit but often on a father's status. The questions again plagued him: Who was his father, and did it matter?

TWENTY-FIVE

Brookline at the end of March was rainy with perennial gray skies. Herb felt the weather was a replica of his life. He struggled to gain meaning from his trip to Providence. Although he had found the cartage company, it revealed nothing specific. In fact, his carefully crafted day away had raised more questions than it had answered. He knew little about his father, but his curiosity was welling up, intensifying his determination to know the truth, even if he did not yet understand all the pieces of that truth. But it was the morning after his trip, and he could do nothing except return to his routine.

Herb entered the university to find Shields with a twisted smirk at the top of the entryway stairs. He sighed, presuming the expression must be at his expense.

"Well, well, our vagabond is back," Shields said with a low-throated cackle. "You missed Mr. Watson. He came looking for you yesterday, but I told him you were flitting about on some foolish errand. There's always a penalty for skipping work."

"Did he say what he wanted?" Herb paused at the landing, prepared to go down to the basement.

"No." Shields shook his head with a hint of glee. "He probably found someone else." He pivoted and duck-walked toward his office.

Herb descended the lower stairs, hanging his coat on a hook on his way to the supply cabinet. *What could Watson have wanted? To move something?* Herb turned on the faucet to fill a bucket. *All their supplies are gone from here. There is nothing to carry.* Shrugging, he started up the stairs to the fourth floor, deciding to work top to bottom that day. Students had tracked in mud during the rainy weather while he was gone.

Cleaning the top three floors required a dozen trips to the basement for fresh water. Finished with those, he decided to have lunch before tackling the first floor. He settled on his wobbly chair, drinking a glass of water before proceeding to the bread and cheese he had arranged on the table beside him. A noise made him listen attentively. He could hear the repeated opening and closing of the main door and footfalls on the stairs to and from the laboratories and classrooms. Then, steps sounded closer, and a figure came down the hallway toward him.

"Herb, I timed it right." He moved in a purposeful stride down the hall, his mid-calf coat flowing behind him. "I thought you might be at your lunch. I like a man with a routine."

Startled, Herb stood up. "Mr. Watson?" He grasped the hand Watson thrust at him.

Watson peered down the hallway one way and then the other. "Do you have another chair? I'd like to have a chat."

"Here," Herb said, opening the closet door. "I keep it away since it's rarely used." Herb moved the extra chair over to the other side of the table. "I don't guarantee it will hold you. They gave me leftovers."

Watson settled slowly. "It's holding . . . I hope." He smiled cautiously. "I've come with an inquiry from Professor Bell."

"For me?" Herb's mind darted to the recollection of Bell's indistinct mention of working at the central laboratory.

Watson stared at Herb's bread while he spoke. "Not only have you helped carry things here and there—"

He stopped talking when Herb reached into his bag and brought out two more slices of bread and another hunk of cheese wrapped in waxed paper. "I packed too much food today; would you like some?" He set the irregularly shaped package on the table next to Tom Watson.

"You're sure?" Watson asked. "I'm much obliged. We'll have a business lunch." He gave a throaty, infectious laugh and peeled back the opaque paper.

Herb was too nervous to eat.

"Well, back to what I was saying. Mr. Bell has noticed your interest in science and your ability to keep quiet about what we're doing . . . and, of course, your muscles." Watson broke off a piece of bread and cheddar cheese. "Secrecy isn't so important now that Bell has the patent," he added before putting the cheese-topped bread in his mouth.

Herb waited for more explanation, afraid to fill his mouth in case Watson asked a question. It seemed to take forever before Watson finished chewing and swallowed so he could answer.

"We have a proposal," Watson said. "We must demonstrate this device we call the telephone to convince people of its potential. That will only happen if we can make it work every time. A lot of money has been put into our research—and many failed attempts. We have to prove the use of the technology but also recoup expenses."

Herb was tantalized by each bit of information, waiting impatiently for the next. *What is Watson's proposal?*

"The United States will hold its first World's Exposition in Philadelphia, from May tenth to November tenth. It's to celebrate signing the Declaration of Independence, but it's really about inventions and showing off this country's industrial advancements. Thirty-one countries have agreed to come." Watson put more food in his mouth. Herb almost regretted sharing his lunch. He wanted Bell's partner to spill everything instead of offering one teasing snippet after another. Suspense tortured him.

"Professor Bell can get exhibit space at the Exposition to demonstrate his new device, but it will take effort to string wires, carry equipment, and keep everything shipshape. We don't have much time—a little over a month before the Exposition starts, although the crucial part is the judging toward the end of June."

"What does this have to do with me?" Herb jiggled in his unstable chair.

"He, *we* want to know if you would come to work for us as a factotum. We really need to have someone like you do all the things neither of us has time for and, in some cases, can't do." Watson finished the bread and cheese and brushed the crumbs off his chest with his long, tapered fingers. "I'm afraid it will be menial, that is, doing anything that needs to be done, but a chance to see the Exposition might make it worthwhile. We can't afford much in the way of pay, but maybe we can match what you earn now. Do you mind telling me how much that is?" He looked at Herb with respect as if trying to woo someone important instead of proposing an opportunity that Herb could barely conceive.

"Two dollars a day," Herb responded.

Watson nodded. "We should be able to come up with the same amount. Shortage of money is dire for Mr. Bell. Don't tell him I said so, mind you. I earn money from my outside mechanical job. We'll come up with travel expenses, and you'll share a room with me in Philadelphia. I'm afraid you'll have to pay for your meals." Watson's brow furrowed. "You'll start at our downtown laboratory right away, and when it's time to go to Philadelphia, the three of us will find rooms until the Exposition ends in November." He paused, clearly waiting for a response.

Herb's thoughts toppled one after another. The job would be over in November, and he would again be out of a job. The menial work meant he was not progressing in his career. On the other hand, he would be working for Bell and Watson in Philadelphia at an exposition filled with world inventions. An hour seemed to tick by as he deliberated.

"I'd be pleased to take the job, Mr. Watson. I'm honored." *Was there any question? The opportunity outweighed everything.* "When would you like me to start?"

Watson leaped up from his chair, sending it over sideways with a crash. His handshake came as Herb rose with him. "We're a bit behind, so as soon as you see a way to come, do so."

"I better give Mr. Shields a few days' notice. He's not going to be happy."

"Anything we can do to smooth things over, let us know. We'll have a contract at the office. You know the address. I best be on my way to tell Graham Bell. He'll be pleased."

Shields's face contorted—his response was almost a snarl when Herb told him he was leaving and why. Herb was not surprised by his wrath. Shields was losing someone of value he had been able to control and threaten, and perhaps, most of all, because two of the world's most well-known scientists had hired him away from the university, Herb, for once, was in command.

On Herb's final day of work on Friday, the last day of March, Shields counted out his pay and not one cent of overtime compensation. There were no thanks and no well wishes. Instead, Shields turned and, in his odd gait, marched to the staircase toward an upper floor.

Herb walked to the door but stopped. He had left his bucket and a rag outside Shields's door before he received his last pay. *He may not say goodbye to me, but those are his standards.* As a parting goodwill gesture, he decided to clean the office since Shields had trundled upstairs. Herb quickly cleaned the windows and all the shelves. Removing books and papers to get to the corners, a stack of envelopes spilled apart. He grabbed them and began to put them back in order. One envelope startled him. He looked at it once and then again. It bore his name. Without a stamp, it must have come by messenger, but how long ago, Herb did not know. Hand shaking, he slipped it into his shirt pocket.

"How dare you go through my things," Shields said from behind him.

Herb turned, forcing any hint of guilt from his countenance. "I'm giving everything one last thorough cleaning before I leave." He was sure Shields could see the outline of the stiff envelope in his pocket, but Herb had only taken what was his. He wiped the shelf and put the remaining stack of envelopes back in their place. "That's it. I'm going down to get my coat and be on my way. Maybe we'll meet again." As he exited, he could sense, rather than see, Shields moving toward the envelopes. He would know the one addressed to him was missing. Herb rushed through the hall and down the stairs, sloshing drops of water from his bucket in his wake. Shields had little to challenge Herb since the letter was addressed to him in Anna's round penmanship.

Should I open it now or on the train? Confusion slowed his breathing. Was it her final goodbye? He raced to the train station, hand over his chest to protect the precious missive. He was afraid to retrieve the letter from his pocket while he stood on the platform. It would be just his luck to have a gust of wind spirit it onto the tracks, and he knew he would leap down after it, death-defying or not.

When he boarded, he looked for a seat with an empty one beside it, hoping for the extra privacy, but every seat filled quickly at that time of evening. He leaned toward the window, gently breaking the seal without tearing the paper. Her script was familiar from her previous notes. The date at the top was thirteen days ago! A chill tingled up his back. He might never have seen it if he had not encountered it while dusting. He fumed. Shields's withholding of it had not been accidental. He read on.

18 March 1876
Dear Herb:

Thank you for your letter explaining your circumstances. I worried that something had happened to you when you weren't at McLaughlin's at the usual time. It was a relief to get your letter and know it was because of your temperamental boss. I've missed you. Thursday had become my favorite day. When my brother saw how sad I was without you that night, he told my parents. My family is so protective! You would think I was still a schoolgirl instead of a woman with a job. They were out of sorts that I might have a beau

they had never met and who isn't Irish, which was one of their
first questions. I'm no longer allowed to go to the pub.

I need to say more about that. It was my family that assumed
you might be a beau. I don't want you to think I am so bold as to
make that assumption.

This predicament was not my brother's intention. Sam made an
offhand comment, not thinking how my parents might take it. He
has seen your respect for me and approves, as long as he can keep
an eye on me to be proper.

Meeting seems impossible now that Ma and Da don't want
me to go to the pub, but I have an idea. A friend from work, the
only other Irish girl, lives in a ladies' boarding house. Agnes
doesn't mind having mail sent to her. My parents know her family
and have permitted me to visit her occasionally. Gentlemen are
allowed to come to the parlor after dinner until 9:00 at night. The
proprietress is always present as a chaperone. It is respectable and
might be a proper place to see each other.

In the meantime, if you wish, and only if you do, you may send
correspondence:

c/o Agnes O'Hare
13 Freestone Street
Boston, Massachusetts

With sincere desire to see you again
Anna

Anna's letter was better than he could have dreamed—as close to a
love letter as he had ever received. Her response sent shockwaves to his
heart and down through his groin. He had received few letters, none
from a girl. Then, he met with a conundrum. He had heard from Anna
and had an address, but he had nowhere to receive future letters from her.
Seeing a woman was natural at his age, but his relationship with Anna

was too tangled with his quest to know about his father to risk rousing his mother's curiosity.

His muddled mind almost made him miss the Brookline stop. Dazed, he stumbled down the train's three iron steps to the platform. Perhaps he could ask Professor Bell for permission to receive letters at his Boston lab. It wouldn't be long before he traveled with Bell and Watson to Philadelphia, where he would have a new address.

Herb began to whistle as he exited the station. The gloom of March had ended, and a new phase of his life had begun.

"Mum, I'm home," Herb said at the kitchen door, where the aromas of dinner were already evident. "My last day at the university is over!" His emotions were a jumble—happy to be away from Shields, trepidation and enthusiasm about working with Bell and Watson, and a mixture of joy from Anna's response and concern about not having responded.

"Have you learned more about your new job? I'm walking on air about where you're going." She set down plates of steamed cod and turnips. Fish was not his favorite, but he had long since given up the gagging histrionics of childhood when forced to eat it.

"I'll do anything that needs to be done. I had to look up the word factotum." Herb glanced across to see if his mum knew—she did, but he said, "The dictionary defines it as a person having many diverse activities or responsibilities. In other words, it's not much different from what I did at the university. I'm still a sweeper and upkeep man." He felt more apprehensive about the new job than he wanted to admit. "It may be a break or amount to nothing more than one more job search after the Exposition closes."

His mother did not yield to his insecurity. "You used your work at the university as a stepping stone. You'll keep doing that." She had been overjoyed with the news, even if the work was menial. She had idolized the Bells since she heard the father and son pair speak about deafness and electricity five years earlier. She watched for anything written about them and used the articles for dinner conversation.

"I'm happy you get to go, but it will feel empty here without you, just like when you were in Lowell. At least this is a happy situation."

He nodded, swallowing a wedge of turnip. It was true. He would miss his mum . . . John . . . Brookline . . . and most of all, Anna.

Am I regretting my new job?

"I've been reading more about the World Exposition," his mother interrupted his thoughts. "Did you know there's going to be a pavilion to display inventions by women?"

Herb shook his head and swallowed a bite of fish. The cod in creamy sauce was not bad, and a change from meat and chicken.

"A lot of people believe only men invent." Her narrow-eyed look conveyed *you wouldn't dare to be one of those* before continuing. "The display was originally meant to be in the main building, but more countries wanted to participate than expected. That's good news." She swabbed the remaining cream sauce on her plate with a piece of bread. "Women were pushed out, but they rallied to raise money, hire an architect, and have a separate building constructed. A great-granddaughter of Benjamin Franklin was a big help in getting donations."

Herb suddenly realized he did not know all he should about the Exposition he would soon be part of.

"Maybe I should attend," she added.

He looked up, startled. "Attend?"

"Why not? The Women's Pavilion may attract women working for the vote or others who attend Lyceums. I shouldn't have trouble finding travel companions."

"Hmm," Herb wondered if everyone's mother had such an intrepid spirit as Sally—his mum. *Doubtful.* "I might be able to introduce you to Professor Bell and Mr. Watson if you come. I'll most likely be in the background with the equipment. I don't know how it will work, but if I get a chance, I'll tell Bell you heard his talk." Herb was silent for several moments. He had no idea whether Bell and Watson were among the many who discounted the fledgling women's movement. They might consider his knowledgeable, attractive mother to be forward, pushy, and loose simply because she supported the cause. Whatever their sentiments about women did not mean his new job would afford him the status to introduce them to her. He was an odd-job person, not an inventor.

"I think I'll start inquiring at meetings if anyone plans to attend. I've overheard talk that tickets and lodging are already in short supply. I'd better do it quickly." His mother pushed back her chair and began clearing the table.

Herb took his plate and the empty fish platter to the sink before going to his desk to write to Anna. He wanted to finish before his mother washed and dried the dishes and noticed him writing a letter when she came into the library to read. He withdrew to the library, where he put Anna's letter in a desk drawer. He was anxious to write a second apology. The first had been for not showing up at the pub. This one was for his delayed response because her reply had been hijacked—both problems caused by Shields. The letter needed to be posted the following day, Saturday. There was no delivery on Sunday. On Monday, he started working for Bell.

He lit the lantern, pulled Anna's letter from the envelope, and reread it. Warmth spread through his body with the second reading. *Heartwarming. I never knew it was real.* His physical reaction magnified the importance of his words. He was tempted to fill the page with his feelings and dreams of kisses—a proper love letter, but the risk of an emotional letter falling into someone else's hands, especially her family's, would doom any chance for their relationship. Instead, he politely thanked her for her letter and contact information, adding that his mailing address would follow soon. He explained why it had taken so long to respond. When he irritably described Shields's role in the delay, he bore down hard with his pen, making thick and misshapen script. His mood calmed as he wrote about his new job. Enthusiastic descriptions of what he hoped to see at the Exposition filled two pages. *My only regret about Philadelphia is being away from you for so many months.* Finally, he recounted his visit to the cartage company. He knew seeing the owner would surprise her. *He was well-dressed with square shoulders, gray hair with remnants of brown, and a full mustache of russet and gray. His clerk told me his name—William H. Sinclair. What luck.*

Herb sealed the envelope and addressed it in care of Anna's friend, ready for the postbox in the morning.

Undressing for bed, Herb glanced in the washroom mirror. Something about his description of the cartage owner in the letter he had just written impelled him to trim his amber-streaked, brown mustache. His chestnut eyes twinkled as he preened. Was he trying to look like an aristocrat? He chuckled. Finally satisfied, he cleaned up and went to bed.

Sunday morning, Herb promised himself he would tell John Brannan everything—or almost—certainly about his new job and Anna, but probably not about his trip to Providence and the cartage company. Truthfully, there wasn't anything to tell about the visit anyway. The weather had warmed, prompting hyacinths and daffodils to push through the dirt. Herb and John sat in the study, drinking the hot tea Eliza had served them.

"Would you mind telling me what you know about the World Exposition? I've been faulty about keeping up with more than general plans." Herb felt his brow furrow. "I don't want to seem like an ignoramus when I go to work at the downtown lab tomorrow."

John clapped his hands in delight. "The interesting thing about you, Herb, is you make me learn as much as I edify anything for you." He rose from his reading chair. "Let me think for a moment where I might have put it." He ran his fingers through his hair. His thick chestnut hair, parted in the middle, was probably brushed each morning, but his habit of idly combing it with his fingers when deep in thought made the hair fuller, accentuating his broad forehead and narrow chin.

John stepped to a shelf and removed what appeared to be a stack of newspapers from his usual organized clutter. The room resembled a microcosm of a science library. "Aha, I've got it. The World's Exposition has so many names that it wreaks havoc with my filing system." He sat down again, ruffling through the papers on his lap to find the page he wanted. "Here's its shortest title: The 1876 World Exposition. It's important to note that there have been many world fairs, but this is the first one the United States has hosted." He looked up from the paper to Herb. "You will be part of history."

Herb swallowed another sip of tea. The importance of the event was beginning to bloom, like the new spring flowers in John's yard.

"Let's go on," John said, smoothing out a full sheet of paper. "It is also called: The Centennial of the Signing of the Declaration of Independence in Philadelphia. Hence the location."

Herb spotted the delighted twinkle in John's hazel eyes. He was hitting his stride.

"But this is the official name. The International Exhibition of Arts, Manufactures, and Products of the Soil and Mine." John thumped the paper with his knuckles.

Herb had heard the first two titles but not the expanded one. "That's a mouthful. May I look at the article?"

"Here," John said, handing him the newsprint. "It was a special edition of the *Boston Globe*; you must have missed it with your extra work hours."

Herb nodded, although he was surprised his mother had not brought it to the dinner table for conversation. She collected back issues of newspapers on her return from trips to catch up with the news.

"Maybe it was a special edition only sold at newsstands and not delivered."

"Why don't you borrow it and return it next week."

"I'd like to. My mum will want to read it, too. I'm one up on her for once."

Eliza came to the door, holding a steaming teapot to refresh their cups. "A little more, gentlemen? You look knee-deep in some discussion, as usual. I hope I'll get a full account later." Her glance at John was one of fondness as she poured. So intent was he on the Exposition, John had barely noticed Eliza adding heated tea to his cup and slipping out the door, but Herb had. The Brannans had a marriage he wanted to mimic if he ever took that step.

"Here's what you should tell your mother . . . and anyone else. The Exposition celebrates one hundred years of a new country, but it's more than that. We're tooting our own horn." John could no longer stay seated and rose to take short steps in the cramped room. "This is all about what we've accomplished. Your telephone will be only one among many inventions to brag about."

"*My* telephone?" Herb lifted his eyebrows at the hyperbole.

John pivoted, retracing the three steps the room allowed. Herb could almost imagine the sound of a marching band accompanying his mentor's impassioned eloquence.

"This is all about making a statement. The United States is no longer an ill-conceived British colony but a legitimate country. We're the mold for a new world, not trying to prove we're equal, but a step better." Reaching his chair, John flopped down in it. "You managed an opportunity for yourself; don't let anything pass without your notice at the Exposition."

Brannan's finale almost seemed like the end of the day's conversation, but instead of getting up to leave, Herb asked, "Do you have time for something else?"

John's posture straightened, his sharp glance signaling Herb had his full attention.

For a moment, Herb said nothing. "I've told you a little about Anna. We've only known each other for a short time, but I want to see more of her. When I leave for five or six months, I'm afraid she won't be here when I return."

"You'll be so busy, and the time will pass quickly."

"Unfortunately, Philadelphia isn't the only complication. Her parents are protective. She's Irish, and we had been meeting at a pub where her eldest brother works. Pubs are like a family gathering place." He looked at John and exhaled audibly. "We can't do that any longer because her parents discovered our meetings. Not being able to see her or even communicate is pure anguish." Herb twisted in the sagging cushion of his chair. "All you say about opportunity at the World's Exposition is right, but I hope it doesn't end our relationship."

John's look was sympathetic. "What about letters? A lot can be said and done with a few strokes of a pen."

Herb nodded. "Anna believes her parents would confiscate letters sent to her home. We may have found a solution—for me to send letters to her via a friend of hers. Once I'm settled in Philadelphia, I'll have an address she can use." He began folding the paper about the Exposition to protect it in his jacket pocket during the walk home. "My reluctance about Philadelphia is leaving Anna."

"You're facing hurdles, no denying it." John shook his head. "But keep trying. If the relationship is worth continuing, you'll find a way. This may strengthen the connection or let you know it's not worth all the work."

"It's worth it. I know that already." Herb stood up; his determination to make his relationship with Anna work rang in his ears.

"I'd like to hear more about her next time. Her name is Anne?"

"No, Anna. It's really Á-I-N-E, accent on the first A, but she Americanized it to be easier to spell and pronounce. She's smart and always curious about things." Herb sighed again. "I'd like you to meet her . . . if it's ever possible."

"I'm eager when the time is right. Until then, let me know if there's anything I can do."

Professor Bell's lab occupied the third-floor garret of the Charles Williams Machine Shop at 109 Court Street. The architectural details of the red-brick building gave it a stately appearance. Each of the four stories had different-shaped windows. Those on the first floor were long rectangles. The second row was somewhat shorter and rounded at the top, with cone-shaped brickwork above. The third was a repeat of the second, without the topping brickwork. The fourth story had four narrow windows just beneath the mansard and two square ones. Bold block letters above the third row stated CHARLES WILLIAMS JR and below, MANUFACTURER OF TELEGRAPH INSTRUMENTS. The company supplied machinery to large telegraph companies and provided a place for inventors to experiment. Thomas Edison, at one time, had rented space there.

When Herb first arrived at the building to unload equipment from the university laboratory, the room seemed spacious, but with what Bell had added, it was crowded. An office for private meetings was at the end of two long equipment-laden tables for working scientists. The owner, Charles Williams, had an office on a lower level.

Like John Brannan's study, what looked like chaos had methods and organization known only to the third-floor occupants. A dozen or more hand-powered, metal-working lathes were set up beside the front and back rows of windows. There were also two small engine-powered lathes. The leather belts and pulleys of the machinery mostly hid the ceiling and beams of the shop. In the center of the room were wooden racks holding steel, iron, brass sheets, and brass rods, all used as raw materials. Piles of castings curled on the floor.

Herb's job was to clean the workshop, repair broken parts, and run errands. After Shields's constant monitoring, running errands or picking up supplies from nearby shops provided unexpected freedom to explore the city streets. Herb was fascinated by what still lay in ruins from the Great Fire and equally surprised by the new buildings rising like Phoenixes from the ashes. Some trips were little more than a goose chase to find a piece of equipment that Bell imagined or hoped existed but did not.

"Herb, are you sure you understood what I'm looking for?" Bell frowned when Herb came back empty-handed. "Did you explain it in detail?"

Herb nodded, hating to disappoint Bell when the item he retrieved did not do what Bell expected or if he returned without anything. The inventor spent hours trying to perfect voice by wire or other inventions—failure sent him into visible despondency.

Herb's place at 109 Court Street was a straight-backed, wooden chair in the corner, next to a wide table, where he ate lunch or made repairs. Watson and Bell were constantly discussing parts that worked or did not, including the timing of when something else they were working on was ready for a patent application. They closed the office door when visitors came but returned to the big room with all the machines and men, still talking and forgetting about any needed secrecy. Herb tried not to eavesdrop since he was unsure what needed to be kept secret, but sometimes, overhearing what was likely private conversation was inescapable.

Two men visited most often: Gardiner Green Hubbard and Thomas Sanders. From putting together bits and pieces of conversation, Herb learned they were Bell's financial backers and the fathers of Bell's two remaining deaf students, five-year-old George Sanders, who had been born deaf, and nineteen-year-old Mabel Hubbard, who had lost her hearing as a child from a near-fatal bout of scarlet fever. Mabel, ten years Bell's junior, was also Bell's fiancée.

With the increasing demands of his telephone research, Bell relied on these investors and the two classes in elocution he taught at Boston University for his income.

One April day, when a week of rain had abated and the sun shone, Hubbard arrived on the third floor. He flung off his soft-brim hat and tossed it on the corner of one of the long tables. "Alec, I've been following other inventors, and the ones who succeed in selling are those who demonstrate what they've made." Hubbard was a tall, heavyset man whose expansive white beard spread over his chest and down to the second button of his waistcoat.

Bell cleared his throat nervously. "I'm not sure it's ready to demonstrate publicly. It worked once when I talked to Mr. Watson from one room to another and then a couple of other times, but it still needs refining. It's frustratingly unpredictable." Bell began pacing the room, his hands curled into tense fists by his side. "I haven't had enough time—either to perfect it or even make up final examinations." He spun, raising his hands in an exasperated motion. "Someone else needs to demonstrate it for the crowds. Let's have Willie do it."

"What?" Hubbard's eyes widened. "My nephew's only a college student. He'd have no credibility. What if something went wrong? No, Willie can assist but can't be on his own."

"Mr. Watson will go, too, and Herb." Bell nodded toward Herb, but Hubbard ignored him.

"Damn it! I said no." Hubbard hung up his topcoat with such vehemence he almost toppled the coat rack. "People want to see the inventor. The Exposition opens on May tenth. I've secured a reservation for the entire Exposition demonstrations and for the judging in June. You must be there for that."

"Impossible," Bell said helplessly. "Sometimes, sound travels only a short distance and can't be understood. I've had to resort to music or a familiar poem so people recognize what's coming across."

"I've thrown money at this without payback. We're finally close, with a chance at a prize." Hubbard stamped his foot. "You cannot delay any longer!"

Everyone in the big room had gone silent, watching the two.

"Teaching is my livelihood." Bell began pacing again, massaging his forehead. "I may fail at both teaching and inventing." Bell looked like he was about to be crippled by one of his headaches. "Here, Mr. Hubbard, let's go into my office and discuss a schedule." Bell reached for Hubbard's hat and hung it on the coat rack. He took the investor's arm, led him to the office, and closed the door.

Twenty minutes later, they came out, Hubbard still adamant. "June twenty-fifth, for the judging. Not a day later. People need to see the inventor before they buy into the idea." He plucked his hat from the rack and put it on, followed by his overcoat. "An award would go a long way in selling the invention and recouping my money." With that, Hubbard turned and descended the stairs with echoing footsteps.

In addition to Bell and Watson, a handful of scientists daily crowded the third-floor garret. Some devised specialty machinery for the Charles Williams Machine Shop customers. Others optimistically tinkered with unproved inventions. Herb was employed by Bell, but the other scientists quickly noticed his ability to fix and assemble devices and asked him to work on their projects or run errands in his "spare time." Each day brought new requests.

By the Friday of his second week, scientists surrounded him with their requests. They loudly moved forward, demanding his time. Herb took one backward step after another until he was pressed against the wall. He could feel their breath their faces were so close to his.

"I'm not sure I can help with that," Herb kept repeating. Desperately, he scoured the room for a way to escape. "Mr. Watson," he called across the room. "I have a question."

With a few long strides, Watson stepped into the melee. Unable to understand the overlapping voices, he ordered, "Quiet! There's a misunderstanding."

The demanding scientists fell silent, looking moody.

"Professor Bell pays Herb's salary. Any request for his time must have my approval and will come with additional payment for the extra work." The men dispersed to their stations, grumbling about the lost opportunity for free labor.

"Maybe we missed a chance to hire you out," Watson joked. "But we'll have plenty for you to do, and if you have spare time, they'll come through me for it."

"Thanks; I didn't want to get off on the wrong foot, but I didn't know how to dislodge myself."

"They're good fellows who saw a prospect that wasn't there."

Herb tamped down his nerves. "Thanks again." He hesitated. "May I ask another favor? Would you mind if I used this address for my correspondence? There won't be much." Watson's eyes showed an inkling of surprise, but if he wondered why correspondence couldn't be sent to Herb's home, he didn't say so. "I see no problem. I'll tell the building owner, Charles Williams." Watson returned to his office, showing no concern about the melee or the mail request.

TWENTY-SEVEN

Herb wrote to Anna about the delay in leaving for Philadelphia. *There are differences over whether giving final exams at the university or demonstrating the new voice-over wire device at the Exposition is more important. Mr. Bell's investors think one way, and he the other. We're all on pins and needles, but the delay may give us time to see each other before I leave.*

Anna's response reached 109 Court Street in two days. Too busy to read it, Herb stuck it carefully in his pocket for the trip home. He spotted the last vacant seat in the train car, crowded with after-work passengers. He squeezed into the seat, half occupied by an overweight passenger. The man's blubber pressed against Herb's arm. Even worse was the smell of his fetid breath. Leaning to the other side, Herb pulled out the letter, sure that it would smell like undigested onions when he returned it to its envelope. Forgetting his surroundings, he let Anna's words cheer him.

She wrote about her new job, improving the filing system in the city's storage rooms.

It was supposed to be a promotion, but it took me away from working with the public. Once I finish, I hope to get my old front desk back again, but I won't complain. I'm lucky to have my job.

She continued, saying she badly missed the pub's lively environment, but her parents would not listen to her arguments about going back.

This may be bold, but I believe the boarding house where my friend Agnes lives would be a proper meeting place if you are willing. Agnes says that the landlady is so strict that she sometimes uses a ruler to make sure a gentleman is not sitting too close to a lady.

I'm interested in the cartage company and anything else you want to share regarding your project. I'll bring a pencil and paper so I can take notes. Maybe you're close to uncovering something.

Would you like to come to Agnes's at seven thirty next Thursday?

The words of the invitation danced on the page. He responded that night, slipping his letter into the metal postbox with a clang on his way to the train station the following day. Then, apprehension fogged his mind. How was he expected to behave at a ladies' boarding house? He had never been in one. His one good set of clothes showed wear; he desperately wished he could afford something new for seeing Anna and for Philadelphia, where he might be in public view despite his menial job. The shapeless jacket, trousers, and shirt he worked in labeled him as a drudge. Pretending to be someone above his station was not his intent; looking respectable was.

That night, at the dinner table, his mother refolded the World's Exposition special edition of the newspaper John had lent to Herb.

"This article makes me even more certain that I have to go to the Exposition." Her eyes gleamed with enthusiasm. "Please, thank Mr. Brannan for it. Attending will be like ten Lyceums . . . or more." She tipped forward in her chair and looked down at the front page again. "I've had my library of books to learn from, but you'll have something even better—exposure to the world's latest inventions. You need to study every single one. This will be like a college education." The idea seemed to make her giddy.

"Mum, I don't know how much extra time I'll have." Her expectations set off an alarm bell. "Maybe I won't even have a chance to leave Professor Bell's exhibit." The thought of leaving the exhibit reminded him about his wardrobe. "I've been worrying about my clothes. I think I need a second set. I've saved enough from my pay, but I have no time to shop." Herb looked across the table. Her violet eyes were still bright from their talk about the Exposition. "Would you mind looking? You can take my graduation clothing for size." He paused. "Can a tailor make something without me being there? One size up, if possible."

She paused. "I think so. Adjustments should be able to be made when you pick it up." She smiled at him. "Let me give it a try. I'll go tomorrow."

"Mum, something else. You said you once lived in a boarding house for ladies. What was it like?"

He read her puzzlement.

"It's hard to remember. I haven't thought about my life there for a long time. Do you want to know about the people or the house?"

"How does it work?" he felt tangled up asking her. "Were you allowed to have visitors?"

She unfolded and refolded the newspaper as she remembered. "We were allowed to have other women visit with permission, but if they stayed for a meal, they had to pay. Men were allowed into the parlor occasionally, after dinner, when the landlady was present. Going out with a man was forbidden unless you took a chaperone approved by the landlady. Of course, some chaperones were more diligent than others." She smothered a giggle with her palm. "We formed friendships, but girls came and went. I haven't kept in touch with any of them; it was so long ago." Her eyes glazed over as if she had drifted back to the past. "None of us liked the landlady. Miss Dill was a large woman with small, round, ferret eyes. She was always observing and prying. We could tell she went through our things when we were at work. Nothing was private. Our doors locked so other roomers couldn't get in, but Miss Dill had a key, and we knew she went snooping while we were gone."

Herb buttoned his jacket buttons one at a time and then unbuttoned them, considering whether divulging anything about Anna would be a mistake.

"My friend doesn't live there, but a girl she works with does. She asked Anna and me to go after dinner next Thursday. A very strict woman runs the rooming house, and Anna's parents know Agnes's parents. It's respectable."

Her lips curved. "I'm glad there are rooming houses that allow men to visit with propriety. Young people should have a place to meet. You said your friend's name is Anna?"

"Yes. I haven't known her long, but I like being with her." He could not disguise the affection in his voice.

"Where did you meet?" She looked at him with genuine interest, and her violet eyes expressed goodwill, not reproach.

"At city hall." He frowned. "Right now, she's organizing files, but usually, she's at the front desk, answering questions about all sorts of things." He tripped over the words.

"Have a good visit. Please give me a report about the rooming house. I'd like to know how different it is from the one I lived in." She picked up dishes to take to the sink and paused. "I'd like to hear more about Anna. Her job sounds interesting. Maybe there will be an opportunity to meet her parents so they would be confident in letting her visit here."

When Herb lifted his plate and fork, they rattled together in his shaky grasp. His mind would not quiet. His mother was not suspicious yet, but he doubted he could keep the inquiry that had led to his meeting Anna a secret forever.

Following Anna's carefully written directions, Herb arrived at the rooming house ahead of time. The architecture of the two-story red brick rooming house, with its four black-trimmed second-floor windows, could be categorized as either residential or commercial. Long stone stairs led up to a doorway protected by a triangular overhang.

Guests were not allowed before seven-thirty, so he used his spare time to walk through the neighborhood. Commerce encroached on what appeared to have been, at one time, the residential street of Freestone, with businesses now occupying some former homes. When he returned from circumnavigating the block, he was a few minutes late. Taking two stairs at a time, Herb reached the front door and clanked the brass knocker. He heard voices inside, but no one answered. Just as he considered knocking again, the door opened. An ample woman with steel gray hair and splotchy cheeks filled the doorway.

She brought a lorgnette to her gray-blue eyes and peered through the lenses. "Mr. Andersen?" she asked, still guarding the entryway.

"Yes, I'm Herb Andersen." He extended his hand, and she offered her fingertips. Taking them, he bowed slightly over her hand, hoping the gesture was proper etiquette.

"I'm Miss Hall, the proprietress. Two young ladies await you. First, may I remind you of the rules?"

Herb knew she would, whether he answered her question or not, so he nodded.

"Gentlemen sit in single chairs, not on the settees. We serve coffee and cake left from dinner. Hours are strictly enforced. When the clock chimes nine, you must depart promptly. Will you comply?"

"Yes, ma'am. I'll be on my best behavior." Herb only just refrained from rolling his eyes. He summed up Miss Hall as a female version of Mr. Shields.

She stepped aside and closed the door, gesturing for him to follow her past the ornate staircase that all but filled the entry hall. When they entered the large, formal parlor, Herb was surprised that a dozen people occupied it. Some were seated, while others stood chatting. There were two other men, both appearing every bit as out of place as he felt.

When Anna walked toward him, he wanted to rush forward and encircle her in his arms. *Fie the commitment to good behavior.* Her green dress highlighted her red hair, which shone as if touched by flames.

Instead of the wished-for embrace, he held her warm, soft hand. The touch had him lost for words until his mind registered a repeated smacking sound. Miss Hall was whacking her palm with a ruler in warning. Herb dropped Anna's hand and took a step back.

"Herb, it's so good to see you, I . . ." Anna hesitated. "Let me introduce you to my friend, Agnes O'Hare."

"Anna has told me all about you, Mr. Andersen. I'm glad you could visit." Agnes was slimly built, with dark hair and a pale complexion that accented her vivid, jet eyes. "Come and have a seat." She walked gracefully to a straight-backed chair with a worn needlepoint cushion and gestured for him to take it. "I'll sit on the settee on the other side of Anna. I brought a book to read to keep me occupied. But first, may I get you coffee and cake?" Her slender lips tipped up, blushing pink against her talcum-colored skin.

"If it's not too much trouble."

The murmur of other conversations rippled in the background. Gilt-framed pictures hung in tight array against rose-patterned wallpaper. Fringed chairs and plump settees made the room feel overstuffed. It was a fussy, feminine setting, but all that mattered was being with Anna. They read each other's eyes, not speaking, until Agnes returned with coffee and a slice of chocolate cake with dark, creamy frosting. She set the plate and coffee cup on the table between the settee and his chair.

"None for you?" he asked Anna.

She shook her head, "My waist. And, anyway, there's so much to say. Let's not squander the time." She waited until he had taken a sip of coffee before saying, "I'd like to hear more about your trip to the cartage company. Tell me everything you remember." She smoothed the shimmery green fabric of her dress but kept her sparkling, eager eyes on his.

Herb moved his plate to the end of the table, interested more in talking than eating for once. "It wouldn't have happened without you," he said. "I would have been stuck with the name Andersen and would have been at a dead end." He sipped his coffee. "Your sleuthing was my first stroke of luck. The next came when I stood at the reception counter, persuading the clerk to give me a bid on my made-up transportation needs." He rolled his eyes, remembering the lie. "I wanted to find out more about the company. As I spoke to him, I noticed two men taking their time coming down the long stairway while they talked. I had time to observe them. Mr. Sinclair, I later learned, was the taller and older of the two and had especially broad shoulders."

He would have stopped there, but Anna asked, "What did his face look like?"

Herb tried to remember the details. "His gray hair had remaining brown and had receded, making his forehead large with obvious lines of age. His nose was prominent, and his bushy mustache was a little redder than his hair." Herb pulled the plate of cake closer, having second thoughts about not being hungry. "You're going to think less of me because of my fibbing, but no harm was done. I didn't give the clerk an address. How could I?" he asked with a shrug. "I told him I'd contact him if I wanted to ship equipment."

Anna did not speak; she just watched him. Her sapphire blue eyes moved while she scanned his features.

"Are you disappointed in me for telling fibs?"

She shook her head so vehemently her hair loosened from its netting, cascading over her shoulders. "Discussion of a bogus order is a small fib." She looked in Miss Hall's direction and quickly bound up her hair before the landlady noticed. "Loose hair, loose morals," she whispered.

"Why were you staring at me?" he asked.

"It's funny. Except for the forehead and gray hair, your features resemble what you described."

"It's probably my mustache—it's finally turned bushy instead of scant." He returned to his cake, but as he ate, he remembered what he had said to the desk clerk. "Can you tell me the man's name? He looks familiar."

"Maybe, but not every man is tall and has broad shoulders," Anna said.

He leaned forward in his seat. "It's one of the many things I admire about you—your attention to detail, unlike me." He returned to his cake.

Anna broke their silence. "Herb," she moved her hand as close to his as possible without risking reprimand, "you don't have to answer, and you can tell me to mind my own business, but is Mr. Andersen . . . or the man you're looking for, your living father?"

For a while, Herb could not answer. He had suspected she guessed before then, but she deserved to hear it from him.

"Yes. I never knew him. My mother told me he died before or soon after I was born. I wanted to know what he was like and understand if I might have some of his traits. It was his characteristics I was looking for, not a person."

"What we've encountered is probably a coincidence." She fumbled in her reticule and brought out a handkerchief. "People have come to city hall convinced of a connection to a relative that, after more investigation, was nonexistent. I've seen hurt . . . and worse, anger. I don't want that to happen to you."

Herb swept away the ghost of his father. He had so little time with Anna; he simply wanted to be with her. For precious moments, they were unconscious of their surroundings, only aware of each other. The clock ticked, but time went on without them. Reality intruded when the clock chimed nine, and without wasting a second, Miss Hall announced: "It's time for guests to leave," just as she said she would.

Everyone hurried to say their last goodbyes as guests wriggled into their wraps. Anna walked with Herb to the entryway, daring to defy the rules by leaning against his arm, unobserved in the mingling crowd. She would spend the night in the rooming house and leave for work with Agnes in the morning.

"Anna, can we see each other again before I leave for Philadelphia?"

"Yes," she whispered. "Agnes will help. She's on our side. I'll send you a letter to—"

"It's time to go." Miss Hall's firm hand propelled him forward, preventing him from glimpsing Anna for a last time.

Outside, Herb stood immobile. He wanted all thoughts to disappear except those about seeing Anna. He let out a dispirited sigh and began his walk to the train.

TWENTY-EIGHT

Most of his arguments with his mum had resulted from his childish behavior or not meeting her expectations. They were tiffs that found resolution before long. For the first time, Herb's irritation over unknown facts about his father threatened their relationship. His mother had been clever at circumventing specifics. She'd always said his father "had gotten sick and never recovered," which had led Herb to assume, all these years, that his father was dead. But he had become unsure about that and whether he should question her credibility about other information.

He lay in bed after seeing Anna at the rooming house, unable to fall asleep. His feelings toward his mother, the mystery of his father, and his desire to know the truth—all of it—clogged his mind. He tried to will those confusing thoughts away. He had to find a way to see the enchanting woman he had fallen in love with.

At work, Professor Bell's frequent remarks about his visits to his fiancée, Mabel Hubbard, intensified Herb's longing for Anna. He retreated to the back of the room to complete his assigned tasks, avoiding the lively banter of the third-floor workshop.

"Herb," Tom Watson said, interrupting his gloom. "Graham Bell wants me to explain the workings of the telephone—when it works, that is." His chuckle was half-hearted. "It would be beneficial to have more than just ourselves understand it. Of course, Hubbard's nephew, Willie, will learn, but it won't hurt to describe it to you, too."

Herb wondered if the good-hearted Watson sensed his mood and wanted to distract him, hoping his worry was not that obvious.

For weeks afterward, Watson spent snatches of time teaching Herb about the telephone and then other of Bell's inventions.

"You pick things up quickly," Watson said.

"Thanks. I've always liked to learn about inventions and how they work." The compliment warmed him. "I'm learning how much trial and error there is. It seems once there's success, the mechanics are not so hard to understand."

"You're right. And now that you've said that, I want you to not only understand the basics of the telephone but to understand it well enough to explain it in case we have to call on you."

Herb jerked to catch the hammer that almost slipped from his hand. "Me?"

"There's always that chance," Watson said as he strode away.

From that moment, Herb spent spare moments inwardly reciting the parts: "The speaker is a cylinder, with paper covering one end and attached to a needle. A wire connects the needle to a battery, and another connects the battery to the receiver. When someone speaks into the open end of the cylinder, the voice makes the paper and needle vibrate. The electromagnet turns the vibrations of the voice into an electric current with enough voltage to transmit the sound along the wire to the speaker."

I might be able to give a rough explanation. God help me if I have to make the finicky thing work. He was sure he would not sleep well until the Exposition was over.

The third-floor laboratory was electric with tension more than machinery. Tinkerers swore and fumed over ideas that seemed to refuse to become a reality. The pressure on Bell from examinations and judging deadlines was in full view.

"I'd much rather be teaching university students," Bell said morosely, "or even more, to be tutoring deaf students."

Out of Bell's hearing, Watson whispered to Herb one morning, "He's resorted to his old habit of staying up most of the night to work out the snags of an invention. Sleeplessness always causes ferocious headaches."

Stress had not left Bell when he called Herb and Watson to his office in mid-May. In the chair beside Watson, Herb listened to the pallid, dark-haired inventor. "I've made my final plan. Mr. Watson, you'll go to Philadelphia at the beginning of June. You'll need to see that the wires are strung properly and that the stations for sending and receiving messages are in place. Hubbard's breathing down my neck." He massaged his forehead with his palm.

"Herb, we've asked you before, but there's only money to cover your salary—you'd bear your own expenses." Dark crescents hung beneath the inventor's eyes. "I'm sorry."

"I've already said I'd pay for the room," Watson interjected. He turned to Herb, "We can stay together."

"I can manage my expenses, Professor Bell," Herb agreed before estimating the costs.

Bell pressed his fingers against his temples. "Take all the wiring we'll need. I'll send the rest of the equipment, so it gets there before I arrive with Willie a week before the judging." He groaned. "Philadelphia—hot, muggy, and without air. I dread the thought."

"Not much different than Boston," Watson said, smiling at his dour companion. Any concern he might have had about the long-sought contraption's readiness was not evident.

Annoyance about his mother's furtive behavior permeated Herb's mind, although she had apparently not picked up on his tense mood. He watched her spoon stew from a pot, forcing his thoughts away from his family to his job. He still could not believe that Bell and Watson had asked him to help at the World Exposition, and with not so much as a moment's hesitation, he had ignored the risks and agreed. It was a leap of faith to risk everything for an opportunity. Only later did chances for potential mishaps occurred to him. Expenses might be more than he expected or could afford. The experience could end up with nothing gained for his effort and leave him jobless. Herb shrugged, realizing he had learned or inherited the ability to take risks from his mother. She easily dismissed adversity to travel and learn. Herb seethed about her secretiveness, but he knew he benefited from many of her personality traits.

He watched her shed her apron before setting down the bowls of lamb stew brimming with pearl onions, mushrooms, and new potatoes. She turned back for a basket of flaky biscuits to dip in the broth. On the side, she'd made a lettuce salad—everything fresh with spring.

"Mum, it's definite now. I leave for Philadelphia in two weeks."

"That's good news." Her eyes shimmered. "I worried you'd have to stay back if Professor Bell decided not to go." She frowned lightly. "It's too bad you missed the Exposition's spectacular opening, but never mind." She smoothed her napkin on her lap. "That was only one day; you get to go for much of the rest. Do you think you will get to stay to the end?"

"Maybe." Herb could not resist the fresh, warm biscuits. He cut one open, releasing a curl of steam, and savored the taste before continuing.

"Money is tight; a lot will depend on how Bell's demonstrations go and, of course, the judging." Herb took a spoonful. "It's good. I'm hungry."

"You're always hungry," she laughed, "but what about the demonstrations? Is there a risk they won't be successful?"

"The risk is real. On any given day, the apparatus works, and then something goes haywire. Bell needs to have it work consistently." His voice lowered as he thought about failure. "It's only a toy if the proto-type sits on a shelf and doesn't become a useful invention. He needs new investors. His current ones have extended themselves as far as they're willing."

"I hope it works for everyone's sake. I'm still trying to find a way to go." She was quiet for a moment. "Maybe in October, when it's cooler, but even if I do come, it will only be briefly, so I'll never see all of it." Distress crossed her face. "You must write to me about what you see. I want to know everything."

He realized that was the essence of her life, wanting to know every-thing. Was it something they shared? Did that explain his curiosity about his father? He ran his fingers through his thick mustache. "I'll probably be busy, but I'll try to find time to write."

"Are you able to manage financially?

A drop of broth spilled from his spoon. The thought of running out of money in Philadelphia was a worry he could not put aside.

"My salary will be the same as it is now, but I'll have to pay for all my expenses. It may or may not be quite enough." He quickly tried to rub the drop out with his napkin so it would not stain the tablecloth. "Fortunately, Mr. Watson has invited me to stay with him. That will help, and I've been saving what I can." He looked up apologetically. "I won't be able to give you part of my paycheck for a while, and who knows if I'll have a job when the Exposition ends."

"Herb," his mother said, setting down her spoon. "Let's not worry about money. We'll somehow make do. This is such an opportunity," her violet eyes twinkled. "Think of how much lower my grocery bill will be. We'll call this an educational expense. It's a good investment."

Relief flowed through his exhale. "I should start thinking about getting my own place when I return instead of always counting on you." Sunny thoughts of living with Anna enveloped him, followed by the dark cloud of his uncertain future. "Remember, no one knows my exact role at the Exposition yet, and they may have to cut expenses and do without me. I may be back in Brookline sooner than we think."

"Make yourself indispensable to Bell and Watson," she said, drawing her shawl tightly around her shoulders. "Voice over wires is a gamble and may not pan out, but make them unable to do without you while they roll the dice."

He tensed. It was much easier to say "be indispensable" than to accomplish it in the competitive world of invention, and yet, it was typical of her to have that kind of attitude. Her secretiveness about the past rankled him, but he could not deny how much her influential intelligence had benefited him, both when he was growing up and at that moment.

His bad temper about his mother's seeming deception about certain facts had made a slight turnabout when it dawned on him that he was about to indulge in his own deception to see Anna against her family's wishes. In her most recent letter, Anna proposed a way to be together before he left for Philadelphia. She'd gone on to explain, *"This was Agnes's idea, but I fully agree."* Herb had imagined the white gleam of her smile as he'd read their plan. *"Let's meet at a bakery for supper. Agnes will come as a chaperone. After dinner, I will spend the night at Agnes's boarding house. My parents won't know about dinner, and crotchety Miss Hall has already given her permission for the night's stay."*

The morning of the appointed supper, the third-floor workshop crackled with tension. Bell had spent another late night complaining that any noise, or even sunshine through the window, made his head throb and ruined his ability to think. Everyone avoided making unnecessary sounds, moving through the lab as if trying to walk on eggshells without breaking them. The mood added to Herb's worry about being able to meet Anna. In the afternoon, he checked his watch so often that he was sure he had worn down the fabric of his pocket. He could not stomach the thought of missing another dinner with Anna because of a work conflict.

When Bell left the lab for a moment, Herb moved next to Watson. "I'm meeting my girl for supper after work." He paused. He had never used that term or even thought of Anna quite that way.

"Oh, you, too," Watson interjected when Herb hesitated. "Men besotted by women surround me. You've heard Graham Bell go on and on about Mabel. I've never seen such a case. That's one of the reasons he doesn't want to go to Philadelphia—he'd be leaving her."

Herb turned to Watson in surprise. He thought the reason was Bell's university students.

"He's in serious difficulty because her father *and* benefactor is of the opinion that he *must* go, as am I. His fiancée agrees with us. It's three against one, with Bell drawing the short straw." Watson shook his head. "I presume it might even be four against one, with you on our side."

"No, I mean, yes." Herb's cheeks warmed. "I agree about Philadelphia, but I'm not in the same boat about a girl." He stumbled to explain. "Professor Bell is engaged; Anna is a friend or . . . I don't know." His shoulders rose in indecision. "What I mean is, there's no commitment yet."

"Well, I wish you luck, whichever way you want it to go." Watson gave him a reassuring smile. "Sorry, I interrupted. What was your question?"

Herb shook his head. "Not a question. I want to make sure I leave work on time so I'm not late. It's the last time I'll see Anna before we leave."

Watson nodded, his attention clearly distracted by Bell. The inventor had returned, huffing from climbing the stairs from the toilet on the lower level, and seemed lost in thought as he entered his office.

Schneider's Bakery was a popular place. Mostly women, but occasionally men lined up, eager to buy baked goods. When Herb arrived, he found a queue of people waiting their turn, snaking through the bakery and onto the boardwalk. Customers came from all backgrounds. Those in sophisticated finery mixed with factory workers to purchase the delicious loaves of bread, pastries, meat pies, and pasties for which the bakery was famous. They could take their purchases home or eat in the small dining area.

From Anna's instructions, he knew the three of them would meet inside, but he wasn't sure how to get through the crowd. At the front of the line, a couple stood behind a glass-cased counter, hurrying to fill orders. They were an older couple—he was bald, while she had iron-gray hair. Both were plump. Herb guessed being overweight was probably from sampling their baking, knowing he would have the same temptation.

Making apologies, he squeezed through the line into the dining area, with bright flooring of red and white alternating linoleum squares and eight tables for four. He quickly picked out Agnes's jet curls and Anna's red coif. Their physical features were as dissimilar as their hair color—Agnes had an angular thinness and porcelain-white complexion, the opposite of Anna's rosy cheeks and zaftig shape. In common, they had alert and intelligent eyes—Agnes's dark and Anna's blue. They waved when they saw him.

"Ah, my fellow conspirators." He gave a mock bow when he reached them before sliding into an empty chair. "I am overjoyed to see you . . . both," he said, finally pulling his gaze away from Anna long enough to acknowledge Agnes. "Aren't you worried someone will see us?"

"A little," Anna admitted. "But everything here is so proper, surely it would seem acceptable, and there are two against one." She gave him a cheerful smile, visibly as happy to be with him as he was with her.

A stocky brunette, who appeared to be a younger version of the woman behind the counter, set down three glasses of water and took their order. Agnes ordered vegetable soup; Anna pork with sauerkraut; and Herb, despite his resolve to save every penny, ordered two meat pies.

They talked of work and the upcoming Exposition until their food arrived and then quietly ate. Herb found the food as delicious as the aroma permeating the bakery.

When she finished her soup, Agnes said, "It won't give you much privacy, but I'm going to turn my chair around and read my book. You'll have to look at my back, but I'll *try* to concentrate on my reading instead of listening." Her smile was mischievous.

"Thanks, Ag; I'm in your debt." As soon as Agnes reversed her chair, Anna faced Herb. "I wish you didn't have to go away." She stopped while the waitress refilled their water glasses. The younger woman gave the group an odd look, perhaps puzzling over whether there had been a falling out among friends, given Agnes's backward chair. "I know it's an opportunity, but Philadelphia seems so far away." The skin between her eyes creased. "I wish I could come and see all you're going to experience." She put her hand on the table, moving it close to his without touching it. "I'm afraid you'll get so smart you'll forget about me."

"No." He shook his head. "It's the other way around. You're the one with a steady job. Your family will find you a nice Irish lad with a future, and that will be the end of me."

After giving him a startled look, Anna sighed. "Let's not think about that now. I have some ideas." Her blue eyes brightened. "I need to see what you think."

"Your ideas are always remarkable," he said with a smile. "Let me hear them."

Agnes's slender shoulders gave a little shrug as she shook her head back and forth, obviously overhearing the comment.

"It may be going too far . . ." Anna hesitated.

"Go ahead. I haven't started my second meat pie. I'll listen and eat while you talk, and then we'll reach a verdict." He cut off a bite with his fork.

"You just remarked about my job, and you're right. I'm fortunate to have it." She tucked a loose strand of red hair into the netting at the back of her head. "Many Irish girls end up being maids. There's great prejudice against the Irish, although things aren't much better for Italians or Germans." She frowned before continuing, apparently deciding not to get sidetracked by different cultures' animosities. "Irish maids have an intricate network. That's how they find jobs and learn who needs help, who is good to work for, and who isn't. You can get taken advantage of when you're poor and defenseless, with no one to come to your aid. Woe to those who aren't wary."

Herb nodded, although it wasn't only immigrants who found themselves defenseless and needing employment.

"We need to learn more about William Sinclair before we make any assumptions." She smiled at Herb slyly. "I was able to find his home address in Providence."

He struggled to swallow without choking. "How?"

"It wasn't hard," she shrugged. "It's in the city directory. His wife's name is Eugenia, but the directory doesn't include children's names if they have any," she said.

He had put William Sinclair out of his mind because he was not sure he wanted to know any more about him. As he pondered, he remembered Anna's comment about people searching through city records only to find the connection they sought nonexistent. What did finding William Sinclair mean? Did continuing to learn more outweigh the unknown consequences of finding out? His mind tumbled with conflicting feelings.

"Herb, are you mad at me?" Anna's face paled, and the corners of her eyes creased. "I'm sorry. I just thought you would want to know where he lived." She put her elbows on the table and clasped her hands. "I always get too eager and go too far. I'm driven—I'm not sure if it's more of a curse or a blessing that I'm that way."

"No, we should check this out to put a dead end behind us. Then maybe I can stop thinking about this and go on to some other endeavor." He ran his fingers through his mustache. "I don't expect to find a living person, just a little more about someone who died a long time ago." He took a deep breath. Tracing a real person was peculiarly unsettling. He did not want his madcap search to involve anyone but himself.

Anna's expression was grave, and Agnes's figure had become as motionless as a mannequin.

"It's my fault for starting, not yours," he told her.

Their silence contrasted with the ongoing chatter and motion around them—their world of introspection and hazard against the bakery's pleasure and sustenance.

The search for his father had become more complicated than learning someone's traits. It was intertwined with Anna, and the outcomes of the search might be higher stakes than he had imagined.

"I won't go any further unless you tell me to."

"This is different than I thought, making it hard to know if it's worth continuing. If this is a dead end, I can put it behind me with relief." He observed her pale, anxious face and wanted to reassure her. "Here's what I do know. I want *you* in my future, and I hope you might come around to that feeling, too." He searched her eyes beseechingly.

Anna leaned toward him, nodding. "More than anything."

The room had quieted, with an empty table or two; the line had receded, so the door was no longer propped open to accommodate a queue. Customers still came and went, but the after-work rush had ended.

"I'll send you my address in Philadelphia once I know how the mail works at the event. It's not the same as seeing you, but at least we'll keep in touch." He looked at her intently, searching for the same eagerness he felt. He read sincerity in the depth of her ocean-blue eyes.

"Herb, you're sure you want me to keep researching?"

He paused, breathing heavily with inner struggle before he replied. "Yes, otherwise, the unknown will haunt me." He sounded surer than he felt.

Agnes's chair scraped as she turned it around to face them.

"Did you get some reading done?" Anna asked.

Agnes rolled her eyes. "Honestly . . . Jane Austen isn't nearly as dramatic as what I heard from the two of you." She shook her head, noticeably nonplussed by the seriousness of their discussion. "It's hard to end this, but I'm the chaperone, after all." She placed her reticule on top of her book and stood up. "Miss Hall will never let you stay again if we don't return on time. Maybe we can walk arm-in-arm back to the rooming house without attracting too much attention. Then you two can touch, as you're dying to," she smirked.

As they exited, Agnes laced an arm through Herb's, and he entwined his other with Anna's.

"What would I do without both of you?" Herb said.

When Herb went to the Brannans on the last Sunday before his departure, John greeted him and immediately began searching his shelves for information he had compiled about what Herb should know before leaving for Philadelphia. "The more you know, the more useful you can be."

"I may be back soon if they run out of money."

"That would be a real shame because I've drawn up a list of exhibits you simply can't leave Philadelphia without visiting." After a few seconds of looking on the shelves, he found what he wanted, thrusting a sheet of paper with writing on both sides at Herb. "Have a seat."

Herb sank into the familiar leather chair and perused the paper, crammed with so much writing that it was difficult to read.

"Thanks. This is a big favor." He looked at it again and laughed. "It may take me a while to decipher."

His mother had said the trip would be akin to a college education, and John had ensured it with his quintessential interest in teaching. Their mandates revealed the best of their personalities and also expectations he had qualms about fulfilling.

John poured two glasses of water and handed one to Herb before sinking into his burgundy chair. "I really should have included more, but it's a start of what you can expect to see there and what you should know. Take steam engines. There is a modern version of James Watt's original steam engine from a hundred years ago—another centennial celebration. And the modern-day Corliss engine, built just for the Exposition, will power everything at the site. It's forty-five feet tall," John gestured with his hands as he described the size, "weighs six hundred-fifty tons and produces fourteen hundred kilowatts of electricity." He dropped his hands onto his lap. "You'll be using some of the electricity, so you should know what produces it." He shifted in his chair. "And don't just get captured by the machinery. Look for unexpected exhibits. Colorado will celebrate statehood. That should be interesting—it's a part of our country we know little about. And think of all the foreign countries. They'll be bragging, just as we are. Imagine what you can learn." He almost looked sorrowful when he asked, "Herb, would you do me a favor? Write down anything of interest and send it to me . . . or bring it back to save postage. I'm not going to make the trip. I'll have to see it through your eyes." He stopped, breathless, as he often did after fervently delivering full-fledged sentiments.

"I'll do my best." Herb thought of the machinery building, which he read covered thirteen acres. It was only one of 200 buildings. "I promise."

They quietly contemplated their individual thoughts until John asked, "What does your girl, Anna, think of your going?"

"I think I *can* finally call her my girl," Herb told him about their meeting, then hesitated. "I should tell you something more about Anna. I told you she works at city hall. I went there because I thought there might be something in the records about my father. She didn't find anything."

"Hmm, I knew you wanted to know more, but I didn't know your interest had gone that far. I'm sorry it didn't pan out."

"Anna's still working on it. Finding information is part of her job. Neither of us is optimistic, but we're going to keep going until we run out of clues."

"Your mother?"

"Questions about my father somehow upset her. I want to find what I can on my own."

John shook his head without saying anything.

"I'm putting aside my interest in my father while I go to Philadelphia. This will be an even bigger job than I imagined," he laughed. "I hope I have enough paper and ink powder for the encyclopedic reporting I've promised."

Herb left the Brannans, relieved that he had finally told John his interest in his father had taken a new form, but it still unsettled him every time he thought of it.

TWENTY-NINE

Philadelphia was sweltering, just as Professor Bell predicted. Even slight movement raised drops of moisture on Herb's brow, and exertion sent rivulets running under his arms and down his back. He and Tom Watson unspooled the stovepipe wire and strung it behind the walls in preparation to connect it from the transformer to the receiver for the demonstration from one room to another. The job took them two days. Watson and Herb could not do anything more until the machinery came from Bell.

The Exposition had designated judges for each category of invention. Those for electrical awards were to decide which, of all the electrical devices displayed, deserved medals. Economic success or failure was at stake for every inventor with each award, especially the top award of gold. Bell had also submitted a proposal for visible speech in the education field, and since it was not technical, demonstration could be done by others.

Assuring themselves that everything was as ready as possible without equipment, Herb and Watson left the hot, claustrophobic exhibit space to explore the World

Exposition. High temperatures had not diminished the crowds. So filled were the walkways that moving from one site to another was slow-going. Inside buildings, they pressed through throngs of enthusiastic spectators who inspected inventions, chatting and fluttering fans in lively back-and-forth conversations as they tried to understand the workings and applications of what they viewed.

The diversity amazed Herb. Some were logical ideas to save time and work, like an automated dishwasher, and some were as far-fetched as a portable bathtub for traveling. He scribbled notes in the small leather notebook Anna had given him for Christmas. It barely stayed in his pocket, with so much he wanted to pass on to her, his mother, and John.

Returning to their lodging after the second day of touring, they found a letter from Bell. Watson expectantly slit it open. Bell reported that he had packed all the necessary equipment and sent it off by a carter. He expected it to arrive by June eighteen, three days away, a few days earlier than Herb and Watson had anticipated. That news was followed by Bell's decision to stay in Boston to help his students prepare for their final examinations. Hubbard's nephew, Willie, would demonstrate the telephone in his absence. Herb and Watson looked at each other, shaking their heads.

"Hubbard will be furious when he finds out," Watson said. "Frankly, I don't understand how Bell can do this to his benefactor *and* future father-in-law."

The news worried Herb. "It's not good for demonstrations, is it?" he asked. *And maybe for my job.* Watson shook his head again. "Graham Bell's real desire is to help deaf people and promote visible speech." He ran his fingers through his hair. "Of course, simultaneously, or maybe secondarily—I'm not sure he knows which—he's committed to succeeding with the telephone." Watson sat down on the narrow bed. "Sometimes he's at the edge of a breakdown; he works so hard. He wants everything to be perfect before he tries to sell it—the opposite of Edison," Watson's jaw flexed with obvious dismay. "Edison starts promoting the minute he has an idea, long before he knows if it will work."

"Is Edison part of this competition?" Herb asked.

"Yes, Bell is up against the top inventors. Edison's quadruplex telegraph sends two electronic messages each way simultaneously, a valuable invention but not a transmission of voice. It's still worthy of a prize. Elisha Gray, from Western Electric, who submitted a patent request, has a concept design to transmit voice by electricity." Watson stood up and made small pacing pivots in the confined space. "There are many others. Dash it all; Bell will lose out if he isn't here to demonstrate! With one decision, he may throw away all our efforts."

They jumped at a loud knocking. Watson opened the door and took a yellow telegram. He read it, and his face dropped. "It's from Hubbard. He wants us to pick up Bell and Willie at the train station in half an hour. Let's go, Herb. I'm not sure who's going to notify Hubbard that only his nephew is coming."

Philadelphia's Market Street station was a melee of passengers coming from and going to the Exposition. Watson stood on the tips of his toes to try to see Willie over disembarking passengers.

"Mr. Watson, I've never seen Willie, but look over there. It's Bell, and he has a younger man with him."

Elbowing their way through the throng, they waved frantically. "Graham Bell, over here," Watson called.

Bell finally responded, bringing his companion in their direction.

"We thought you weren't coming," Watson said, sounding almost delirious. "You are a sight for sore eyes." He clapped the mercurial inventor on the back.

Bell scowled. "Mabel threatened not to marry me if I didn't come." He wiped his brow. "It's stifling, just like I said," he fumed. "I don't want to be here."

"We're most grateful you are," Watson said, reaching to take Bell's satchel from him. "Good day, Willie. Please meet our factotum, Herb Andersen. We'll take the streetcar to our lodging. We have work to do. The equipment is to arrive tomorrow."

Early the following day, the cart driver knocked at Bell's door. They rushed to open it, prepared to unload and put all the pieces in place. "It's not my fault," the hauler cried out, wringing his hands in despair.

"What's not your fault?" Watson asked.

"Damage. It was that way. Not my fault."

The four ran out to the cart to look. Lifting the tarp, they found their delicate equipment in a jumble of damaged cartons, some spilling broken implements. They stood silent in motionless misery while gay spectators passed by, oblivious to the catastrophe. "There's no chance of making the judging now." Bell held onto the edge of the cart, his knees folding in a near swoon. His voice was a mixture of despair and exhaustion.

"We're not giving up yet," Watson began opening boxes. "Herb, start moving boxes out to survey the damage. Graham Bell, assess what needs to be done. Willie, write it down," he almost shouted orders.

They spent the day frantically searching shops in Philadelphia to have some equipment repaired and to buy parts to fix what they could on their own. They tinkered for four days to make their equipment workable.

Judging had been scheduled for a Sunday when the Exposition was closed to the public. The four arose early to set up their repaired instruments. The sun's gold orb, low in the cloudless sky, promised intense heat. The room they chose to exhibit the receiver was designed with an oversized hood above a huge, multi-keyed organ. The room maximized acoustics but lacked ventilation. The space for the speaker was smaller but just as claustrophobic.

The four had stripped to their singlets, quickly damp with fresh perspiration. Herb stood with Willie in a larger room, ready to follow orders, watching Bell and Watson rush from one room to the other to ready the device. Herb's every muscle twitched. The two scientists made one delicate adjustment after another, hunched over either the receiver or the mouthpiece. All the while, the sun pierced the Machinery Hall's glass window panes. Tension was as high as the heat. An insistent knocking at the door made everyone jump. Without waiting to be invited, a heavyset man in colorful military regalia, replete with medals and gold-fringed epaulets, hurtled in.

"Alec!" the man's voice boomed. "I heard you were here and came to see what is happening."

"Dom Pedro? Do I imagine it?" Bell staggered up from his cramped position to greet the corpulent man with graying hair and beard.

"It *is* me," the animated man exclaimed. "I heard you were here and needed to know what you're doing."

"Let me introduce you to my assistants, Messrs Watson, Hubbard, and Andersen."

Herb felt his face flush at the promotion. *If only I were his assistant.*

Bell's face was radiant with astonishment. "Dom Pedro is the emperor of Brazil and a patron of the Exposition. I met him when he visited Boston to see my work with visible speech."

Dom Pedro vigorously shook each man's hand. "This looks like something different. Tell me—what are you doing now?"

While Bell explained his apparatus, Dom Pedro peeled off his heavy jacket. "Voice over wire. I don't believe it," he said. "You will have to prove it."

"All right, men, let's try it," Bell said. Willie took the emperor to the organ room and placed the receiver against his ear while Bell ran to the small room, out of sight, to use the speaker. Dom Pedro was silent, then shouted, "My God, it talks! Let me hear it again."

Just then, a scrawny young man entered through the already-opened door. "I've come with a message for Mr. Bell." He looked at each of the disheveled men, still wearing only their singlets, and at the emperor, who looked regal even without his jacket.

"I'm that man." Bell stepped forward and took the folded notepaper. "No." His shoulders slumped when he read it. "This just can't be true." Bell pressed his hand against his forehead; new lines showed around his dark eyes. "The heat is so oppressive that the judges have decided to postpone judging for the day."

"Wait, you're supposed to be the last one," Dom Pedro said. "It doesn't make sense. They've judged all the exhibits in electronics except yours."

The Brazilian, accustomed to tropical heat, seemed unbothered by the temperature. He grabbed his elaborate jacket, pulled it on his rotund body, and catapulted out the door. "I'll gather them," he said over his shoulder.

The astonished four men hurriedly donned their damp shirts, jackets, and ties and waited.

Within twenty minutes, Dom Pedro was back gleaming, the wilted and displeased judges in tow. Herb was unsurprised that they had found it impossible to turn down the emperor. He had read that Dom Pedro was both a sponsor and one of the celebrities with President Grant who had fired up the Corliss engine at the opening ceremony.

At first, the judges watched Bell demonstrate. All Herb's heat-soaked fatigue vanished. One by one, each judge demanded a turn using the speaker in the small room and then listening to the "magical contraption" emit sound from the receiver in the organ room. They split up to ensure no tricks were played. Three stood in the speaker room while the other half crowded into the one with the receiver. Each time, Herb could not breathe until he heard the machine work. The expressions of Bell, Watson, and Willie told him he was not the only one struggling to breathe normally.

The judges' rapid questions overlapped as they examined each piece of the apparatus. Once Bell had answered all their questions, the judges huddled by the outer door of the sweltering space, volubly conferring about the invention. Bell rested in a chair with his eyes closed. None of the four spoke.

Finally, the judges shook hands with one another, and a gray-bearded man, who appeared to be the leader, came over to Bell. "Mr. Bell, the committee awards your speaking telegraph the Exposition's gold medal for electronics. Congratulations. And a word to you," the whiskered judge declared. "This magnificent device must be demonstrated to everyone who comes to the Exposition. Without seeing what you call the telephone—or maybe I should say without hearing it," he chortled, "no one will possibly believe it."

Dom Pedro jumped up and down, making the floorboards sway. He exited with the judges. Herb heard his booming voice echoing as they moved down the hall.

Herb almost disbelieved what he had witnessed. "If it had not been for Dom Pedro," he mumbled.

Another knock at the door froze them. Their ebullience vanished like notes played on the organ. The skinny messenger who had brought the previous note extended his head through the doorway. "Mr. Bell, I was asked to deliver this before you left."

Herb's breath caught. Had the committee changed its opinion?

Trembling, Bell opened the envelope, unfolded the letter, and read it out loud. "The Centennial Exposition awards Visible Speech the gold medal in education!"

"Two gold medals! Electronics and education." They whooped, danced, and clapped the smiling Bell on the back, words tumbling out about the day's happenings. Then, they packed up. They would take the batteries, magnets, receivers, speakers, and containers of acidulated water to their lodging for safekeeping.

The heat was still oppressive when the four went to dinner after the judging. The World's Fair's eateries lured visitors to try unfamiliar food. While they rarely splurged on dining out, when they did, Herb and Watson were game for any foreign fare.

"I don't care if it's fish, fowl, or mammal, I'll try it," Watson exclaimed.

Willie demanded familiar food. "I won't eat anything I don't recognize," he pouted.

"Don't you even want to have one taste?" Watson once chided him.

"It could be worms or reptiles, for all I know," Willie replied while guarding his mouth with a napkin.

They had relied mostly on inexpensive markets, with their hanging tubes of sausages, cheeses, and loaves of bread. Rye and pumpernickel had become Herb's favorites. Friendly conversations came with their purchases from owners who understood thin budgets. Often, Herb ate dinner alone, sitting at the round wooden table in their apartment before Watson and Willie returned. Their lodging had no cooking facilities, and they could not keep anything perishable.

That night, they chose an inexpensive restaurant with American fare to celebrate. There was no money for anything extravagant. Herb experienced a newfound sense of belonging as they took turns telling stories about the elusiveness of new inventions. Each had memories of problems that, for months, defied solutions and sent them into despondency. Watson said, "We still have to sell the invention. The common attitude toward new things is apt to be pessimistic. The average man thinks what hasn't been done, *can't* be done, or perhaps doesn't *need* to be done."

More than triumph, Bell expressed relief—the judging was over, and the equipment had worked. "Perhaps now, people might believe and invest in voice over wires *and* visible speech," he said, and for the first time in a long time, he looked free of his persistent headache.

Hubbard's congratulatory telegram after learning of the awards was one of jubilation. *Your presence paid off. Money is bound to follow both projects.*

Bell merely nodded after reading it. "Willie and Tom, you can give the demonstrations for the rest of the Exposition. Herb, stay if you wish. I'm catching a train in the morning to return to my students . . . and Mabel."

Little lanterns flickered on and off along the pathway beside the Schuylkill River—dragonflies sending messages in the thick evening sky. All four men had gone to bed, but Herb could not sleep. Instead, he got up and went outside in his shirtsleeves to tamp down his churning emotions from the tension of Professor Bell's demonstration. Not until the final second was it certain the experiment would work as hoped. He began walking to consider the day and his future. Success was good news for Bell as the inventor and for Hubbard as the main investor. In addition, it was an opportunity for the public to experience verbal communication by wire. It was a new chapter for everyone, but the uncertainty of his future had kept Herb awake. With Willie at the Exposition, there was little need for another assistant and no money to pay him anyway. Herb's life always seemed to be an unanswerable question mark. How would he make ends meet? How should he build a future? Would he always be a sweeper? What about Anna? Why seek his father? He longed for a roadmap for the future instead of constant aimlessness.

Suddenly, his arms jerked out reflexively to catch himself as he hurtled forward. He barely maintained his balance. Breathing hard, he looked down. His foot had caught on a rough spot in the path in the dim light. Distracted by his thoughts, he had walked well beyond where most Exposition visitors came at night. Lamplight was scarce, with long stretches of obscurity ahead. He needed to turn back.

Walking often clarified his thinking, but he wasn't sure it had that night. Only one idea occurred to him for his future. The message board—a central place to post information or inquiries about the Exposition. It was all he could think of trying since job prospects in Brookline or Boston seemed futile. Spending time with Anna beckoned him, but he did not want to return as a failure, a former sweeper looking for a job. Besides, the ingenuity and determination of the inventions intoxicated him. He had to see more. Whatever he did had to be fast before money and time ran out.

The haze-dimmed sun had barely crawled up from the horizon when Herb walked to the message board in the morning. Night had done little to help cool the air. Under the eaves of the main building, organizers had hung an oversized cork board with slips of paper and tacks for messages. If he had not been so desperate for new employment, some of the notices would have made him laugh:

"Lost, one small black leather boot, right foot, size 3, kicked off during a temper tantrum."

"Lost, one drop pearl earring, given by a fiancé who may not be if the earring isn't found."

"Found, one top hat; a much superior article was taken. Please return the fine beaver hat in place of the inferior one of rabbit skin."

Most jobs did not match Herb's skills: seamstress, cook, expert woodworker, laundress, and dozens of others. Then, a neatly written card caught his eye. "Mechanic needed to make basic repairs. Inquire to David Mason at the Machinery Hall office. Reference required."

He had made repairs for his mother all his life and then for Shields. Tom Watson had taught him additional skills. He seemed to have a talent for repair work, but the advertiser would want someone with paid expe-rience, and Herb had no such reference. He choked at the humiliation of a reference from his mother. What about asking Watson? Would he consider it an affront? Herb copied the information before returning to his room.

The two men were waiting for him.

"We thought you'd abandoned us," Watson said. "Graham Bell just left. Join Willie and me for breakfast." He lifted his eyebrows. "Have you tasted the Liège waffles at the Belgian exhibit?"

"No, and I'm famished," Herb said, although uneasy about the cost.

"As always," Watson said with a smile. He picked up his coat and motioned to Willie.

"I was too busy absorbing everything to eat much at dinner last night." It was a slight apology; he knew teasing was a part of their friendship.

The steamy aromas of yeast, sugar, and coffee welcomed them at the small venue. They talked between bites of the syrup-drenched waffles and fried sausage.

Herb downed his first bite and then asked, "I'm thinking of applying for a job. What do you think?" He slid his penciled copy of the ad across the table to Watson.

"Hmm," Watson said after reading it. "I'd like to know what they mean by basic repairs." He took a careful swallow of his steaming coffee. "You better find out if there are guidelines. The way it's worded, it could mean anything, from the Corliss engine to a microscope." He searched the room for a waiter. "What about another round, gentlemen? This one's on me." He placed the order and said, "You have the ability, Herb; I'd see about it right away."

"What about the reference?"

"I'll write one; you've earned it, and now that Bell's name is on every-one's lips," Watson smiled, "my recommendation may even carry some weight." His smile grew wider when the waiter set three plates on the table. "If you get the job and run into problems with mechanics, we can consult." He cut a square of the waffle and popped it into his mouth.

"Just on the quiet, though," he mumbled around the bite. "I'm willing to problem solve, but I don't want another job. The telephone is all I can handle!"

Herb began eating rapidly.

"Are you trying for thirds?" Willie asked while Watson laughed.

"What's so funny? I need to go right away before someone else applies. If I get the job, I'll need to find a room."

"Room?" Willie asked. "Do you remember Bell's and mine? It's bigger than the one you're in now—not luxurious, mind you, but big enough for three of us for a few months. Do you agree, Watson?"

"No doubt at all. Splitting the rent three ways will help all of us. Good luck, Herb. We'd like to see you stay."

Herb set off at a lope to reach the Machinery Building before anyone else. Watson's hastily written reference did little to lessen his feeling like an imposter. Herb entered the office through the main entrance. He found a man sitting at a desk strewn with machinery, parts, and paper. Herb assumed it was the man whose name was on the advertisement. He wore a lightweight jacket without a waistcoat, apparently readying himself for another airless day.

"I'm Herb Andersen, here to see about the job. Are you Mr. Mason?"

The man nodded, scrutinizing Herb as he walked toward him.

"First off, did you bring a recommendation?"

Herb pulled out Watson's folded paper. Mason nodded toward the empty chair for Herb to sit and then lowered himself into a swivel-back chair on the other side of the desk. Recognition came to Mason's eyes as he read the brief lines. "Bell's assistant?" he asked.

"Yes, that's Mr. Watson."

"No, I mean you." Mason was a slender man; his gray hair was his most distinctive feature. Silky strands covered his head, floating down to his sideburns into a beard and a mustache that swept out on each side, dancing with the movement of his lips.

"No, sir." Herb shook his head. "I've been working for them as their handyman. I carry, clean, and fix things. I'm a general worker." Even those words might aggrandize his position, but he refused to say he was a sweeper.

"Well, let's see what you have to offer. I have a maddening pile of broken or flawed parts and other complaints about things malfunctioning throughout the site. You can work on these ones here, and we'll talk at the end of the day." He swiveled his chair around and stood up again. "Follow me to the workroom. I'll show you the forge and various other tools. There's running water here and a toilet outside, down the path. Find me in the office if you have questions; otherwise, I'll come back to the workroom in the early evening." He turned to leave but stopped. "Take a break for lunch, but let me know when you leave and return."

The workroom was dirt-floored, with rough brick walls. Like the rest of the Exposition, it had been recently built. Some tools hung on the wall; others were piled on the workbench. Parts of all sizes and compositions were jumbled on a long worktable in the middle. Herb took stock quickly. First, he mounted the rest of the tools on the wall in a systematic order, pounding in additional hooks when necessary. Next, he tackled the broken or non-working parts, separating them into three groups. In the first, he put things he believed he could fix right away. The second comprised work that would take more thought or parts. So far, so good, but the third, smaller pile worried him. He did not understand how the parts in that group malfunctioned. He groaned. *Maybe I should take a train back to Brookline.* Instead, he returned to the first pile and began fixing what lay on the table. He skipped lunch, cupping his hands beneath the tap whenever he needed to quench his thirst. Unlike Shields, Mason left him alone. He was exhausted, but when Mason returned at seven, Herb explained what he had done.

"I've fixed all these," he pointed to the newly repaired items. "With additional parts, I think I can fix these." He had arranged them in a neat row. "These at the end of the workbench," Herb swallowed back his nervousness, "have me puzzled. I might be able to fix some of them, but I'm not sure."

Mason stroked his mustache like a cat preening its whiskers as he surveyed the space Herb had straightened and organized.

"You say you *might* be able to fix these?" The supervisor picked up a metal contraption.

Herb wanted to say "yes" because he desperately needed the job. Instead, inspiration struck. "Would you let me take this one overnight and give it more thought?"

Mason gave his mustache another stroke. "Are you sure you'll bring it back? It's worth something, broken or not."

"I'll have it here in the morning, at seven."

Mason stuck out his hand. "All right. We'll talk about the job then."

They shook on it, and Herb left, carrying the metal pump. He wanted Watson's opinion, but he needed food first. His stomach pinched from hunger. He stopped at an understated market and bought four loaves of bread, a round of cheese, and a long cylinder of inexpensive salami. Unlocking the door of their lodging, he washed his hands and his tarnished pocket knife and then sagged down at the room's small table, tired and ravenous, and began cutting pieces of his purchases, arranging them in stacks—bread, a circular slice of salami, a slice of golden cheese—sampling pieces as he cut. He washed down the food with swallows of lukewarm water. After consuming the first loaf, he relaxed and reexamined the mechanical part. He scraped the rust off the pump and ran water through it but could not make it work.

Watson and Willie returned before Herb had finished eating. After examining the pump, Watson quickly identified a defective bolt. "I hate to guess how many malfunctioning mechanical gizmos are on this site." Watson shook his head in warning. "Broken parts and frustrated owners will take a thick skin. You'll get quite an education—trial by fire if you can stand the flames." He put the pump on the table. "Think about the hazards before you accept the job."

Convivial conversations about the day followed their meal until late. Herb stayed in the anteroom of their combined lodging after Watson and Willie said goodnight and had gone to bed. He sat on the couch and stretched his legs across the small round coffee table to reread Anna's latest letter. She had been faithful to her word about writing, as had he. His letters were enthusiastic but straightforward descriptions of daily events. By comparison, hers were chatty embellishments of what was happening at home and work. Even though she never asked, her words pulled at him to return to Brookline and Boston. He glanced at the pump lying on the table, wondering how many impossible tasks he'd face if Mason offered him the job. He mulled his options and then thought of the exhibitions he had not seen. It was already the end of June. The Exposition would end in a little over four months when the buildings would be dismantled, and exhibitors dispersed to global destinations. There was no question. He had to stay.

Twirling the ends of his mustache as he talked the next morning, Mr. Mason offered Herb the job at a dollar fifty a day, six days a week, with half an hour for lunch. "It's a trial. You're younger than I wanted, and if there are too many complaints, we'll part ways pronto." Mason fiddled with the blotter on his desk, hesitation in his voice. "You're to fix the working mechanics of the fair, not individual inventions. Orders for your work will come through me; I don't want exhibitors or inventors conning you to do something they're responsible for."

Herb swallowed hard and accepted the job, knowing he was a hire of convenience and likely to be let go when someone with more experience showed up.

Work *was* a trial by fire, as Watson had conjectured. Herb had to steel himself not to tremble when exhibitors stomped in Mason's office, red-cheeked with spittle-flying, complaining of malfunctioning equipment. The angrier the exhibitor, the less understandable his English, resorting to languages Herb could only guess at. "Go!" Mason would say, waving his arms at Herb. "Fix whatever it is. That's what I pay you for."

Herb quickly learned to shut out the exhibitors' expletives—most of which he could not understand. He worked on large and small equipment, slowly growing better and faster at troubleshooting. At the end of each long day, he wolfed down supper and collapsed into bed, his clothes stinking from exertion, tension, and the relentless Philadelphia heat.

"I knew I was wrong in hiring you," Mason said when Herb failed to make a repair, but he did not fire him. As weeks went on, the weather cooled, and, ever so slightly, praise from satisfied exhibitioners edged out belligerent complaints. Herb gained skills through his accidental apprenticeship. His need to consult Watson diminished but never completely ceased. There were repairs that even Bell's assistant declared "unfixable."

An occasional extra coin for his work added to his meager salary and protected his sanity after a day spent being called an "incompetent nincompoop," or probably worse, in unknown languages. He learned how to adroitly dodge offers of sub-rosa payment to fix the exhibitor's own equipment.

As his exhaustion lessened with experience, Herb stayed up later to share stories with Watson and Willie. They had plenty of tales to tell. Theirs were usually about visitors, turned giddy by a machine that carried sound or the miseries when the telephone failed to transmit sound.

Non-working equipment took Herb to many sites. Once a problem was solved, exhibitors relished explaining their varied displays. It was a private tour of an exhibit. Their contagious enthusiasm inspired Herb, especially when they described obstacles they had conquered before what they hoped to invent had succeeded and qualified for display at the Exposition.

At first, weariness and constant invective kept Herb's inkpots stoppered. "It's the worst of jobs and the best of jobs," he explained in letters to his mother, Anna, and John. "I hope I survive to the end." He wrote to John about the celebration of Colorado's becoming the Centennial State on August first. Herb chuckled, remembering that John had suggested that he might consider Colorado Territory for college, where there was less competition than in more populated areas. In a letter to his mother, he reminded her of the jigsaw puzzle she had given him of Pikes Peak, and he wrote to Anna about the Colorado exhibition, which depicted breathtaking landscapes unlike anything he had experienced. To all, he wrote of meeting Nathaniel Hill, who, he learned, served on the Centennial Commission to finally bring Colorado to statehood.

Herb had been sent to the Colorado exhibit to resize frames and cases that did not meet the exhibitor's requested dimensions. He spent the first day in the machine shop adjusting them.

"Can you give me a hand in inserting the pictures and hanging them?" Hill asked when Herb returned the frames. Herb hesitated, unsure of Mason's reaction, but soon agreed to help the affable man, who was enamored of his adopted mountain home. Herb found the panoply of geography within the new state astonishing, made all the more vivid by Hill's enthusiastic descriptions as they put paintings in frames. Cases displayed minerals and unfamiliar animal furs, like bison and antelope, feathers from birds like the magpie, and dried specimens of columbines and other plants. Hill described all those and also agricultural products. A natural raconteur, he told Herb that he had been Brown University's professor of chemistry. Despite his prestigious position, he had succumbed to the first territorial governor's invitation to join a party prospecting in southern Colorado in 1864. They failed to find gold, but Hill had become intrigued by the difficulty of extracting metal from ore. "Chemicals bound the precious metals to the ore," he said, taking a piece of ore from the case as an example. The problem had seemed unresolvable, and with it, the viability of the territory.

"I wish my wife, Alice, were here," he interrupted his story. "She'd know how to arrange these to interest visitors." He grunted as he leaned over to rearrange the shelves. He was portly, with a drooping, bushy mustache laced with gray. Otherwise, he was cleanly shaven, and his receding hairline showed an expanse of bare skin. Herb guessed he was in his fifties.

"I didn't invent anything but found a process that worked. The Swansea system of smelting rescued mining and the territory." Finished with the display, he reached for his jacket that he had slung over the back of a chair. "Everyone thought we'd become a state shortly after that, but that was not the case. One proposal after another failed. Here we are, fifteen years after it was named a territory, finally a state."

"You should be proud of the exhibit, Mr. Hill." Herb put on his jacket. "Everyone who sees it will be tempted to visit, or even move there."

"It's a place of new starts, discovery, harsh reality, and whatever else you make of it." Hill reached into his pocket. "I had cards made to give to Exposition visitors. Take one and look me up if you ever venture west. Thanks for your help. I'll let Mr. Mason know I'm pleased." His broad smile revealed even teeth. "I confess I was in a swivet when I went to him demanding help."

THIRTY-ONE

The Exposition's closing month of November had a carnival atmosphere. Cold weather had turned Indian summer into winter in a snap, but exuberant crowds of over 100,000 people a day braved the cold, and often rain, determined to get a last view. Closing brought a natural letdown from the excitement of exhibiting. Some had been there for the entire six months, others less. Tempers grew short with the work of dismantling. People who would never see each other again said their last goodbyes; regret of leaving and anticipation of returning home hung in the air. Carters were in high demand. Herb was tempted to suggest Sinclair Cartage to transport Bell's equipment but more wisely left the decision to Watson.

Herb's duffel bag was packed and latched, resting near the door two days after the closing. Despite the lodging's small size, it had suited the trio. Confined spaces and work tension rarely resulted in discord. Their conversations centered on science and considering future inventions. Ideas flowed so readily that occasionally they all talked at once. "One at a time," Tom Watson, the natural leader, commanded to their laughing response. Herb regretted that those mind-elevating discussions had come to an end. Willie planned to return to earn his degree from Harvard, and Watson intended to devise additional parts for the telephone.

"I want to come up with something to let people know there's a call. We can't expect someone to sit with a receiver to his ear, waiting for someone at the other end to say something," he remarked, with his usual zeal for invention and a pinch of humor. "What's next for you, Herb?"

Herb envied his teammates' smooth progress up to the next rung. Watson's question daunted him as if "what's next?" was his life's motto. He shrugged. "Back to Brookline or Boston, most likely. Searching for a job in a tight market." His spirits flagged. "Maybe someone needs a sweeper."

"You know what occurred to me," Watson interjected. "What about querying Charles Williams? You worked in his building, even though it was for Graham Bell."

"About being a sweeper?" Herb tried to joke, but it sounded snappish.

"After so many months away, I don't know what's available, and I may go there myself to tinker with my ideas about a ringer." Watson's tone was consoling. "Don't forget how much you've learned about mechanics and the nature of man—or men, from all over the world." He smiled. "I'd be glad to write up my impression of what you've learned and what you offer. You couldn't fix everything thrown at you, but you fixed a lot, kept learning, and never gave up. Those are inestimable qualities."

"I agree," Willie added. "You've developed a new sense of yourself since you came."

Impulsively, Herb thrust out his hand to shake theirs. "Thanks. I still can't believe my luck in rooming with you or being at the Exposition." Herb knew what they said was true. He felt a pride of accomplishment and new confidence. If only an employer would see that and hire him for something other than sweeping.

"Okay, gentlemen, it's time to catch the train," Watson said. "Centennial planners must consider the Exposition a success."

"America should be pleased, too," Willie added. "The world will hear more from this country going forward." He closed and locked the door for the final time.

Wrapped in their warmest coats and mufflers, the three walked down the road to the station, stopping at the office to leave the key and the Exposition behind them.

The afternoon of Herb's return, frost shimmered on the bare November tree branches. He walked home from the Brookline train station, calmed by the familiarity of the natural beauty. Even though it was cold and stark, the surroundings were a release from the constant pressing of crowds and buildings. He could not deny that there had been a certain exhilaration of meeting pressure-filled demands . . . of the next challenge . . . of the latest mind-sparking invention . . . and of the effort to make stress elevate instead of defeat him. He would never forget the Exposition but had had enough of it and of Philadelphia.

Opening the front door for the first time in five months, Herb stepped onto the worn Brussels hallway carpet, calling out to his mother so he would not startle her, even though he had written her when to expect him. The aroma of dinner cooking pulled him like a magnet.

Sally, as he occasionally and teasingly called her, had made a trip to Philadelphia in early September with three friends she knew from Lyceum lectures. Herb had been able to see her once for a quick lunch together during her three days at the Exposition. Lunchtime was usually fictitious time off. Frantic exhibitors constantly pulled him from one site to another, demanding repairs every minute of the day.

When she heard Herb's voice in the foyer, his mother rushed into the hallway and wrapped him in her familiar hug, one arm around his back, the other across his shoulders, her cheek against his, the assurance of her presence warming his heart.

During dinner, she wanted to know more, ardently asking his opinions about what she might have missed during her visit and beyond what he had written in letters.

"And now what?" she asked him.

Herb had an odd sense about her question. Natural curiosity was in the gently phrased query, but he noticed reservation—a subtle shift in their relationship as if his plans would affect hers. During the meal, he had told her Professor Bell had returned to his family's home in Brantford, Ontario, Canada, to experiment more with the telephone in his laboratory there. "I've heard he's working on increasing the range—he calls it a long-distance call." He put his utensils on his empty plate. "He'll be back in Massachusetts, off and on. Mabel's here, and he can't stay away. They've set a date to be married next July." Herb gulped down envy of Bell's commitment, wishing it were his own to get married. "Watson will travel with Bell when he demonstrates the speaking machine."

She frowned. "Are you disappointed not to be working with them any longer?"

"Yes and no," he said. "I didn't expect it. Professor Bell still can't afford another worker. Hopefully, finances will change with his two first-place prizes. Unfortunately, I can't wait around until that day comes." Herb finished dinner and leaned back in his chair, satiated. He curled his fingers to comb the crumbs from his bushy mustache, looking across the table at his mother and guessing why she was concerned. "He gave me a bit of a lead."

"Professor Bell or Mr. Watson?"

"Mr. Watson. That's what I call him when anyone is around; when it's just us, he's Watson. I owe him a lot. He taught me skills in both Boston and Philadelphia. I might not have kept my job there without him." The memory of working with the scientist who was almost as well-known as Bell still gave Herb chills. At the Exposition, he'd only asked him for help as a last resort. When Watson had given advice, it had been collaborative, with Herb learning from problem-solving together rather than stepping aside while Watson did the work.

Herb's attention returned to his mother. "He's suggested I see if Charles Williams is hiring. Remember, that's where I worked before Philadelphia, but I worked for Bell, not Williams. Of course, Watson hasn't been employed at Williams for half a year and has no idea if the machine shop is hiring, but he's written me a letter of recommendation. Since I worked in the third-floor garret, Williams might even recognize me."

"What a relief." His mother clasped her hands as if it were a sure thing rather than a potential interview.

He straightened in his chair. "Be careful not to get too optimistic, Mum. Williams may have nothing. The economy is still in a squeeze." He grasped the irony of warning *her* to be realistic while straining to rein in *his* racing hopes. It was a bit of a stretch, dreaming that his experience qualified him to be a mechanic in Williams Machine Shop. He certainly could not take over for the irreplaceable Thomas A. Watson. Herb's ideal would be a job below mechanic, but somewhat similar. "I'll go to Williams the day after tomorrow. I need a day to catch up." He stroked his mustache idly. "And I've been writing to Anna." His earnestness rang in his ears. "Now that I'm not in Philadelphia, I've asked her to send letters here."

She smiled supportively. "Your future is unfolding." Her violet eyes reflected her pride in him.

He guessed only with effort did she suppress questions—she was willing herself not to intrude. Instead, she pushed back her chair and stood up, smoothing her skirt. "I wish you the best of luck on both fronts. I can't wait to hear more news." She began taking empty dishes to the sink.

Her well-intentioned words made Herb cringe. If he and Anna kept up their project, the future might involve his mother in ways she did not suspect nor he could predict. He took his dishes to the sink. "Good night, Sally . . . Mum," he murmured and went upstairs to the peace of his solitary bedroom for the first time in almost half a year.

Anna was the bold one. They had been plotting throughout their correspondence regarding how to get together in Boston, but options were scarce, and the consequences worrisome. Herb had an unnerving suspicion that if they met without a chaperone—no, if they even met—Anna's father or one of her brothers, all of whom he imagined to be as big and muscular as Sam, would hunt him down and shoot him . . . or maybe only pummel him. That notion was far-fetched. More likely, it would be the end of their relationship. Anna had written that her parents had established a list of suitors for her to meet at their Catholic church or social gatherings. The pressure on her to choose someone was mounting. She feared if she did not decide on her own, her parents would do it for her.

No one comes close to you in intelligence and personality, she'd written in her most recent letter. It had not taken him long to tick off characteristics her parents would consider shortcomings. He was not Irish or Catholic and worked as a sweeper or, at best, an odd-job man. Maybe even his lack of a father would count against him. It was easy to believe that he was cursed by the ongoing shortage of jobs and everything hoped for was unattainable. He was without social influence to open doors. His life seemed out of his control.

The best suit he had taken to Philadelphia now revealed wear in the elbows, knees, and cuffs, even when he stood out of direct light. He needed a new suit, but it would have to wait. Tom Watson's letter to Charles Williams was tucked carefully in his pocket. He would happily return to the business at 109 Court Street, only blocks from Boston University.

He paused in front, gathering the courage to meet with Williams. He had come up with a justification for being hired. Since there had been profit in equipment for the telegraph, there would be for the telephone, too, but so far, Herb could not think of what else would be needed. Watson, he knew, was working on a ringer to announce a phone call. That necessity was evident, yet Watson had not devised a way to create it. If the telephone became popular, there would be other add-ons. He straightened his tie; he had no inventions to present but had to get on with it. He entered the front door.

The man behind the desk was slender and middle-aged, with smooth black hair and a trim mustache. Herb's immediate impression of him was one he had experienced when delivering messages after school—a desk clerk's job was to protect those inside from outsiders rather than to welcome strangers.

"I'm Herb Andersen. I have a letter from Mr. Watson. Tom Watson. He recommended that I see Mr. Williams." Herb saw the man's look shift from ennui to interest.

"Ah, Mr. Watson, one of our favorites. Do you have an appointment with Mr. Williams?" he asked, doubt returning to his eyes.

"No, I'm sorry," Herb apologized. "I just returned from the Philadelphia Exposition the day before yesterday." Herb noticed that mention gained him one more notch of credibility. "I came as soon as I could."

"May I see Mr. Watson's letter?" The clerk took the letter from Herb, turning it in his hands to inspect it. "Let me speak to Mr. Williams. I don't know his schedule. Wait here."

Herb watched the man, who had never introduced himself, walk down the hall. He had a military bearing but a stiff gait. His left knee didn't bend, as if injured, maybe in the war. Herb waited, wishing he had used the train station lavatory after two cups of morning coffee.

After a few minutes, the assistant limped back. "Follow me. Mr. Williams is willing to accommodate you."

Down the hallway, they entered a modest room, spare in furnishings. There was a desk and three hard-back chairs. Shelves, cluttered with mechanical devices, filled two walls, and curtained windows the opposite walls. Mr. Williams came around his desk, extending his hand in a warm gesture.

"Mr. Watson speaks well of you," he said. "Have a seat so we can talk." He pointed at the chair opposite his desk. "Thank you, Mr. Burrows," he said to the lingering assistant. From the curious expression on the man's face, Herb suspected he would have liked to stay and see how the interview went; instead, he withdrew, gently latching the door behind him.

Williams was dressed in an informal, dark suit and appeared more like a tradesman than a business executive. He had thick, brown hair, a similarly colored mustache and beard that flowed together, almost hiding his mouth. Herb guessed he was in his mid-forties.

"Mr. Watson said you're seeking employment. Why don't you describe some of your skills?"

"You may remember that I worked here on the third floor before the Exposition. My job was mostly cleaning up, but Watson . . . Mr. Watson, taught me how to fix equipment and even about the workings of the telephone. At the Exposition, I had a job repairing an assortment of equipment, mechanical and otherwise." Herb kept his posture erect, feeling more confident than he usually did during an interview. "I'm interested in mechanics and inventions." He took a deep breath and decided to take the plunge. "I know your company designs equipment for the telegraph, and Professor Bell's telephone will also need mechanical devices. I want to work on those."

"Have you considered any devices the telephone might need?" Mr. William's smile broke through his coalesced beard and mustache.

Herb felt his cheeks warm. "It's so new; it's hard to imagine what extras will be needed until people start using it, but understanding how the telephone works will help me think of things."

It was a bluff, and he knew it; Mr. Williams probably did, too.

Williams paused. "We have enough tinkerers around here. My only need is for someone to clean up after them."

Everything inside Herb constricted. "I hoped for something more after my work at the Exposition." He needed a job and should take *any* offer, especially at the well-known Williams Machine Company, but he couldn't restrain himself. He needed to take a step up, not down. Only then could he have a future with Anna.

The room was quiet. Herb almost broke it by blurting out, "I'll take it. Anything." But he did not.

"How old are you?"

"Twenty-one last August."

"Just under half my age." Williams rubbed his whiskers. "I remember the age; the title can be as important as the job."

His hesitant pause sent a touch of acid to Herb's throat.

"I think I have room for an assistant," Williams said with a smile. "Assistance cleaning up and keeping things straight, and possibly just a little time to fix things and tinker." He raised his hand firmly. "Your pay depends on the first two. And that will be two dollars a day, half an hour for lunch, and six, twelve-hour days." His expression was paternal. "In time, there may be an increase, depending on what transpires."

"Thank you, Mr. Williams. I'll earn my pay." He stood as Williams rose, and they shook hands. Herb had wanted to be a mechanic, but the title assistant was better than a sweeper. He probably would have had nothing without a recommendation from Watson.

"See Burrows on the way out and tell him to add you to the payroll at starting pay. Be here tomorrow, and I'm afraid there will be some catching up to do as . . . assistant," Williams said as he sat down and began looking through papers on his desk. Herb thought he saw a slim smile, but it was hard to tell through all the whiskers.

The morning was cool and still. Herb was buoyed by getting a job quickly and, at the same time, daunted by the decisions ahead of him. Some were easy, like a stop at the Brookline tailor to buy a suit. His mother would have obliged a request to order one, but maintaining the independence he'd established in Lowell and regained at the Exposition felt urgent. And he had almost a full day before starting work.

"Good morning, Mr. Iverson," he greeted the owner as he stepped inside. "I've come to order a suit."

"Good morning, Herb. Welcome back from Philadelphia. Talk of the telephone is on everyone's lips."

Herb looked with envy at the tailor's tapered dark jacket trimmed with a checked collar, cuffs, and coordinating plaid trousers. His lean physique showed off his clothing like a calling card for his and his wife's stitching talents. A perennial tape measure hung around his neck, and powder ringed the trouser pocket where he kept his marking chalk.

He looked Herb up and down with a smile. "I see you've gotten quite a bit of use from the last suit I made for you. Tell me, is the suit for a special occasion?"

"Just every day. My new job starts tomorrow at Williams Machine Shop." The lowly position did not lessen his sense of pride.

"Splendid. The scientists at Williams are the talk of the town."

"Since it's a mechanical shop, the suit needs to be something that can take physical work." Herb was sure it was obvious that physical work meant "clean-up man," but he could not hold back saying, "I'm an assistant."

"Good for you. Let's take a look at what would be appropriate."

The small shop run by Iverson and his wife was filled. Sketches of different clothing designs for both men and women covered the walls, touting the newest fashions, suggesting that even recent styles were out-of-date and should be replaced. Rows and rows of fabric samples, from silks to wools, hung from racks. Most of them, Herb knew, cost more than he could afford.

Iverson unhooked a sample for Herb to examine. "The brown especially doesn't show soil."

Herb rubbed the sample between his fingers and several nearby.

"You know, Herb, when you and your mother moved to Brookline, and you delivered messages after school, I knew you'd make something of yourself. The whole town did. It's good to see you on your way."

"Thank you." *On my way, slower than sludge.* "I think you're right about the brown. How much is it?" Herb closed his eyes, preparing for the answer.

"Three dollars for a jacket and pants. I'm sorry. I know that's a great deal, but it's an investment. It can be worn to work and is smart enough to wear to church or out in the evening. Adding a waistcoat would only be another fifty cents."

He thought of Anna. "I'll order the suit. And the waistcoat." He hesitated. "I don't have much with me, not even a dollar."

"Give me what you have, and I'll write a receipt. Let's take new measurements—you keep gaining muscles. Bring the remainder when you come in for the fitting."

Herb worried about managing a fitting in his lunch hour but slid his coins into Iverson's palm before standing in front of the looking glass to be measured.

When he finished with his tape measure, Iverson said, "Congratulations, Herb. You make Brookline proud."

Herb rolled his eyes. *A born salesman.* "Thanks, Mr. Iverson. I'll see you next week." He opened the door, making the bell jingle again.

His next errand was a stop at the bank to deposit the little he had saved in Philadelphia. He planned to contribute financially and assist Sally with maintenance projects, even when he had a place of his own. Then, like a serpent raising its head, he wondered how the research into his father's background would affect their relationship. He had been able to put those thoughts aside during the hectic atmosphere in Philadelphia, but they had reappeared with his return to Brookline.

At home, his mother was reading the newspaper on the couch in the library when he told her of his job.

"An assistant? That's good news, Herb. To whom?"

"No one, and everyone." The irony was clear. "It's cleaning up again. I can't seem to get past the bottom rung." He plopped down on the couch next to her. "It may not be that bad, certainly not as peeving as working for Shields. And, I won't have my ears scorched from swearwords, like at the Exposition." Recollections of furious reactions to impossible requests still made his heart pound. "Keeping that job was miraculous, but I wish I had a chance to use what I learned in Philadelphia as an occupation."

The skin at the edge of her eyes crinkled sympathetically. "With jobs so short, it's hard to be picky." She folded the newspaper and put it on the table beside her. "Are you discouraged or hopeful?" She seemed relaxed and relieved that he had found a job, although he guessed she must be tired of repeating his latest job was a stepping stone to something better.

"I like what goes on at Williams. Inventors are interesting, and my first meeting with Mr. Williams was favorable. He was willing to be flexible about a title, if not the job. I'll start low, but he hinted about opportunities to rise." Herb stroked his mustache. "Maybe Mr. Williams realized that working under fire at the Expo gained me more than mechanical skills." Herb let himself remember some of his newfound skills—how to stand his ground, negotiate, and judge what could be fixed. He could have added keeping a handkerchief close by to wipe off the spittle that flew in his face from the lips of a shouting customer.

His mother nodded. "I was impressed with your confidence when I visited."

Herb felt an undercurrent of tenseness since his return from Philadelphia. Their conversations seemed stilted and forced, like two wires touching and sending off sparks without relaying a message. He could not identify anything specific causing his mother's unease, but her mood, in tandem with Anna's research, unsettled him. He was tempted to divulge what he had learned and demand that she fill in the missing pieces . . . if she could . . . or would. Constantly living life in uncertainty sapped his spirit. It was time for him to be on his own, whether the past was uncovered or not.

His earlier time at the Charles Williams Machine Shop with Bell and Watson was so brief that Herb knew little about the building, but he learned more with his new job. Williams had moved to 109 Court Street in 1862 because he had outgrown his building. Businesses in 109 Court's other floors included a battery manufacturer, periodical dealer, clothing wholesaler, and paper box manufacturer. William's office was on the floor above a billiard hall.

The specialized machinery on the third floor catered to inventors and entrepreneurs who worked on experimental designs, especially for the telegraph. Of the ten men, Herb was the lowest. He cleaned, ran errands, and repaired equipment while the others tinkered to get their inventions to operate. Yet, it was different from the university. Mr. Williams introduced him to everyone as a full-fledged member of the team, whereas Shields treated him like a lower-class dunce. The tinkerers, as the ten men called themselves, nicknamed Herb "Mr. Fix-it," with a hint of humor and a dose of respect.

The lab's layout was the same as when he worked for Bell and Watson—machines, tables, and ceilings laced with wires, but schedules and personalities were different, even though Bell and Watson were often there. Learning the routine preoccupied Herb's time, but seeing Anna again filled his mind. Since he was back, they were determined to meet regularly but had not resolved how. Her parents would be suspicious if she frequently asked to spend the night with Agnes.

Besides, weekly meetings are too much to ask of Agnes, even though she has become curious about 'the research.' Anna had written. *What about Sundays? After early church at the Cathedral, parishioners, especially young people, gather to make baskets for the poor. I can join in putting them together. As congregants go out to deliver them, I'll take a detour to the park pavilion. It's covered and has benches. We'll have to wrap up during the cold days, but it might give us an hour together.*

Herb had wasted no time in responding. *It's a risk, but let's try next Sunday.*

At the end of the week, Herb told his mother he was going to Boston to see Anna for a short time on Sunday but offered to do projects before and after his afternoon meeting with John Brannan—his first in five months.

Herb caught the earliest train into Boston on Sunday and arrived in the pavilion at the time they had set. He strode up and down the structure, beating his gloved hands together and watching his frosty breath spiral away with each exhale in the mid-November cold. Anna had been right about bundling up. Even in his warmest clothing, he was cold. At first, Anna's lateness did not concern him, but after fifteen minutes, his mind painted dire scenarios. Had her parents discovered her plan? Had something at church prevented her from coming? Or had he confused the meeting place?

Herb scanned the park for other structures but saw nothing he could have mistaken as the pavilion. Turning back to look toward the cathedral, his worry changed to joy. She was a block away, her skirt and coat swirling around her boots in her fast, barely ladylike pace. He walked quickly down the two steps and onto the path, his long strides unencumbered by petticoats and skirts. When they were close, he shoved his gloved hands in his pockets to resist embracing her. The cold and her fast walk made her cheeks rosy. *She's even more beautiful than I remembered.* Silently, they walked to the pavilion from the lawn. He took her arm at the two marble steps to keep her from tripping, reveling in the momentary chance to touch her. They sat on the bench six inches apart—without physical contact, yet he could feel her warmth. The cold had reduced the number of Sunday strollers, but there were some. They had to maintain propriety.

"Thanks for suggesting a place to meet. I'm delirious about seeing you." He paused, smiling. "Although we may freeze and look like sculpted figures to match the marble here." His whole being responded to her presence.

"Except for being together, it wasn't such a great idea." She laughed. "Everywhere warm is closed on Sundays, apart from some of the pubs and churches, and, of course, we can't go to either." She shifted to face him directly. "Speaking of church, do you mind that I'm Catholic? And Irish?" Her expression told him she was serious.

"We went to church only occasionally while I was growing up," Herb answered. "Religion wasn't part of my upbringing. As far as my heritage is concerned, I don't know exactly what it is. So, neither is something I have a strong opinion about."

"Some people do care ... strongly."

"Do you care that I'm a sweeper and don't know who my father is?"

"Of course not." A nudge with her gloved fist sent electric waves through him. "You're smart and have so many possibilities. I hope I get to see all the things you'll do."

"Thanks for your confidence."

She nodded and then sat up straighter. "Is it okay to go over some of what I've learned? I've written it out in charts, but it's too cold to go over them outside."

"I remember your charts. I've missed them," Herb said wryly. "You'll have to tell me everything to satisfy my curiosity. It's been growing for five months. You only hinted at things in your letters."

"I'm sorry I was so circumspect." Fine lines creased her brow. "You can never tell who will read something; I was leery about mentioning names."

He was eager to hear what she had to say.

"There are a lot of Irish maids; some people think it's the only thing Irish girls can do, as I've said before." Her look was one of disgust. "I've worked for months using Agnes's address, contacting and asking questions of Irish maids in Providence."

"I wonder what Miss Hall thinks about all the mail."

"That's a good question, and we have to be careful. There has not been that much. I'm frustrated that the girls I sent letters to aren't quick to answer, if at all. And, too often, I followed scant information that led to families unrelated to what we're looking for."

"I wish this hadn't taken so much work."

"You know I like following clues," she smiled. "That finally paid off. I received a letter from a girl whose friend has worked for a Sinclair family in Providence for five years. When I wrote her friend, I was careful not to ask for too many details—not wanting to raise alarms by seeming to pry." Anna's expression was solemn. "One morning at work, Agnes slipped me a letter—from the girl who worked for the Sinclairs. The head of the family is the owner of Sinclair Cartage. She described him as still having most of his hair and a full mustache. His wife, Eugenia, is slender and pretty for her age. They have three grown children: two sons living with their families in Ohio and a daughter who travels and visits occasionally. Sometimes, Mr. Sinclair's business takes him to Boston, leaving Mrs. Sinclair alone. My contact found the Sinclairs pleasant to work for."

When Anna stopped, they were both quiet.

"I don't know what to make of it," Herb said. He blew on his gloved hands. The temperature had notched up, but sitting on the marble bench chilled them. "You've spent a lot of time uncovering this. I'm grateful." He searched her eyes. "Why are you doing all this work?"

"I'm a natural researcher—in school and at my job. I always get involved with my projects." She hesitated. She carried a muffler of soft rabbit fur on a cord attached to one wrist and stuck her gloved hands in opposite ends with a shiver. "That's part of it, but it's mainly because I care about what it means to you." She held his eyes until he looked away.

"Frankly, I'm grasping to figure out what it means. We've discovered a man who travels to Boston, where my mother and I happened to live for most of my life." He was shifting around on the bench, from cold or agitation he could not tell. "Sally—I've started calling her that more lately—also happens to travel to Boston now that we've moved, and to Providence . . . for more than meetings." That thought made him stand up. "I envy all those layers women wear. They must make the bench warmer and softer." He rubbed his hands against his backside, which had become numb from the cold. "Did I tell you that when I applied to college—I wasn't accepted because of finances?" He knew he scowled when he said it. "There was a financial connection in Providence that my mum, Sally, seemed certain would help at first. When money did not come, she was more than disappointed, almost angry." Herb shrugged. "That's my impression. She didn't explain it, and I'm not sure it has relevance."

Anna stood up, excitement in her blue eyes. Together, they paced alongside the pavilion's rows of carved Corinthian columns. "I've had many situations in my job where you think a clue means something, and it turns out to be nothing. We need to learn more." They had come to an end of the pavilion, turned, and started the other way, side by side but not touching.

"We need to find out if Mr. Sinclair and my mother were in Boston and Providence at the same time."

"Even if they were, it could still be a coincidence rather than a meeting, but it's a start." Anna looked at him seriously. "As we get information, I'll add it to my chart."

He gave her a teasing grin. "I knew your chart would figure into this somehow." They both started to laugh, but the moment's importance stopped them.

"The hour went fast." Anna gave an extra wrap to the scarf around her neck. "I must get back to church. Let's check the weather next week to see if we can meet here again. Ugh, it's just the beginning of winter." She gave a sideways motion of her hand for a goodbye instead of saying anything and stepped down to the sidewalk.

More than anything, he wanted to walk beside her as a companion, a friend, a lover, but it was not allowed.

THIRTY-THREE

Returning home, he discovered his mother moving fur-
niture in the kitchen. "What are you *doing*?" His teeth
still chattered from time in the park and the unheated
rail car from Boston to Brookline. "Do you need help?"
He stood close to the stove's warmth, unwilling to part
with his outer wraps. Her brown checked work dress
showed areas of mending and fit more snuggly than he
remembered. A measuring rod lay on the floor, a piece
of chalk in her hand. "While you were in Philadelphia,
I looked hard at how tawdry this place is getting." She
put her hand against her back as if it ached from bending while she measured. "Mr. Abernathy isn't a bad
owner, but he's not going to do anything unless forced
to." She pointed at the floor. "The wood is almost worn
away." Herb noticed chalk marks in a line. "It's paper thin,
except under the table."

She explained that the owner would not replace the
wood but had agreed to pay for linoleum to be laid on top
with adhesive. "It comes in attractive patterns and is easy
to clean. That's why it's known as sanitary flooring." She

sat on one of the chairs at the edge of the room where she had moved it to measure. "I chose a pattern, and Mr. Abernathy ordered it. It's supposed to arrive tomorrow. Would you consider installing it for me? The baseboards must be removed and put back on, and the floor will need a light sanding before you apply glue." She wiped drops of perspiration from her brow.

"I'd be happy to," he said, stuffing his gloves in his pockets before unwrapping himself from his coat. He felt warm for the first time in hours. "We had linoleum at the university, although I never installed it. It shouldn't be hard."

She looked somber, but her violet eyes flickered with relief. "I hate to ask you to work around here when you have a new job, but new flooring would improve where I spend so much time." She looked around the kitchen again with a dissatisfied expression. "Look at all the nicks and scratches on the wall—they were here when we moved in, but recently, I've learned of a new product similar to linoleum that's embossed, called Lincrusta and used for wainscotting. Mr. Abernathy said I'd have to wait until the beginning of the year before he'd pay for that. Linoleum and Lincrusta would be like having a fresh, new kitchen!"

Herb took out his pocket watch. He had a couple of hours. "Let me change my clothes. I can at least take stock of what needs to be done and get out my tools before going to John's."

Once Herb had changed into the clothes he'd worn routinely at the university, he got on his hands and knees, checking the figures his mother had noted. Everything was exact, except that she had not accounted for an extra half inch to go under the baseboard. He also realized he would have to borrow a jack to get the linoleum under the stove. After recording the measurements, he returned the table and chairs to their original position. His mother had left him on his own to work.

When he was doing chores as a young boy, she had hovered over him, advising him what to do. Her talking had made him unable to think, and in a rare fit of temper when he was twelve, he refused to do chores unless she let him figure things out by himself. She had sent him to his room without dinner for being impertinent, but after that, she let him work on his own. It was a routine they had maintained.

For Herb, working on projects was time for contemplation. The quiet allowed him to consider how to complete the task and settle any extraneous thoughts somersaulting through his mind. Today, Anna's vision lingered. Spending time with her made him hunger for more time together. He had to find an easier way to see her.

Other problems jumbled his mind. He brooded over the information Anna had uncovered. In frustration, he shoved a chair out of the way of his marking stick. He had to work up the courage to ask his mother questions. *Do you know William Sinclair? Have you ever met with him? If so, do you still?* Herb's gut twisted as his hypothetical questions progressed. *What was . . . is your relationship?*

The task of measuring the floor was simple compared to the complications of his personal life. When he was through, he lined up his tools, ready to remove the baseboard before dinner, and then went upstairs to change his clothes again.

<hr />

John Brannan greeted Herb with a bear hug. "Come in, come in. Eliza says I've become a grump on Sunday afternoons without male conversation. She's heated mulled cider for us. Let's go to my study; there's no time to waste. The Exposition, the telephone, a new job. Tell me all of it!"

You've mentioned only half of what's going on in my life. Herb sighed.

For over an hour, Herb relayed all that had happened since they last met. Explaining it crystallized what he had gained in five months. He described sitting in the same room with Alexander Graham Bell, possibly the most talked about man in America at that moment, and how the great man, not so much older than himself, had struggled to make his invention work. Then he moved on to his fix-it job at the Exposition, which had provided him with new skills and a thicker skin. Last, he explained how he felt about being relegated to sweeping again, this time with better prospects if he could think of something to invent.

"I'm astonished! So much in such a short time. Good on you. And, I want more details down the road, but I'm not sure an invention is the only way—"

"If you don't mind, I'd like to tell you more—not about work." Herb's face must have looked grim because he saw John's eyes change from softly praising to piercingly alert.

"You once told me I'd know when I met the right girl." He reached forward to set his empty cider cup with a clunk on the table. "I have. It's Anna."

"I remember your fondness for her. Congratulations," John stuck out his hand.

Herb could not take his offered hand. Instead, he shook his head. "No, it's impossible."

"Why?" John sounded dismayed.

"She's Irish." Since John showed no reaction, Herb continued. "Ironically, while immigrants feel the sting of being shunned, Anna's family finds me unacceptable because I'm not Catholic and, of course, not Irish. Their attitudes make seeing each other almost impossible. We want to be together; society keeps us apart. It's frustrating."

John cracked open a long pause. "It's not all easy being young and in love." He patted Herb's knee as he stood up. "Let me put some thought into it while I get more hot cider. The room is chilly today. You can look through my shelves and see what I've accumulated since you left."

Fifteen minutes passed before John returned, carefully protecting himself from the heat of the teapot he carried with a hot pad. He poured steaming liquid into their cups, set the pot on the circular table, and settled into his chair.

"Society is altogether too segmented. We're a new country—a land of immigrants, and yet firstcomers look down on new arrivals, and of course, that's not the extent of it. The wealthy have fancy-dress balls, while the less well-to-do socialize in pubs and churches. Men and women have different spheres. Women are mostly excluded from office work and, of course, men's clubs. Instead, they visit each other over tea or charity work. Even at a dinner gathering, men excuse themselves to smoke, drink, and talk after dessert, leaving women behind." He cleared his throat. "Maybe living with three females makes me more aware of that separation," he said, sighing. "It's natural, but all this separateness makes it especially hard for young people to meet—"

"Especially if they're from different cultures," Herb broke in. "This morning, we had to be together outside, in a freezing-cold pavilion, to have a conversation. Even then, we risked someone who knows Anna seeing us and telling her parents."

John was quiet for a few moments before saying what he must have gone over in his mind. "The library is closed, as are eateries on Sunday afternoon. You've already said meeting at the pub is no longer possible; she's a Catholic, and you are not, so no church socials. Eliza would be happy to have you both around our dinner table, but Anna's parents' confidence would be lacking, even with my position as a teacher."

Herb nodded, feeling glum. "Her parents and brothers are *very* restrictive. What's worse is that her family is introducing her to eligible men, and I'm not one of them."

John rubbed his forehead with his fingers, again hesitating before he spoke. "Do you have a sense of how she feels?"

Herb got out of his chair and walked to the window and back. "I think I do. She wrote to me regularly when I was in Philadelphia and suggests how to meet with me now that I'm home."

John stood up and clapped Herb on the back. "I think that's affirmation. I wish I had some magic to make things easier, but when it seems right, Eliza and I would like to invite her here."

Herb knew the afternoon had come to an end without consulting his watch. They had not delved into science or world issues, as they often did, and saying more about his search for his father would have to wait. Nevertheless, having John aware of his burdens was comforting, even if he had no solutions.

"I'm anxious," Anna said, "but at least a little warmer." The green and blue plaid wool cape wrapped around her shoulders highlighted her red hair.

"Maybe people will think we're brother and sister, taking a trip," Herb knew it was ridiculous but said it anyway.

"Not with the way you look at me." Anna smiled. "Please don't stop!"

He laughed. "A railroad depot passenger station is one of the only public places open on a Sunday mid-morning, and there isn't much traffic. We couldn't possibly be doing anything improper here, but people love to gossip."

The polished wood of the high-backed benches gleamed in the light of the gas chandeliers. The room was long and open, with travelers going in different directions; some were followed by a porter pushing a cart stacked with luggage. Herb and Anna had chosen to sit near the exits for long-distance trains, lessening the likelihood of being recognized by local travelers.

"Have you thought more about searching for your father? It must be hard not knowing anything and then wondering what you might find."

They sat next to each other but remained a foot apart. She had brought a leather-bound notebook with a loop to hold a pencil.

He nodded, agreeing with both her question and her statement. He retrieved a folded piece of paper from his breast pocket beneath his outer coat. "I've written down all my mother's trips to Boston or Providence that I remember. I wasn't as successful as I wished." He ran his fingers through his mustache. His mother's trips had been commonplace since he was a child, and he'd never given much attention to when those visits had happened until recently. He gazed into Anna's alert blue eyes. "There is a little good news. When I was little, my mother bought me a journal with several pages for each day of the calendar. I added the year when I wrote. When I was young, she helped me mark down when she was going away and coming back so I had something specific to look forward to. I kept it up pretty much until we moved to Brookline when I got distracted by changing high schools. It ended altogether when I went to Lowell, of course."

Anna brightened. "Anything's helpful. I'm guessing that if your parents travel a lot, you don't keep track. Mine don't, so I'd remember if they took a trip." She stood up and removed her cloak. "I'm warm because the building's heated. Fancy that." She scanned the room as if looking for anyone she knew before folding the cloak neatly. "Did she go anywhere other than Boston and Providence?" she asked, sitting down again.

"I vaguely remember a suffragist meeting in New Haven, but that's the only one. I can't remember about New York."

"Thank you for making a list." She took the paper he had unfolded and held out to her. "It's going to be helpful."

How had he not remembered the light spray of freckles across her upper cheeks—like a sprinkle of fairy dust on her creamy complexion? "Are you going to make a chart?" he teased, smiling at her gently. He could not stop looking at her.

"I am," she said seriously. "I'm going to list all the times your mother was in Boston and, below that, make another column for Providence. After that, I'll try to discover William Sinclair's actions to see if they were in the same place."

"How are you going to do that?"

"I have some ideas. Irish maids work in residences *and* hotels," she said with a smile. "And I know a lot of Irish maids. It's like having a whole brigade of detectives. I've already learned that Sinclair Cartage has monthly board meetings—sometimes more often. In even-numbered months, they are in Providence, and odd months, in Boston. The company does business in both cities, and maybe there's a business advantage to meeting in each."

"Have you written down the dates?" Every nerve in his body prickled.

"I have. Now I must chart the dates and compare his locations to hers."

"Should we do that now?" Herb asked.

"I'll do it at home, where I can spread everything on a table. My family will think it's a work project. By the way," she met his eyes, "I get to go back to the front desk of the records department next week. The higher-ups liked my organization of the files in the back. I may get snide remarks from the other girls—I'm the only employee from Ireland at the front desk—but they can't dispute my work. I'll keep my job as long as the men above me continue to get positive marks for my work."

"Like take credit for it?"

She nodded.

They met mid-morning the following Sunday at the same railroad station, with its prominent clock tower jutting out from the exterior. As before, the depot was comfortably warm, but Herb felt edgy. What would he say if someone recognized him and asked: "Herb, what are you doing at the depot? Taking a trip? And who is this lovely young lady?" He knew a surprising number of people who might remember him from his days as a message boy. What worried him more was if a family friend recognized Anna. That would end everything. He staged an internal debate about whether or not it was worth the chance they were taking. But the alternative was to give up seeing her. That was not a choice.

"Have you found anything new?" Herb asked, sitting down next to her.

"I think you'll be interested." Anna pulled her gloves off, fingertip by fingertip. Herb took the soft, supple kidskin and pressed it between his palms. The gloves were still warm from her hands, and he savored feeling them as if he were touching her skin.

"Tell me." He was unable to erase the black cloud over their constricted existence.

"On quite a few dates, your mother was in the same location as Mr. Sinclair."

Anna took her gloves from him, folded them, and tucked them in her reticule. "I can't afford to lose any more gloves," she told him. "I've tracked down the hotel where Sinclair Cartage holds its board meetings in Boston. It's the Liberty Hotel. The meetings only last a day, and board members outside of Boston typically spend the night before, but not after that." She scanned his face before continuing. "From the dates you gave me, I know your mother often arrives the same afternoon the meetings are held, but she's never registered at the Liberty, at least not under her name."

A chill breezed up Herb's spine. With a start, he realized he'd been assuming that a connection between his mother and Sinclair was far-fetched and amounted to nothing more than so much hocus-pocus. Instead, facts were pointing in just that direction—an idea he wanted to will away but which stuck like warm tar.

"I haven't figured out where your mother does stay on her visits. Unfortunately, the Sinclairs' maid doesn't know where he stays when he's away, but a housekeeper at the Liberty found from the register that he only stays there the night before each board meeting, even though he is gone for two or three days." The skin over the bridge of her nose wrinkled in apparent frustration. "The timing is beginning to look less coincidental, but the evidence to unravel the truth gets harder to find."

The weight of an anvil settled in Herb's chest. After a long pause, he asked, "Do you know anything about the Standard Hotel or Parker House? My mother often returns home from Boston, saying she prefers the Parker House but stayed at the Standard." He looked into Anna's intense, cerulean eyes. "The Parker is where well-known authors, like Dickens and Twain, stay." He frowned. "I never question her—"

"They might be leads," Anna cut in encouragingly. "I should follow all the threads." She shook her head. "I don't think I know anyone at the Standard or the Parker, but I'll send out feelers." She wrote down the names, although Herb knew she would remember without recording them. "Do you think they would use their own names? They might prefer to remain anonymous."

Herb watched passengers come and go. A train must have just arrived. He was looking for any distraction from thoughts of his mother meeting a man in secret—a man whose looks he favored. He considered going to the toilet, which would provide only momentary refuge from his thoughts.

"This can't be easy for you, Herb," Anna said. She reached out and touched his arm, immediately withdrew it, looking around furtively.

He shook his head in response, his emotions jumbling one on top of another. Anna had scooched closer, improperly close, as if sensing his inner turmoil.

"Do you know what occurs to me?" He swallowed, trying to rid his voice of the anger inside him. "We're doing the same thing." With a sweep of his arm, he gestured to the expansive public space. "Meeting secretly. I know why we do it, but I can't even speculate why Sally—my mother—might have met a man clandestinely."

"We're still not positive they know each other," Anna said, her eyes soft. "Are you sure you want to keep at this? Neither of us imagined it would be so painful."

He reached for his overcoat. "You may think I'm selfish, and probably I am, but I want to know as much as possible."

Anna glanced at the round, gold watch at her waist. "Mercy, I didn't know it was so late. I need to hurry before I'm missed. Shall we meet next Sunday? I don't know how much I'll uncover by then."

"I want to meet whether you find anything or not." They both reluctantly rose. In a gallant, stiff-armed gesture to keep the act proper, he helped her with her green and blue plaid cape. "Next Sunday, we're going to talk about us," he said. "If anything happens to thwart our plan, can we communicate through Agnes?"

Anna nodded. "She's cheering us on."

THIRTY-FOUR

Sunday mornings at the railroad station were their revered time together. Yet, only occasionally were they able to laugh with the delight of being with each other. The more they met, the more inevitable someone they knew would see them. Herb knew Anna also worried that church members began noticing her disappearance after each service. Herb's greatest anxiety came from her family's matchmaking.

"Ma asks me what's wrong with each man, fuming, 'You're too particular.' Da says I'm close to being an old maid and complains he'll have to support me forever." She narrowed her eyes. "I've worked hard to contribute to my family's income, but it seems all they can think of is getting rid of me, without my consent of how." She shifted toward him. "None of my suitors measures up to you, Herb. They're Irish and Catholic. That's all. They have none of your personality or intellect." Her eyes glistened.

Bitterness caught in his throat when he thought of Anna being forced to marry someone. His sour mood was exacerbated by each shred of information she'd uncovered about his mother and William Sinclair.

"I have an odd question, Herb. Would you describe your mother, please?"

Herb stroked his mustache for a moment. "The first thing I'd say about her is she's smart because she reads so much, not only books but newspapers. She's interested in everything and wants to know as much as possible."

"That's important, but what does she look like?"

He smiled. "Sally has a slender figure, is fair-skinned, and has blonde hair. From how people regard her, I know she's attractive, but to me, she's my mum, who cooks good meals and makes conversation while we eat."

"Interesting," Anna said. "I found nothing under Sinclair or Andersen at the Parker House, Liberty Hotel, or the Standard. I'd almost given up hope, but then I connected with the Standard's morning housekeeper. She goes to our church. Martha agreed to peek at the hotel's register on some of our circumstantial dates." Anna looked at Herb with a grimace more than a smile. "It was the room number that jogged her memory. She said a couple routinely reserve room 417 for two days every other month and sometimes more often. Apparently, they've been coming there for years. She's seen them periodically, leaving early in the morning. She described a slender, light-haired woman accompanied by a muscular man with a bushy mustache. Martha guessed the man was more than a decade older than the woman. They register as Mr. and Mrs. Simpson. On the first date Martha checked, your mother's and Sinclair's visits align with one of the Simpson's visits."

The news made Herb dizzy. "Did she check the other dates?"

"No," Anna said, "she didn't have time."

"I don't know where the Standard is, which doesn't mean much. I don't know many Boston hotels."

"From what I know about it," Anna said, "the hotel fits the name—a basic place to stay, not fancy but clean, and one where a person's more prominent friends might not reserve a room." With trembling fingers, she tucked a loose strand of hair back in place.

Herb tipped his head back in disbelief, staring straight up at the unlit chandeliers before focusing on her. "I'm tired of spending so much time on them. What about us? That's more important. You've taken so many risks—meeting me like this." He could hear the severe sound of his voice and tried to lighten it. "You know," he joked, "women who behave too freely can be sent to an institution."

"Or a nunnery!" They both tried to laugh but could not—the possibilities were not far from the truth, and an arranged marriage was even more real.

The waiting room had gone still. The time between trains made sounds echo against the solid walls. Through the leaded-glass windows, traces of sun blinked on and off between the wispy clouds.

Herb's eyes drank in the subtle spray of freckles on her unblemished complexion, her crimson hair above those always-alert azure blue eyes. He did not want to stop being with her. He almost asked her again, "What about us?" Suddenly, another question crowded out that question. He slid off the smooth wooden bench onto one knee.

"Herb, what's the matter?" Anna looked at him and then frantically twisted to survey the room for witnesses to his bizarre behavior. "Get up before someone notices."

"Anna, will you marry me?" He clasped her hands in his, feeling her warmth and momentary tug to pull away, followed by acquiescence, leaving her hands wrapped in his.

Eyes wide, she nodded. Then, she shook her head. "When? How? How can we possibly marry? I'm C-Catholic," she stuttered, her lips trembling. "My parents, your mother. . . ." Her voice trailed off.

He moved back on the bench to sit a foot from her in their usual, proper position. "I've been thinking about this. I didn't intend to ask so soon. It would be best to consider everything you'd give up because there's more. I want to leave Boston. We both have too many encumbrances here. I've told you more than once about meeting Nathaniel

Hill. He told me about the West and its opportunities when I helped him set up his exhibit to celebrate the Centennial State—Colorado. I wrote to him, and he responded, saying he'd do his best to help me find work. It may not be much at first." Herb turned to slip his arms into his coat. "I don't want your answer now. Christmas is two weeks away. Maybe that gives you enough time to consider the consequences. I may be asking you to give up more than I can give you. But I offer whole-hearted love."

"And I for you." She lifted her arms, then dropped them, and Herb felt her desire to embrace as intensely as he did. Instead, she fidgeted with her watch. "Oh, no! Look at the time. I must race and hope no one has missed me." Lifting her skirt an inch to make movement easier, she ran across the terrazzo floor toward the exit. Herb moved around on the bench after she disappeared, letting what happened sink in. He had pro-posed to the person he wanted to spend his life with and then concocted a half-formed plan to quit a job he liked to move west. In less than ten minutes, the planets of his universe had altered. His job and paycheck would end with nothing sure to replace them. He would trade the only state he had known for distant, new, and uncertain land. But he would have Anna. His breathing accelerated at the thought.

Knowing he would be leaving his mother, he had two choices. He could say nothing about her possible relationship with William Sinclair or confront her, hoping to discover the truth.

But as he walked home, his thoughts weren't of his mother. If he mar-ried Anna, he would become responsible for her—and his savings would not stretch far.

The sketchy morning sunshine had retreated behind pillowy clouds when Herb walked to John Brannan's in the early afternoon. Herb wrapped his scarf tightly against his neck, tucking the ends in his overcoat to ward off the frosty December air. Bare, thorny rose stalks lined the Brannans' front fence. The yard was tidy—he imagined leaf-raking was a big occupation on fall weekends. The clang of his rap of the knocker met with only a short delay. An instant after opening the door, Eliza shook his hand, pulling him from the cold outdoors into the warm interior. "I don't know why it has to be so dank and freezing. We're trying to inject some cheer by preparing for the holidays. Here," she said, smiling and reaching for his coat. "Let me hang it on a peg."

Herb relinquished his scarf and overcoat and inspected the cheery Christmas tree wedged in the corner of the parlor. Cranberry and popcorn chains looped through the branches, and paper cutouts dangled in between. Diane and Vicki had been creative with their handwork. It was reminiscent of the decorations Herb and his mother had put up when he was young. A wave of melancholy washed through him as he remembered happy times instead of the current dissension.

"We have an extra fire going in addition to the kitchen stove. With luck, some warmth will make its way into John's study. Ah," Eliza rubbed her hands together. "Here he comes now."

"I've just been reading about Bell and Watson's demonstration the ability of the speaker and receiver to communicate sound farther away from each other than at the Exposition. Quite remarkable," John said, shaking Herb's hand. "All the more so, knowing that you got a look at the original. Come back; I'm eager for a chat."

The air was sweet with the aroma of hot clove and cinnamon tea that Eliza served them as they speculated on the maximum distance sound could travel over wire. "Maybe it's unlimited," John said, tasting the hot liquid cautiously. "Can you imagine picking up a phone in Boston and talking to someone in Brookline?"

"How about someone in San Francisco?" Herb scoffed at his improbable thought.

"Like the fantastical fiction about future science that some authors write—letting their imaginations run away with them. I admit the stories are enjoyable, if unbelievable. Speaking of inventions, how's your job? Has anyone come up with something new? Are *you* close?" Herb felt John's eyes studying him.

"It's the best job I've ever had. I think the work could hold my interest for a good, long while. I've already gotten a raise, and I like the men I work with, but I'm going to quit."

"What?" John twitched in surprise, sending tea over the brim of his cup. He whisked his handkerchief from his pocket and dabbed up the drops of liquid. "Tell me why."

Herb usually cut short the details; this time, he could not suppress his emotions. "Do you remember you once told me, half in jest," Herb attempted a smile, but his lips merely quivered instead, "that I should consider applying to college in Colorado?"

John inclined his head. "It was only in jest, but it might not have been such a bad idea. Tuition is more affordable, and maybe the West has more jobs."

"Well, I also have a jigsaw puzzle of Pikes Peak. You know, the Colorado gold rush. Then, at the Exposition, I met Nathaniel Hill from Colorado. I've told you the story. He was on the Territorial Council, promoting statehood, which finally succeeded."

John's eyes were trained on him with curiosity.

"Colorado keeps turning up, poking and jabbing at me to find out more. Hill's friends call him Professor Hill because that's what he was at Brown University before he moved to the territory—now state. He's moved from a mining town to Denver and said he will try to help me find employment if I move out to the Centennial State." Herb stroked his mustache, waiting for a response.

It took time. Herb watched John's gaze moving under his tensing brow. It was his usual visage when grappling with a problem.

"What about your girl—Anna? What does she say?"

Herb's words cascaded out, describing his marriage proposal and his greatest fear: Anna could not say "yes" because he was asking too much. "I'm not Catholic or Irish and plan to move to Colorado. If she agrees, her parents will try to separate us. And I can't forget that going west means abandoning my mother." He stood up. "Would you mind if I used your toilet?"

"Do, by all means. You know where it is down the hall."

In John's study again, Herb found his mentor clasping and unclasping his hands in thought. "My, my, my, there's no denying the challenges." As Herb returned to his sagging leather chair, John looked across with a troubled expression. "Let's take it one step at a time. My guess is that not being Irish doesn't matter to her, but it does to her parents."

Herb nodded.

"Are you asking her to give up her religion?"

"Certainly not." Herb frowned, "But I don't believe a priest will marry us if I'm not Catholic. And becoming Catholic would take some serious thinking on my part. Plus, it's not something I could accomplish quickly."

"I believe a priest will marry you if you agree to raise your children in the Catholic faith. Would that bother you?"

Herb had not considered children, much less their religious affiliation. It took him a moment to consider. "I don't know why it would. A child's education falls mostly in the mother's realm of responsibility anyway." Agitated, he stood up, walked to the window, looked at the gray, overcast sky, and paced back. "I hope they all have red hair," he said, feeling wide-eyed from looking far into the future.

"One of the great advantages of being a teacher is seeing all my students leave school, grow up, and live very different lives. Some of them stay in touch. One of my students, Peter Hyder, now Father Hyder, became a Catholic priest. I think he would be willing to talk to you and Anna and answer your questions about a mixed-faith marriage."

"I suspect her parents wouldn't consider it a marriage at all, whether a priest married us or not."

"It's the two of you who need to be satisfied, although, admittedly, standing up to parents is daunting." John produced a reassuring smile. "And, since I'm giving opinions, your relationship with your mother is especially close since it's been just the two of you. You've made it more complicated by your reasonable interest in your father." His voice was low and calm. "I suspect most mothers regret it when their children leave home. It doesn't stop most from doing just that. Some go farther than others." He paused and blinked. "I'm glad I don't have to think about Diane and Vicki leaving home quite yet.

"Your mother *will* be sad to have you far away, but she seems to be an independent woman with a life of her own."

Herb sucked in his breath. *If you only knew.*

"Would you like me to get in touch with Father Hyder?"

"Would you?" Herb said, relieved to have something positive to consider.

"I will. I'm flattered by your confidence."

"Thanks for your advice." Herb almost added *If I had a father, I could have asked his advice.* Instead, he apologized, "I've used up so much time that we haven't discussed the telephone or other inventions. I'm sorry."

"Not at all. Your important decisions should be given time and thought. I've met your mother, and I look forward to the privilege of meeting Anna one day," John said as he stood up. "I'll contact Father Hyder. Let me know if there is anything else I can do. Anything!" He clasped Herb's shoulders as he stood next to him. "And you can be assured that Eliza . . . no." He shook his head. "Eliza, Vicki, and Diane join me in the offer of assistance. We, too, will regret having you far away if that's the eventuality. What will I do with my Sundays?" he exclaimed, lightening the mood. "I'm still counting on you next week."

"I'll be here. Thank you again."

THIRTY-FIVE

Herb's life was as upside down and scrambled as puzzle pieces dumped upon a table. What was his put-together puzzle—his future? He had to know and commit to it before organizing the pieces logically. Anna's answer was most important. If she said "no," he would escape from Boston forever. If she said "yes," staying in Boston was also an impossibility—they could not be married against her parents' wishes and remain. A half smile played on his lips. At least the geography of his future was decided. He was going to leave Boston one way or another. Part of the puzzle was in place. Piecing together the logistics of moving to Colorado was urgent. His heart rate picked up speed. He would plan for two. Taking a train to travel across the country made the only sense. His few possessions made one oversized piece of luggage realistic, although he had no idea how much Anna had to bring . . . *if* she said "yes."

At his desk, Herb opened the leather-bound notebook Anna had given him to a blank page. He began to pencil out a budget. He estimated costs for travel, meals, and short-term expenses in Denver, then built in a little extra for unforeseen costs. His savings barely covered it. He'd have to get a job soon after they arrived in Denver. There were other matters, like resigning from his job, a wedding, and determining what to say to his mother; he could not get married, wave goodbye, and move across the country without talking with her about the past—known and unknown—and then the future.

His original reason for searching for his father had been settled. His success was not tied to his father. He had had no father figure to influence him—contact and guidance were more important than some biological link. That resolution comforted him, but the question of William Sinclair still loomed. The man had the first and middle name of his father, he and Herb had a similar appearance, and Sinclair worked in the cartage business as had his father, according to Sally. The two had apparent proximity. Was there a link?

That unexpected part of the search was more complicated. Pulling apart bits and pieces of information to connect Sinclair with his mother might satisfy his curiosity and make others suffer. He had to be sure before he made accusations. William Sinclair appeared to have a wife and three children. His mother was a widow . . . wasn't she? Could she have had a child out of wedlock? Untangling the web could threaten the Sinclairs' home life and his mother's comfortable, possibly false, backstory. And what about himself? Who sired him? As the days cascaded toward Christmas, Herb struggled to keep his emotions locked away.

In the weeks before Christmas, Boston and Brookline store owners decked their windows with wreaths and ribbons to entice shoppers to spend money on gifts. Office buildings, too, sported gaily-trimmed windows and doors, although colorful decorations could not erase the presence of the dire economy.

Herb brought home a small evergreen tree and set it near the window in their library, far away from the danger of sparks from the fireplace. His mother had already retrieved her boxes of carefully packed ornaments.

With their cups of eggnog on a side table, they tied decorations to the tree's branches. Over the years, they had handcrafted many of the ornaments and reminisced about their makeshift creations while comparing them to a few manufactured ones they'd purchased at museums or other memorable places. His mother had marked the date on each with a fine ink nib. Each ornament recalled memories of their lives at the time.

But, the usual joy of the tradition escaped Herb. He was moody instead of merry, and Sally, too, seemed removed from the holiday spirit. Every ornament made him wonder what other life she may have lived at the time. Warily, he sought an appropriate time to tell her what he and Anna had learned. Nervousness tightened his chest and then up his neck and into his skull. Each time he started to ask her about the past, an excuse muted him. Only in the dark of his bedroom did the words demanding an answer come, but they disappeared in the dawn.

The Sunday before Christmas, Herb and Anna followed their usual routine at the train station. Whoever arrived first chose an out-of-the-way bench and waited for the other to come. The station that day was almost empty. Everyone seemed to have gone or come to wherever they were going for the holiday. They had not met the previous week because their meetings had begun to feel too risky.

Usually, Herb got there first, but he found her sitting at the east end, her posture stiff. Herb gently sat down beside her, as usual, a foot away. He was weary from his sleepless night of worry about his mother.

"We only have a few minutes; there are extra deliveries because of Christmas."

He noted shadowy half-circles under Anna's eyes. "I shouldn't have come, but I can't think of anything else except us." She locked her eyes with his. "I can't imagine life without you, but . . ."

Herb gripped the bench. Her answer was no.

"We have to be married," her lips trembled, "by a priest. I can't do it any other way." She looked at him searchingly.

"Is that all?" Herb asked. Relief almost spilled him off the bench. "If your answer is yes, I agree," he said.

"No! You don't understand." A tear slid over her curved cheek. "Father Coughlin won't marry people outside our faith. He's very strict." She obsessively checked the room and, seeing no one, reached for his hand. "I want to be together, but it's not possible."

He enclosed her hand in his. "Would you be willing to be married by a priest other than the one from your church?"

Her expression bore a touch of annoyance with her surprise. "It would be the same problem."

"Not necessarily." Herb shook his head cautiously. "John told me one of his former students is now a priest."

"Catholic?"

"Yes, and his provision to marry us is that I agree that our children," his eyes pressed shut with the incredible image, "are raised Catholic. And I agree."

He felt her hand twitching in his while she stumbled over her words. "I've heard of that provision, but I'm still not sure it's possible. Most priests refuse, and I can't demand that you become Catholic. Anyway," she said, scowling, "being married to a non-Catholic would still be insurmountable at home. My parents came to a new country, but they desperately want to maintain what they grew up with—they've lost their country, so keeping their culture is paramount, including who their children marry. It's ironic, but I think the prejudice against the Irish in this country, and against most immigrants, makes them want to hang on tighter to their traditions."

He watched her with sympathy, regretting that he was the source of her turmoil. "I can't imagine how hard it must be to be asked to give up your family and culture, and, even more, to go away . . . a long way away. Only you can decide if I'm asking too much. I may be miserable, but I'll understand if you say no."

"Let me consider the idea of a different priest. Right now, I have to go back to church."

When they stood, Herb embraced Anna, kissing her without restraint, exhilarated by her eager response. Then, reluctantly, he let her retreat from his arms. "I'll wait," he told her, but he knew he was asking too much.

Christmas fragrance filled John Brannan's study the Sunday before Christmas. Vicki and Diane had each studded oranges with cloves and saved two for Herb to take home—one for him and one for Sally. The oranges sat on the round table beside the teapot, exuding their citrus and spice aromas. John relayed his conversation with his former student, Father Hyder, who had agreed to meet with Anna and Herb to officially discuss "Holy Matrimony And The Covenant Between Spouses And The Procreation And Raising Of Children."

"I may be rushing the gun, but if Anna says 'yes' as you hope, there will be a flood of things you have to do with little time to spare. Father Hyder mentioned the need for witnesses. I would be glad to stand up for you. I don't know how your mother figures in, but know that my offer is there. And," John gave a throaty laugh. "if you need flower girls, there are two champing at the bit in the adjacent room."

Herb knew John was trying to make any potential ceremony more festive than a ten-minute technicality of taking oaths and signing documents—another validation of the luck he'd had to have John in his life.

After Anna officially said "yes," Herb and Anna had their first meeting with Father Hyder. Herb had asked, not once, but three times if she was sure she could leave her family and still be happy.

"I wish I didn't have to choose between family and going with the man I can't live without. I'll miss them, but I'm ready to start my own family . . . our family."

"And your job? You've said it was miraculous luck that the city hired an Irish girl for something other than a maid. It won't be easy to replace. There are few miracles in life. I have mine—that you're marrying me."

"Jobs are never certain, and I'm thinking of something different to do. I want to try to be a teacher. I'd like to teach boys *and* girls the rewards of investigating and learning. It may not be possible, but maybe prejudice against immigrants isn't as severe in the West."

"I don't have much money, you know that."

She nodded. "I can add a little. I was expected to give Da most of my pay, but I held some back—in my lower dresser drawer, not a bank. Women aren't allowed accounts."

"How much luggage will you have?" he asked gently.

Her smile was mischievous. "I can get everything in a trunk. I bought one and sent it to Agnes's rooming house. Every day I go to work, I bring her a satchel of my belongings to add to the trunk."

<hr>

The holidays were over, and the new year had begun. Herb and Anna continued to meet with Father Hyder. Sally packed away the Christmas decorations he knew he might never see again. Herb noted an edginess as she told him of meetings in Boston. Her usual eagerness to travel was absent. He had promised himself he'd tell her his plans at dinner, but the conversation drifted as they spoke about the new year's events. Abroad, Queen Victoria had been named Empress of India, and the cricket season had started. A furious political battle raged in the United States to determine whether Democrat Samuel J. Tilden or Republican Rutherford B. Hayes had won the 1876 presidential election.

Herb's skin burned, but he could no longer procrastinate when she stood up to do the dishes, the usual end of the evening together.

"Sally . . . Mum, I have something to tell you. Will you sit a little longer?" He felt lightheaded as she slowly sat down, observing him quizzically. He had planned to ask her about her relationship and finish on a happy note with news of his plans with Anna. Instead, the words rushed out as if someone else were speaking. "I've proposed to Anna, and, unbelievably, she accepted. We're getting married.

His mother's eyes widened, and it took a moment for her to absorb what he had said. "Oh, my gracious. I knew you were communicating but had no idea how committed you are." She twisted in her chair, "I'm overwhelmed and happy at the same time. Congratulations, Herb." She stood up and stepped toward him, reaching up to wrap her arms around him as he stood. "Please tell me your plans. When may I meet her and her family?"

Herb felt disoriented as she released him, and they sat down again. "It's complicated." He pressed his eyes shut, not wanting to continue, but he could no longer stall. "I'm going to Colorado. *We* are moving to Colorado to work, live, and start our family."

She slumped against her chair, looking baffled. "So far away? Why? Why can't you live here?" She stuttered, losing her usual control. "I haven't even met her," she said, her lips quivering.

"Her family won't approve of our marriage. It's not me," he explained. "They won't accept anyone who's not Irish or Catholic."

"Why would you choose someone whose family is like that?" She frowned.

"No family is perfect. We *both* have family issues," he said slowly and carefully. "In fact, it's past time that I know more about ours." He could not eradicate the anger in his tone. "I'd like to know if you have a relationship with William Sinclair."

His mother gasped as if he had struck her. The color drained from her face, making her features look crumpled and old. She began to tremble. "My relationships are not your business."

"If it concerns my father, it *is* my business."

Her usual *sang-froid* disappeared. "How do you know about him?"

"I saw Mr. Sinclair by accident—I look a lot like him. I've always wanted to know about my father. It's natural. Lately, it's become a . . . well . . . somewhat of an obsession."

Sally hesitated and then got up. "I'm going to get a glass of wine." She walked into their compact pantry, and Herb could hear the noise of her trying to uncork the bottle but did not get up. He remembered someone had given her a bottle of wine years before, and it had sat in the cupboard since then. In a few minutes, she returned with the bottle and two glasses.

She set one in front of him, but he shook his head. The deep red caught the chandelier's light as she filled her crystal glass and began her story.

"My parents were poor and had little to give me. I was rarely asked to other homes and never considered inviting anyone to my rundown house. It sat at the end of a dirt road on the junky side of town. I was always embarrassed by having so few clothes, which, as I grew, got tighter, shorter, and more worn before my parents replaced them—oversized to allow for growth and save money. From the way people regarded me, I knew I was considered pretty, but my real advantage was being a good student, and I tried to prove myself through my grades, although I was often discounted . . . because I was poor and a girl.

"My mother died when I was thirteen; she had been sick for a while. Daddy sank into a shell of misery and gave up what little attention I ever had. I cleaned, shopped, cooked, and did the laundry and cleaning. The day after I left high school, I went to work in a factory, sewing clothing for children. It was a dreary place, crowded with sewing machines, where we worked twelve hours a day, with three short breaks to eat the food we brought. We were docked for every mistake—or what they called a mistake. Not that they could squeeze much out of our poor pay. We huddled together to walk to the trolley, never letting the managers find us alone. We'd heard about the girls they took to the back corners. When my father died two years later, I was terrified of the leering factory bosses and left to work as a maid at an inn in Boston's commercial center. My father hadn't owned our house, so I had no place to live. I moved to an inexpensive boarding house—one considered respectable for ladies. I met a man at the inn who gave me a job at his office. I've told you that part," she said tensely. "I'm sorry, you'll have to excuse me."

When she returned from the washroom, she poured more wine. He almost never saw her drink and suspected she needed the wine to bolster her courage to tell her saga.

"My employer had a small office in Boston; his principal business was in Providence. Mr. Schultz, his salesman and assistant, managed the Boston office. I found the assistant lazy and happy to have me do as much as I was willing. He was fat and often unshaven, but he didn't bother me. One time, when my employer arrived in Boston from Providence, Mr. Schultz had sent word that he was ill and couldn't come to work. My employer asked me to tell him what had occurred at the cartage company since he had last been in Boston. When I finished, he was more than complimentary. Schultz had never given him so many details. In a month, Schultz was gone."

His mother looked sad as she continued. "My employer asked me to be his secretary in Boston. He raised my paycheck, probably by more than I deserved, but he said I saved him money because it was less than he had paid Schultz. Even though I earned more, I still scrimped on expenses to buy dresses and look like an office worker rather than a maid. I was in his debt. I was so thankful to no longer be a needy girl working as a maid or in a factory.

"When he came to Boston, we began having meals together, and conversation flowed easily since I knew almost as much about the business as he did. I took home newspapers to read when he had finished with them. He gave me the gift of a hundred books in appreciation for my work. It was the education I could never have, even when using a public library."

Her eyes were cast down as she explained that one thing led to another, and they spent one night together and then another. "It was a momentary transgression on my part. I never planned or wanted it to happen," she said pleadingly. "Finally, he bought me a small apartment where we stayed when he visited. He said we would both be there when we were married."

She looked at him with more sadness than Herb had ever observed.

"He told me he had not had a loving relationship for many years and was going to leave. Yet, something always came up, something that delayed a divorce and marriage to me."

She took a deep breath and poured another glass of wine. Her speech had become looser. "When I discovered I would have a child, Will was furious. I was, too, not about the pregnancy, but that he didn't understand the time had come for a divorce. He made more excuses. I could have exposed him, but what good could it have done? I don't think he would have ever thrown me out, and I had kept his many passionate love letters with promises of divorce. When you were born, I fabricated the story of being a widow."

Herb's breathing and heartbeat increased. "So, William Sinclair is my father?"

She nodded.

Herb could not tamp down his disbelief. "Why didn't you tell me the truth?" He didn't look up at her for the unanswerable. She had begun to cry.

He quietly considered everything she had said. He felt raw. Small shards of realization about why she had fabricated her story did not make him feel any better. "And you still see him?"

"Yes," she dabbed at her eyes. "He has given me everything, including something to live for—*you*. Before him, I had nothing. I was always peering through a window and never invited in, tightly bound by convention and the inability to escape poverty."

He gave you everything—everything but himself and marriage. It was too sad a sentiment to say out loud.

Herb and Anna met with Father Hyder for their last counseling session the day before their wedding. He concluded by saying, "God bless you. I give you my approval to proceed with the Rites of Holy Matrimony." Coming close to them, he joined their hands and folded them within his. "Congratulations," he said with an approving smile. "I look forward to performing the rites tomorrow morning."

They left the church, and Herb took Anna's arm. "Are you sure you're okay with Father Hyder marrying us?"

"More than okay."

They had managed a major hurdle, but the nerve-wracking details roiled his mind. Any failure could end their plans . . . and future together.

Herb sent Professor Hill an expensive three-word telegraph with their arrival date after Anna had said yes. His response had come a week before the wedding, giving Herb the name and address of a widow with a room to let. He wrote: "Finding a job will be more successful in person, but I will be happy to provide a reference," and added, "With the growing number of children in Denver, teachers are needed. Mrs. Andersen should be able to get an interview."

His mother's confession was a thick, murky fog clouding his ability to think, but he would have to because he had not told her he planned to leave so soon. He had one more night at home and needed to say goodbye. Thinking about what to say bounced between relief and distress. Now that she had told him the truth, he yearned to sort out what it all meant or even how he felt about knowing. He glanced at Anna. Her expression told him she was traversing her turmoil. She would not be able to say goodbye to her family.

They had quit their jobs the day before, both with remorseful apologies about leaving so abruptly but knowing the short notice meant less chance of accidental disclosure of their plan. Anna had arranged to go to Agnes's rooming house half an hour after work usually ended. She would stay the night, as she occasionally had. The following morning, Anna and Agnes would take a carriage with Anna's trunk—the one Agnes had surreptitiously filled over the past weeks—to the small chapel where Father Hyder would perform the ceremony. Agnes had agreed to be a witness.

His mother had left the previous day "to settle things in Providence." Herb was too preoccupied to question what that might mean.

"We're almost done," Herb said to Anna as they walked.

"There's still so much to do. We're bound to get caught." Her voice quaked.

"Let's follow our plan." He wanted to reassure her by taking her hand but could not. They were in public.

Anna nodded, her eyes darting from one place to another as if too nervous to light on one object.

They took the train from Boston to Brookline. He sat at the front left of the car, and she at the rear right. There were few people and no other solitary woman. His breath came in rapid rhythm, fearing discovery until they arrived at the station and exited the train. He had plotted a route that took them out of the way of most pedestrians. When they were close to his apartment, Herb extracted his key from his pocket. "We must be fast so no one sees us enter together." He ran up the stairs, Anna behind him. When he unlocked the door, they burst through.

"Mum?" he called. There was no answer. She was gone, as expected.

His hands shook as he took Anna's coat and led her to the library. "Come in and have a seat." She was pale and speechless, trying to catch her breath. "I'll light a fire and try to recover from almost dying from apoplexy." The thin, reedy sound of his voice in his ears was not reassuring.

When the fire glowed in the red-tile fireplace, he sat beside her, sinking into the sofa's soft cushion and leaning against her warm shoulder. "Touching without worry about someone seeing us. It will take a while to believe," he said, relief not yet calming his nerves.

"This is how it will be if . . . we succeed," Anna said and looked at him with pleading eyes . . . "and if not. . . ."

"One more day."

"Is this your puzzle?" She leaned closer to the coffee table.

"Pikes Peak. I haven't made much progress. I moved it from the dining room to this familiar spot, hoping I would work on it."

"I tried to imagine where you put together your puzzles."

"I don't think I'll finish it, but better yet, we may see the actual mountain."

She scrutinized the pieces spread around the periphery of the already completed border. "Hmm," she said with glee, reaching for a piece and locking it in place.

Impetuously, he took her hand before she reached for another and pulled her close, feeling her shiver. He circled her with his arms and pressed his lips against hers. They were soft and moist. They had always resembled raspberries, but he had not imagined they would taste sweet. Their chests were so close that he could feel her heart beating, or maybe it was theirs together. Her response intensified his need for her. Breathing combined breaths, they stretched lengthwise together on the sofa, their bodies locking. Their fingers urgently fumbled for buttons to undo. The heat was not from his recently built fire but from the feel of her against him. Their bodies belonged together, but they stilled and separated in unison.

"I agree," Herb murmured, although Anna hadn't spoken. "Not yet. Sally made that mistake."

Anna nodded her head on his shoulder. "Waiting until Colorado is unbearable, but it's right."

"Herb, I'm home," his mother called late in the afternoon. She came into the library and looked at the coffee table. "How did you manage to finish the entire puzzle? Didn't you go to work?"

"It's a long story, Mum. Would you come to sit down so we can talk?"

She removed her coat and laid it on the back of the couch, taking a seat at an angle from him, her expression troubled. The fireplace glowed with replenished coal, warming the room from a fire he had been stoking since morning.

He turned to face her, "I quit my job, and Anna quit hers, too. We spent the day here, so we completed the puzzle together. She left a short time ago in a carriage to spend the night with her friend, Agnes. Tomorrow is our wedding day."

She shook her head in incomprehension. "Tomorrow? So soon? But I haven't met her."

"I know. I wish you could; you would like her," he said, and it was true. For the first time, it occurred to him how much Anna's independence resembled Sally's. He read what she must be thinking. He was getting married without her. "I'm sorry, Mum, but we're getting married and leaving for Colorado. There is no other way. We have to leave to build a life together."

"I won't attend my only son's wedding?"

"No," he fumbled with her hurt. "We wish this could be a family celebration, but it's not possible," he said. "Our families cause too much difficulty right now—both of them."

Sally remained quiet in the face of his accusation and then turned to go to the kitchen. Before leaving, she turned back and leaned over, encircling him in her familiar hug. "I can imagine how happy you are, and it spills over to me. It makes me sad that you're leaving, but I want to know your plans. Let's talk over dinner. I have news of my own. Now, I better go make us dinner." Her voice caught. Herb knew as well as he suspected she did that it might be the last time she said those words.

"Thanks, Mum; I have a few things to get ready." When she left, he took apart the puzzle and put the pieces in the box. He had no room to take it.

At dinner, Herb told her about his communication with Professor Hill and Anna's desire to teach. Her response was a sad jumble of pride and regret about his moving so far away so quickly.

"We're not going to another country, just west. The railroads bring it closer all the time."

He read the sorrow and skepticism in her eyes.

"Sally . . . Mum, you said you have your own news." He took a forkful of dessert she had bought on her way home from the station.

Her head bowed. "I've finally ended my relationship."

"With William Sinclair?" Herb could not say, "With my father."

"Yes, that's what my trip was about." She looked up at him. "It was overdue, and maybe I should have done it long ago. I enjoyed his company, but a night here and two nights there, worried that we would be seen, is not a relationship. I stayed because it provided a life I would not have had without it—not prosperous, but not working as a maid or in a sweatshop. It allowed me to raise you in comfort—neither poverty nor luxury. I also had a certain amount of independence without someone telling me what I could or could not do. I eventually came to accept that lifestyle and ultimately realized that we would never get married, but things changed." She stopped and took a sip of her water.

"Changed?" Herb was not sure he wanted to uncover more secrets.

"Will's refusal to pay your college tuition removed the blinders I had worn about our relationship. Not only had he not married me, but he also denied his son a college education. You are his son, acknowledged or not. I was angry—and still am. He has enough money; it was selfishness. The whole, long relationship tipped in his favor. He allowed me a lifestyle I would not have had otherwise, but with an incomplete family. I paid the price of continual secrecy. He enjoyed living two lives, with little responsibility for ours."

"I thought the money came from a trust?"

"It does, one he provided, but he refused to add more for college." Her troubled face blotched red.

"Yesterday, I told him our relationship was over and told him why—it met his needs more than mine. I'm not sure he understands. The trust he set up for me long ago has been invested well and has survived the depression. I will have to be frugal, but I'm free now. I wish I had done this a long time ago, and I wish I had told you the truth, but I couldn't. I hope someday you will understand and forgive me."

Herb's breath was heavy. Ending the relationship seemed to have brought his mother some measure of peace, but it would take him time to know if realizing who his father was and that he was alive would do the same for him. His father had been a fixation, but after hearing his mother's story, he had lost all interest in meeting or knowing the man who had sired him. Creating his own identity was what mattered. Self-invention was the key: figuring out what to live for of his own volition, not driven by someone else's traits. With the most extraordinary luck, he had found Anna to do that with. His worldview had changed.

Mid-morning was an unusual time for a wedding, but no one present cared. After the priest's vows, Herb slipped a slender gold band on Anna's finger, and they said, "I do," with Agnes and John as witnesses. Herb kissed Anna for the first time as his wife, bringing congratulatory cheers and hugs from Eliza, Diane, and Vicki in the absence of family members.

Knowing her family would have forbidden her to leave, Anna told Herb she had not said goodbye. Instead, she had written what she described as a long, sorrowful parting letter without any destination details. She had left it on a kitchen shelf where it would be found, hopefully, after their train left.

Bright sun had broken through early morning clouds, and the January temperature was cool but pleasant. After the ceremony, Herb sat in the carriage so close his arm rubbed against . . . his wife's. In the boot behind them was their luggage. The sound of last good wishes trickled into the distance after the driver flicked his switch, and the horses moved the carriage beyond the well-wishers. They were on their way to their new life.

At the station, they loaded their luggage and found their seats. They could not afford a Pullman, so they would sit upright for the trip, but at least they could touch with impunity.

The conductor blew a long, high-pitched, five-minute warning. Anna glanced out the window. "Oh no, no, no! Herb, it's my father and brothers."

He turned to see four men running down the platform toward the train. "Quick, come with me." Running, he pulled her through their car into the next one. Its compartments would prevent other passengers from noticing them cramming into the washroom together. They frantically pulled and pushed at her petticoats and skirt and managed to shut and lock the door seconds before voices and heavy footsteps sounded in the corridor. "Anna, are you in there?"

"Use the next car; I need a few more minutes," Herb shouted.

"Check the baggage compartment for her luggage," a man's voice boomed from the other side of the door, followed by heavy, running footsteps.

"I'm caught," Anna whispered.

The conductor blew the whistle again. "All aboard! Ticketed passengers only!"

It felt like an eternity before the engine vibrated under their feet, and the train slowly gained motion. Herb cautiously opened the bathroom door and peeked out. There was no sign of Anna's father or brothers. Working to keep their balance in the train's motion, they walked back to their seats. Anna drew the curtain across the window while Herb held their tickets for the passing conductor to punch.

"I thought we were doomed." She was pale and gasping. "Why didn't they find my trunk? It was right there—one of the last on."

Herb steadied her within his embrace. "I put name tags on. Yours reads Mrs. Andersen and mine simply Mr. Andersen. They don't know my last name. Everyone at the pub, including your brother, just called me Herb."

The Ring of a Bell is about the introduction of life-changing technology of the telephone. It is a story of inventors and ordinary people during the Gilded Age—a revolutionary time of technical innovation. Only through ingenuity and intrepid perseverance was the telephone invented. Early on, it was considered a toy or plaything and therefore discounted. 19th-century society could not imagine that the telephone would become indispensable.

The inventors, particularly Bell and Watson, are real. Conversations and scenes are fabricated to provide a sense of time and place. *The Ring of a Bell* reveals the lives of real and imaginary people coping with challenges, and I hope it will allow readers introspection of their own lives and challenges that are as real to them today as they were to my 19th-century characters.

The backbone of the current book is historical fact, but many of the characters were created from my imagination. Herb Andersen is purely fictional but represents the dilemmas and aspirations of a boy coming of age. His mother, Sally, is also fictitious but typical of women of the time before they had the right to vote or to negotiate the circumscribed lifestyles imposed by society.

As part of my academic training, I became interested in the history of technology. It ignited my interest in invention and entrepreneurship. Many years later, quite by chance, I began writing fiction about those topics. To my surprise, I learned "history and fiction seek the truth." I wish I knew who said those wise words, but nonfiction and fiction use different styles to portray the truth. Fiction's advantage comes from transforming past moments into pictures for the reader's imagination and, therefore, giving a greater sense of the events.

ELLEN FISHER, 2024

ACKNOWLEDGMENTS

Writing historical fiction takes countless hours of imagining a story based on facts relevant to the time and contemporary society. Many additional hours are spent researching events to give the narrative accurate context. And then, there is the time it takes to write and put the story in literate form. It is exhilarating to achieve a complete draft, but it is only the beginning. Outside readers with keen eyes give essential, objective input. I am incredibly grateful to my editors, who plow through the jumble and find areas to praise and others to modify or discard.

I especially appreciate Hadley Fisher, who was the protagonist's age when he read the first draft. As my Beta reader, he gave me invaluable insight into the coming-of-age process, which has similarities in every century. Eva Fox Mate combed the manuscript to strengthen the writing and find gaps in the story's historical underpinnings. Hers was a gallant and vital effort. My copy editor and close friend, Cotheal Linnell, agreed once again to take a final look, over three or four thorough readings, to rid the document of errors, large and small. Joel Johnson, Sherry Kenney, and Eva Mate—my early morning writing group—are always there to cheer me on and offer invaluable friendship and advice.

And special thanks to Fred for sixty years and more!

I can't imagine writing without these thoughtful, patient people.

www.ingramcontent.com/pod-product-compliance
Lightning Source LLC
Chambersburg PA
CBHW020646120726
47906CB00001B/154